Dead Love

A Dark Stalker Romance

Audrey Rush

Dead Love: A Dark Stalker Romance by Audrey Rush

Independently Published

Copyright © 2022 Audrey Rush

All rights reserved. No portion of this book may be reproduced in any form without permission from the publisher, except as permitted by U.S. copyright law. For permissions contact: audreyrushbooks@gmail.com

Cover Design by Kai

Paperback ISBN: 9798351887449

This title was previously published as The Art of Ruin Duet. Part I was titled *Cruelty & Fire*. Part II was titled *Innocence & Ashes*.

This is a work of fiction. Names, characters, places, and incidents either are the product of the author's imagination or are used fictitiously. Any persons appearing on the cover image of this book are models and do not have any connection to the contents of this book. This book is intended for mature audiences only. Any activities represented in this book are fictional fantasies only.

Dead Love

Part One

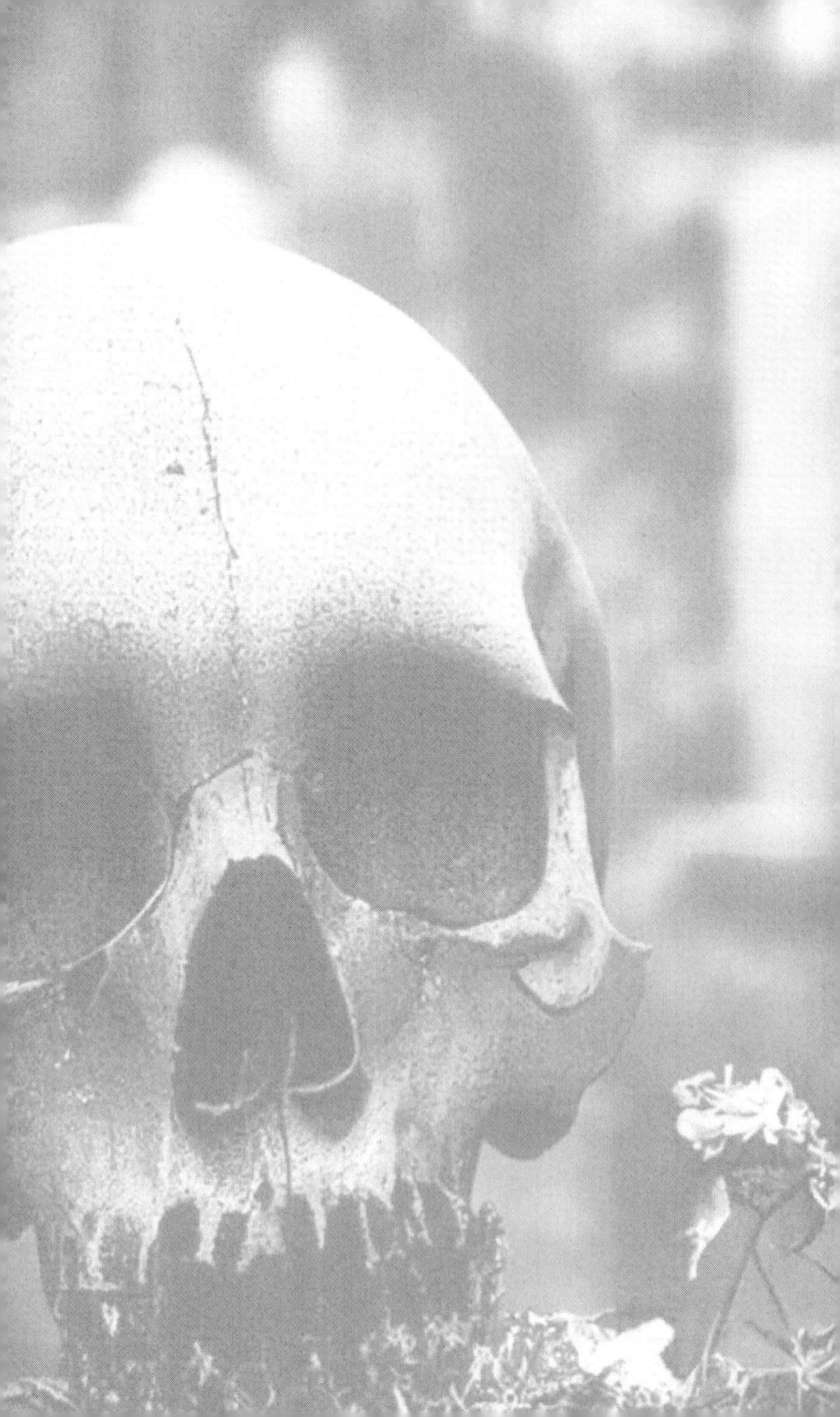

Chapter 1

Vincent

three years earlier

I STILL WANTED TO BURN THE BASTARD. BUT EIGHT FEET DEEP INTO the ground, I ran through the motions: bury the man like he wanted, give him the respect he deserved. Like I had been taught. But as I stabbed my shovel into the dirt, the urge to ruin perfection simmered inside of me. To break and destroy all the fake virtue rising above us.

I grunted, leaning my weight on the metal to go deeper. The healing cuts on my palm ached and the plot was more than big enough, but I kept digging anyway. *I don't want to become a painting on your wall*, my older brother had said. *I don't want to watch you live your life while I'm stuck on a canvas.* He shoved my shoulder. *Don't you dare burn me, asshole.*

You wouldn't feel it, I said.

His lips pinched together. *That's not the point.*

An unsettling sensation crawled in my gut. I couldn't stop myself from digging. Wouldn't let myself.

"Cops are here again," a voice said.

My employee's shadow hovered in my peripherals, watching from above. The employee was new; she had been at the funeral home for a few months now, but eventually, she would move on too. I kept digging; the dirt caking my face. At this depth, you had to toss it high over your shoulder, and if you weren't careful, some of it rained back down on you. I threw another scoop up to the ground and she darted out of the way.

"What was that for?" she asked, as if I was trying to aim for her. I didn't care that much.

The rectangular hole of blue sky had finally begun to darken. The sides of her head were shaved, the short gray dyed hairs glowing like peach fuzz in the dim light.

"I could get the excavator," she said.

I sucked down a scowl. We had machinery that could do this, but I preferred to do it by hand. I liked keeping myself occupied.

"The sheriff?" I finally asked.

"Nah. The other one. White hair. I always forget his name."

I touched up the grave with the back of my shovel, smoothing the edges. I should have hired a contractor to dig his grave. Should have needed to take time off. But I was removed from it. Guns. Overdose. Disease. It was all the same. I'd rather go with a knife, the blood leaking out of me. Or better yet, a fire so that I burned with every possible agony in those last seconds. But in the end, it didn't matter how you went. Life continued on. I felt nothing, only an emptiness that I filled with work.

"I'll stay here," she said. "You need the time off. Go. Mourn. Take care of that officer. I'll finish up here."

"You'll stay until sunrise?" I asked. She nodded. Not being around on Halloween—a night where the teenagers in Punica loved to vandalize the cemetery—was a reprieve I would not pass up. She could learn the hard way about Halloween. I climbed up the ladder.

"You want tomorrow off?" I asked.

"That's a given."

I muttered my thanks, then went inside the funeral home. A young officer in full blues waited in the lobby, his thumbs in his belt loops.

"Evening, Erickson," he said. My scalp prickled; we weren't on familiar terms, but he and his sheriff had been around a lot lately. He tipped the imaginary hat above his white hair. "The toxicology report came back. Heroin."

"Doesn't surprise me," I said.

"Didn't you have an incident a few years ago?"

I had been out at a bar when a fight broke out over some drugs. The charges were dropped, but that didn't mean that there weren't arrest records out there. The officer must have been digging around to find that.

"Almost a decade has passed," I shrugged. "But yeah. There was an incident."

The officer tilted his head. "Coincidental," he said.

"Lots of people do drugs." My jaw stiffened. "But you know that, don't you? And we both know my brother did."

He wrinkled his brow. "What are you saying?"

"What else is there to report?" My tone was biting; I had endured enough of law enforcement in the last week to cover a lifetime. "You could be serving the citizens who need you. Instead, you're wasting your time investigating someone who OD'ed."

"A bullet. Cuts. Drugs," he sighed. "Why so many options?"

"He must have been very determined."

"What are you hiding, Erickson?" the officer asked, glaring at me. "You seem awfully reluctant to scrutinize your brother's death. Apathetic, even."

"Trust me, officer. We all mourn in different ways," I said. I tipped my imaginary hat, mocking him. "Catie will be back in a few minutes. She can take care of anything else you might need."

Without another word, I headed up the winding path between the grave markers to the trees that lined the edges of the property, separating my house from the funeral home. I unlocked the door to my house, then fixed dinner for the only housemates I had left. When it was ready, three rottweilers came trotting into the kitchen. I kneeled down to pet them. They sniffed at me, noticing the dirt on my clothes, and huffed away. I could have changed, but I wasn't trying to impress anyone.

Restless, I drove to the downtown area, where children with holey sheets, witch hats, and superhero jumpsuits ran down the sidewalk, shouting *trick-or-treat!* to each shop owner. I parked down one of the side streets, then walked past the jack-o'-lanterns and stringy cobwebs decorating the storefronts. I crossed the street, to the scenic viewpoint; it was one of my favorite haunts. I leaned my back on the railing, observing. Directly across from the viewpoint, was Poppies & Wheat, the town's only flower shop, with its typical wreath decorated with orange and red flowers, and a single giant pumpkin carved into a rose outside.

Three figures strode down the sidewalk. The sheriff wrapped his arm around his wife's back, an older woman with her brown hair twisted into an elaborate updo. She owned the flower shop, and though my late brother used to do most of the business negotiations, I still spoke with her from time to time. But behind them was a young woman I had never seen before, the daughter everyone knew about, but few had seen. Wearing the same ankle-length black and orange dress as her mother, her hairstyle identical, she was her mother's mini-me. But her leafy-green eyes gleamed in the light, full of longing that made her stand out, even as she hovered behind her parents.

"There's something I wanted to ask you two about," the young woman said.

The parents continued talking, and the daughter walked quicker, trying to catch up to them. The door to Poppies & Wheat jingled, opening and closing for them. In the window, the assistant manager moved to the side, letting the family take over. The daughter gave a small, timid speech, while the mother's face contorted until she stormed out of the room. The sheriff's eyes widened with each word he spoke. The daughter's wrists shook as she tucked hair behind her ear. Her stare fevered, her eyes full of tears.

Part of me wanted to mock her; *oh, how tragic, her paradise was ruined, all because mommy and daddy hadn't given her everything she wanted.* But a thought stopped me: the people she lived for, turned away from her. I knew what it was like to look at your family and know that they didn't give a shit about you.

I stared down at the mouth of the stream pooling beneath the viewpoint, the water glimmering under the full moon. Part of me wished I could destroy their perfect family: a florist mother; the sheriff father; the sheltered, likely virginal, daughter. My brother and I had seen our parents die before we were teenagers. And when our uncle took us in, mentoring us to take over his business, it became even more clear that we were the anti-family. Two orphans, being raised by a mortician.

For a perfect family like theirs, it would be easy to pick them apart. To steal the heart that kept them together. To watch them crumble like ashes. Passion burned inside of me when perfection was destroyed like that.

A stream of trick-or-treaters trailed behind me, one whispering, "Is he a dirt monster?" My brother would have been amused by that. I had forgotten I was covered in dirt.

I turned to head back to my car when the jingle of the flower shop's door carried over the street. Footsteps dashed across the asphalt, then two hands slammed into the railing. The young woman—the daughter—panted frantically, like she didn't know what to do with the emotions boiling up inside of her.

I shouldn't have given her a second thought. She wasn't anything to me. But I didn't care about what she wanted or needed, only that those tears on her face were delicious, wrought full of pain. I couldn't stop myself from staring. Those full quivering lips. A thin, breakable neck. Thick, bushy eyebrows, so young and full of promise. Cheekbones blushing deeper the longer she endured my gaze.

She turned to me, wavering.

"Is that your costume?" she asked, her voice hesitant. A grin flitted across my face. I was in my thirties, and yet, she thought I was dressing up for Halloween. How innocent.

"I was working," I said.

"What do you do?"

"I dig graves."

She wrapped her arms around herself. Heat pumped through my veins. I loved rubbing that in people's faces; it was a useful tool to intimidate others. Her dense brows furrowed, then her forest eyes searching me intently, the tears finally stopping. She shifted her weight, uncomfortable with the silence. I should have asked her a question, but I wanted to see what she did under the pressure to speak.

"I didn't know they still dug graves by hand," she finally said.

"Most don't."

She let out a soft breath, then pulled out the ties and pins from her hair until it all fell down her back in long curls, past her hips, like strings of rope.

"Maybe I should just cut it all off," she muttered.

"That will show them."

She glared at me, and I lifted my brows. Caring about hair so much was ridiculous. Maybe if my brother hadn't died a few days earlier, I wouldn't have been so callous. But right then, I really didn't care.

"What's your name?" I asked.

"Kora," she said. "Kora Nova. My mother owns the flower shop. You might know my father—he's the sheriff?"

Telling me everything when she knew so little about me? What a trusting girl.

"What's your name?" she asked.

The door to the flower shop rattled open, interrupting our conversation. The sheriff exited, heading toward his squad car parked a few shops down. Kora faced the stream below us again.

"Why were you crying?" I asked. I couldn't help myself; I wanted to poke at her shallow pains.

"My parents," she said. "They won't let me go anywhere. This," she smacked her hands into the railing, "*This* is the first time they've ever left me alone. Why did I think they would let me go to college? I'm just their precious little flower." She turned to me, baring her teeth. "But you don't help a flower grow by blocking out the sunlight."

I grinned to myself. Poor little girl couldn't go to college. But there was venom in her voice like she was holding back parts of herself, knowing they couldn't escape. I wanted to mold that, to squeeze her until she erupted from the seams.

"Your life isn't over because you can't go to college." I chuckled to myself. "You're—what, eighteen? Your life has barely begun."

"It's not just that." A cry rattled through her chest, the tears rushing back. "Even though I want to go, I can't leave. No matter what I do, I'm stuck here."

"And you always will be," I said. She stiffened, and I turned to the moon's reflection on the water. "This world traps all of us."

And it always would, until we were rotting in the ground.

Those tears shuddered to a halt. The trails on her cheeks shined blue in the moonlight. I took another step forward, jasmine filling my nose, as if she steeped in its scent. I grabbed her chin; she flinched, but her round eyes widened, taking me in. Her lips parted. I must have been the first man to ever touch her like this.

"One day, you'll wake up and you'll realize none of this matters. Your dreams. Your failures. These tears." I wiped the wet trails from her cheeks and her green eyes traced mine. "None of this will matter. I promise."

Because one day, we'd all be dead too.

She blinked rapidly. "Who are you?" she stammered.

I bent down, kissing her forehead, the dirt on my cheeks smearing her skin. "I'm no one," I said. Then I turned, heading across the street. A twitch of adrenaline surged through me, my steps lighter than before. I imagined breaking her apart, watching her cry until her eyes shriveled, until she was nothing but an empty husk of herself.

This was what I needed: to ruin Kora Nova and her family.

I headed back to the funeral home, letting the weight ease off of my shoulders. I knew what I had to do. Without acknowledging my employee, I moved my brother's body to the crematory retort and immediately started the process. He had spoken his desires when he was alive, but now, he was dead. There was no one to check on his last wishes, except for me.

And what did I care what he thought?

As the cremation proceeded, my mind buzzed with thoughts of her. Kora's laughter transforming into tears. Kora gasping for her last breath. Kora with her face down in the dirt. Kora on her back, her blank eyes staring up at me. Once the machinery beeped, signaling the process was complete, I went to the far end of the cemetery, finding a new plot that I would dig specifically for her. She was fascinating: she was stuck in her parents' shadow because it meant pleasing them, even though she knew she would never be happy.

She shouldn't have cared so much. No one was worth that kind of trouble. Not even family.

Ruining Kora's innocence, then making her forsaken body into a painting drove me forward. I imagined creating a memorial painting in her cremains, delivering it by hand to her reluctant father. Then I pictured painting a bouquet, then giving it to her mother, watching her throw away my hideous art, not knowing exactly who it was. And as I made it past the first two feet of dirt for her grave, the energy I had longed for was back. I needed to paint *now*.

All because amusement had found its way into my life in the form of a precious little flower.

I rushed my brother's ashes through the pulverizer. And once I mixed his ashes with paint, I dashed my brush across a blank canvas, staring at the work. In a few moments, the clear form of her swan's neck, her pouting lips, her blushing cheekbones, her furiously childish eyebrows, all came to life. But something was off.

I dug through my drawers until I found blue pigment, then added it to a fresh bowl. I dragged the brush along her cheeks, fixing the canvas with tears and moonlight.

Living or dead, Kora would fuel my art.

Chapter 2

Kora

present

"Nyla, dear?" my mother, Shea, asked, her voice calmer than usual. I glanced at Nyla, knowing what was coming. She bit her lip.

"Yes, Miss Shea?"

"Did you read the date on the printout, or did you forget to check that part?"

Nyla's nostrils flared, and she subtly shook the yellow hair out of her face. A gold ring with a giant onyx stone flashed on her finger as she tightened her fists at her side. Almost as if she wanted to use that ring to punch my mother.

"These are yesterday's orders," Shea continued. "Did you read the computer?"

Nyla's eyelids fluttered, holding in her frustration. "I must have missed it."

"Try a little harder next time, then. I already made a boutonniere when I realized that the school dance was yesterday," Shea said. Which, of course, meant that my mother hadn't been reading the orders either, but it was easier for her to blame everyone else, to give her a false sense of control, than it was to admit that she was wrong too. She peered at me. "That arrangement looks lovely, sweetheart," she said. "You've really developed an eye for it."

"Thanks," I said quietly. My head hurt; a braid went across the top of my head like a headband, the rest tucked into a fat, messy bun at the nape of my neck. I liked having long hair, and my mother told me I would regret it if I cut it, but I always kept it in a bun anyway. I straightened the stem of the white rose. The baby's breath stunk in the air, but if you skipped it, the customers always noticed. Especially the brides.

Once Shea was in the storeroom, I turned to Nyla. "You know she didn't read it either," I muttered.

"Uh-huh," Nyla said. "But it's probably my fault that she forgot her reading glasses again."

"Yours, or mine."

Nyla knocked into my shoulder. "Watch it." She nodded at my hands. "You cut yourself again."

My palm was bleeding, a knick from a tool.

"Maybe it was the scissors," I said. I grabbed a bandage from my dress pocket and slapped it on. The only thing good about a mother-boss that picked all of your clothes, was that when I said I *needed* pockets for work, she listened.

"Your dress is cute by the way," Nyla said.

The dress was mauve and flowy. I beamed. "Thanks!" Like my mother, Nyla cared about style, but I tended to like Nyla's clothes better than my mother's, and it wasn't often that Nyla actually *liked* the stuff my mother picked out for us. We were usually wearing the same thing. *Like mother, like daughter,* Shea often said.

I opened the drawer underneath the counter and got a handmade card with a pressed daffodil on the front.

"Happy Birthday," I said.

Nyla grinned; daffodils were her favorite.

"You shouldn't have," she said. "Thank you, Kora." She tucked it out of the way so that my mother wouldn't see it. My mother had a way of making things weird when it came to my friends. Nyla leaned over and whispered: "You know I got her a mocha, right?"

A smile spread across my face. "What? Not a chai latte?" I

reached over and shoved her arm. "How dare you get a mocha for the Queen of Poppies & Wheat!"

"Off with my head!"

"She just might kill you," I joked. Nyla's eyes flicked back to the computer as she printed out the correct order list, her chin sinking lower. "Or, more likely," I added, "fire you."

"I'm not even sure if I want this job anymore." She shrugged. "Maybe that's what I should do: get her the wrong coffee drink so many times in a row that she fires me over a latte."

"Don't quit yet," I pleaded. Two years ago, when Nyla had first been hired, I had begged my mother not to fire Nyla. My mother went through assistant managers like tissue paper; no one was ever good enough for the store, or to watch over me. But unlike the others, Nyla and I quickly became best friends. I knew my mother would never fire her after I asked her not to. It was easier to do the simple things that I wanted, than it was to try and appease my bigger dreams. "At least wait until you can open up your own place," I said.

"Won't that affect your mom's business?"

It was true; there wasn't enough room for two florists in Punica, but that didn't matter. My family would find another way.

"A little competition never hurt anyone," I said. "You know she's only hard on you because you remind her of herself." Nyla looked up at me, a question in her eyes. "Seriously. She thinks you'll be better than her one day."

"What do you think?"

"I think you already are." My mother was good, but her style was traditional, where Nyla's was adventurous. "Don't quit yet though, okay? I'll cover for you." I nodded towards the storeroom. "I'll tell her that I ordered the coffees today."

"Got it."

Shea floated into the room like a sunny sky. She seemed even-tempered for once. Now was my chance to talk to her about my latest plan.

Shea headed to the display cooler, and I followed behind her.

"You remember I said there was something I wanted to ask you about?" I said.

"Not now, sweetheart," she said, thumbing through the boxes of daisies and roses. "I'm trying to see if we have any Middlemist Red camellias. Someone told Quiet Meadows that we'd have them in stock, and *now*, they have a special request."

Everyone always had a special request when it came to flowers. Especially funeral customers.

"In a few minutes?" I asked.

Shea folded her arms and faced me. "What can I help you with, Kora?" It was her words for customers, as if she knew that whatever I wanted to ask her about, was going to irritate her. On any other day, I might have backed out, waited until a better time to approach her. But this was it; my only other friend besides Nyla was bringing in the final draft of the business proposal today, which meant I had to broach the subject now.

"You know the empty lot next door?" I said. Shea raised her brows, then shoved a lock of dyed brown hair behind her ears. "I was thinking maybe I could build a greenhouse."

She blinked, then leaned in, lowering her voice: "Did you say *build* a greenhouse?"

"I could be right next to you, and I'd still be able to learn about growing, rather than—" I shrugged, "—arranging flowers."

"What's wrong with arranging?"

"Nothing," I said, my voice squeaking into a higher pitch. I always had to be delicate with my mother. "I just like growing things. And the independence of owning my own greenhouse could be a great learning experience for me. And I would be nearby, so we could always—"

"Sweetheart," Shea said, letting out a long, exasperated sigh. "How on earth do you think you'll be able to manage Poppies & Wheat when I'm gone, *and* a greenhouse? It's hard enough as it is running this shop with just you and Nyla. And if I'm gone and you're managing the flower shop and the greenhouse, just imagine how stressed you'll be." She put a hand on my shoulder, her grip heavy. "It isn't good for your health. Now, I appreciate that you're trying to make it work for both of us, but you have your garden at home. Don't mistake a hobby for a career."

I held my breath, fire burning inside of me. "I—"

The store's phone rang. The three of us startled.

"I'm sure it's Quiet Meadows again," Shea said, clicking the phone's answer button. "Poppies & Wheat," she said, then she waited. "I told you to tell Vincent that I would look. But Middlemist Red is sought after for that very reason. It's extremely rare. Yes, I know that there's a rumor that it grows on Mount Punica. But I can assure you—"

Shea disappeared into the back rooms. I finally exhaled. *Vincent.* That name sounded familiar. He worked at the funeral home, didn't he?

"At least you tried," Nyla said.

I forced a smile. "Try and try again," I muttered. There was no use in fretting over what my mother had said. I would have to find another way to take care of her, and still do what I wanted.

The door chimed. I turned to go to the storeroom, but when Shea whipped around and saw that it was Andrew, one of the county cops, she smiled and motioned me forward. Shea had watched Andrew when he was a baby, before I was born. And though he was five or so years older than me, my mother and father had always dreamed of us getting married. His crisp uniform fit his muscular body, and the color brought out his blue eyes. Hair so white, it shined around his head like a halo. And while Nyla practically drooled over him, he was just Andrew to me. Shea lifted the phone, showing Andrew that she would be available in a few minutes, then returned to the storeroom again.

"How are you, Miss Nyla?" Andrew asked.

"Just fine, here, Officer Andrew," she winked. He tipped his imaginary hat, thumbing his belt loops, showing off his stature. His eyes landed on me. "I see you're looking well today, Miss Kora."

He laid the charm on thick, no matter who it was. But Nyla always said he had eyes for me, and yet that was easy when he was one of the only men my mother would let me talk to—the only other man, besides my father, that she trusted. Andrew lifted a manilla folder, holding up the business plan. Over the last few months, he had worked with the banks and some of his lawyer friends to get me a solid plan to open up my own place. Andrew was good with his connections, and it helped that he worked at the police department.

"I asked her about the lot next door," I said.

"How'd it go?" I sucked in a labored breath, and Andrew let out a whistle. "That good, huh?" I nodded. Shea returned to the main room, and Andrew turned to me. *I'll talk to her,* he mouthed. Relief swelled through me.

"I told Quiet Meadows that if Mr. Erickson wants a Middlemist Red, he'll either have to go to Wild Berry Trailhead to look for it himself, *or* he'll have to, heaven forbid, come down here to Poppies & Wheat so we can discuss his options." Shea turned to Andrew, a smile springing to her face. "And how are you today, Officer?"

"Fine as ever, Miss Shea."

She smirked. "You make me feel young again."

"And my, what a fine lady you are." He took her hand and kissed it. She fanned herself, a blush creeping across her cheeks. Nyla's chin dropped. Andrew put an on Shea's shoulder. "Now, Miss Shea, I heard about something here. You know the lot next door?" He led her into the storeroom.

Once they were gone, I smirked at Nyla. "Pick up your jaw," I said. Nyla stripped another rose stem.

"I don't understand how you don't see it," Nyla said. "He's like a popsicle on a hot summer day."

I rolled my eyes. "Like he melted all over the place."

"He makes me all sticky."

"Gross!"

As Shea and Andrew returned to the main room, Nyla jumped up. "Miss Shea," Nyla said, in a sweet tone, "It's my twenty-third birthday. Will you please come out to 52 Peaks tonight?"

"You mean, will *Kora* please come out to 52 Peaks tonight?" Shea corrected, raising her eyebrows.

"I couldn't imagine celebrating it without my best friend," Nyla said.

We both knew that the only way I could go anywhere, was if Shea was with us, which luckily, usually had its perks, like a private suite or VIP service. Shea knew most of the people in the county; it was part of being on so many committees and being the sheriff's wife.

"What about the Echo deaths?" Shea said, turning to Andrew.

"There has been a surge," he said. I sighed. *Thanks for the help, Mr. Popsicle.*

"What even is an Echo death, anyway?" Nyla asked.

"It's a synthetic drug, masquerading as the new equivalent to MDMA," Andrew explained. "Doesn't hit people until they're driving home. Then they're dead." He shook his head, his chin heavy. He turned to me. "It's a good thing your daddy is on the case."

"Wait. Why would it only give them symptoms when they're driving?" Nyla asked. "That doesn't make sense."

"Maybe it has something to do with the lights on the road, inducing a seizure or another reaction." Andrew shrugged. "All I know is that I don't like it. Too many funerals for twenty-somethings lately."

We were all quiet for a moment. The funeral orders had been good for my mother's business, but it was never fun to put together white lilies, carnations, and roses. Even if they were beautiful, you could never forget what they were for. Especially with the parents. No one wanted to survive their children.

"That settles it, then. We're busy tonight," Shea said firmly. "But we can have a cake here tomorrow."

"Miss Shea," Nyla started, her eyes round like two giant sunflowers, "I never do drugs. And I would *never* let Kora do drugs. I would never even let her out of my sight!"

"And I volunteer to escort them," Andrew said.

"Yeah! We could take Andrew with us," Nyla said. "And with Andrew there, no man would even try to talk to us, and he would make sure—"

"The answer is no," Shea said, her eyes cold. "Now, come here, Andrew. I want to show you something…"

The two of them disappeared once again, and I stared off into space. I might have been home-schooled and barely let out of my parents' sight for the last twenty-one years, but still, I could survive one night at a club. But in a small town like ours, people talked, and my mother hated when she was in the middle of unfavorable gossip. It was our responsibility to be the perfect image for my father's career; we owed it to him. And when we failed, she spent days in bed. Letting me go out would risk all of that.

"What's that face for?" Nyla asked. "No frowns allowed on my birthday."

"I just feel like I'm always missing everything." My shoulders sank. "Like I'm stuck in quicksand."

"Don't worry," Nyla said, rubbing my shoulder. "Once I open up my own shop, you can come work for me. Or if your business plan with Andrew falls through, maybe we can own the shop together. See if he can work something out for us."

My heart fluttered. "That sounds amazing," I said. "We can call it Best Buds, you know. Like two flower buds."

"What about Buds & Buds?"

I squeezed her arm. "I love it."

"Don't worry, Kora." Nyla beamed at me. "We'll get you out of here one day."

She was right. I shook away the fear, the shame, the anger, burying it deep down. There wasn't any point to those feelings; all they did was remind me of what I didn't have, and that's not how you lived: you had to appreciate the beauty in each moment, even if that moment was dreaming about a future that might never come.

"Nyla, for heaven's sake!" Shea yelled from the storeroom. "You know I'm sensitive to mocha syrup. I always get a chai latte. How could you forget?"

Nyla and I exchanged a look. "I put in the order today," I shouted. "Nyla just picked it up."

"Well," Shea emerged, her eyes bloodshot. "*You*, of all people, should know better." She rolled her eyes. "Let's go to Nectar Latte." She threw her purse over her shoulder. "Maybe we can get you a birthday drink."

"And the shop?" I asked. My heart raced; Shea rarely let me leave the shop or our house. Going to Nectar Latte was like sneaking out to go to a house party.

Shea glanced at the computer, then flicked a finger at Andrew, ordering him to follow her. "No pickups until the evening. But I need to stop by the grocery store first," she said. "And it will give us a chance to talk things over too. Andrew has a fantastic idea. He asked to partner with you on the greenhouse, but there are some conditions."

Partners? That wasn't part of the deal. My chest tightened. "What conditions?"

"Marriage."

"*Marriage?*"

"Well, dating first, of course," she laughed, exiting the shop.

I switched the *Open!* sign to *Be back soon!* then followed my mother, my best friend, and my childhood friend, down the street, happy for this small adventure, pleased with the chance to actually *discuss* the greenhouse proposal, and hoping, for all the plants and flowers in the world, that I had misheard the 'conditions.'

Chapter 3

Vincent

"Another one," my employee, Catie, said, her voice sullen.

"Echo?" I asked.

She nodded and I rubbed my forehead. "Same thing as before, though."

Catie ran a hand through the gray-dyed mane on the top of her head, the sides shaved. She wasn't what you'd typically expect of a funeral director, but as long as the families were comfortable, I didn't care what she looked like. She was the face of the business; I worked behind the scenes.

We headed to the holding room, our footsteps clacking on the tile.

"The wounds don't make sense," Catie muttered. "A car accident wouldn't do that. Even I know that."

We weren't medical examiners, and Catie had only done embalming while she was in mortuary school, which made it eerie that she could tell something was up. A stillness settled over us as we reached the room. A black pouch was sprawled on top of a gurney. I unzipped the bag, the mild scent indicating that this person had died recently. The skin smooth, then rippled with blood and impact. Broken bones, gashes in his face. Parts of his body crushed like a trash compactor. He couldn't have been much older than twenty.

And the one mark that stood out from the rest: a puncture wound through the chest bone, straight to the heart. Just like the last several Echo victims.

With my eyes steady on that hole, I asked, "The coroner's report?"

"Car crash, induced by driving under the influence of Echo," Catie said. "But that—" she pointed to the wound, "—that's too clean to be from a car crash."

There wasn't any reason for me to care about these young adults, dying for the new drug that was as rampant as a plague in Acheron County. Deaths were deaths. It was part of the business. But when it came to suspicious reports that glossed over certain patterns, curiosity struck me. Who was behind this, and what was their reason?

Go ahead, rob someone of their life. But do it with reason.

I went to my office and grabbed my keys and jacket. Then, in the bright light, I headed to my car, then drove to the Acheron County Coroner's Division. We were a small county that hadn't been able to hire an actual medical examiner. So, outside of the steel doors, Bill pushed up his glasses.

"Mr. Erickson," he said.

"I came to ask you about Echo," I said. Bill nodded and stepped to the side, letting me past him. The chill of the room crept over my shoulders. A muted television hung to the side, local news flashing on the screen. The polished nine-body morgue gleamed against the wall.

"A lot of Echo deaths lately," Bill said quietly.

That was an understatement. "A lot of driving under the influence, even for Acheron County," I said. "Did the police mention the state of the vehicles?"

"Always totaled, sir."

"There's one missing piece, though." I rubbed my finger over my chin, then went toward the body cooler, dragging my fingertips across the smooth steel handles. A drug epidemic was possible, but the puncture wounds didn't add up. "Do they all drive the same car? Crash in the same spot?"

"That would be impossible," Bill mumbled. His shoes

squeaked against the tile floor. "Too many possibilities. The county would have done something by now. A recall. A traffic stop."

I grabbed the handle of one of the cooler doors, pulling out the tray. A long white sheet covered the body, the toes sticking out of the bottom, the tag hanging to the side. *Nicolette Larson, 19, Folium City.* Not for our town, but for the city that held 52 Peaks. Likely another Echo death.

"Mr. Erickson, I—"

I yanked back the sheet. Sure enough, there was blood soaking her chest.

"How is it that out of all the Echo victims, and I do mean *all* of them, have the same puncture wound on their chest?" I asked, slamming the door to the refrigerator shut. I snapped around to Bill, then stepped closer. "Right here," I punched a finger into his chest bone, "as if someone stabbed them," I knocked my finger into him again and he twitched, "and yet, there's no mention of this in your reports?"

"Mr. Erickson. Sir, I—"

"Funny, isn't it?" I said. "You know, maybe if they drove the same cars, drove the same exact streets, and all had the same GPS or some other bullshit instrument attached to their windshields, then *maybe* that would explain how all of them were impaled." I paused, staring down at Bill. "But that would be impossible. It doesn't make any sense, does it, Bill?"

Bill swallowed a dry gulp of air. "N-no, sir."

"Perhaps they were stabbed."

"M-maybe, sir."

"And yet your reports mention nothing of that." I grit my teeth, looking down my nose. "Who are you covering for, Bill?"

"No one, sir."

While Bill was likely working for someone, my gut instincts told me that he wasn't directly a part of it. I stepped back. It was better to keep a close eye on Bill, to see who he had contact with, than it was to pursue him as the main perpetrator. Crimes came with consequences, and death came with a price. Once I found the perpetrator, I could figure out how to use that person to my advantage.

"It was all from the crash," Bill said. "I'm sure I mentioned it. But my reports—"

Sheriff Mike's familiar brown hair filled the television screen.

"Turn that up," I said, gesturing at the image. Bill quickly found the remote, eager for the break from his interrogation.

The Echo Crisis won't terrorize our people any longer, the sheriff's voice boomed. *Our children deserve to grow up in a world that's safe and nurturing. As your sheriff, I promise I will continue to take care of this county, every step of the way. The Echo Crisis will always be my greatest concern in protecting our people.*

A still image of the sheriff with a red and blue label plastered across the screen. *Reelect Sheriff Mike!* a male voiceover chimed. *I'm Mike Nova and I approved this message.*

Sheriff Mike's concern sounded genuine, but he was good at acting. It was probably mostly a front. Everyone was obsessed with Echo; it was fitting that the sheriff would latch onto the latest crisis to help boost his reelection campaign. Did he have the same doubts as I had, or did he truly think that the Echo deaths were a drug problem?

"If you think of anything, let me know," I said to Bill, then headed out. I mulled over these thoughts as I made my way back to Quiet Meadows Funeral Home. I would have to ask Sheriff Mike about it in person, or perhaps start investigating the crime scenes myself. There was always someone at the other end of the rope, and I intended to figure out who it was.

Catie rushed at me as soon as I came through the entrance. "Shea said she won't look for the Middlemist Red anymore. She said you either have to come down to the shop to negotiate, *or* you have to find it on Mount Punica by yourself."

"But it isn't for me," I said. "It's for the Cliftons, who specifically asked for the Middlemist Red."

"I know," Catie sighed. "I tried. Believe me."

If the Cliftons had been mourning someone who had lived a long, fulfilling life, I might have been tempted to tell Catie to redirect the family to Shea, so that they could discuss by themselves. But their daughter was barely twenty-one when Echo supposedly took her life, and I knew that this was the last thing they wanted to do.

Besides, it gave me a chance to check on my flower.

I drove the short distance, parking on the side street, then came around to the front of the shop. The same empty lot was next to it, now filled with wildflowers. *Be back soon!* hung from the door, the shop lifeless, the white bouquets in the coolers like the silhouettes of ghosts peeking out from the darkness.

I walked down the sidewalk, heading for the coffee shop, joining the line waiting to order from the cashier. Punica was a small town, and yet Nectar Latte never seemed to have any breathing room, as it was the only locally owned and operated cafe. A minute later, the door opened, and the latest customers entered.

"It's not that difficult," an older woman's voice rang through the room. I turned and glanced; it was the florist, as I had expected. I had been watching her, her husband, and her daughter for years now, and they were all creatures of habit. "It's not like he's proposing you get married right now."

"You did mention marriage though," Kora said, her voice tense.

"And a wedding," another woman said. Her yellow hair was familiar; she had worked in the flower shop these last few years. Officer Andrew stood behind the group, his hands on his hips, literally shielding them. I scoffed; he and I hadn't been on good terms since my brother's death.

Kora's lips pressed into a thin line. "The point was that I do this on my own. That it's *my* place."

"Sometimes, compromises have to be made," Andrew said. "It'll help with any future loans you might need. It's simply an idea, Miss Kora."

"But wouldn't it be your business, then, if my name isn't even on it?"

"Which means I'll take the fall, should you fail," Andrew said. I wanted to smack the smirk off of his face. "I'm sure we can think of something else if this idea doesn't work out for you."

"Andrew!" Shea gasped. "But I thought—"

"I will not force the girl, Miss Shea." Andrew tipped his invisible hat. "That isn't how you respect a lady. You have to earn her gratitude."

My lips curled, a sour taste in my mouth. If Kora had wanted him, I would have stepped in to remind her of her place.

But Kora was too smart for that.

After I ordered my drink, I leaned against the wall. The mother was too busy lecturing the yellow-haired assistant manager to notice the strange man staring at her daughter. Kora hesitated, pushing the hair behind her ears, smiling at Andrew, then turning to her yellow-haired friend, bobbing her head along with the conversation. So obedient. So ready and willing to do whatever Mommy and Daddy wanted, even if it destroyed her.

I wanted to take that desire to please and wring it out of her, making her kneel before me in a way that would kill everything her parents had worked so hard to protect. It was amusing to me, meddling with the perfect family. Kora was a detached fascination for me, like a fly trapped under a pin, waiting to die beneath the glass case. A grin crossed my lips; I had enjoyed observing her like this. Through the glass storefront. From the walls of Nectar Latte. Just inside of her bedroom window while she slept. In the last year, she had started leaving the window open every night, like she couldn't sleep without fresh air. Like she was waiting for me.

Once I figured out who was behind the Echo deaths, I could exchange my silence for adding a Kora-look-alike to the list of victims, so that no one would notice when she disappeared with me, or if her body turned up later. Not even Coroner Bill, Officer Andrew, or even her father, Sheriff Mike.

Kora's eyes locked with mine, recognition flashing across her face. Her bottom lip dropped slightly, and her fingertips touched her forehead as if she could still rub the dirt from my kiss off of her skin. I held her in my gaze, ripping each layer of protection from her soul until I imagined she was barely there.

The barista at the end of the counter announced my drink and I lifted my cup in Kora's direction, giving her a silent toast. She stared at me, her eyes blank.

Oh, my little flower, I thought. *Petal by petal, I'll rip you apart.*

I drove to my house. It was behind the funeral home at the bottom of Mount Punica, on a slight hill, so that I could look down through the trees to Quiet Meadows. It had been my uncle's home; my brother and I were supposed to inherit it. At first, when they were both alive, I had always thought there was something missing from the house, and yet now, literally monitoring the graves by myself, I could forget that emptiness.

As soon as I turned off the engine, three rottweilers barked in a chorus, waiting at the edge of the yard for me to open the car door. Sarah, the big sister of the three, barked at me, dropping a wet red ball at my feet. Bernie jumped up, resting his paws on my chest, and Ulysses circled around the three of us, waiting for his turn. They were rescues. It had been an off chance that I had seen them that day, but now, they had a home too.

"All right, all right," I said. "We'll play after dinner." Bernie and Ulysses started wrestling with each other, grunting in response, waiting for me to jump in. Sarah barked at them, and a few seconds later, the three of them trotted inside, following me into the stone-paved kitchen. I pulled out their food from the fridge, putting it into a saucepan to heat before dumping it into their bowls. The two brothers lapped away hungrily, while Sarah put her head on my knee, waiting for me to stroke her fur, before heading to her own meal.

It was a little early to feed them, but with the Echo deaths, I never knew how late work would run. But while I had a minute to spare, I contemplated my plan: if Shea hadn't noticed me watching her daughter at Nectar Latte, then it was time. Echo deaths would begin piling up soon, so before then, I would have to get to work.

Perhaps I would stage Kora's death to add to the list of Echo victims, but not before destroying her with my own hands first.

Chapter 4

Kora

The next day, Shea crossed her arms over her chest, peering out of the store windows. She fixed the hem of her turquoise dress, then glanced at me, to make sure that my dress was in place too.

"Nyla is usually here by now," Shea said.

"It was her birthday last night," I said. "Give her a break."

Shea rolled her eyes. "Maybe she's getting us coffee."

"A mocha, I'm sure."

"*I* was the one who got the order wrong, remember?"

"Uh-huh." She winked at me. She pulled the orders from the computer, cursing at the machine under her breath, and I went to the back patio, grabbing the sanitized buckets from the storeroom to fill them with water. I watered and trimmed the new shipments, placing them back inside of the cooler, then handled the phone while my mother was working with walk-in customers.

An hour went by. And then another. The sun was high, roasting the asphalt and treetops beneath it. A tension pooled in my stomach. Once the store was empty, I turned to my mother.

"Do you think she's sick?" I asked.

"What happened to it being her birthday?" Shea said, squeezing my shoulder. "Leave the worrying to me, sweetheart. Nyla's just enjoying her first hangover."

But Nyla didn't drink.

"I'll call," she said, right as the next customer walked in, "after I finish with her."

My stomach buzzed while I waited, and I swear I stripped the same rose six times before I realized it. I moved onto the next stem, staring into space, imagining Nyla dancing in a flashy nightclub. The phone rang, startling me out of my thoughts. I answered it; another vase of white roses for the funeral home. I added the order to the correct day, then went back to stripping roses.

A drop trickled down my finger, like a bead of sweat. Blood. In the storeroom, I put on a bandage, and when I returned, my mother picked up the phone and smiled at me, then began dialing Nyla. Her eyes shifted to the figure eclipsing the sun; my father's tall frame, in full police uniform, filled the window. He bowed his head. He never came to the shop while he was on duty.

I knew, then. *Nyla.*

The world went white, a ringing pulsing in my ears. My calves throbbed with dull pain and my stomach dropped to my ankles. My face was hot; the air vacuumed from the store. My mother spoke and my father rubbed my back. But I couldn't breathe. Couldn't think. Couldn't stop myself from feeling.

She had more promise than anyone I knew. It should have been *me*.

Why Nyla?

I ran to the back patio and retched my guts onto the cement, the orange juice sour and burning my throat. I wiped the back of my clammy wrist on my forehead, then leaned against the building, slumping down to the ground. The sweet scent from the lot next door, full of wildflowers, blew toward me, but my stomach flipped even more. I covered my nose. Nyla and I had planted those seeds for the lot. And now she was gone, leaving the flowers in her place.

No. I couldn't think about it.

I swallowed it down: all of those emotions, all of those thoughts. Pain wasn't useful. It consumed you, making it so that you couldn't be present. And if Nyla was gone, there was nothing I could do now. This was why no one could dwell on the future; anything could be ripped away from you in an instant. That's why the present moment mattered, more than anything.

The door to the back patio swung open.

"Kora?" Shea asked. "We can close shop for the day, or I can call one of the seasonal workers. Let's go home, sweetheart."

My breath caught in my chest. "No," I whispered.

"Kora, I think you should—"

"I said, 'no,' Mom."

Shea's eyes softened. I rarely ever told her 'no.' But now, I couldn't deal with my mother's smothering need for control.

"Nyla never did drugs," I said confidently. "Never. Not even weed. She waited until she was twenty-one to have her first alcoholic drink, and she didn't have any after that."

My mother laughed politely. "Oh, sweetheart, almost every kid at least *tries* alcohol before they're of age. Maybe she—"

"Not Nyla," I interrupted. "So *why* would she do Echo? After everything Andrew told us?"

Shea's brows drew together. "Maybe she was drugged."

That's what I was afraid of. "We need to tell Dad, then."

"I'm sure your father already knows, sweetheart. This is his profession, after all." She stroked my arm. "You need to rest. We can go home; I'll make you some tea. And we'll watch old movies…"

I zoned out, not listening to what she was saying. I needed to talk about something else right now. To get my mind off of it. Before I sunk underneath these consuming thoughts.

"Does Vincent still need the Middlemist Red camellia?" I asked.

Her head flinched backward slightly. "From Quiet Meadows? I don't remember mentioning Mr. Erickson's name."

It was for a funeral; I knew that much. And even if she hadn't explicitly mentioned his name, I knew from eavesdropping on the hushed conversations of our customers, that Vincent Erickson was from the Quiet Meadows Funeral Home.

"If you want any chance of finding it, you'll have to go to the flower field on Mount Punica," I said. "The one by Wild Berry Trailhead. I want to come too."

"You'd be better off sitting out for this one. I can have one of the seasonal workers come in and watch you, and then—"

My eyes burned. The only way I could ever leave Poppies & Wheat was by inserting myself into my mother's errands.

"Mom," I said, tears filling my eyes, "I need this."

This. A distraction. Anything. So that I didn't have to think about how she was gone.

Shea's chin sank, then she forced a smile. "Of course, sweetheart. Let's go now."

After she asked a seasonal worker to handle the shop for a couple of hours, we drove through town, up to the Wild Berry Trailhead off the side of the road. Mount Punica was considered an active volcano, with areas where the sulfur was heavier in the air than others. It hadn't erupted in centuries, but the soil was still ripe for flowers, even ones like Middlemist Red camellia. It was rumored that John Middlemist sold it to a traveler who planted it here for good luck, as a peace offering to Mount Punica. If it was anywhere, there would be one in the flower field.

Focus on the flower, I reminded myself.

"All right," Shea said, stepping out of the car. She surveyed our surroundings. "No one is ever out this way, but you know the rules. You check over here, and I'm going to hunt up there. I think I saw red and pink flowers the last time we went hiking." She fixed the collar of her dress. "But if you see anyone, and I mean *anyone* —you come and find me."

I nodded, but my mind instantly glazed over, ready to get lost searching for that mysterious flower. Between the fir trees that lined the mountain, there was a clearing, with the sun's rays resting on it like a spotlight. A fence of black huckleberry bushes lined the area. And in the center, poppies and lupines sprung up. Glacier lilies and windflowers swayed next to the sprawling edges of the western wallflower. I scanned the field; there were no symmetrical kaleidoscope petals of reds and pinks. No Middlemist Red camellia. But my eyes stopped on a flash of yellow: in the middle of the field, a single daffodil stretched up.

I had never seen one in this area before.

I bent down, kneeling in the middle of the stretching stems, wrapping a finger around the daffodil. It's not like Nyla's spirit was inside of this flower, and yet, I was drawn to it; it was the same color as her hair. I pictured us the day before, standing in the middle of Nectar Latte. Her easy-going nature. She was so good, she even made my mother relax sometimes. And yet Nyla *and* my mother didn't notice the man in the corner, watching me. No one did. Not even Andrew. But I did. A flash of gold sparked in his eyes as his gaze sunk over me, those golden specks disappearing into the darkness.

Vincent. That's what the barista had said. Like the funeral home worker.

How many Vincents were there in Punica?

It was so rare for my mother to leave me alone, that I sat there dazed, almost like I was inside of a daydream, staring at that daffodil. It reminded me of a teacup; bright enough to warm your day, tender enough to drink from. It was almost like hypnosis was seeping into my skin, urging me to drink from it. To eat it. I raised it up, bringing it closer to my lips—

"Go on," a deep male voice said. His voice coaxed me, wrapping a hand around my gut. I sat up quickly. In the shade of a tree, a man stood tall, his shoulders wide and sturdy. Muscular. His skin was abrasive, dark from the sun, with white streaks of scars dashing across his skin, deep valleys and bumpy keloids that had long since healed. His dark hair was a mess, stubble tracing his chin and jaw. His eyes were dark as if no light could penetrate them. He looked older than me. Maybe he was in his mid-thirties. "The ambulance will have an IV. And if that doesn't work, I'll take you to my home."

My skin flushed. His home?

"What are you talking about?" I asked.

"Those flowers are poisonous."

My hands started shaking. I knew that.

Suddenly, I knew where I had seen him. He was the man from Nectar Latte yesterday and from Halloween night, all of those years ago.

"You work at Quiet Meadows Funeral Home," I said. He must have been *the* Vincent I had heard about. "Is that what you mean by home?"

He smirked at me, teasing me for the obvious connection.

"I don't work at Quiet Meadows," he said. "I own it."

My skin flushed. Working and owning were two completely separate things. I knew that. "Did you name it after this place?"

"Now why would I do that, Kora?" he asked.

He knew my name. Had I told him it years ago? And did he remember me from back then too?

I bit my lip. "This is a quiet meadow. It's peaceful," I said.

He stayed on the edge of the clearing, his obsidian eyes penetrating. I pulled the daffodil apart in my hands, not realizing what I was doing until there was nothing left to shred.

"The narcissus," he said, gesturing at the broken petals. "An interesting flower. Has quite the history. They symbolize rebirth and spring."

My breathing hitched. Even when the voice inside of me warned me of all the things my mother had said, about why I couldn't trust men—I wanted to know, to understand why he was here, why he was telling me this.

I shouldn't have been talking to him. But I wanted to. A distraction. *Anything.*

"What's the history?" I asked.

He leaned on the tree trunk next to him. "The myth goes that Persephone was distracted by the narcissus until the earth opened up and swallowed her down into the underworld."

I touched the damp dirt hidden under the stems. "Why would the underworld swallow her?"

"Because Hades wanted her."

My stomach twisted into knots. I dug my fingers into the dirt, unsure of what to do. I had never spoken to a man like this before. The only two men I had ever had conversations with were my father and Andrew, and they didn't seem to count. This was different. *He* was different. The way he kept looking at me, lit my skin on fire. But I wanted him to keep going.

"How do you know so much about flowers?" I asked.

"After working with your mother for ages, I've learned a few things. I'm sure you have too."

My mother. That's why we were here, wasn't it? For him. For his funeral home.

"So you're searching for the Middlemist Red camellia?" I asked. "Like my mother told you to?"

"I'm here for you." A violent flash of heat coursed through me and disappeared as quickly. My heartbeat thumped in my chest, my skin turning red. He must have read the panic on my face because he grinned and added: "You inspire me, flower. I've been using you for my art."

I reflexively tucked my hair behind my ears, even though it was all tied in a bun. Was it flattering that I inspired his art? Or strange?

"So you're an artist?" I asked.

"Not really."

I blushed, the color creeping across my neck and cheeks. How was it that he made me feel like this, just by answering a few questions?

"What are you, then?"

"No one," he said. A chill ran through me. Those were the same words he had said all of those years ago. He chuckled, his dark gaze scrutinizing me like a test subject. The sun hid behind a cloud, covering the meadow in a shadow. His form grew black in the darkness.

I turned back to the daffodil, holding the remnants in my palm. They would be withered and dry soon, and then, like Nyla, they would be gone. A single tear fell down my cheek.

"How long did you know her?" he asked, his voice softer than before. He already knew about Nyla then.

"Two years."

The wind blew through the leaves, rustling the fir trees, the piney scent swirling around us, mixing with the pungent flowers. The torn petals scattered in the wind. This was the only place on Mount Punica where I had never been sickened by the bursts of sulfur from fissures, the only place where we could forget that this soil was rich, only because of its potential to destroy everything around it.

"I'll take good care of her," Vincent said.

I narrowed my eyes at him, daring him to make my friend into a joke. But for once, there was no ridicule behind his words. As if he took pride in his work, in preserving her memory for me.

"Is she going to be buried?" I asked.

"Embalmed for the viewing. Her ashes buried on the grounds."

A tree burial would have been better, but the current plan seemed like what her parents would have wanted.

"Kora!" Shea screamed, her words splitting through the quiet. My eyes watered and I turned to her.

"Yes, Mom?"

Her eyes softened for a moment. I rarely ever called her that, only when I knew I needed her on my side.

"You know better than to talk to strangers," she whispered. She stood behind me, grabbing my shoulders. "Why are you speaking to my daughter?"

"Mount Punica isn't private property." Vincent smiled, extending a hand. "My business often seeks your assistance. I'm Vincent Erickson."

"Oh," Shea said, her cheeks turning red. "I'm sorry, Mr. Erickson. I had no idea that you would actually—"

"My funeral director said that I had to come to retrieve my order from you personally, or that I had to find it myself. What better way than to ask your daughter about the rumored rare flower?"

His eyes landed on me again, setting every part of my body ablaze.

"I hope you understand, Mr. Erickson," Shea said, squeezing my shoulders as if she could literally shield my body from him by keeping me in place. "But my daughter has a delicate composition. We prefer she doesn't talk to strangers."

"No need to explain," Vincent said. "I understand the importance of treasuring something special."

My mother's body stiffened, but she forced a smile. "Thank you, sir. Now, we haven't found the Middlemist Red, so I'm afraid you'll have to tell that client that we'll figure out another comparable flower." She moved her body, standing in front of me. "You know, most clients will be satisfied with a rose."

"I'll speak with the family." He turned to me, looking past my mother's shoulder. "It was good to see you again."

Shea watched him closely. "Likewise," she said. He disappeared down the path, and she let out a harsh exhale.

My stomach clenched.

"Why were you talking to him?" Shea snapped.

"I—" I stammered, glancing at the torn petals in my palms, then quickly said, "He's taking care of Nyla. I was asking about what he was doing to her."

"He's going to do what he always does," Shea scowled. "Pump her with chemicals or burn her to ashes.

I clenched my fist. "Don't talk about Nyla like that."

"What?"

"You're acting like she doesn't matter. But she matters to me." The tears burned inside of me, threatening to boil over. "She's my friend," I added in a quiet voice.

My mother sighed, then whispered, "Was." She put a hand behind my head, pushing me into her shoulder, expecting me to sob, to seek comfort from her. My body tightened. I had no desire to hug her right then. "You can't think of her like that anymore. Nyla is gone. This pain you feel?" She tapped my breastbone like it was the only place I could hold sorrow. "There's no use for it. It'll make everything worse, sweetheart, and you shouldn't dwell on what you can't change."

If anyone understood that, it was my mother. She was right. I couldn't bring Nyla back.

But I couldn't move on without her. Not yet.

"I want to organize the funeral," I said.

Her lips pressed into a fine line, suppressing a condescending smile. "That's the funeral director's job, sweetheart," she said. "I don't know if we can go, honestly. We've been so busy with the funerals lately, and something like that, it's really too difficult for your temperament—"

"I want to celebrate her life, Mom."

She gave me a quick smile, then tapped her lip. "In a funeral, all you do is say goodbye to the flesh and bones. But Nyla is still inside of you, sweetheart. You carry her memory with you everywhere. It's—"

"I'm going to the funeral," I said, raising my voice.

"What about Andrew?" She glanced around frantically. "What about the wedding? Your proposal? The greenhouse—"

Was she dangling that in front of me on purpose? "Don't change the subject," I warned.

Her lips flattened, all of her features tightening. The forced kindness vanished from her face. "Haven't I taught you not to speak when you're emotional like this?"

I narrowed my eyes. "I'm going to the funeral."

"You have no idea what you're committing to. What you're committing *us* to. You can't let these feelings take control of you."

I grit my teeth together. She didn't get it at all. How many more times did I have to say it?

"I *am* going to the funeral," I said, more determined than ever.

"And I need to protect you."

"Protect me from what?" I threw a hand toward the mountain. "This is the most dangerous part of Punica. If it erupted, we'd both be dead right now."

"I'm protecting you from men like Vincent Erickson," she hissed. Her eyes were seething, steam practically bursting from her sides. I shrank back, the flowers brushing against my legs. "A man like him will rip you to shreds and laugh at what he's done." Veins pulsed in her face, and I hated myself for upsetting her. "Do you think I *want* to do this to you, Kora? To cage you like a little bird? To clip your wings so you can't fly?" Her whole body shook. "I don't want you to end up like Nyla."

I stared at her, shifting between her bloodshot eyes. I pleaded that I hadn't pushed her over the edge. I wasn't the delicate one; my mother was. It was never worth doing this to her.

A pain throbbed in the back of my throat. I hated when this happened.

But I wasn't going to let this go. I needed to do this for Nyla, even if it meant risking the consequences.

"All I want is to say goodbye to my friend," I said quietly, my voice calm and measured, despite the tears blurring my vision, threatening to fall. "She was my only friend, Mom. I need to do this." I took a deep breath, bracing myself for her wrath, then added: "I *am* going to go to her funeral. Whether you like it or not."

The wind blew through the flowers, and finally, the clouds moved away from the sun, letting its light burst forth. The rainbow of colors shined bright, and at the sight, my mother sighed, rubbing her forehead. She closed her eyes briefly.

"Fine. We'll go to the funeral together." She motioned for me to follow her back to the car. "But pick yourself up. Tears aren't useful. You know that."

The sky was blue between the trees. I blinked until the tears disappeared. At least Shea was letting me go.

Shea headed back down the mountain road. Finally, she broke the silence: "*I* don't want to go. It's too real," she said. "I don't know what I would do without you."

That was it, then. Seeing Nyla like that meant imagining what it would have been like if she had let me go to 52 Peaks with her. But the pressure to be everything my mother wanted me to be swelled inside of me. The perfect daughter. Her protégé. Her garden of possibilities that she could nurture and cherish and sculpt into the perfect arrangement, pretty and wonderful, until it went limp in the vase. Nyla had always been able to shake those thoughts from me, to remind me that there was life outside of Poppies & Wheat. Nyla had even given me hope that one day, I could be on my own.

I'll take good care of her, Vincent had said.

Vincent's dark eyes filled my mind. He might have been the kind of man my mother was afraid of, but somehow, I knew I could trust him when it came to Nyla.

Maybe he would have the answers I was searching for.

Chapter 5

Vincent

They argued through the trees while I dragged my boot along the dirt, scattering the seeds inside of a thin valley. With the bottom of my shoe, I moved the dirt back into place.

"I *am* going to go to her funeral. Whether you like it or not," Kora said, her voice uncharacteristically raised. I leaned to the side, watching her closely. Her body was tense, her palms clenched into fists. Her skin was blotchy and red, her body pulsing with energy. The florist made sure that her daughter was insulated, that she never felt anything, not even anger. I smiled. This was new, then.

Soon after, they left and my amusement died with it. To everyone else in Punica, they were the perfect happy family. A sheriff, a florist, and a pure, sheltered daughter. Even three years later, the thought of ruining their image entertained me. What else could destroy that perfection, more than a disappearance of the one thing that brought the happy family together?

Leaving Mount Punica, I drove down the road back to the edge of Acheron County, to Folium City, where 52 Peaks was located. Most of the Echo victims died along Willow Highway, a two-lane road lined with fir trees, the sickly vapor of the volcanic vents hanging in the air.

And now, another young person had died there. Nyla Nerissa.

Once I recognized her name from Poppies & Wheat, I decided I would investigate the wreckage with my own eyes. Whoever was behind these deaths had come too close to what was mine. Kora could have been with Nyla that night.

A few squad cars were parked along the highway. A silver car, the front mangled like a gnarled branch. The windshield broken, the glass shattered on the car and asphalt.

"We appreciate your concern," a familiar voice said, "But we don't need the mortician to survey the scene. Aren't you needed back at Quiet Meadows?"

The white hair fell into view. Andrew Pompino, the supposed protector of the innocent, the only non-blood-related man allowed to speak to Kora. The high-and-mighty cop needed to be kicked down a notch. Naturally, I found ways to mess with him.

"I thought your team would have been done by now," I said, motioning at the car. "What's this about? Aren't you going to wrap it up and call it another Echo death?"

"I am here on orders from Sheriff Mike," he said, narrowing his eyes. "The Echo Crisis is ravishing our county. We need to protect our citizens. I will do whatever is needed, whenever it is needed, as directed by the sheriff."

"The sheriff only until the next election," I said evenly.

"Sheriff until the people vote otherwise." He sneered. "What are you doing here?"

"Investigating." I walked toward the caution tape, peering over the side. Nyla had been removed, placed into a body bag, her eyes staring up at the blue sky. A stain of blood marked her chest, but the coroner, Bill, zipped up the bag quickly. Bill hid his eyes, hunched as he pushed her toward the van. I waved, knowing he would ignore me. Then I walked back toward Andrew, my footsteps crunching the glass. "Do you read the coroner's reports? Examine the bodies for yourself?" I laughed. "Perhaps you assign some intern to do that for you."

"How dare you imply I—" Andrew started, then stopped. "I read the reports."

"And do you ever check the bodies before they come to Quiet Meadows?"

"Now why would I need to do that when I trust my coroner?"

"There's a pattern," I said. "Looks closer to a knife wound than a car crash injury."

"I trust our coroner. He's a good man."

"Is Bill one of your friends?" I asked. "Must be nice to be given a government job."

"We are a separate government entity," Andrew said sternly. "Nepotism is against policy."

I tilted my head, studying Andrew. We were both tall, but where he was thin and fit, I had more bulk to my muscles. White hair, blue eyes, completely different from my brown hair and black eyes. He was an officer that lived by the rule book, the exact opposite of me. I had been to detention centers a fair amount of times as a teenager, even overnight as a young adult, but Andrew had only ever been in jail to lock someone up.

"You know what I find strange, Erickson?" Andrew asked. "You see, your brother—what was his name?" He cracked his neck like he forgot when I knew that asshole had memorized my brother's name. He loved using it against me. "Justin. Right. Well, Justin had a peculiar thing about his situation too. He was drugged—"

"Shot the heroin himself," I corrected.

"But there were knife wounds too."

"The coroner determined it was suicide."

"Yeah, and yet these kids—" he said, tilting his head. "Drugged too."

"Or they took it themselves."

"You know, I was good friends with Miss Nyla, and she never took me as the devious type." He shook his head, his expression pained. "And, if what you are saying is true, that they have knife wounds? Then that's like your brother."

My jaw clenched. This was bullshit. "My brother killed himself," I repeated.

"According to the reports."

I sighed, shaking my head. "You trust your coroner, don't you?" I scratched my chin. "And isn't it convenient for these deaths to be right around Sheriff Mike's reelection, right when he needs a cause to rally his voters behind?"

"Convenient for you too. Being that death care *is* your business."

Andrew had a point; business had been better than ever. But I shrugged my shoulders.

"Check the reports," I said. "Then come by Quiet Meadows and check the bodies yourself. There's a pattern I'd like for you to see."

"Like I said, I trust my officials to work according to our good law." He tipped his imaginary hat. "As you should too, Erickson. We are all simply doing our jobs."

I chuckled to myself. As I was doing mine.

Back at Quiet Meadows, I finished my tasks for the day. Once the evening settled in, I went to my studio. Each space on the wall was covered with a painting: the curve of her neck, her pouting lips, her eyes gazing at me. Most of the paintings were in black and white, created to look as if they were done with charcoal, but were actually a combination of acrylic paints and abandoned cremains. And there were a few rare dashes of color, a deep blue. The color swirling in a portrait of her at the viewpoint, the moonlight on her cheeks, the trails of tears running down her face.

Using the ashes and acrylic mix, I dashed the brush across a blank canvas, creating her form in the middle of that vast field. The broken petals in her palms. I loved mocking her for her pain, but I knew firsthand that it was hard to lose someone you loved, especially when that was the last person you had in the world.

In the backyard, the firepit was unlit, the extra freezer storage humming almost as loudly as the insects. In the darkness, red fruit shimmered like a deep purple wine on the dark mountainside. I went through the woods, finding my favorite tree, then tapped on one of the fruits. It made a metallic, hollow sound. I ripped it off, carrying it with me.

I went to Rose Garden Neighborhood, where the Novas lived. Naturally, it was one of the nicest communities in Punica, with a vine-covered archway leading inside. The plain bushes in the Novas' front yard shook in the wind. I slunk into the backyard, using the latch on the side gate like I had many times before. The sheriff was too confident to lock anything. It was a pity, really. I would have enjoyed the challenge.

The rose bush across from Kora's window had been removed recently. And this time, she was sleeping on her side, facing the wall, as if she couldn't bear to look out her open window and see the blank space. The windowsill was full of young plants, drooping slightly. I stepped over them, my shoes landing faintly on the floor. A bowl of plain yogurt and granola sat on her desk; she usually finished her evening snack. Dried flowers were strung up on a long branch of driftwood against the wall, other dried flowers pressed in tiny glass frames. Trinkets and pretty knick-knacks of all kinds covered her walls and counter spaces. A white comforter with a giant red carnation printed on the fabric was pulled tight over her shoulder, the bedspread accented with red and green blankets. To the side of the room, a few plants hung from the ceiling, their vines dangling below, and another large window with dividers showed the fence to the side of the house.

Her shoulders heaved slightly, then a whimper came from her throat. She wasn't asleep at all; she was crying.

I placed the pomegranate on her windowsill next to one of the potted plants, letting my boots make more sound than usual. Kora turned over, and as her eyes cast upon me, realizing that I wasn't a shadow, but an actual figure, she sat up quickly.

"What are you doing here?" she asked.

"It's all right, Kora," I said. "You remember me from Mount Punica? I'm here to see if you're alright."

"And why wouldn't I be all right?"

"Your friend died."

Her expression went white, then as the color returned to her cheeks, she gritted her teeth. "My father is the sheriff. My mother will—"

"Tell me, flower. Is that what you want to do? Go to your parents for protection when you and I both know you're capable of handling me, all by yourself?"

She shifted, her eyebrows squeezing together, not backing down. To say that she could handle me by herself was generous, but I knew it would appeal to that independent streak buried inside of her.

"For all they know, you're dreaming," I said. "Sleep-talking in a grief-induced dream."

She tucked her long hair behind her ears, the need for sleep evident in her sunken eyes. "Why are you here?"

"Isn't it obvious?" My lips pressed into an eerie curve. "I'm here to save you."

Her jaw dropped. "From what? What could possibly be more dangerous than a man breaking into my bedroom?"

"You enjoy thinking of it that way, don't you?" I tilted my head. "But you knew I was coming. That's why you started leaving the window unlocked for me. You knew I was watching over you. Waiting for the right chance to speak."

She held a hand to her chest, her eyelids fluttering. "I don't know what you're talking about."

Lying to herself, then. What a silly flower.

"Do you enjoy your life here?" I asked. "Staring out barred windows. A view of a fence. A garden on your windowsill." I gestured all around us. "I could give you more than this."

A slight tremor ran through her body, and she unconsciously spread her legs. "You're the man from Nectar Latte."

I nodded.

"The man from the flower field."

I nodded again, a smile spreading across my face.

"The man from the viewpoint years ago."

"You recognize me, then."

She trembled, her eyes flickering around, searching for a sign, *anything*, on what she was supposed to do. But she found nothing.

"You want to save me?" she whispered. "From my home?"

"Yes."

"You can't." She pulled the blanket up under her chin. "My mother would die without me."

"There are far worse things than death," I said. I stepped toward her, and the blanket fell from her grasp, dropping to her waist. The creamy silk of her babydoll shined in the moonlight.

"Trust me." I took another step closer to her bed. "This will all be easier if you go of your own free will."

She shook her head. "I can't leave my mother right now. She needs me."

"Your mother wants someone to obsess over. Someone who will fall in line. But what about you, Kora? What do you want?"

Her eyes widened, those bushy brows tense. But she leaned closer to me, and with my boots touching the comforter of her bed, I knew I had her. I peered down at her body.

"Show me," I murmured.

Keeping her eyes trained on mine, she slipped the comforter down past her hips until it rested at the foot of the bed. Her legs were bare, a few black and brown beauty marks speckled her thighs. The space between her thighs was a damp pink. The silk shimmered against her skin, curving against her thin breasts.

"What do you want, Kora?" I asked.

Her lips quivered at the thought. "I don't know."

"Lies," I growled. "Tell me something real."

I touched her chin, rubbing a finger across her cheek, staring at her plump red lips, swollen as if she bit them while she sobbed, too lost in thought to give herself true relief. The urge to make her entire body swell with that tenderness burned inside of me, making me ache with resentment at her untouched existence. Full of lust to ruin her.

"Are you a virgin, Kora?"

I dragged a finger across her lips. She shivered. I dragged my hands down, caressing her bare shoulders, her arms, then grabbed her hips, pulling her to the edge of the bed. Spreading her. Then I skimmed her thighs with my fingertips.

Her lack of an answer was all I needed.

"Take off your underwear."

She slowly slid them off, her cheeks red, her eyes on me the entire time. My cock hardened as I watched her. Her hesitant movements. So unsure of herself.

"Spread yourself for me."

She widened her legs, pushing her breasts forward, then hunched her shoulders, unsure of herself. I took both of her hands, arranging them so that she pulled apart her lips, showing off that beaded clit, glistening with desire.

She was an incredible sight. I kept my eyes on her pussy for a moment longer, salivating, then focused on her dilated pupils.

"You could order me to leave," I said, my voice full of gravel. "You could even scream. You could yell to your mother that a stranger broke into your bedroom. But you haven't done any of that, have you, Kora?" Her eyes flicked away, but I grabbed her chin, pinching her tight, forcing her to look at me. "No one is stopping you. Scream all you want. I dare you."

But she didn't move. Her breath caught in her throat.

"No?" I grinned to myself, and she gave a subtle shake of her head. She wanted me here then, just like I thought. "Show me how you touch yourself."

She blushed, her mouth open and panting. Her fingernails dug into her pussy lips, trying to suppress her nerves.

I laughed. "Don't tell me you've never done that before."

She shook her head, gazing down at the bed underneath her. My cock swelled with heat.

"I'm going to show you, then," I leaned down, lowering my voice so that my words brushed along her collarbone, "Would you like that?"

"Yes," she whimpered.

Her cheeks burned red, and I moved her hand, pressing a finger along her lips, making her touch her own wetness. "You're a smart girl, aren't you, flower? You know what this means." I moved her slick hand across her clit. She shuddered, so damn sensitive it was maddening. "I want you to touch here," I said calmly, "with this hand. And with the other?" I moved her other hand to her pussy lips. "Press a finger inside. See how it feels. Try moving it. Slowly."

She opened her mouth, her body quaking with need, her breathing quickened, and she pressed into herself. I bent in closer to her neck, dragging my teeth against her throat, and she whimpered, the cry so sweet and full of surrender that my cock jerked in my pants, begging to be shoved down her little mouth. I inched my hands closer to her delicate pussy and her hips writhed, begging for more. I wanted her. There was no doubt about that. She was feminine putty, melting to my touch, desperate for more. How could anyone resist someone so pure, *so innocent,* knowing exactly the kind of pleasure and pain that would ruin their very beliefs about themselves? My cock tingled with aggression, knowing that I would destroy her, ruining everything her mother and father had hoped to protect, creating my own version of her in her ashes.

But not tonight. When they were all distracted by the others that were dying, *that's* when I would take Kora for myself.

Tonight, I'd make Kora desire her own destruction.

Her mouth quivered, hungry with lust, and I bent down, my eyes heavy, breathing on her lips, about to touch her.

"Flower," I said, "You want me to take you right here, right now, don't you?"

The glazed look in her eyes told me she had no idea what that meant, but she wet her lips and waited for me.

"Beg me," I growled. She blinked rapidly. "Go on. Tell me what you want. Make me believe you."

"Please," she whimpered.

"Louder."

"Please," she cried, her voice slightly louder. She was hesitant, not wanting to wake her mother. I coaxed her on, tickling her inner thighs with my fingertips, then moved on, playing with her slick folds, relishing in the way her entire body shivered with my touch. Then I ran my hands over hers, massaging her clit. "Please. Yes. More of that. I need more. Please."

My head rushed. I loved it when women were so full of lust that they couldn't speak.

In one sharp movement, I pressed my finger inside with hers, her velvet clenching, her slick heat swallowing me. I curved my finger, making hers curve with mine, and her eyes rolled back into her head. A little moan escaped her, making me growl. I pressed on. She bucked her hips into our hands, her face covered in sweat, but I never increased my speed. I kept the same agonizing pace. She was going to tear me apart.

As her breathing reached new heights, I stepped back, a wide grin falling across my face. She blinked, her cheeks flushing red. I locked eyes with her, then licked my fingers clean. She tasted as sweet as I knew she would.

"Why did you stop?" she asked.

I stepped back toward the windowsill. I checked to make sure the pomegranate hadn't moved, then I exited through the window.

"Vincent?"

I turned, waiting for her. Her lips hung open, unable to speak. Finally, she asked: "Why do you call me 'flower'?"

I smiled. That was her question?

"Precious little flower," I mocked her words from so many years ago, how much pain she thought she felt when everyone else knew her life was a small slice of paradise. She put her hand to her chest, checking her own heartbeat to make sure she wasn't dreaming. "You don't grow by hiding from the sun."

Once I was back at Quiet Meadows, I pulled open the body cooler's tray, finding the latest decedent. Removing the white sheet, her yellow hair was lifeless against the metal.

I moved her to the table, then scrubbed her body. The same puncture wound was on her chest. Staring at Nyla's body, a towel over her for modesty, I thought of the day that Kora would be stretched out before me like this. Dead. Helpless. Not a thought in the world. All it would have taken was one lapse in judgment, and Kora would have joined her best friend much sooner. In fact, they could have had neighboring refrigeration units.

Perhaps there was a benefit to her mother's oppressive obsession. Kora wasn't dead yet.

But I looked forward to changing that.

Kora was consumed with the living and growth, while I was here, pumping a chemical solution into her friend's body, preserving her corpse so that her friends and family could pretend that the destruction of death could actually be prevented. But I knew better.

And soon, Kora would know too.

Chapter 6

Kora

In the morning, I stared at the pomegranate in my hands. It hadn't been there the night before, and though I could have chalked up last night to a weird lucid dream or hallucination, the evidence that Vincent had been there—or someone, at least—seemed to lay inside of that pomegranate.

I had never had one before. My mother said they were too sour, so she never bought them, but Nyla had always loved pomegranates. I was beginning to sweat, wearing two layers. And yet something inside of me felt powerful and rebellious. I tore at the outer peel. When it didn't bend to my nails, I threw it on the ground. The flesh split open. Tiny ruby seeds sprinkled the carpet, their juices staining the fibers. I quickly wet a washcloth, wiping up what I could, then slid a green rug over it.

I picked up one seed, studying it. It was probably sweeter than my mother had said—she was pretty sensitive. I put it in my mouth, curious.

The back of my tongue scrunched up. I spit it out. That thing *was* sour. I coughed, then gulped down some water. But maybe it was a bad seed. I had to try again. For Nyla. This time, I shoved in five seeds—just to make sure—and though the little seeds burst in my mouth, full of flavor and as lush as citrus, it still punched my taste buds. I took the entire fruit and hid it in the washcloth, then threw it in the trash bin. I would have to find a time to take out the trash when my mother wouldn't see.

Gazing down at it, my insides burned. My mother hadn't noticed that Vincent had been in my bedroom, despite how loudly he had made me moan. I closed my eyes; I could still feel his hands manipulating me. What would Nyla have thought about Vincent leaving behind a pomegranate? Would she have liked him as much as Andrew?

Someone banged on the door. My stomach twisted.

"Are you all right, Kora?" my mother asked. "It's time."

Every available space around the corridors of Quiet Meadows was decorated with elegant standing sprays, wreaths full of white carnations, floor baskets, vases, even a single white rose propped up next to an arrangement. A chandelier full of sconces lit the lobby, the shadows of the electric flames flickering inside the votives. Beige walls. Clean tiles. Dark wooden double doors were propped open on either side of the viewing room, as if they opened up into a giant coffin, big enough for all of us. An older couple, maybe Nyla's grandparents, admired her in the casket. The rest of the room was filled with cushioned chairs, like we were all expected to stay.

A black off-the-shoulder dress cinched my abdomen, flowing and loose everywhere else. Nyla had bought it for me. *A little black dress,* she had said, winking at me, *Every girl needs one.* But the only opportunity I had ever had to wear it was here. My mother had chosen a floor-length dress with full sleeves and a high neck. But once I had gotten to the funeral home, I had taken off to the bathroom, faking illness, and changed out of it. This funeral was one of the few times my mother would let me out of her sight. She was going to lose her mind when she saw me. My stomach turned. I still didn't know if it was worth it.

I clenched my fists at my sides, holding my breath. I had argued for this, told my mother that I was going, one way or another, and yet, I couldn't bring myself to see Nyla. I should have done something. Should have prevented her death. Why hadn't I asked her not to go? Why hadn't I convinced her to stay in with me, with rental movies and candy, like we had done so many nights before?

But thinking about those what-ifs wasn't useful. Instead, I judged the arrangements for their tight designs, none of them showcasing the flowers' natural beauty. These people—Nyla's friends and relatives—obviously knew that Nyla loved flowers, but they didn't understand anything about her floral style. I went through the arrangements, propping up their petals, restructuring them into patterns that were more whimsical and outgoing. Like Nyla.

A hand landed on my shoulder. My mother. I knew she wouldn't leave me alone for long.

"What are you wearing?" Shea muttered under her breath.

"Nyla gave it to me," I said.

"You look like a—" She stopped, holding back her words, the derogatory term itching to get out. "People will talk, Kora. This isn't a good look for the daughter of the sheriff. They'll think—"

"I honestly don't care what they'll think."

I stared at her; my mother's stare seared back. She wouldn't make a scene in public. It was one of the only places I had a small amount of power.

"We'll talk about this at home," she said under her breath. Then she fixed her frown into a tight smile. "Remember, this is a time to celebrate Nyla. No tears today, remember?"

"I'm not crying."

"Good." She pulled up my dress. "Only happiness."

As Shea found another person to talk to, I looked down to a glowing window at the end of a hallway, in the middle of a door. I went forward, drawn to the light. I didn't know where it led, but I knew it was better than here.

The door slammed shut behind me. I breathed in deeply. The air hummed with insects, a cool humidity clinging to my skin. Hexagonal stones lined the dirt, leading around the funeral home. I glanced back; through the door's window, my mother had her back to me. For once, she wasn't following me.

Maybe there were positives to a day like this: a chance to be by myself.

I followed the path around to a garden in the back, full of a mix of flowers: gardenias, roses, hydrangeas, azaleas, and lilies—everything white. They were arranged in a brick enclosure, blocking off the funeral home from the cemetery like a gate. If Nyla were here, she would have made a comment about the lack of color.

But I couldn't think about her right now.

I closed my eyes, forced myself to erase her from my mind, to think of anything else, so I wouldn't cry. *Vincent.* Where was he? He must have been somewhere on the grounds.

Just thinking of him woke my senses. It had felt like my entire body was coming apart from the inside. Like he was calling to a different side of me.

When I opened my eyes, the same lifeless colors were there, like beautiful ghosts. Footsteps knocked on the stone steps behind me. From my peripherals, I could see him: the tall frame, the deep white scar slithering up his neck. He stood to the side of me, his suit fitted to his body, drawing attention to his broad shoulders.

"Do you like it?" he asked. My chest tightened as I stared at him. Was he actually asking me that? A flush covered me from head to toe under his gaze, but I grit my teeth. Where did he get the nerve to manipulate me like he had last night and act like everything was normal now? And how was it he could have a garden in his funeral home, but I, the florist's daughter, could only nurture potted plants in my own bedroom?

"It lacks color," I said.

"They were left behind."

I winced; maybe I should have said something nicer than that. Why didn't he throw them out, like the families that neglected them?

I couldn't stand it. These feelings inside of me. Anger. Sadness. Frustration. Envy. *Guilt.* I wanted to bury it all deep in the ground where I'd never find it again.

But it bubbled up.

His gaze didn't waver, but I turned quickly, heading back

inside of the funeral home. Being around him didn't help anything; it just forced me to face it. Charging through the lobby, my mother smiled and lifted a hand toward me, but I ignored her, going straight into the viewing room. I marched toward the casket, displayed on the bier, alone in the front of the room.

I held my breath, lowering my chin to look down at the casket. Her yellow hair was bright, her cheeks smooth, with a hint of color. Her eyes and lips were shut, as if she was simply breathing through her nose. There was no visible damage from the car accident, but the pink blazer covered her neck and wrists; maybe it was hard to tell. It seemed like she could wake at any second and say that she had finally gotten the rental agreement. Buds & Buds could be our new reality.

But none of that would happen now. This was what happened when you contemplated the future. When you hoped for something else. Something better. I had to be in the moment. With my friend's body. *Here.*

A dark figure appeared at the edge of the room. Vincent's presence was heavy, as if he was scanning my body. He stepped forward, standing by my side once again. I bit my lip. Was he following me? The coffee shop, the flower field, my bedroom, and now, here?

No… He worked here. There was a reason for him to be here. A good one, at that.

But that didn't explain all the other times, or why he kept talking to me.

"How are you?" he asked.

"Fine," I said automatically, trying to end the conversation.

"Really?" he asked, scratching his jaw. "Tell me something real."

His eyes were earnest and questioning, and yet, it brought me back to the night before. He could see past my facade. Inside of me. Like my world was crumbling down, and his words were adding to the weight. I was trying so hard to hold myself up. To keep it together.

I huffed out a breath, turning back to the casket. Her expression was serene, more peaceful than I had ever seen in her living life.

"I wonder what it feels like," I said, my voice full of air and light.

"What?" he asked. He turned toward me.

"This," I gestured at her body. "She doesn't feel anything, does she? What does death feel like?"

I reached down and touched her rosy cheek, but her skin was cold, and I yanked back my hand. I crossed my arms, covering my fingers, as if my fingertips burned, like I had broken some kind of barrier.

"Don't be afraid," Vincent said.

"I'm not." But I wasn't sure if that was the truth.

"People would rather pretend like this doesn't happen every day," he said, looking down at her body. "They're afraid. But pretending like death doesn't exist never stops it from coming." His brows drew together. "Trust me. I know."

I didn't understand him. He was threatening and venomous. And yet I got the feeling that he wanted to teach me, that he was speaking to me more than he cared to with most people.

But that didn't change the fact that my mother was going to be livid if she saw me talking to him.

"Why did you come to my bedroom the other night?" I asked. "My mother wouldn't like to hear about that."

He tilted his head. A sly grin crossed his lips. "You haven't told her?"

I raced to the back of the room, my cheeks red. A woman with the sides of her head shaved, the top of her hair in an elegant braid, smiled at me. As someone passed by, she patted their shoulders, handing them a tissue box. A black jacket covered her lace-lined shirt, and her name tag reflected the fluorescent lights. *Catie,* her tag read, *Quiet Meadows Funeral Director.*

"How are you holding up?" she asked, as if we had known each other all of our lives.

"I'm fine," I said, but this time, I *knew* I was lying. "No. I'm not." I shook my head. "Yes. I'm fine." I shrugged, frustrated with myself, trying so hard to be someone who wasn't affected by any of this. I took a deep breath. "You did a great job." I motioned toward the casket at the front of the room quickly, then turned back to her. "She looks beautiful."

"Considering everything that happened, she looks fantastic," Catie said, a sad smile on her face. I was glad I hadn't seen her before the embalming. "I'll let Vincent know you appreciate his work. He always likes to hear that."

I blinked at her, trying to process. *His work?* I turned back to the front of the room, expecting to see Vincent still standing in front of the casket, but he was gone.

"Vincent does the embalming?" I asked. "I thought he just owned the place."

She nodded. "Cremation, gravesites, and yes, embalming. He's an expert at it, actually. I can't seem to do makeup on anyone but myself," she laughed.

That made sense then. *I'll take good care of her,* he had said.

Another person approached us, asking for Catie's help in announcing the reading of the eulogy, and I stood there, pretending to listen, my mind swirling with Vincent. I had been taught to be cautious of everything, including death. But he truly wasn't afraid of death. I had never met anyone like him.

"There you are!" Shea said. She put an arm around me. "I've been looking everywhere for you. You shouldn't be by yourself."

I hadn't been by myself. And yet, I wasn't sure that I had wanted Vincent's company either.

Maybe my mother was right. If Vincent treated the dead with more respect than he treated the living, then maybe he could rip me apart.

Still, I had such little experience with anything at all. What would being torn apart feel like? Would it hurt?

Or would I like it?

Chapter 7

Vincent

I stepped into the lobby. The forlorn shapes of the artificial ficus trees hovered between the groups of people. It was better that way; I simply dusted the trees and none of the families had to worry about them dying too. A woman with black hair cut to a chin-bob emerged from the hallway offices. My bookkeeper, Lee.

"Boss," she said. While men had primarily dominated the funeral business in the past, more and more women had entered the field. Lee and Catie were evidence of that. Lee scratched her chin. "The Nerissa family paid their last invoice this morning," she said, anticipating my question.

"Good," I said. It was better not to put additional stress on the families on days like today, but the death industry was still a business, and it was *my* business, one I had inherited from my uncle. Even if the all-in-one cemetery, crematory, embalming station, and funeral home, was a dying model, between the three of us—Catie, Lee, and I—we ran a smooth business. Luckily, once I had hired Lee and Catie, I was able to avoid dealing with the families almost entirely. I was better at crematory work, embalming, digging graves—anything to keep my hands busy and my brain occupied. Lee headed back to her office and I rubbed my hand over the sleeves of my jacket, the scar thick under the fabric.

It had been like this since I was seven years old. It started with an accidental cut on my arm. When my mother saw my arm bleeding, dripping all over the floor, she had screamed in a shrill voice, then pulled me to her body, clutching me tighter than she ever had, caving into herself, like I was the only one who could hold her up. Dizziness overcame me, like my body was floating under all of her weight, more powerful than I had ever been. I didn't understand how sick she was at the time, but I figured out new ways to inspire that reaction in both of my parents, sometimes even my older brother. To find the passion that I knew lived inside of them, somewhere.

So I lit my desk on fire. Pulled apart our treehouse. Made a bonfire from the planks. Nearly burnt down our house. Hit my head on a boulder until my forehead bled. Cut my neck with a kitchen knife. All the while my mother grew weaker, until finally, she could barely hold me.

That was when I finally understood that she was dying. But I had never expected my father to die so soon after.

You'll understand one day, he had said.

But that understanding never came. Not even when I saw the exit wound on the side of his head. My brother rushed to our uncle's house, but I stared at the two of them. My mother's body was in later stages of decay, the ripe stench of rotting meat fogging the air, metallic with my father's blood. My father hadn't done anything with her body; calling the funeral home seemed like an impossible task. Now, she was tinted bluish-purple. Blood from my father's gunshot wound caked across my mother's face, so dark it was brown.

Back then, I knew nothing about death.

I touched their faces: my mother's cheeks squished under my fingers, but my father was still firm, still warm. The blood had cooled, and when I touched the hole in his head, a sharp fragment pained my finger. A piece of the bullet. I flinched back; I couldn't tell if it was his blood or mine, but my finger hurt. It fascinated me. It was incredible to witness, to see the human body, so utterly destroyed. A machine without power. The shell of light. My mother had died slowly, but my father was gone in an instant. The difference between a treehouse destroyed plank by plank, versus lighting a match underneath the structure until it was engulfed in flames. And still, they were both gone.

When the funeral finally came, I had been enraptured by how normal they both looked. Though there were obvious signs of decay, the embalmer had made my mother seem as if her body had never gone through the trauma of illness. Like she was her old self in some ways. Like she could give me a hug and it would be all right. And the side of my father's head had been smoothed with wax, then colored to match his hair; he looked good too. Like he had died peacefully, and not full of guilt and failure.

My uncle smiled down at me. *Sometimes, death is less painful than we think,* he had said. *Your mother needed the final rest.*

How do you explain my father? I asked.

He blamed himself, he said. *Your mother wanted to go, and your father begged her to stay. And when he realized how selfish it was, he felt it was the only way to make things right.*

That didn't make sense to me. *So why did he go?* I asked again. *Why did they leave us here?* My uncle was taking care of us, but we didn't know him well, and my brother refused to talk about their deaths. I was alone.

My uncle was silent for a while. *I'm afraid there is no explanation,* he said, *only acceptance.*

The need for destruction intensified, with drugs, fire, pain, and violence, until finally, after getting expelled from high school, my brother asked my uncle if he could train me in the field earlier than planned. Now, I was here.

Catie came to my side, then motioned to the viewing room. "I came to check on you. Figured you might need some help."

What she meant was that I rarely attended the services themselves; it was odd behavior to be here for a decedent I didn't know.

"Everything is in order," I said. My eyes landed on Kora, standing in the doorway to the viewing room. Her mother put an arm around her back, her grip firm, as if she was afraid of letting her daughter go, and Andrew bowed his head, his hands in his pockets. I understood her mother, but what did Andrew want with Kora?

"Do you know her?" Catie asked, tilting her head toward Kora.

"The florist's daughter," I said.

"Shea Nova?" she asked. I nodded. "She's off-limits, then."

"Nothing is off-limits."

She raised a brow at me, but I didn't move, my gaze still cast on Kora. A black dress showed off her bare shoulders, flaring out to the sides, more of a dress for a nightclub than a funeral. A smile danced across Kora's face, soft and pleasant, as if Andrew was being amusing.

My hand twitched. I wanted to rip off his head and feed it to my dogs.

"I'd stay away if I were you," Catie warned. "I hear Shea is like a barricade when it comes to her daughter."

"There's always a way around the fence."

That's when Kora finally looked at me, right as her father, Sheriff Mike, slapped me on the back and Catie disappeared.

"Didn't expect to see you here," the sheriff boomed. "You came to join us for once?"

"We worked with Nerissa directly," I explained. "We have a good relationship with your wife's shop."

"Ah. It's another tragic Echo death, isn't it?" He shook his head. The man didn't know restraint when it came to the volume of his voice. "It goes to show you why the town needs a strong sheriff to represent them and make sure that this crisis is put to rest."

He said those words louder, to make sure everyone heard his political soundbite.

"Every gathering is a campaign opportunity," I said.

"Of course it is."

I didn't care one way or another whether Mike was reelected. But I had my suspicions.

"It's quite timely that these deaths occurred so close to the election," I said, tapping my chin.

"Don't I know it," Mike said, lowering his voice for once, grabbing my shoulder. He rambled on about his campaign platform, and my eyes glossed over to Kora. Her mother was no longer in sight, but Andrew was close to Kora, the back of his hand knocking into hers. Too close for my liking.

"What do you think of Andrew?" I asked, cutting Mike off.

"Andrew?" he grinned. "He's like a son to me. My wife used to babysit him, you know," he winked. "He wants to be sheriff one day." Sheriff Andrew? I scoffed. "Shea wants him to marry our daughter. I can't imagine a better match." Mike laughed. "Wouldn't you say?"

Another addition to their impeccable family.

"I don't trust him," I said.

He smacked me on the back. "You don't seem like the type to trust anyone."

It's not that I didn't trust anyone; it's that I didn't care *for* anyone. There was a difference, or rather, a lack of interest. But Andrew struck me as off. Kora backed away from him as he leaned into her. If he did that one more time, I was going to have to remove him myself. This was my funeral home.

"He's not good enough for her," I said.

"No one will ever be," Sheriff Mike said, beaming at his daughter. "But you know it's not up to me. Shea runs the show when it comes to Kora. Always has. Always will." He chuckled. "The only way Andrew might get to Kora is by kidnapping her himself!"

He laughed hard, but I didn't find it amusing at all. Not when I knew what I had planned.

"She can't expect your daughter to live, grow, and die in your family's house," I said.

"Shea has her own plans. Says we take care of the children, then the children take care of us." Mike shrugged. "But she'll never let anything hurt her."

She had no idea what was coming, then.

"How is the Echo investigation coming along?" I asked, changing the subject. "I heard your team is getting close to an arrest."

"I'll tell you what." He put a hand up to his mouth, guarding his words for once. "There's a suspected Echo ring we're busting tonight. I'm taking the force with me."

I patted his back. "That's exactly what we need right now," I said, knowing the words he wanted to hear.

"Can I count on your vote?"

"Always," I lied. We shook hands, and he found another person to chat with, his voice shaking the room. I turned toward the hallway that led to the garden.

"Vincent," Catie appeared at my side. I turned to her. Kora's eyes burned into my back.

"What?"

"There's a home pickup," she said. "South of—"

Andrew wrapped an arm around Kora and she rubbed the back of her neck, looking around as she did. For someone to help her.

I crossed the lobby to her side.

"If she doesn't want your attention, take it elsewhere," I said in a low voice. "This isn't a bar, Officer Andrew."

"We were just talking," he said, a grin on his face. "And I believe it is none of your business, Erickson."

"If you make someone uncomfortable in my establishment, it *is* my business."

"Establishment?" Andrew laughed. "Go figure. Erickson thinks his funeral home is an 'establishment.'" A few people chuckled with him, but Kora crossed her arms.

"Leave her alone," I said quietly, "or this won't be pretty."

"Are you threatening an officer, Erickson?" Andrew asked.

"You both need to shut up," Kora said, staring daggers at us. We both silenced, turning toward her. "Today isn't about your egos. It's about Nyla." She shook her head. "You're both acting immature right now."

"Miss Kora," Andrew started.

"I can take care of myself," she said, her gaze snapping to me. "Now, if you'll excuse me." She walked back through the hallway to the exit.

I clenched my fists, glaring at Andrew. "You're supposed to be a cop."

"And I am here to protect Miss Kora," he said, sticking out his chest. "And you heard her. She can take care of herself."

"Then why are you still here?"

"I'm not," he said, turning to leave.

The door swung closed to the garden, and I grit my teeth. Even if she was strong enough to put us in our places, as soon as anything had happened, Kora had fled. She couldn't handle anything real.

And yet a part of her was drawn to the darkness, where pain and death and grief and longing all existed in the same space, boiling with each other. Where you had no choice but to feel everything.

Don't be afraid, I had said.

I'm not, she had said, triumphant in her words. *What does death feel like?*

I had wondered that same thing with my parents and my brother. It was rare to find someone like that.

I went through the back door, exiting around the side of the building. Kora's slender frame stood gaunt to the side of the garden, but I went past her, not giving her a second glance.

"Thank you," she said.

I stopped, turning my head for a moment. She crossed her arms, blocking herself off from me.

I resumed my walk, heading back to my house. *Don't thank me yet, flower,* I thought. *It's time you were plucked.*

Chapter 8

Vincent

In the studio, I stared at the blank canvas. I turned on the police scanner, the crackling audio surging through the room.

10-25? Sheriff Mike's voice called through the scanner. I browsed the code guide I had purchased years ago; he was asking if the person had contact with whomever they were investigating.

A slight pause, then the line crackled. *Affirmative.*

Then another voice piped in: *10-49. Possible Echo use.*

They were getting close, then.

Visions of Kora surrounded me, paintings I had created: Kora's mouth wrapped in agony; Kora being crushed under the weight of the earth; Kora and her innocence, protected behind a gate. She had been my spark over the last few years. But right then, I felt nothing. A stern indifference always overcame me right before I was about to do something destructive. My body always saved energy for those moments.

A few seconds later, another voice: *10-70. And let's go with a 10-38. Backup requested at the scene. Lake Drive and Willow Highway.*

That was closer than the others.

It's totaled, he continued. *We need another officer down here.*

A 10-70? Echo? another voice asked. I checked the code guide: a possible dead body.

Another pause, then: *Affirmative. 10-71.*

Sending the team down now, Sheriff Mike said. *Andrew?*

Andrew: *On it.*

An array of codes was read off, but my mind glossed over once I confirmed that Sheriff Mike had been telling the truth. Having a potentially dead body was a curious situation, especially so close to a supposed arrest for Echo distribution. And who better than to assist at the scene first, than the golden boy, Andrew Pompino, himself?

It left me the prime opportunity to finally take Kora.

In the kitchen, Sarah lifted her head from the ground, grumbled, then laid back down between her paws. Her brothers snored beside her. I gave her a scratch on the head, and she huffed, annoyed that I was leaving her.

"I'll be back," I said. "Soon."

Another huff.

The night was quiet; Punica saw little action after the moon came out, which was when I liked to work. But as I turned onto the main road, blue and white lights flashed in my rearview mirror. I pulled over, waiting for the officer. When he finally came, I rolled down the window. Andrew's white hair came into view.

"Officer Drew," I said.

"Andrew," he corrected.

"What can I do for you on a night like this?" I smiled. "You must have something—" I shrugged, "—more *pressing* to take care of right now?"

Wasn't he supposed to be on his way to a car wreck? Not dealing with a traffic stop.

"Always the clever one," Andrew said. "According to the paper, this is about the time the dealers sell Echo."

"Interesting," I said. "Do you know where I can get some?"

Andrew stiffened, not appreciating my joke. "Do you know why I pulled you over?"

I pointed at the chip in the glass. "The crack on my windshield?"

"Tail light out. Something like that isn't safe, especially at night."

"I could think of worse things."

He tapped the side of my car. "Fix the tail light. And don't let me catch you with it out again."

"Of course, Drew," I said. He glared at me, then walked back to his vehicle. I pulled out, taking the long way to the Nova house, and finally found a new parking spot a block away. I went through the gate in the fence. The master bedroom's blinds were shut, but Kora's window was open. She faced the wall again, not wanting to see out.

Back at the car, I took out the wet rags and canisters of gasoline, then scattered the liquid on the sides of the house, avoiding the areas around Kora's bedroom. The walls near the kitchen. The living room. The sides of the house. The master bedroom. My head itched, the sensation crawling down my neck, expanding in my chest. It had been a long, long time since I had done something like this. I had been waiting for it.

I hit the match against the striking strip, then dropped it. The flames burst to life in a flash of blue and red, crackling across the house. The heat brushed my skin.

For a moment, I thought about leaving them both inside of there. Locking the doors. Letting Sheriff Mike find the bodies of his family. With a fire this big, it wouldn't take long for the police to be notified about the house. And by then, Shea would likely be dead.

But I wasn't finished with Kora yet.

Holding a wet cloth to my face, I went through the window to Kora's room. The smoke seeped through the cracks at the bottom of her door. The fire hadn't reached her room yet, but it would soon.

She stirred, coming to life.

"Vincent?" she asked, rubbing her eyes. "What are you doing here?" I smacked a wet cloth over her mouth and her eyes widened. Her muffled screams vibrated through the cloth, but I pressed my palm firmly on her mouth. The fire around the house flickered in her eyes, and she panicked, twisting in my arms.

"We need to get out," I said.

She thrashed just long enough to get out the words, "But my mom!" Then I tightened my grip with the wet cloth around her mouth and nose, cutting off oxygen, until she fell silent. I let myself out through the gate, then threw her in the back of the car, pinning her body down with my weight, using cable ties to bind her wrists and ankles. She woke again, coughing as she did. I removed the wet cloth, the drops of water dripping down her face.

"My mom," Kora said, her voice hoarse. "My mom."

Her breathing was shallow, her skin flushed. She squeezed her eyes shut, trying to wake herself up.

"Your mother is a smart woman," I said, as if brains could save a person from a fire. I almost hoped that Shea *would* survive; her reaction to the abduction would be intriguing. I strapped Kora's body lengthwise to the seatbelts. "Don't move."

Back at the house, the dogs came to the car, panting at my feet. Well-trained, they didn't make much noise after dark, but once I opened the back seat, Kora kicked my shin. I grunted, stunned for a second. The pain seared through my bones, and I grinned. The dogs growled, their eyes glowing in the night. I crawled over her, enjoying the sharp pains turning to a dull discomfort. Then I held her neck, gripping her tightly as her eyes widened. She pleaded with those green gems: *Don't do this.*

But I squeezed harder. I had waited for this for years.

Her body went still, and a calmness settled over me. I sat back in the seat, looking down at her limp body. The babydoll was pushed up, exposing her thighs, the cotton underwear pushed to the side, a few trimmed hairs poking out of the fabric. Sarah sat by my side, and Bernie and Ulysses paced next to her. A few seconds later, Kora opened her eyes, gasping for air, and I leaned down to her.

"Make a noise, and it's the chloroform next."

"What?" she asked. "Chloroform?"

Well, then.

I went to the front and grabbed what I needed. She inch-wormed across the back-seat, and Sarah growled again in warning. I moved the dogs out of the way, then pressed the cloth to Kora's face. She struggled, thrusting her body as hard as she could, but there was only so much you could do without your hands and ankles. I held the cloth there for several minutes, putting more pressure on her face each time she squirmed.

Finally, she relented.

I stretched for a moment, the pain in my shins surging to my thighs, but then I leaned down, about to pick her up, when a woman's voice interrupted.

"What are you doing?" Catie asked.

Her flashlight beamed at me. I straightened. From her position on the other side of the driveway, she likely couldn't see inside of the vehicle.

But that didn't change the fact that she had come here unannounced.

"What do you want?" I asked.

"You didn't sign off on the Andersons' invoice. You were acting strange today—"

"Did I ask you to come here?" I said. She was like the little sister I never wanted.

"Whoa, there." She lifted her hands. "I thought I heard someone scream. I just wanted to make sure you were okay."

"Probably the dogs." I needed to play this off. I leaned down and scratched behind Bernie's ear, and he whined affectionately. "You know how they are."

"Right," Catie said, hesitation in her voice. "They can be loud."

Which didn't explain what I was doing this late at night, but Catie knew better than to ask any more questions.

"I'll see you tomorrow," I said.

"Yeah," she said, her voice drifting off. "Tomorrow."

"Before you go." She turned around quickly, waiting for my words. "Can you tell me if my tail lights are out?"

She stayed where she was. "Go for it."

I slid into the driver's seat and tapped the brakes. When I got out, she lifted the flashlight. "All good," she said. Just as I had thought; Andrew had made it up. Catie turned back to the funeral home, but paused at the top of the path. "You sure you didn't hear anything?"

"I will take a look." She nodded, pleased with that answer, then started down the path. "Have a good night, Catie."

"You too."

Once she was out of sight, I pulled Kora out of the car and carried her into the house. Thumbprints were visible on her neck, and she would likely wake up with an excruciating headache. Down through the house, to the basement. The entry point to the room was a loft to the lower level, and a spiral black staircase took us down into the depths, creaking with our weight. The bottom level was two stories deep, with brick walls, brown leather chairs, wooden crates that acted as tables, and a scarred cement floor. A decorative artificial fireplace shimmered to the side of the room. I set her down on the leather couch, her body sinking into the material.

Kora laid there lifeless. The pale green babydoll shined on her skin, her pink lips open. Her chest rose and fell. My shin throbbed. I pulled the tracking device applicator from my back pocket and pressed the tip to her arm, inserting it. A drop of blood formed at the incision point. After, I ran a hand up her thigh; the warmth of her body sent a wave through me. I could use her right now, and she wouldn't know the difference.

But ruining her perfect life didn't mean simply stripping her of her innocence. It meant so much more than that. And that took time.

She startled awake, a long gasp shuddering through her chest. Her eyes locked on mine, and a subtle smile twitched against my lips.

"Welcome home," I said.

Chapter 9

Kora

I pulled against my wrists, the plastic bindings digging into my skin. A smug smile hung on Vincent's face.

"Untie me," I demanded.

"Now, now," he said, "Patience, my flower. The best things in life are worth waiting for."

When he saw my jaw drop, he gave an arrogant laugh.

"You think this is funny?" I narrowed my eyes at him. "My mom might be dead because of you. My father is the sheriff. He'll put you in jail—"

"Who said that I started the fire?" He raised a brow. "Did you see me light a match?" I stared at him intently. No, I hadn't. I had been asleep, like any normal person would be at this hour. "As far as we both know, I saved you from that fire. So why don't you thank me?"

He cocked his head to the side, then glared down his nose at me. Every part of my body was hot. I held my chin high.

"You are a jerk," I said. "This isn't a game."

"But why wouldn't I want to have fun with you?"

I looked around frantically, taking in my surroundings. There were no windows. No doors. An old-fashioned staircase led to a higher level. There must have been a door up there.

"Let me go, and I won't tell anyone that you abducted me." *Only that you burned down my house,* I thought.

"What a fair trade." He leaned down, his hands on each side of me. His dark eyes swallowed me whole, a gold gleam of light reflected in them, like a monster peering out from the depths of a cave. He was bigger than I remembered, his shoulders expanding as he peered down at me, like he was curious about his next meal. Gasoline traced his skin, mixed with musky earth. It was him; I knew it.

He pressed his thigh between my legs. "How does it feel to be restrained, knowing that I have you at my mercy?" he asked.

Adrenaline shot through my system. My mother was right. Men were obsessed with power, with influence, with domination. Whether that was law enforcement, like my father and Andrew, or a man determined to control me, like Vincent. *Trust me,* his words reverberated in my mind, *This will all be easier if you go of your own free will.*

A cold sweat broke out all over me. He had planned this all along.

But I didn't have to be at his mercy.

I let out a breath, trying to calm myself. Being panicked wouldn't help me.

"Please," I said, trying to find the right mix of fear and compliance in my voice, "At least undo these cuffs. It's not like I can run." I nodded to the staircase. "You would catch me before I got to those steps."

He stared at me, then pulled a pocket-knife out of his pants and broke each of the ties. A glimmer shined in his eye. It was just another game to him. Even letting me have my wrists and ankles.

I rubbed my wrists. "Why am I here?"

"What does it look like?"

I glanced around, tension throbbing all over. "I haven't done anything to you."

"That's right," he said. A grin tugged at his lips. "You've never done anything wrong in your entire life." He motioned around us. "Your mother and father can't help you here. You'll actually have to work for it. Make decisions on your own. Fight for your life."

My skin flushed with heat. What was he talking about? "I saved you from your cage."

I snapped my teeth. "And put me into another."

He scowled at me, the frustration and rage evident on his face, his cheeks red, a vein in his neck throbbing under that white scar.

"It doesn't have all the pretty flowers you're used to, but perhaps the bricks will be more comforting, seeing as you don't have to pretend that you're living a free life."

I narrowed my eyes. My heart beat hummed through me, a steady ringing throbbed in my ears. My fingernails dug into my palms. How could he say something like that?

"What is wrong with you?" I seethed.

"There it is!" Vincent clapped his hands together, and I slammed my fists down at my sides, holding myself back. I had never wanted to hit someone before, but I wanted to punch him in the eye. "Get angry. Feel it all. Don't let it go." He leaned in closer, bending down to me. "What does it feel like, flower?"

He moved my knees apart, like he had done in my bedroom, his fingertips skimming the inside of my thighs—but this time, I didn't lose myself in the sensations. I couldn't let him touch me like that. Not when he had burned my house. Not when he pretended he had saved my life.

But I knew I had to tread lightly. I had never met a person—man or woman—like him, and I knew he was volatile. One wrong move and I could give myself a death sentence.

I lifted my chin higher. Why were my cheeks so hot?

"What's the matter?" Vincent grinned. "You can't handle the way it makes you feel, can you, flower?" He gripped my thighs so tight that his fingernails dug into my skin and I cringed. "Fight me." His eyes locked with mine, gold embers burning deep inside of those black voids. "Show me your rage."

It was like he knew exactly what I wanted to do. A strange part of me thought he *wanted* me to hit him. It was a mind game, a way to use my emotions against me. I had to stay strong.

He stroked the back of my head, playing with my hair, his fingers dragging through the tangled locks, chills going down my spine. He grabbed the back of my head, dragging his lips against my ear.

"You're too weak for this, aren't you?" he whispered.

I grit my teeth and rammed my fist into his face so hard that it cracked through the room. He held his face, the inner part of his eye socket red, a grin spreading wide across his face.

"There it is," he said again, satisfaction ringing in his tone. "I knew you had it in you."

"You're disgusting," I hissed.

He lunged at me, grabbing my throat so tight that the blood rushed to my face, lifting me off of the ground. Then he put his leg between my thighs.

"So disgusting you can't help but get wet for me," he said.

He dropped me to the ground and I fell to my hands and feet, then scrambled away as far as I could, pressing myself against the couch.

"I thought you were different," I panted. My mother's warnings blared through my head. I touched my neck; it was warm where his hands had been. "But my mother was right. All men are the same. You're nothing like what I thought."

"Funny you should say that." He ran a hand under his chin. "I'm more of myself than I have been in a long time."

He studied me, waiting for my next move. Then his phone buzzed, and he glanced at it, then exited up the stairs, disappearing behind the click of a closing door. Once he was gone, I let out a breath, my arms and legs shaking, trying to force myself to stay calm. But the emotions trickled in so high it felt like I couldn't get my head above water. I punched my fists into the couch cushions and screamed.

That helped. I took a deep breath and looked around. Now, I needed to get myself under control. I had to think with a clear mind.

A fake fireplace flickered to the side, and two modern chandeliers hung from the ceiling, each one decorated with crystal icicles that resembled dripping tears. A faint glow came from within each fixture. Wooden crates and a few leather couches littered the room. This must have been a place where he could store his toys.

The thought made me shudder. I was sick to death of being my mother's doll. I wasn't going to let him use me like that too.

I went to the stairs, carefully going up the twisting staircase, my gut rolling with each creak, not knowing if Vincent could hear me. Up on the loft, a black door was shut, with a long couch against the wall. I tried the handle, but it didn't budge.

I squeezed my fists together. I pictured my open bedroom window, knowing that I could have snuck out so many times before, but I never had, no matter how many times I realized I was living in a cage—my mother and father's house, cage, where I would live, breathe, and die being the perfect daughter. Instead, I had left the windows open, because I knew someone was watching over me. Because I wanted that guardian to come in.

And he had.

This was insane. My father had been on duty, but my mother? She could have been dead.

A drop of liquid landed on my foot. A red dash on my toe. I looked up, trying to figure out where it had come from, but then I realized the liquid was smeared on my arm and nightgown. A small cut was in my arm. I pressed my finger to it; a firm piece of metal was under my skin, like a tiny data chip.

My eyes widened. What the hell was it?

I had to think. Had to figure out a way out. Couldn't let my fear take over my mind. Prying my fingers under the material, I pulled the thin sheet of carpet from the ground, revealing the wood underneath. I threw the couch cushions to the side, looking for anything—a key, a toothpick, a hair pin—but it was cleaner than our disinfected floral buckets.

I went down the stairs, holding my breath as the metal screeched with my weight, then searched the bottom floor. Underneath the loft, there was a toilet, a sink, and a narrow shower stall surrounded by glass walls. A large painting hung on the back wall of a smoky form, almost like a human body, scowled down at me, making me small.

What was I doing here? Why was I so unprepared?

Everything that my parents did was because they wanted the best for me. And yet, Vincent's words seemed terribly true right now: *I saved you from your cage.* It was only this year that my mother had finally started letting me come on errands outside of the flower shop. And this situation, being in Vincent's den, was the farthest I'd ever been away from home. The only time I had ever been without her. In a way, I was free. Maybe if I had been allowed to meet people, to go anywhere, to interact with someone other than the women that came into the shop—maybe I would have a better idea of what to do.

Was I stupid for hitting Vincent, if that's exactly what he wanted?

Surrounded by brick, the light was sucked from the room. Something in my heart told me that my mother was okay, and I held onto that instinct because it was all I had. But my mother had depended on me for her serenity for so long; what would she do without me?

What would I do now?

The walls stretched up, as if I had been swallowed into the earth. I grit my teeth, tapped my fingers on my sides, pushing everything down. I had to think clearly. I had to find a way out.

Chapter 10

Vincent

In the morning, a knock rang through the house. No one came here, and never this early. I closed the door to my studio, locking it behind me. I peeked through the peephole: Sheriff Mike stood proudly. I opened the door.

"Erickson," he boomed. He blinked at me. "What happened? That's quite the shiner."

A deep red bruise, turning a shade of purple, was in the corner of my eye.

"Was rough-housing with my dogs," I said. "Fell on a rake."

He laughed, hitting his chest, then glanced around. "Where are those pups now?"

"Morning hunt." I gestured to the backyard where the house rested against Mount Punica. "There's a squirrel out there, they just know it."

"I miss having a dog." He shook his head. "Shea is allergic, of course. Swears Kora is too."

I'm sure Kora had never been exposed to a dog. I gave a patient smile. I didn't care about their weird family life, only watching them fall apart.

"So, what do I owe this pleasure?" I asked.

Mike let out a small breath. "You mind if I come in?"

I stepped to the side, and we went through the brick archway to the small table in the breakfast nook. The natural fauna from the mountain filled the window. In the distance, the heavy red petals of pomegranate blossoms flashed through the trees.

"Our house burned down last night," he said.

"Holy shit," I said, leaving my mouth open for effect. I sucked in a breath. "You're okay?"

"I was on duty, but my wife—" He stopped, then leaned on the table. "She's being treated for smoke inhalation."

"Wow," I whistled. "You're not in the hospital with her?"

"I'm doing what I do best: trying to figure out what happened so I can put that asshole in prison where he belongs." He shook his head. "The only solace that I have is that my daughter is missing, which means she made it out. She's out there. Somewhere."

His eyes were dreamy, staring off into space, tears welling in his eyes. I didn't believe a second of it.

"Anyway," he continued, immediately shaking off those emotions, "She was at Quiet Meadows yesterday. Right before she disappeared. Did you see or hear anything?"

I looked up at the ceiling, mulling it over in my mind. He could pretend to care about his daughter like I could pretend to not know who started the fire.

"The only person I saw her talking to was Andrew," I said. It was partly true. "He seems to be eyeing her."

"Andrew and Kora have always been close. Grew up together." Mike ran a hand over his head. "Andrew was out on duty with me. He's devastated. Maybe more than I am."

I'm sure he was.

I patted him on the back. "I'll keep an eye open." He smiled. "How did the Echo arrest go?"

"Found the distributor, but he never goes to the nightclub," he shrugged. "Arrested him anyway, but still on the lookout." He puffed his chest. "Still, it's good for the county. Especially Punica. Makes the people feel safe, you know? The source has been brought to justice. Now we need the seller."

"You'll find him soon." But I would find him first.

I followed Sheriff Mike out to the patio, exchanging meaningless pleasantries, when he stopped and turned to me.

"There's one other thing," he said. "There's been another Echo death. Keep it quiet for now, but it might be murder." He glanced at his squad car, then focused on me. "The media will find out soon, but you wouldn't know anything strange about those deaths, would you?"

Finally, he had figured something out.

"Puncture wound to the chest?" I asked.

"You saw, then."

"Your coroner is the one who missed it. Not me."

"Damn it," he hit his forehead. "I can't talk much about the case." I stifled a chuckle; it's not like that had stopped him before. "But you know what they're saying. It seems like you're profiting off of the deaths."

"So is Poppies & Wheat," I sighed. "Plenty of places profit when people get together."

"But none so clearly have an advantage when it comes to murder."

I studied him. His face was expressionless, but I got the feeling that he was hiding a secret. That he knew he was accusing me of something that had nothing to do with me.

Something else was at play here.

"I wanted to warn you," he said. "You know. As a friend."

Friend? "Think of the positives," I said, lifting my head. "It's given you something to fight for when it comes to your reelection campaign. *You* profit as well."

He plastered his usual smile across his lips. "As long as I can find the scoundrel, I will deliver punishment swiftly, all for my people." He winked. "The votes help motivate me, you know."

"I'm sure."

Once he was gone, I checked the surveillance footage of the basement—Kora paced, checking the walls for a secret exit. There was water in there, some blankets too, but it would take her a while to find them if she was still concerned with finding an escape.

At Quiet Meadows, we didn't have any services that day, but Catie was there early. She must have gone to pick up a body, perhaps the one the sheriff had mentioned. A few minutes later, the coroner called, putting Nyla's cremation on hold. But when the time came to burn Nyla, would Kora want to witness it? It gave some closure. Others, it made the grief worse. I would give that to her, then. If nothing else, it would be intriguing to see how the cremation process affected her.

Until then, I worked on a decedent that had died of natural causes. Once the body was prepped and placed in a rigid cardboard casket, I slid open the metal doors to the first retort, then pressed the button to start the process. The conveyor belt brought the casket into the retort. The door shut automatically. A beep from the computer signalled that it had reached the desired temperature.

A few hours later, I pulverized the bone pieces to ashes in the granulator machine and grabbed a temporary plastic urn. As the grains fell into the container like sand in an hourglass, I thought of Kora.

Kora on her knees before me. Her mouth level with my cock.

Once I said my goodbyes to Catie and Lee, I made my way back to the house. I put some fresh yogurt with granola in a bowl, then added a cup of lukewarm tea to the tray, then brought it down to the basement. I checked the surveillance footage; she was on the couch, biting her nails, her long, ragged hair tucked behind her ears.

When I met her, her eyes were cast in front of her. Blank.

I lifted the tray. "You must be hungry."

She whispered something, her lips moving with her inaudible words.

"What was that?" I asked.

"I said, I will *not* be eating anything from you."

I laughed. "It's food. Not poison."

"How would I know?"

"Because if I wanted to poison you, I would open your mouth and shove it down your throat."

She glared at me, her eyes narrowed. I lifted the spoon to my mouth, my eyes glued to her as I swallowed the bite. She watched my throat, glued to it. I leaned forward with the tray, about to place it in her lap, when she smacked her hand underneath the tray, sending the bowl and glass to the ground, white liquid and chunks of oatmeal flying through the room. A glob landed on my cheek.

I stared at her for a moment, those pine eyes seething with anger. If that was how she wanted to play, then by all means.

I grabbed her by the hair and forced her down to her knees, burying her face against the cement.

"So this is what it takes?" I growled. "Ripping you from your home, a few mere hours in a basement—and finally, you feel something more than the fake happiness you wear like a second skin?"

"You know nothing about me," she hissed.

I pulled her hair, lifting the skin from her scalp, and used my other hand to pry her mouth open. She snapped her teeth together, snarling at me, and I dropped her, letting her fall to the ground, then grabbed the knife out of my pocket. I flipped it open and she gasped. She stumbled on all fours. I pulled her up by the nape of her neck, maneuvering her around until the blade was on her throat. She pressed against me, trying so hard to inch away from the knife. Blood rushed to my cock, swelling with heat.

"What does this feel like, Kora?" I pressed the metal into her skin, not enough to break it, but enough that she choked down a labored swallow. "Is it fear? Is it lust?" My dick twitched against her and she grimaced. "I bet you get wet when I hold this knife to your neck. Don't you? You don't know why it turns you on, but it does, doesn't it?" I laughed. "I know you better than you think."

"You would never turn me on," she howled.

"When will you stop lying to yourself?" I took her hand and shoved it down until it was inside of her cotton underwear, then pulled it out, her fingers gleaming with desire. I licked them, one by one, sucking it all in, her sweet, mild taste. She stared at my lips, entranced, then shuddered deeply. In disgust. In fear. In lust.

My mind raced. Her fear was thick on her skin, making her ripe, mixing with the hint of jasmine that still lingered. Her hair tangled in my fingers. I pressed the blade into her throat even more, but still not cutting her, and she whimpered. My cock throbbed: *Ruin her already.*

Not yet.

"You think you're too good for everyone," I whispered in her ear, "But make no mistake, Kora. You will never be good enough for anyone." I bit her earlobe between my canines, and she flinched at the pain. "Not even me."

I let go of her body, and she wavered, finding her balance. I headed toward the stairs, but stopped before I ascended.

"This mess will be gone by the time I get back," I said in a low voice.

Then I went up the stairs and left her alone.

Chapter 11

Kora

Each day, Vincent brought another tray of food and left it on the ground. I took the bottled water, but other than that, I refused. I had this feeling that he was telling the truth, that if he wanted to poison me, he would have done it already. And I knew he was more than willing to hurt me.

But that didn't mean I trusted him.

Still, when he gave me a bag full of mismatched clothes: a pair of socks, a sweater, sweatpants, everything in shades of black and gray—I didn't hesitate. The dirty nightgown stunk. I put on the sweater and some leggings, slightly too big for me. Then I washed my underwear with the plain bar soap at the sink, letting them air dry.

I glanced at a large wooden crate in the back, in the space under the loft. It occurred to me that he might have been keeping something inside of boxes, but I hadn't checked any of them yet. It hadn't seemed important; they couldn't help me escape.

But what did I have to lose now? I checked a few tops, but they were stuck. Then, after moving to a fourth crate, the lid opened.

The dusty scent of wood fluttered toward me. Inside, there were canvases: white edges, grays and blacks bleeding over from the front. I pulled one out: a painting of a man dripping with dark liquid running down his face, gathering on his chin. The next one was a woman in the fetal position near the foot of a bed, her back to the viewer. Then, another person covering their mouth, their eyes wide. The bleeding mouth. A severed head. And at the corner of the crate, a plastic container the same size as a coffee canister. Inside, there was a gray powder, almost like a cement mixture.

I closed the lid, then put it back, staring at the paintings. Each canvas had another person, all of them in different states of agony. Another crate contained paintings of destruction; ruined farmhouses, a volcano erupting on a town, a house burning in the night. The colors seemed as if it was all done with charcoal, but the texture was off—clumped on the edges, then lacquered in place.

You inspire me, flower. I've been using you for my art.

These were Vincent's paintings, then. Why did he have them boxed up?

They were beautiful. In a desolate kind of way.

I ran my hand over the gritty bumps, when a thought popped into my mind and I dropped the canvas. The texture—what if it was ash? I pulled out all the canvases, propping them against the wall, staring at each of them. A twisted mouth. A crying face. A bruised cheek. All the surfaces were bumpy, with gray grains of sand.

Had he killed these people, using the funeral home as his cover-up? Or did he know these people? Was he using the dead as his models, trying to represent them in life?

My head floated as I stared at the paintings. It was like looking at a graveyard. Was Nyla here? No—there had been too much dust on the crate for her portrait to be here somewhere.

I'll take good care of her, he had said.

It was one of the only times he had seemed sincere, like he took Nyla's afterlife seriously. Like he knew what it was like.

But of course, he knew. He owned a funeral home.

Emotions began to swell within me, the light dimming, threatening to overtake me, but I couldn't shut down. I had to stay here. Had to be present.

I went to the next crate. A large coffee-table book was on top.

I lifted it. Underneath, pomegranates layered the bottom, their rich merlot flesh some of the brightest colors I had seen in days. I picked one up, marveling at it in my hands. My stomach growled.

I hated pomegranates. But I was hungry, and this was just fruit. It's not like Vincent had cooked it.

I threw it at the concrete. The flesh split open, and I scrounged the seeds off of the floor, not giving myself time to second guess it. My mouth puckered up, my taste buds clenching, but I closed my eyes and chewed, letting them explode in my mouth. A stomach cramp twisted through me, but I kept eating. Stared at the brick wall, trying to ignore the sour taste. Until I could pretend like I liked it.

The next crate had bottled water. As I was downing the second bottle, the door in the loft opened.

"You want to come up?" Vincent asked.

He was going to let me out that easily?

"Yes," I said.

"Then come."

Once I was up in the loft, we faced one another. He loomed over me, heat radiating from his body, his black eyes peering down. My fingers twitched. The bruise on his eye had faded, but it was still obvious, and yet he made no attempts to hide it. Almost like he was proud, showing off what I had done. Scars twisted around his arms and neck like they had always been there. My bruise was just another mark.

He lifted his arm, showing me his gun in the holster. He probably still had the knife too. He pointed to my arm. The skin was red and tender.

"That's a tracking device. If you try to remove it, poison will be released into your bloodstream. We'll clean it up for now." He tilted his head. "Like I said, flower, if I want to poison you, I will."

Chills ran through me as he dressed my incision. Then we walked down a path from his front driveway, down through the trees, into the cemetery. I hadn't realized he lived so close to the funeral home. Sulfur snuck into my nostrils, and I cringed, but as we went deeper into the cemetery, the blooms of hydrangeas and roses overpowered it. As the Quiet Meadows building came into view, relief coursed through me. It would be easier for my parents to find me here.

The building was empty and quiet. He pointed where to go, and soon, we were in a large, open room with a brick and metal rectangular structure, with two small doors, like a giant oven. A large cardboard box was in front of it, resting on a conveyor belt. Vincent pressed a few buttons on the side, and the box moved into the structure. It must have been the furnace for cremation.

A television played in the corner: *The police are now saying that it is likely that Echo is used to subdue victims before murdering them. It is not as simple as driving under the influence of a new drug, but something much more sinister,* the newscaster said. *And now, we have Sheriff Mike here to bring you the details.*

We will find the Echo Killer, my father said, his fist clenched in front of him. *Once and for all. I will not rest until the people of Acheron County are safe!*

Commercials for pharmaceutical companies began playing. Relief swelled through me. The fact that my father *looked* normal and that the newscaster hadn't mentioned anything about my mother must have meant that she was okay. I hadn't gotten to watch a lot of news, but I knew that the worse the news was, the better it was for ratings.

Vincent typed into a computer to the side of the furnace. Did that computer have the internet? I hadn't used it much, but Nyla had let me use her smartphone a few times when my mother wasn't looking. I knew how to get around a computer, enough to search for instructions on texting a phone number from a computer. But I still needed time, and I wasn't sure if I had that.

A landline hung on the wall, but I knew the computer was the best option. If I could type out a message when Vincent left the room, then he wouldn't hear me.

Breaking News! the reporter chimed in. *Echo found inside of Sheriff Mike's house, in his daughter's room!*

The television flashed to a picture of my house with pieces of the exterior missing. The cream-painted walls were now stroked with black, decimating the structure. A few beams stood in place, but it was like a skeleton of itself.

83

I don't care what happened anymore, my mother cried into the camera lens, my father's arm clutched around her. He rarely touched her like that, and she seemed to soak it up, leaning into him. *Please bring my daughter back.*

My stomach sank. The reporter continued: *Police have not yet confirmed whether there is a connection between the Echo murders and the arson of the Nova house, but we expect a full statement from the sheriff soon.*

A few seconds passed with a discussion between correspondents from the network, but my mind went blank. Could the Echo deaths really be murders?

Did that mean Nyla had been murdered?

My father filled the screen. A sense of serenity washed over me for a moment. He might have been an absent father, but he cared about justice. About his image. He would figure out the truth; his career depended on it. *It is my belief that the arson and the murders are connected. While this might not be the same criminal, it is highly likely that they are working together. If you have any information about the crime, please contact the police department.*

Vincent stood to the side, crossing his arms in front of him. Was Vincent the murderer? Adrenaline surged through me, and I let out a haggard breath. No... I couldn't let myself shut down now. I had to *think*.

He threw a hand toward the screen.

"Don't believe that crap," he said. My shoulders tensed. "They just need something to say so that the people don't get antsy."

I stared at him. Why was he telling me this?

"The Echo deaths have nothing to do with your mother's house," he explained.

"The Echo *murders*," I corrected. He didn't say a word, so I continued: "You burned my mother's house down so that you could abduct me."

"How many times do I have to say this? I could have left you there, but I didn't. I saved you, Kora. From more than the fire."

"Saved me?" I laughed. "Wow. How lucky for me."

He stepped forward slowly, making me shrink.

"Tell me, how many men have you met in your life?" He

tapped his chin. "What about people in general?" I looked off to the side, but he stepped closer, and his body heat radiating toward me; I couldn't concentrate. "I may have abducted you, but I rescued you too."

He stood up straight. My eyelids fluttered as I tried to push down the guilt. The shame. The fear.

"Don't shut down, Kora," he said. Anger flickered in my veins, pulsing through me. He may have had me cornered, but I refused to believe he could read me like that. "You can't shut down every time you feel something." I balled my hands into fists. He put a finger under my chin. "I have to check something." His words were careful, his eyes searching back and forth. "You will not leave this room or I *will* hurt you."

Then he left.

I sprinted to the computer. *Password:* was on the screen, and no matter what I typed, it flashed, *Incorrect password!* A hot sweat broke out all over me, but I kept trying anyway. After the fifth attempt, I went to the phone. I dialed my mother's number. Vincent's shadow stretched into the room, and I turned, my face going white.

"Hello? Mr. Erickson?"

Vincent smacked a hand over my mouth and held the phone to his ear.

"Hey Shea," he said like he was ringing her himself, "I saw the news. I was calling to see if you were all right."

"Oh. How nice," she said, her voice cautious. "My husband said you were very helpful during the investigation. I'm afraid that's all you can do—"

I tried to scream, but Vincent tightened his grip around my mouth, pinching my nose shut.

"Let me know if I can be of any help," he said, then hung up. He let me go and I gasped for air. He narrowed his eyes. "What did you think you would accomplish?"

I glared and he grabbed my chin, forcing me to look up at him. My heart pounded.

"I don't understand what you want with me," I snapped. My body pulsed with frenzied energy, every muscle laced with heat.

"I enjoy ruining perfection." His voice was calm, as if he were simply talking about the weather. "I want to make your pain into my art."

My heart clenched. Those paintings. The ashes in his basement. I knew what that meant.

"You are evil," I said, forcing the panic down. "You are selfish to your core."

"Selfish?" he laughed.

"Sadistic."

"That's not where it stops, flower."

The words made me shiver and cringe all over. I hated that he called me that—and yet it made me feel like I belonged too. I wanted to hurl the words into his mouth. It made me angry and frustrated that I liked it, like he somehow owned me. Like he could manipulate me. Like he knew I would like it.

He had broken so much of my life already, and yet I couldn't control the ache between my legs.

"You burned my home," I shouted, trying to get the strength inside of me to come to the surface, to stand up to him. "You almost killed my mother." He smiled, and I scowled in response, then said, "Why don't you just burn me too?"

A wicked smile crossed his face. He went to the computer, hitting a button. The second furnace rumbled on, and he opened the hatch, the fire blazing. The machine started beeping an erratic alarm, as if something was wrong. My heart raced.

I ran toward the door, but he grabbed my shoulders, his grip so tight I could feel the bruises forming. He threw me down on the conveyor belt in front of the open machine. He pulled my long hair against the metal, using it to pull me taut against the belt, stretched out before him. The heat from the furnace blanketed my face. My eyes burned. What had I done?

"Tell me," he commanded. "Why shouldn't I burn you?"

"Please, Vincent," I begged. A tear slipped down my cheek. "I don't know why I said that."

"Tell me, is that what you want, Kora?"

I looked back and forth between his eyes. My breathing was heavy and rapt, and his body pressed into me, holding me down.

Serenity settled over him. A surge of adrenaline shot through my limbs, awakening all of my senses. He wanted to hurt me.

And what would it feel like to end it all?

If I wasn't here, I would be with my controlling mother, my practically non-existent father, living a life *for* them. And here? There was no facade with Vincent. I was his prisoner. And I knew if he was crazy enough to put a tracking device inside of me, then I would never escape. What difference would it make if he burned me too? What would it actually change?

Sometimes, it seemed like the only way I could move on. Even when I was with my parents. Like it would always be the same.

And I couldn't bury those emotions right then.

"Tell me what you want, flower," he said. He dragged a hand up my thigh, tickling my skin through the thin fabric. My body trembled. He grabbed my cheeks, forcing me to look at him.

"Burn me," I whispered.

He studied me, his eyes roaming my face. Then he turned on the conveyor belt, and it rolled toward the machine, the heat rolling toward my head. I closed my eyes, tears slipping down the sides of my face. The heat blasted hotter. I squeezed my eyelids together, rocking back and forth, pushing it all down, waiting for the inevitable. My heart pounded and my hair sizzled, the burning fragrance filling the room. The machine whirred, the fire crackled, and I turned my face to the side, looking straight into Vincent's dark eyes, reflecting the crematory's golden fire.

Suddenly, he shoved me off of the belt, knocking my head to the ground. My whole body was feverish, my hair still warm, the tips charred and brittle. I lifted myself onto my hands, then Vincent pinned me to the ground, staring intently into my eyes. There was a vacancy inside of him as if he was trying to see what was really there.

He had been wrong about me; he was realizing that.

He switched off the furnace.

Chapter 12

Vincent

After I threatened Kora in the crematory, I brought her back to the basement in silence. She had enough food and water to last awhile, and with the tension to kill each other higher than ever, we needed space.

She was supposed to be an object to watch die. My inspiration. My spark. My art. And yet, the flash of rage and hope and fear in her eyes had set me on fire. She could no longer escape down into that place where she felt nothing. She had to face this.

There *was* passion inside of her. And that made her interesting.

I closed the basement door, reminding myself that I couldn't burn her yet. Not mentally, emotionally, nor physically. She had so much more that I wanted to take, that I wanted to ruin. To show her what it meant to be alive.

To destroy her like that would take time.

The next day, I took a pair of scissors down to the basement. The room reeked like melted plastic. Her ponytail was frayed at the bottom, blunt like a bush. I handed her the tool, then rested my palm on my gun. A gun could kill a lot faster than a pair of scissors could.

She cut the ends of her hair off quickly. The strands fell to the floor, leaving an uneven cut. I took the scissors back upstairs with me. Neither of us spoke a word.

I drove through Punica, passing Poppies & Wheat. The store was dark, but the plants still filled the window display. Limp stems, the edges browned. Next was the house. The beams were still intact, but the exterior was blackened and weak. What had once been the perfect depiction of a family home was now a shell that could protect nothing. I wet my lips, tilting my head to the side, my body buzzing with power. That sort of conversion always intrigued me. The same materials, and yet, completely different.

I returned to the basement. Kora sat in the corner, underneath the loft, leaning against the wall, the coffee-table book in her lap. It was a book of my photographs. *The Wake*. She glanced through it, bored.

"You like the photographs?" I asked.

"They're fine," she said.

"I have a task for you. Up there."

"Oh." Her face stayed dry and she closed the book. "What can I help you with?"

Her words came with the rigid courtesy of a retail worker.

"Come to my studio," I said.

"Why?"

"I need a model." *And for once I'd rather stare at you in the flesh than imagine you.*

She lowered her chin, her leaf-green eyes assessing the situation.

"If you let me call my mother," she said evenly.

Bold woman. I smirked. "You know I can't let you do that."

"I guess I can't be your model, then."

I tapped the side of my leg, clenching my jaw. "You think bargaining with me will work?"

She shrugged. "I assumed you could be mature and reasonable. One thing in exchange for another."

"I could force you into the room," I growled.

"Then force me."

Every muscle in my body tightened, but instead of scooping

her into my arms and shoving her into the studio, I grabbed her by the throat, her breath quickening as she stared into my eyes.

"We don't have to do this the hard way," I said.

"Let me call my mother," she said. "Or I won't go."

I threw my grip around her throat, and she sank back against the wall. I bounded up the stairs. By the time I reached the loft, almost to the door, a shuddering sob raked through Kora's body, echoing through the room.

Outside of the door, Bernie circled my legs while Ulysses panted beside him. Sarah laid her head down near the door, whining. Once Sarah started, it was a chorus of pleas to let Kora play, because they could tell she was sad.

"Leave it alone," I said. They didn't listen, so I raised my voice slightly. "I said, *drop it.*"

The three of them silenced, and Sarah lifted her head to judge me. Yes, I knew that there was a woman crying in the basement, but that didn't mean that *I* had to make her feel better. She had done this to herself.

But that wasn't entirely true. I had ripped her from her home. Forced her to give up her life. Even if I didn't end up killing her, I could never let her return to her old life.

My chest tightened, a pain swelling in the back of my throat: *If I didn't kill her.* That had never been an option before. I had to change my thoughts, had to remember what she was there for. Sarah's brown eyes widened at me, reading my emotions, and I knew she was right. Only a terrible bastard would do something like this to someone so harmless. Kora was innocent; so were her father and mother. The only thing they were guilty of was having a perfect life.

My skin itched with the thoughts churning in my mind. But there was nothing I could do to change that now.

I was scratching behind Bernie's ears mindlessly when the front door opened. The doormat flapped back into place, indicating who was intruding: Catie.

"Sarah? Bernie? Ulysses?" she called.

The dogs ran toward her, barking, and she bent down to pet their heads.

"Hey doggos," she smiled. "I'm glad to see you too."

"What are you doing here?" I asked.

She startled at my voice, standing up straight. "I didn't think you were awake. You asked me to check on the dogs whenever you missed work."

I had said that, hadn't I?

"I fed them," I said. "Thanks."

"But then it's time for a treat from Auntie," she said in a singsong voice that instantly made all three of them jump. She went to the bag above the fridge, grabbing a few treats and handing them out accordingly. As they licked her face to show their appreciation, Kora's sob, like a faint whimper, reverberated through the house. The dogs froze and Catie looked down the hallway to the basement.

"Now I know I heard something," she said.

The dogs went to follow the noise as if to say to Catie: *We found a friend! It's her!* Catie tilted her head to the side, and I motioned in the hallway's direction. Might as well get this over with. We followed the dogs and stopped at the locked door to the basement.

"Who's in there?" Catie asked.

"I had to cut her off from everything," I explained, "including her parents."

"Who?"

I rubbed my forehead as if it pained me to say this. "You remember that woman with the big green eyes at Nyla Nerissa's funeral?" I asked. Catie nodded. "She told me she was twenty-one, and yet her parents were so controlling that she had never been out of the house by herself."

"Never?"

I shook my head. "She asked if I would help her run away. But, you see, her mother is incredibly—" I paused, trying to think of the appropriate euphemism, "—*determined* to keep her daughter pure and safe for as long as possible. And her father is a cop."

"Mike," she whispered, lowering her head. "How long has she been in there?"

"Since the funeral. She begged me to help her. How could I say 'no'?"

"Oh." She furrowed her brows. "Is that why you were out late that night?"

"You caught me."

She nodded slowly, like it all made sense now, and yet I could tell it still didn't sit right with her. That was the thing about hiring someone intelligent; they caught on to bullshit too quickly. I needed to distract her from what was going on as soon as possible.

"Did Saturday's family come by yet?" I asked.

"Yeah, just left a few minutes ago, actually. They want a plot on the eastern side. Hey, Vincent?" She tapped on the door. "Why don't you let me talk to her? She might need someone to talk to if she's still processing this."

I forced a smile. "That's a great idea," I lied. "But let me prepare her first. I want to make sure she's comfortable."

"Why wouldn't she be comfortable?" Catie asked. "You're not torturing her down there, are you?"

I tilted my chin. If only she knew.

"She can't have phones," I said. "No internet. *Nothing.* If her mother finds her, she'll make up a story to keep Kora locked in a cage, and we can't have that."

Catie bowed her head. I had found Catie camping out in one of the mausoleums before I hired her. She knew that life didn't always make sense, but she trusted me.

"I wouldn't dream of it," she said.

"Tomorrow, then?"

"Tomorrow."

Catie and I discussed work matters while the dogs stood near us. And as soon as the time came, I quickly pushed her out the front door. After she walked away, I grabbed the key from under the mat, put it in my pocket, then locked the door and leaned against the wall. The dogs heard a bird outside and went to chase it in the backyard. I stared at the dog door. I had Kora; what did I do now? If I was supposed to ruin her beyond repair, the end result of killing her and making her into literal art to give to her parents, then what was the next step?

I squeezed my hand closed as tight as I could, watching the green and red veins flush on my arms. Perhaps checking on her once more would inspire me.

I unlocked the basement's door, then descended the stairs. This time, Kora was lying across the couch. The scooped neck sweatshirt exposed the dainty dips of her collarbones, so breakable, and yet, strong too. Her hair was tucked into a small messy bun, the new blunt ends choppy, and though tears wet the strands of hair near her face and her bloodshot eyes were glossy, she seemed lighter then, like the hair wasn't holding her back anymore. Was she finally letting go?

She tucked a stray lock of hair behind her ears, her lips trembling. She was vulnerable, and still, there was so much she didn't know. So much that she needed to understand before I could finally destroy her. A gnawing sensation wrenched in my stomach, surging to my cock, then back up to my brain. What the fuck was wrong with me? Why did I want to brush away her tears? I should have wanted to taste them instead.

She finally looked at me, but before she could speak, I swiftly ascended the stairs, locking the door behind me, then went to my studio. The overhead lights were dimmer than I preferred, but it seemed fitting then.

Using my fingers, I dipped into the oil and bone fragment paint, using harsh smudges to draw her outline—the arch of her neck and clavicle, the puffiness to her cheeks, swollen eyelids, the desperate curve of her mouth. With my thumb, I shadowed across her eyes, rendering them as haunting as she made me feel. Like she saw the evil that lurked inside of me, the monster that couldn't be contained anymore. And yet, she wouldn't look away. Like she knew there was darkness inside of her too. The parts of ourselves that we never showed anyone, but each other.

Chapter 13

Kora

I had no idea what time of day it was, but since Vincent delivered food at regular intervals, and another one had passed. A knock sounded on the door upstairs, like a gentle tapping of a bird's feet on a branch. I stiffened; since when did Vincent knock?

A few seconds later, the door opened and closed. Then Vincent came down the stairs, treading softly this time.

"A friend of mine wants to visit with you," he said. *A friend?* I was starting to believe he didn't have any. "I told her that I helped you escape from your sheltered life."

Sarcastic laughter bubbled up inside of me. I smacked my hand against my mouth. Vincent gave me a strange look.

"You're serious?" I asked.

"Why wouldn't I be?" His gaze darkened. "Your mother never let you free. I *did* rescue you from her."

And from the expression in his eyes, I knew he believed those words.

"I figure it's good for you to have some company," he added.

"How thoughtful of you," I mumbled.

Vincent snatched my chin. "If you tell her differently, I will make sure your mother dies the next time I start a fire," he said. He stared into my soul. "And that's a promise."

He let go of his grip, a chill settling across the room.

"Can I count on you, Kora?"

It made me flinch to hear my real name on his lips. "Yes," I mumbled.

He grabbed my chin again, pinching it tightly. "What was that?"

"Yes, Vincent," I said, louder this time.

He stood, straightening his clothes, then walked up the stairs. A few minutes later, the points of stilettos clicked on the carpeted loft, then rang against the metal staircase.

"I didn't know they still made staircases like this," she said. I recognized her voice. My eyes widened.

"It's you," I said. "From my friend's funeral. You were there. For Nyla."

"Right," she smiled. "You thought I had embalmed her."

"How is she now?" Then I blushed, shaking my head furiously. She was dead. How could I ask something so stupid?

"She was cremated a day or two ago. Vincent did it. He didn't tell you?" I blinked at her. We had been in that crematory room during a cremation. Had that been Nyla in the cardboard box? Catie put a hand on my shoulder. "How are you holding up? Vincent said you had a rough time with your parents."

I stared at her, searching her eyes. She truly believed Vincent. The pure look in her eyes told me she had no reason *not* to believe him.

I didn't want to risk him killing my mother by telling her the truth. I had to find another way out.

"Parents," I mumbled. "You know how they get."

"I saw how your mother was at the funeral."

I cringed, thinking back on that. A day where Shea was being *lenient* with me.

"Vincent isn't much better," I said.

"I know." She patted my back. "Vincent is kind of—" she shrugged, "Well, he can seem a bit off at first. But that's just part of who he is." She smoothed a fold in her pants. "But he's also someone that sticks to his word. If he says he's going to protect you from your mother, then I know he'll do everything he can to make sure you're safe. Even if it comes with," she lifted her shoulders, "weird rules."

To make sure I'm safe? I wanted to laugh again, to repeat all of his threats, how he had almost burned me alive in the crematory room. But then, I thought about his words: *Do you enjoy your life here? Staring out barred windows. A view of a fence. A garden on your windowsill.* In the shadows of my bedroom, he looked as if he had been kissed by the moonlight, his skin tinted a dark blue, those scars glowing along his skin.

I could give you more than this, he had said.

Considering what had happened since he had said those words, I knew he had been honest. It was frightening, strange, and *real.* I couldn't figure out how I was supposed to feel about anything anymore, how to bury those emotions.

Because they wouldn't go away. Nothing would ever be the same after this.

Catie rubbed the top of my hands. "Hey," she said. "I'll bring you more clothes. Better clothes than the stuff from the Lost and Found."

I rubbed my palms against my sweatshirt and pants. "These are from the Lost and Found?"

"Vincent has a habit of looking after things that are left behind."

I wrinkled my nose and she shoved my arm. "Relax. They're washed. Unless it says 'dry cleaning' on the tag. I don't see him taking anything into a shop." She shrugged. "We always wash the clothes. People get weird about leaving their stuff behind at funeral homes. So it's one of our policies."

That was interesting, and sort of nice, but I stumbled over her words: *Vincent has a habit of looking after things that are left behind.* How far did that extend? Did he think that *I* had been left behind?

"Well," she checked her phone, "I've got another family to meet in a few minutes. Another fucking Echo death," she muttered. "But if you need anything, let Vincent know, and I'll bring it by. And the clothes will be here later tonight."

I stared at her. How had Vincent managed to get someone as kind as Catie on his side?

"Thank you," I said.

She smiled. "Don't mention it."

After she left, Vincent brought down a new tray of food, and instead of picking at what I could manage without actually eating, I had several spoonfuls. A strawberry parfait and a protein smoothie.

I flipped through the pages of the coffee-table book, *The Wake*. The photographs didn't have the same prestige as the paintings that he had created, but they had the same mood. People who looked out into the distance, the pain wrought on their faces. On the surface of it, those people seemed normal, but vulnerable. As if Vincent could expose what was actually there.

What did he see in me?

A few hours passed, and while I was dozing off, the door opened, startling me awake. From the loft, Vincent leaned over the railing and lifted a plastic grocery bag full of clothes.

Catie. "Thanks," I said.

"Come here."

My stomach tightened, but I bit my lip, tucking the choppy hairs behind my ear. Retaliation and bargaining hadn't worked, but maybe if I listened and tried to figure out what *he* wanted from me, then maybe I could help, and eventually, get *myself* out of this mess.

It wasn't the best idea, but it was the only plan I could think of.

He led me to a bathroom and let me change. Just like the Lost and Found clothes, most of Catie's clothes were dark. I put on some black leggings and an oversized gray hoodie. I glanced at the mirror; I hadn't looked at myself since before Nyla's funeral. I had changed, somehow. Tired. In comfortable clothes, not the pretty styles my mother selected. And yet, my skin was brighter. Glowing. More alive than before.

My mind must have been playing tricks on me to make me feel better.

Silently, Vincent motioned for me to follow him. As we emerged from his house, the night was peaceful. The insects hummed and the wind rustled through the trees. Our footsteps were soft on the ground, the frogs quieting as we passed. We walked down the path, the familiar fragrance of roses meeting my nose. I sucked in as hard as I could, enjoying the fresh air. The headstones hovered in the night, like hunched over souls, waiting for the darkness to pass.

He kept walking until we came to a statue of a woman with a crown of flowers twirled around her head, loose fabric covering her body, drapes of vines twisting around her like a whimsical fairy. The woman rested her head on a stone. The inscription read: *Nyla Nerissa. Until we bloom again.*

My heart sank at those words. Until we bloom again?

"What is this?" I said. I gripped my hands into fists. "Why would you bring me here?"

"Her ashes were buried yesterday," he said.

My heart plummeted to the ground. I kneeled down in front of the stone, then heard motion coming from behind. Three rottweilers came up, black fur with playful brown faces, the ones I had seen the first night Vincent had brought me here. They bumped into me, greeting me with their wet noses. Vincent stepped away, grabbing a rake leaning against a tree, and started tending to the loose leaves. My heart raced. I rarely got to pet dogs at the flower shop, and never ones that were this big. But the dogs licked and nuzzled my face, and those fears melted away.

"Hi pups," I said, though they were certainly bigger than that. "What are you doing here?"

Then it clicked. These weren't strays that stuck around the cemetery because Catie and Vincent fed them. They were *his* pets.

One of them nudged into me, then sat perched at my side. I stroked her back. We both watched Vincent cleaning the property while the other two dogs followed behind him. I leaned over and pulled her tag out: *Sarah.*

"Hey, girl," I said. "Sarah," I corrected myself, and she panted happily beside me. "You sure are loyal, aren't you?"

I turned and stared at the stone, reading the inscription repeatedly until the letters didn't make sense anymore. *Until we bloom again.* It was like we were all locked inside of a dark winter.

But the seasons never stretched too far in Punica. It came with the climate. It was always temperate here, always steady, as if the earth wasn't supposed to feel anything.

I wondered if Vincent was right. I had always thought my parents were protecting me out of fear for my safety, but what if the opposite was true? What if they were causing more damage by not letting me grow into my own person?

The other dogs joined us, sitting next to Sarah, all in a line. I checked their tags too: *Bernie. Ulysses.* From the shadows, Vincent emerged as well, standing near a tree where he rested the rake once again. He removed an item from his pocket: a ring. A gold band with a giant onyx stone.

Nyla's ring.

"They left it on her. And when I asked them about it before the cremation, they said to keep it."

"Why would they do that?"

He let out a small sigh. "I stopped trying to understand people when they're grieving a long time ago. None of it can be explained. We just have to accept what it is."

After a few seconds, he stepped closer and offered it to me. I stared up at him, waiting for an explanation. But perhaps there was none. Nyla's parents had told him to keep the ring, and he had, like any other thing that was left behind. And now, it was mine.

He was trying to give me closure. A piece of Nyla to take with me.

I took the ring, clutching it in my palm.

"Thank you," I said quietly, those words awkward on my tongue. He nodded, looking into the starlit sky. I had never seen anything as gorgeous or as peaceful in my life, sitting under the stars, waiting in the quiet solitude of the graves. There were no bars against the windows here, no cages to lock me inside, no bricks or divided windows. There was only the dark sky.

Vincent turned toward me. My chest tightened. He held out his hand. "Let me show you around," he said.

I waited for a moment, staring at his hand. And then I took his grip.

Chapter 14

Vincent

Bernie and Ulysses led the way, with Sarah trotting beside our guest. Kora wrapped her arms around herself, looking up at the bright moon. Shadows hovered over each memorial statue, the bouquets stirring in the breeze.

"You know the garden," I said as we approached the edge of the cemetery. The garden, filled with the leftover potted plants that the grieving families didn't want, was a wash of white petals that glowed in the dark, lighting a clear path to the funeral home in the night. Kora sucked in a breath, her nostrils flaring, enjoying the scent. I didn't care for it much; it reminded me of work. But the smell that sometimes came from her skin was different: jasmine and her sweet sweat. For some reason, *her* floral hint never bothered me.

In another corner of the property, we came to the mausoleums. We went through the arches, reaching the squares that were decorated with flowers. I sat on the bench against the wall as Kora ran her fingertips over the names. Punica was a small town, but it had been around for a long time, which meant an extensive history of people who had been born, had lived, and died here.

"It's beautiful," she said. She sat beside me, pulling on the sleeves of her hoodie until they covered her hands. "You take good care of it."

I tried my best. Death care might not have been what I thought I would do with my life, but it was my life. Eventually, I got the words out: "Thank you."

"No," she said. "We," she nodded to the memorial plaques to the sides of her, the moonlight silhouetting her face, "*we* thank you."

Kora petted the dogs for a while, and Bernie brought her a stick to play fetch. We went to the open grass next to the cemetery —an area that was ready to use once the rest of the plots were filled. Kora played with the dogs with joy on her face, stopping to pet Sarah at every chance, laughing when Bernie stole the stick from Ulysses and the brothers started brawling. I remembered her father's comment; Kora had probably never played with a pet before. She smiled at them, bright and playful. It was a smile that seemed to come from within. I had seen her lips take that shape before, but never as naturally, never as *at ease*, as she was right then.

When the morning light stretched over the horizon, I took Kora back inside, bringing her to the basement with a cup of tea, a bagel, and a small bowl of yogurt.

"You should get some rest," I said.

"I'll try," she said.

And for once, neither of us had a smart remark to say.

By the time I was finished with my breakfast, a knock rapped through my door. I must have been Catie. At least she had knocked this time. I opened the door.

"Mr. Erickson," Shea said. She stood on the front porch with her fingers itching at the fabric on her chest. "I'm sorry to bother you this early, but I was hoping you could help me."

A jolt of adrenaline surged through me. Her polite attitude was overwhelming. She had no idea that her daughter was right there, underneath her. I grit my teeth, then soothed my nerves. I had not predicted that she would come to see me like this, but that was the beauty of destruction. Nothing could ever be predicted.

"What can I do for you?" I asked.

"I hope this isn't rude," she said. "I heard a long time ago that you lived on the property, and I..." She looked at her feet, unsure of what to say next.

"It's fine," I said. *Just get on with it.*

"You called the other day," she started again, "And I didn't think anything of it at first. But then I remembered—in those last days before she disappeared, we saw you, remember? In the flower field. Wild Berry Trailhead. On Mount Punica? We were all there, hunting for the Middlemist Red."

That day had played through my mind many, many times. "I remember."

"Did she tell you anything then?" she asked. "Did she say anything? Anything at all?" My chest expanded and I wet my lips. Since I had started watching her family, I had never seen Shea let a flicker of negative emotions cross her face when someone could see her. But now, she was falling apart, more with each passing day. It was fascinating.

"We didn't talk much," I said.

"But you have to know *something*," she stammered. My head buzzed with pleasure. Another crack in the facade. "Please, Mr. Erickson. Is there anything at all?"

I flexed my fingers straight, one by one. I imagined Shea's face when she saw the closed casket, how she'd throw herself over the wood, her sobs reverberating through the room.

But for now, I could point something out to her. It would make the ending sweeter.

"They found Echo at your house," I said. "Right?"

"They did."

"Is it possible that her friend brought it over?"

"What friend?"

"Nyla Nerissa. The one who died?"

Shea grit her teeth, staring down at the doormat beneath her feet, then her chin flicked up.

"You think Nyla is a part of this?"

"I think Nyla might be a key that's been neglected. Maybe her family knows something."

She stepped forward, grabbing my hand. I flinched.

"Please. If you know anything, please help me. Nyla's family has been here, right? They won't return my calls. They're too busy. They aren't concerned with my daughter. But if you could ask them for me, maybe they'll listen to you. I know they're grieving, but—" A tear fell down her cheek. "I don't know what else to do."

We stood there in silence, and heat bubbled inside of me. I let it linger, acting like I was disturbed by Shea's pain, when the opposite was true.

"I'll do whatever I can, Mrs. Nova," I said.

"Thank you," Shea said.

"Sheriff Mike must be able to question them," I offered. "Can't he help you with that?"

"He's so busy with the campaign. You know how he gets right before an election. I can't—" She rubbed her forehead, looking down at her feet again. It must have been difficult to have a picture-perfect life ripped away from you. To have a husband who was too busy trying to get re-elected to focus on his personal problems. To have a daughter that was no longer under your control.

"If I remember anything, I'll call you." I paused, pretending to think it over. "I'm sure she's out there."

"Thank you," she said, tears filling her eyes. Then, without another word, she got into her car and drove away.

Once she was gone, I settled into my tasks for the day. A body removal. Tidying the grounds while I waited for a family to sign paperwork. An embalming finished the day, someone who had lived a long life, dying of natural causes.

That night, I relaxed in the studio, staring at the blank canvas. I thought about Kora in the mausoleum, the way the moonlight seemed brighter then, with her underneath it. I dipped the paintbrush into the jar of blue, then stroked the canvas.

A knock echoed down the hallway. I opened the door to the basement: Kora stood before me in a tank top, leggings on her hips, all the material clinging to her skin. Comfortable. Natural.

"I changed my mind," she said. I tilted my head, waiting for her to explain. "About modeling. Do you want me to pose?"

A heaviness lifted from my shoulders.

"Let me get my supplies," I said. Then I closed the basement door and locked it.

I returned with my easel, paints, and a canvas, setting up inside of the loft. She sat on the couch, and I positioned her so that she resembled that night in the mausoleum. As I brushed the strokes of her neck on the canvas, working next on the shape of her shoulders, I asked, "What made you change your mind?"

"Boredom," she said, a twinge of flirtation in her eyes. Then she let out a small laugh. "I wanted to thank you for taking me to Nyla's grave last night. This modeling," she motioned around us, her new ring flashing under the chandelier's light, "seemed like a good option."

That was unexpected. Something inside of her had shifted. And now, that change was more evident than ever.

"Have there been any more Echo deaths?" she asked.

"None last night."

"That's good." She paused, tilting her head. "I wonder why the killer skipped last night."

"Coincidence. Or the body hasn't been found."

"You're probably right."

For a while, we didn't say anything. The brush stroked the canvas, my empty fingers tapped my leg.

"My father will help," she said confidently, breaking the silence.

"Your mother says he's too busy with the election."

Her eyes darted up to me, her body deviating from the pose. "You spoke to my mother?"

"This morning."

She wrapped her arms around herself. "How is she?" she asked quietly.

I glanced around the side of the canvas. "Holding on." I motioned for her to return to her pose. "Confident that you're out there."

"Good."

After a few minutes passed, I added, "Your father had a big event last night. A charity cookout. That's probably why there were no bodies found. He was too busy using his men to patrol the cookout, rather than finding them."

Kora grimaced. "That makes sense."

"Was the funeral the first time you had been around that many people?"

I don't know why I asked, but the words had slipped out, and I wasn't going to hold back with her anymore. It was part of breaking her down, showing her the flaws in her own existence. Kora blushed, then nodded, looking over the railing to the basement below.

"You shouldn't have let your parents control you like that," I said. "You're young. You have the world in front of you. Do you even want to be a florist?" I put the brush down. "They've put you in a cage since birth."

Her features grew melancholy. "You say that like I'm not in a cage here," she said. My empty hands tightened into fists impulsively. She lifted her chin. "My parents are good to me. At least, my mother is. She has strange habits, but she's never left my side. She's always taken care of me. Gave me a good life, set me up for the future—"

"And did you get to decide any of that for yourself?"

Kora adjusted the strap of her shirt, and from this angle, I could see the outline of her lace bra underneath the tank top. The way her stomach rolled with each breath, giving way to that delicate valley between her legs. On the canvas, I switched to her thighs. Kora parted her legs in front of me, and my eyes were glued to that tight fabric, showing off the outline of her pussy. I licked my lips.

"Listen," she said. I lifted my eyes to hers. "You think you know everything about our life, but you don't. My parents love me. And yeah, I know that my mother has some flaws." She shuddered. "Okay, maybe she has some major flaws. But she's not evil. She's just scared."

I had never considered that someone as successful as her mother could be afraid. But I had also never thought that a young woman like Kora would have any spine to speak of. But I wasn't going to give Kora back just because her mother was having a difficult time. Plenty of people had hard times. Try watching your mother, father, and brother die.

"Everyone's scared of something," I said.

"Yeah," she said. "You're right."

The chandelier's lights flickered in her eyes, as if her hope was changing into something else, an emotion that was more honest. Everything inside of me burned, wanting to push her over the edge, to watch her fall to the ground, to jump down after her. The world might not have been the place that Kora thought it was, but there was so much more it could give her.

And that frustrated me. There was so much I could give her, and yet I hated myself for it. I wanted to destroy her.

But I needed to possess her first.

Chapter 15

Kora

A FEW MORE DAYS PASSED, VINCENT AND I FELL INTO A ROUTINE. Every night—or day, or morning?—Vincent would pose my body, then paint me. He never showed me the final products, but always engaged me in conversation. Something had changed between us. Our dynamic, while it was still one of abductor and victim, didn't feel like that anymore. If I wanted to play with the dogs, he took me out at night. If I wanted to model for him, I did. All I had to do was ask. In a way, I almost looked forward to seeing him.

No, that's not right. I *did* look forward to seeing him. Maybe it was the fact that he was the only person who I *could* see: a case of the victim liking their abductor out of pure survival instinct. Or maybe it was something more. It's not like he had to bring me to my best friend's grave and give me her ring, tell my mother that I was out there, or even speak to me while he painted. We both knew he could force me to do whatever he wanted. But he hadn't.

So I stopped questioning those feelings. Otherwise, I would go insane.

After a few days like this, I knocked on the basement door. He didn't answer at first, but when he did, he huffed down the hallway, exiting the house. He simply wanted me to stop banging on the door.

I glanced at the kitchen, then the door to the backyard, where his property rested on the far edge of Mount Punica. My pulse quickened. *I could run—*

"Tracking device. Poison. Gun. Knife," he said, popping through the sliding doors. My heart raced. Was I that obvious? And would he really kill me? "Follow me." I tightened my hands into fists, took a deep breath, then caught up with him.

We took the path that led to the cemetery. Near the field where I played ball with the dogs, there were two empty graves, and a third was halfway done.

Three graves?

Vincent jumped down and went straight to work.

"You did this all by hand?" I asked. "I get digging a grave every once in a while, but this—" A clump of dirt hit the mound next to the site, interrupting me. I started again: "Isn't this excessive?"

He threw another shovel full over the side. "I prefer to do it by hand." The clod fell onto the pile with a thud. "Keeps me busy."

He hit the shovel into the ground as if it felt good to take out his anger on the dirt.

"Is something wrong?" I asked.

A few more shovels of dirt passed before he finally spoke up. "No one knows what's going on. Murders. Drugging. Arson. Runaways. Abductions." His voice raised in pitch, avoiding something else. "No one cares. No one gives a fuck what their plans are, or what's going to happen." He stabbed the shovel into the ground. "We just keep spinning around in circles until we all fall down."

Was he talking about the Echo deaths? "My father will figure it out," I said. If there was one thing my father cared about, it was justice.

Vincent chuckled. "Unless it's all happening right under his nose."

I shot a glare at him. "What's that supposed to mean?"

He never stopped shoveling the dirt. "The world isn't made of roses, Kora," he finally said. "Not everyone is as perfect as you think they are." He shook his head. "But everyone falls. Everyone crumbles eventually."

I crossed my arms over my chest. "Why are you so bitter?"

Suddenly, he leaped out of the hole, jumping to my side. He wrapped me in his grip, throwing me around until I was locked in his arms. I thrashed, trying to break free, but he yanked me into the grave.

"What the hell are you doing?!" I yelled.

He slammed me against the wall of dirt. I gasped. His eyes hovered over each part of me, the moon's reflection gold in his black pupils. To my bare neck. Down to my covered stomach. My legs. Dirt filled my palm, and I dug into the earth with my fingers, the soil caking my nails.

What did he want from me?

He unzipped the hoodie slowly, letting each slide of the metal teeth send shivers down my spine. I hadn't worn a bra; the tank top was thin underneath it. He cupped my breast. A subtle pain filled my chest. And when his thumb lingered over my nipple, he grinned, then pulled my shirt down until my breasts were exposed. He continued massaging me, teasing my skin, driving me crazy. Every thought erased from my head.

"Is this better for you?" he asked, a grin on his face. That grin made me want to fall to my knees and slap him in the face all at the same time. My eyes traced his strong shoulders, his thick arms that were used to the labor of digging, the dirt flaked across his neck and hands, marking my breasts. Down further to his stomach, the bulge growing in his pants.

"Go on," he said. "Touch me, flower. If you don't like it when I'm bitter, show me how you'd rather I behave."

My fingers flinched. I longed to feel his cock; I had only ever seen one on Nyla's phone when my mother was in the storeroom. But *this?* Sex permeated the air, a heavy, fragrant scent mixed with earth, and yet the smirk on his face made me small. Like he knew exactly what his next move was, and I had barely figured out how to stand on my own two feet.

"I—" I muttered, not sure what to say. "I thought we were getting along well now."

"How dare I confuse the princess."

My skin flushed, full of heat. I clenched my jaw, and he

laughed, though it seemed forced. With the tension building inside of me, I reached forward, grabbing his cock, squeezing it. A growl escaped his lips, his hardness twitching under my grasp. My lips fluttered open, my breath caught in my throat, and he pinched my nipples, digging his nails into my skin.

"What are you doing to me?" I whimpered.

With both of my nipples pressed in his fingers, he twisted until I bit my lip. I tried so hard not to make a sound, and he kept me on my toes.

"How does that make you feel, flower?" he asked. His breath was hot, brushing my cheek and neck, and I squeezed his cock tighter, not knowing what else to do. His eyes rolled into the back of his head, and when he looked at me again, he bared his teeth like a predator.

"I feel—" My whole body was hot. It was hard to think. He brought his mouth down to my neck, grazing me with his lips, sending chills down my spine. I closed my eyes, enjoying it. But then I remembered this wasn't about me. I wanted to know about *him*, why he was so angry. So bitter. All the time. "Answer me," I whispered. He didn't stop, so I said it louder. "Vincent. Answer me. What's actually going on with you? Why are you so angry?"

He bit down on my neck, so hard that white-hot pain burned through my body, making all of my muscles seize up. Then he dug his fingers into my back, getting between the ribs, digging in tight until I crumpled in his arms. My eyes watered, but I held strong, holding my breath.

"I don't understand," I rasped. "Do you want to kill me? Is that it?"

"Kill you?" he laughed. Holding me up with one arm, using the other to play with my nipples, he rotated between massaging my areola and pinching it until I had to bite my lip to stop myself from crying out. "That's only the start of it." Then he shoved me forward, pinning me to the wall, grabbing my neck. The dirt clumps fell down, and he smirked, then squeezed tighter, until my face was hot and everything sounded fuzzy. "You've never known death, have you, flower? Not until Nyla." My lips trembled, trying to say the words, *Please. Vincent.* But he watched me shake in his grip. I pulled at his hands, trying to loosen his grip, until finally I kneed him in the chest and he dropped me to the floor. I coughed, the dirt flying back in my face, but he looked down at me, unfazed. Then he scooped me up in his arms, forcing me to stand. He took one of my fingers, bringing it to his mouth, then bit down harder and harder until the pain shot all the way to the back of my arms. I let out a sob, unable to hold back, and stomped down on his feet, but he didn't move. He simply laughed. Then he relieved the pressure by shoving my hand into my pants. I instantly flushed again; I was so wet.

We stared into each other's eyes. "You've never felt real pain before this. Tell me I'm wrong, Kora."

I didn't know what to say. He was right. I had never known loss like that. Not until Nyla.

"You had never had real pain," he said with venom in his voice. He jerked my hand, making me touch myself. "You've never had anything negative in your perfect life."

I tried to read what was there. Like he was longing for that. Like he saw what he wanted in me. Because Vincent wanted to make me squirm. Because he knew he could make me feel like he did. And that burned inside of me.

"You're jealous," I whispered.

"Don't flatter yourself," he said, gritting his teeth. "You're numb to the world. I'm just trying to fix that."

We stared at each other for a moment, both of us daring the other to speak. Then Vincent let go of me and went back to shoveling. Stunned, I stayed there for a while, then fixed my shirt, zipped up my hoodie, and lifted my nose, but I didn't feel proud. My throat ached, but I stayed still, not understanding what we had just done.

But that was the thing—this was about... something else. Something I didn't understand. A place where Vincent refused to let me be.

I leaned on the wall of the grave. I didn't understand him. I had a feeling few people did.

When I attempted to get out of the hole, Vincent grabbed my hips, lifting me out. A surge of heat roamed through me. He could choke me nearly to death, and a few minutes later, help me out of a grave? As soon as I sat down, Bernie brought me a slimy red ball, but I stroked the top of his head and whispered in his ear, "Not tonight, buddy," then gave him a kiss. He tilted his head, then looked at his brother and sister. The three of them wandered through the trees lining the edge of the property. An idea dawned on me.

"Have you ever thought about tree burials?" I asked.

He furrowed his brows. "Tree burials?"

"You combine the ashes with seeds with soil and other nutrients. Then a tree grows from it."

"That sounds like some hippie garbage."

I gave a soft laugh. Maybe it was, but I liked it. "My mother had a customer who brought in a pamphlet once. She was going to the capital to have her husband buried like that since we didn't have that service here in Punica." Vincent slowed for a second, and I knew he had understood my subtext: since *he* didn't offer tree burials.

He resumed his steady pace. "Not interested."

"Why not?" He ignored me, focusing on shoveling. I continued: "Maybe, something like a tree, something like *life*, could actually show you a different side of grief. One you haven't seen much of." Another clump of dirt landed on top of the pile. "One of hope."

He exhaled deeply. "Would a tree make you feel better about Nyla?"

"I think she would have liked becoming a tree. And I would have enjoyed visiting her."

"And what if she died? As a tree?" He laughed to himself, mocking me. "*Again?*"

I wrinkled my nose. "I wouldn't let that happen."

"Sometimes it's not up to you."

Speckles of dirt covered his cheeks and forehead, sweat beading on his brow, mixing it into a rich brown.

"Look into it," I said. "You might be surprised."

He grunted, still absorbed in his task, but his shoulders relaxed. Maybe he wasn't completely opposed to the idea. I smoothed the grass beside me, picking a few blades to braid, and when he was done, he motioned to the funeral home.

Inside, he led me to a small room with a standard food refrigerator, a microwave, and a small cabinet. He wiped his face with a wet cloth, a streak of clear skin illuminated by the fluorescent lights. But then he rubbed his brow and got some dirt in his eye. He cursed to himself, then, holding one eye closed, pointed at me. My fingers twitched in my lap.

"Don't go anywhere," he said.

As soon as the funeral home's bathroom door closed behind him, I raced to the crematory room. I dialed my mother's number, but it went straight to voicemail. My hands shook, knowing that this was my only chance. I dialed the police department, then asked to speak to Sheriff Mike, and when he wasn't available, I asked for Officer Andrew.

"This is Officer Andrew," he said.

"Andrew," I whispered.

"Miss Kora? Is that you?" he asked, his voice raised. "Where are you, darling?"

"I'm at Quiet Meadows." I clutched the phone to my ear. "Vincent is holding me prisoner. He almost tried to kill me. I need you to get me out of here—"

"Erickson?"

"Yes!" I whisper-yelled, my words picking up speed. "Get here now. And please don't tell my parents. At least, don't tell my mom. I don't want her to worry."

"Whoa, there. Hold on a second, darling," he said, his tone thin. "First thing's first. Are you all right?"

I held my breath. Why was he wasting time asking me that? "I'm fine. But seriously, Andrew. He tried to kill me—"

"How so?"

I cocked my head. "He literally just—"

"Is he doing anything strange to you?"

What was that supposed to mean? And what would that even include?

"He *abducted* me," I said, irritation leaking through my words. "Please. Help me get out of here."

113

He waited on the line, the speaker rustling like he was twisting the phone up to his ear. "You have a second, darling?"

I tapped my fingers. "Not much."

"You are a strong, brave girl, Miss Kora." Those words were compliments, but it made me dread to hear what he was going to say next. My stomach sank. "And you have a rare opportunity. You can look into him."

"*Look into him?* Are you crazy?" I clutched the phone. "You remember he abducted me? He choked me just now. Why on earth would I look into him?"

"He's one of our lead suspects for the Echo murders."

He didn't miss a beat. Nothing fazed him. Not even the fact that Vincent had choked and tried to kill me. A headache throbbed in my temples.

"*The* Echo murders?" I asked.

"None other."

"And you want *me* to investigate him?"

He chuckled to himself. "Like I said, Kora. We don't have enough on him yet, but with your help, we can put him in jail for good. Bring peace to our town. I know your daddy would be mighty proud to put him in jail before the big day, you know? Be the sheriff the county needs. And think, if he saves his daughter in the process, the voters won't have a choice but to vote for him."

My body hummed with confusion. "He's not the Echo murderer," I said. It didn't make sense. If he wanted to kill people, he'd burn them, like he almost burned me. "He's weird, I get that. But Vincent isn't a killer."

"He kidnapped you," Andrew said, his tone firm. "The man is capable of anything, as far as I am concerned. And your father needs to win this election. Your town needs him." The phone filled with static for a second, like he was adjusting his grip. "And I need you, Kora. Can you do this for me? For Nyla?"

My heart skipped a beat. If Nyla *had* been murdered, and I was the only person who was this close to one of his suspects, then I had to do my part. I had to do what was right for her. Nyla.

But it didn't make sense. If it *was* Vincent, then what were the car crashes were for? To cover up the evidence?

My brain pulsed, the headache intensifying. Dirt covered my arms like I had been digging too. I needed a cold shower.

"What if he kills me?" I whispered.

"Trust me, darling. You won't die an Echo death. If he wanted to kill you, you would likely be dead by now, unfortunately. He must like keeping you around," the grin was evident in his voice. "I know I would."

I cringed. What did that even mean?

"I don't like this," I said.

"I don't either, but you are a strong girl, Miss Kora," he said. "Do this for me. For your mother." His tone hardened: "For Nyla."

The bathroom door clicked open. "I've gotta go," I whispered and hung up. With quiet steps, I headed back to the other room, but Vincent caught me in the hallway. He leaned forward, studying me. I swallowed a breath.

"I was checking to see if you had anyone in the crematorium," I said.

"And?"

I couldn't remember any details, so I quickly changed the subject: "This is your break room?"

I walked into the room, then sat down at the table, my entire body shaking with nerves. How was I supposed to take what had happened with Andrew? A cop who was supposed to be protecting me, was telling me to spy on my abductor?

And what exactly would I find?

Was Vincent the Echo Killer?

Vincent sat across from me, his hands bracing the sides of the table. If he was the Echo Killer, what did he want from me?

"What do you want from life?" he asked.

Those words shocked me. I had been thinking almost the same thing. "What?"

"What do you want from life?" A subtle smile crossed his lips. "It's simple."

I furrowed my brows. I needed to be calm. I needed to pretend like everything was fine.

"Is anything ever that simple?" I asked.

"When it's about desire, yes. It's what you want. No one can change that."

His onyx eyes sucked me in, drowning me, and though I knew I was supposed to see a killer inside of him, I didn't. I saw a man who was tortured by a past I didn't understand, possessed with an obsession to see things weaken before him, someone who was struck by the world.

"So?" he asked.

"So," I gave a nervous laugh, "When I was younger—okay, when I was eighteen, so like, three years ago," I corrected myself, "I wanted to go to college. Study floriculture. Maybe even go to one of the agriculture universities on the west coast." I shrugged, trying to play it off like it didn't bother me anymore. "I even got a scholarship. But I couldn't go."

"Why not?"

"My mother needed me. Here," I said in a quiet voice. "She said she couldn't risk me being that far away from home. And rather than risk another one of her episodes, I've been trying to think of ways I can work on learning nature here, in Punica. I was working with my friend to set up a proposal for this business." I didn't bring up the greenhouse, nor did I bring up Andrew's marriage compromise. The whole thing seemed silly now. "Sometimes, my mother gets me books from the library, but mostly it's just reading the catalogs. Scouring the websites when she lets me on the computer."

His jaw ticked. "Your mother kept you from going to college on a scholarship?"

I narrowed my eyes at him, trying to figure out why he was acting like that offended him. "Yeah. She needed me here."

"She doesn't *need* you. She's a grown woman."

"You don't know her."

"Nothing could give her an excuse to hold you back like that."

I crowded my arms around myself. My cheeks flamed; he was acting like he knew my life better than I did.

"You can't dwell on what you don't have," I said. "I'm not going to pity myself, or be angry with my mother, when I can find a new goal. A different way to make things work." He shook his head; he didn't agree. "You have to see the beauty in each moment. Maybe I didn't get to go to college, but I got to help my mother expand Poppies & Wheat. And if I had actually gone to college, then I would never have met Nyla." My muscles tightened. "You have to enjoy life. Even the little moments in between."

He cocked his chin to the side, his eyes focused. He leaned forward, tapping his chin. My skin laced with heat. Why was he scrutinizing me like that?

"What is it?" I asked. "What are you thinking about?"

After a few seconds had passed, he said, "Like," he scrunched his lips, "digging graves in the moonlight. Playing fetch in the dark."

My stomach dropped. Those were his moments in between. Mine too, now.

"You're still wrong," he said.

My jaw dropped. "Excuse me?"

"You're saying it like it's wrong to want something. But what else is life for? What gives us that drive? You've got to want something. Then reach out and own it."

Maybe that was true. And by compromising with my mother, I would be able to find something that would make us both happy one day. Wouldn't I?

He always sounded so sure of himself.

"But what if I don't know what I want anymore?" I asked in a quiet voice.

His gaze was hard. "You know. You just have to listen to yourself."

My scalp prickled. Those words were the truth, but I didn't want to face that right now. I changed the subject, avoiding it altogether: "What do you want, then?" He lowered his chin. "What about your art? Why do you paint? What exactly do you want out of life?"

He kept his eyes on the table, then ran his finger across the surface, rubbing away a red sauce stain from one of the previous days.

"Work keeps me busy," he said. "It's hard to explain. Makes me sound sadistic."

Curiosity simmered inside of me, but fear overpowered that urge. With all the tension in my shoulders and Andrew's suspicions vibrating in my head, I was too nervous to ask what he meant.

"Then what about your art?" I asked instead.

"I come to you."

My cheeks reddened, and his eyes were hot on me, as if he was absorbing everything about me. "What about before you abducted me?" I asked.

"You've been my spark for a long, long time, Kora."

Was it possible that he was there the whole time, making art that was inspired by me?

My breath caught in my chest. I had always known that there was someone out there, watching out for me. It was why I left the window open. Why I stared out the window at night. It was hard to comprehend exactly what that meant. It was both terrifying and comforting, and I was afraid to confirm it, to know that what I had known all along, was true.

"Well," I blushed, "Then *you* should follow your dreams too."

"This isn't about 'dreams,' Kora."

"Then what is it about?"

We both waited in silence, but then I got irritated and finally spoke: "If this isn't about dreams, then what is it about? What do you want for yourself? Who cares if you're sadistic, or whatever you want to call it." I twisted my fingers into knots. "What even is it, anyway?"

He didn't say a word. Instead, he scrutinized me. I shrank before him. I stared into his dark eyes, his thick bottom lip, the stubble that stretched across his neck and jaw. I had always been curious about sex, and luckily, Nyla had filled me in as much as she could whenever my mother left us alone. *It's like explosions in your body,* she had said. What would it feel like to have his lips press against mine? Would it feel like explosions, or would it feel like nothing at all?

I wanted to know. But he was the only suspect that the police department had, and if he was the Echo Killer, then what did that say about my attraction to him? What did that say about me? Was this a mind game I was playing with myself, to convince myself to get closer to him?

"Sometimes I wonder what it would be like to kiss you," I said, forcing myself to say it. I blushed deeply, but his mouth stayed stern. I shouldn't have said anything. But when he tilted his body toward mine and parted his lips, the embarrassment left me. I couldn't think.

"You must be starving," he said.

But I wasn't hungry. Not like that.

Chapter 16

Vincent

The next late afternoon, the embalming machine hummed to life, pumping the decedent's body full of chemicals. I closed my fists, grinding my teeth until my head hurt. A twenty-one-year-old shouldn't have to die when they had hardly lived.

Kora was twenty-one.

I should have been able to pinpoint who the culprit was by now; instead, I was here, embalming another Echo victim. It shouldn't have bothered me, but I couldn't help but think of her. All it would have taken was one lapse of judgment and Kora would never have come home.

For the first time in years, I was tired of digging graves. I had dug three more the night before, and though Kora had helped to release some of that energy, it was impossible to focus on my work. Every corpse that came through Quiet Meadows was another version of Kora. Young. Innocent. Barely there.

In the shower, I leaned against the wall, letting the steam turn my vision blurry. With my blood throbbing, I fucked my fist until it hurt, until I lost control over her. And once I had a second of clarity, I went over my plan: the first step was to figure out who was behind the Echo deaths so that I could either blackmail them into adding a fake Kora to the list, so that no one would ever suspect me; the second step was to completely ruin Kora, to the point that when I destroyed her, she wouldn't recognize herself. Because then, I wouldn't care anymore. Her transformation would be complete. I could kill her, then.

But I wasn't going to do any of that yet.

I drove to 52 Peaks, a nightclub in Folium City. Large columns, ending in scroll-like fixtures, held up the roof of the club. Purple lights illuminated the white paint. Inside, there were two levels; a dance floor with circular neon bars, and a top-level with metal railing to keep the herd inside of the pen. It was a weeknight, but the crowd was still decent. Laser beams shot across the space while metal leaves hung off of the sides of the second floor. Naked metal statues flaunted themselves throughout.

A man acknowledged me. A flat cap sat on his head, a leather jacket wrapped around his arms. I stood beside him, keeping my eyes forward.

"You mind if we hang out?" I asked.

He grinned, his smile more perfect than a dental model's. "What did you have in mind?"

"Where can I find Echo?"

"Echo?" He sniffled. "I never have that."

"I need it *now*," I said, gritting my teeth. "Where can I find it?"

"You realize they're linking that shit to murders, right?"

Which was exactly why I needed to find it and figure who was killing these people. I needed to do something *now*, before things got worse with Kora.

But what did 'worse' mean for us?

Us.

"You're not a cop, are you?" he asked.

Idiot. "If I were a cop, would I be straight up asking for Echo?"

"Find it somewhere else."

He trailed the walls to an area outside. I waited a minute, then followed him out to the back. He knew something; I just needed him to say it.

The door led to an alley with a few patio chairs and tables.

The man was leaning against the wall, smoking a cigarette, joined by a few other people. He met my eyes instantly.

I held out a hand. "Let's start over."

We shook hands, then he offered me a cigarette. I declined.

"Cops like to come undercover to the club now, and there's only so much they'll let slide," he said, letting smoke expel from his mouth. "They are *ruthless* when it comes to Echo."

"They come here often?"

"They think it'll be easy to hunt. But no one knows exactly where the Echo comes from."

My mouth went slack. "You really don't sell Echo," I said.

"I could make a killing if I did. That shit gets you so high, you can't even tell. It's like your senses are on fire." His eyes widened in amusement. "You know they mix it into drinks now? It's all crushed and you think you're drinking a Long Island or a beer and then *bam!*" He smacked the back wall. "That's why I always buy bottled water when I'm here."

A shadow stretched down the alleyway. "Deacon," a male voice said. The dealer shook hands with a man in a v-neck shirt and jeans, his arms and shoulders buff, his white hair shining purple under the exterior lights. "I see you've met Vincent."

"You two know each other?" the dealer asked me.

"We're acquainted," I said, glaring at Andrew. For once, he wasn't in uniform.

"I'll see myself out," the dealer said, shaking my hand.

The dealer went back inside, and the others exited too. For the most part, Andrew fit in with the club's target audience, but that didn't matter. Neither of us was supposed to be there.

"What are you doing here, Erickson?" he asked.

"I should be asking you the same thing."

"I'm here on the job." He rested his hand against his pistol. "Investigating for the sheriff."

"Could I find that in a report somewhere?" I tilted my head.

Andrew widened his stance. "Mike is too busy with the campaign. But I have got to make sure we can catch the murderer." His jaw clicked. "Funny thing is, I didn't expect to see you here tonight."

I cracked a forced smile. "What are you really doing here, Drew?"

He grit his teeth. "Investigating suspects, Vinny."

He narrowed his eyes at me, and I knew the asshole wasn't going to let me do anything. I tapped my chin. "Enjoy the rest of your shift. I'll see you around."

I went through the club to the entrance, and the same man with the flat cap on his head—Deacon, the dealer—was waiting outside. He waved to me before I made it to my car.

"Why are you so interested in Echo, man?" he asked. "It seems a little young for you."

"I'm a mortician," I said, but that didn't explain anything. Not even to me. "Curiosity, I guess."

He studied me closely. "You want to get rid of this sonofabitch?"

He wanted me to say 'yes,' so I nodded, even though that wasn't the true goal. He pulled his hand out of his pocket and shook my hand, a small object palmed inside of our grip.

"I have a friend who got a hold of it once," he said, "but he doesn't know where it came from. I haven't touched it because I'm tired of it." He laughed. "It's bad for business. Can't do anything if your customers keep dying."

I nodded. "Thanks."

"Don't thank me. Get the killer."

On the drive back, my body hummed with energy, agitation leaking into my bloodstream. Nothing had felt right since Kora. The urge surfaced with vengeance—the compulsion to destroy scratching at me like a bad itch that I couldn't reach. I had buried it long before my brother's death, but now it was here. Crawling out. Like it would never give up. But I couldn't take it out on Kora. Not yet.

To the side of the road, a firepit flickered through the trees. I slowed my vehicle and watched: teenagers, maybe college students, were surrounding it, passing around beers. I stared at the green pill in my palm, at the three curved black lines on the top. Why were these kids hanging out in the forest, anyway? Didn't they know that a bunch of kids their age had died here recently? I split the tablet in half, then put it on my tongue. Put the other half back in my pocket.

I parked to the side of the road where I could see the flames. Grabbing my tools, I went through the woods. Even when my boots snapped the branches, none of them cared. They laughed with each other. They were invincible. I poured the canister, going as close to them as I could without being seen. Then I lit a match and dropped it to the ground.

The fire blazed up, swallowing a clear path toward them. I stepped back, letting the flames come close enough to share their heat, but far enough away that nothing touched me. The fire crackled behind them, but no one noticed. None of them had a worry in the world. Finally, one looked up.

"Fire!"

"What?"

"Shit!"

They ran through the trees, scattering like cockroaches. Screaming for their lives. My heartbeat raced. Once they were gone, I returned to my car, then drove. They were smart; none of them would die. But it thrilled me to watch them run.

At the house, I was rejuvenated, but still desperate to feel. I rested the half-pill on the easel in my studio. The Echo hadn't done shit. I had tried cocaine, heroin, and MDMA before, but this?

I felt blank.

There was no monster coming to kill me. The only monster was me.

I debated taking the second half, but I didn't care that much. Anger flashed in my veins, hot and ready. I needed a better outlet. I needed to do something about the problem in my basement, the problem that was burning me alive from the inside.

I wonder what the dead feel like, Kora had said. Was she that ungrateful for her life? I would show her, one fucking day.

I bounded down the stairs into the basement, and her mouth dropped open as soon as she saw me. She trembled, anticipating my next moves.

"Stand up," I ordered.

She stared at me. "What?"

"I will not ask again, Kora."

"I don't under—"

I grabbed her by the hair, yanking her to her feet, then I pulled her over to the back corner of the room. I ripped her out of her pajamas, staring down at her naked body: the softness, the subtle curve of her hips, those ghostly pale nipples hardening under my stare. Getting a key from my pocket, I unlocked one of the special crates, then removed the top. Kora shrank back, so I gripped the hairs on her head, bringing her toes, making her whimper. Finally, I found what I was searching for: a few cable ties and some plastic wrap. *Perfect.*

"What are you doing?" she whispered. Her bottom lip quivered and my cock twitched, yearning to be shoved between those lips.

"I'm going to take advantage of you, flower. In ways you could never dream of."

"Vincent, I—"

I put a finger to her lips, shutting her up. "We're not friends, flower," I said, keeping my voice even. "Never make that mistake. I took you from your home because I don't give a fuck about what you want. Because I decided three years ago that you were mine." I smiled. "Now, I can either show you what I want, or I can leave you here to rot. Be a good girl, and you can decide." Her pupils dilated, her lips parting as she stared at me. *Good.* She made her decision. I gestured at her palms. "Give me your wrists."

Like an obedient pet, she gave them to me, and my cock swelled with heat. She was naturally like this, willing to surrender herself, and yet with her lack of experience, as much as she hated it, she wanted it too. Her mouth hung open, her breathing husky, goosebumps erupting on her arms as my fingers tickled her skin, linking the plastic cable around her wrists. Next, I secured her ankles, though that one I left looser than the other, better to see her squirm. Then I held the arm of the plastic wrap, circling her body until she was layered from her shoulders to her ankles like a mummy. I scooped her into my arms and carried her to the couch.

"What is this?" she cried.

It was an interesting game, especially for the claustrophobic types that couldn't stand the inability to escape. The plastic wrap clung to her skin, slipping with her sweat.

I ran my fingers along the plastic, exploring the curves of her body. She panted, her mouth open, her eyes locked on my lips. She was easy. So fucking easy. She *let* me do this. Wanted me to. And yet it was her mouth that stopped me. I wanted to use that hole until she cried out, until she couldn't breathe, until my come drowned her into an oblivion of lust and need and she forgot who she was.

But this wasn't about *my* pleasure. This was about punishing *her*. I had let her off easily for far too long.

I went upstairs, finding a metal ruler and scissors in my studio then brought them down and immediately started striking her feet with the ruler. She yelped in pain, a delicious cry that made me pulse, her body wiggling on the couch until finally, she fell to the ground like a worm inching back and forth. I laughed. I laughed so fucking hard that my stomach ached, watching her writhe. I rubbed my cock through my pants, hard and thick, the tip soaking my pants. Power surged through me as I looked down at her.

She was no longer her parents' little flower. She was my fucking flower. My complete disgrace. And I was going to pick her apart.

"What is wrong with you?" she asked, exasperated, her voice wiry.

"I don't hear you asking me to stop," I said in a low voice.

She wagged her chin. I leaned down, pressing my body on top of hers, pinning her to the floor. My lips grazed her ear.

"I bet if I ripped that plastic open and touched your pussy right now, you'd be soaked for me," I said. "You might not know what it's like to feel a cock inside of you, flower, but you know what you want, don't you? And you want more of this. You want more of *me*. All you want is for me to use you like a good little fuck toy. To fuck you. To own you."

Her body impulsively moved, her hips bucking forward into me. I grinned and she blushed.

"You're wrong," she hissed.

"You can't fight it, flower."

And neither could I.

I lifted her up so that she was sitting, then propped myself behind her and wrapped her head, encasing her skull in the plastic. She twitched like that, thrashing, her mouth sucking in the little air that it could, the plastic swelling in and out. I studied her, watching her fall apart. She had been relatively calm before, compared to this, but now, she was running on full primal instinct. Life and death dictated her next moves, those breaths that she so desperately wanted. The seconds ticked by, and she twitched in panic. How long could she hold her breath? Would her face turn purple, like lavender? My cock surged with heat.

"I don't care if you die, flower," I said. "Your pussy will still be soaked for me."

She groaned and gasped and finally, I ripped a tiny hole for her nose and mouth. She breathed in deep, sucking in like it might be her last breath. And she was right. She needed to enjoy the air while she still could. My cock twitched against her back; I couldn't stand it anymore. I pushed her to the ground, then ripped a hole in the plastic covering her cunt, and when the plastic proved to be too cumbersome, I used the scissors to cut it off. She was slick: the wettest, filthiest little cunt I had ever felt. I leaned down and tasted her, lapping up what I could, and she let out a guttural moan. She wasn't the same princess locked away in a tower anymore, but a woman consumed by her own needs.

Kora liked this as much as I did.

I yanked out my cock, my mind racing on what to do next. I played with her folds, ripping the plastic so that she was completely exposed, letting my fingers drag across her sensitive pussy lips, and pulled out my cock, stroking myself. She wasn't dead, not yet. But she was helpless, and I couldn't figure out what I wanted to do more: kill her and get it over with, fuck her face into oblivion, or make her come so hard that she passed out.

I leaned down, staring at her closed eyes underneath the plastic wrap as I shoved my tongue down her throat, and the sound she made was a mix of a moan and cry so mournful that she took my breath away with it. My face pressed against her nostrils, my mouth completely closed over hers, sucking the life out of her, but I didn't care. I fucked myself, tonguing her throat, and when she wriggled for escape, I pulled back, gave her a second to breathe, long enough to mount her face, shoving my cock into her throat. She gurgled, but her throat constricted around the head of my cock, and the pleasure ran through me in waves. My eyes rolled back into my head.

"That's it, flower," I said, my voice harsh and hoarse. "Show me what a fucking slut you are for me. Always ready for me. My little worm. My good girl. My flower." I moved my hips, pumping her mouth back and forth, and she moaned. When I held back, letting the head of my cock graze the tip of her lips, she lifted her head, trying to buck herself forward so that she could taste me. I laughed at her; she was so damn pathetic, so desperate for my come, and I knew that every fiber inside of me was exactly like her, driven by my insane carnal need to have her. To degrade someone so precious. To show her what it meant to be alive, to be completely stripped of everything you thought you were, until you were nothing. When nothing could stop you from what you wanted.

She gave a sad little cry, and that was all I needed to fuck her mouth, using her face hole until I came, deep in her throat. With each twitch of my cock, I pushed further inside her throat, the ridges of her esophagus tight, making her swallow all of me.

As soon as the high was gone, I could barely feel my body. I needed to get out of there. I needed to end all of this.

But when my eyes rested on her, relief swelled through me. I cut the cable ties then pulled her into my arms, holding her close, letting sleep overpower me.

Chapter 17

Kora

I fell asleep on the floor, tucked in Vincent's arms, both of us completely spent. Plastic wrap laid in tangles on the ground like the skin of a snake, our bodies wet with sweat and lust. I was too tired to question what we were doing; all I knew was that it felt good to be in his arms, and then, I fell asleep.

When I woke up, I was by myself again. My throat was scratchy, swollen, and sore. A pleasurable warmth crowded my belly, reminding me of what he had done. I pulled the blanket over my shoulders. I was now lying on the leather couch, inside of a heavy, comforting blanket that smelled like Vincent, a new one that hadn't been there before.

Vincent wasn't with me, right then, but he had thought of me.

When he opened the door later, my heart jumped into my throat. Our eyes met, and I smiled—I must have still looked like a mess; I hadn't even washed my face yet—but he stopped in his tracks. His jaw was loose, prickled with stubble, and his eyelids were stuck on me. I blushed.

Finally, he continued down the stairs, and when he reached me, he nodded up toward the door.

"Catie says she'll watch you," he said. I quirked my head to the side. "I've got some errands to run, but you can stay with her."

Unconsciously, I rubbed my arm, the tracking device a flat

ridge under the skin, and Vincent's eyes lowered there too, then flicked back up to me.

"Do you want to, or not?" he asked, an edge of frustration lingering in his voice. I nodded. I showered, dressed, and ate, then Vincent walked me over to Quiet Meadows. Catie's hair was clipped into poofy buns on the top of her head.

"Thanks for doing this," I said to Catie. It wasn't lost on me; she was babysitting me. But like Nyla, for some reason, I had a feeling that Catie wouldn't make it feel like that.

"Of course," she said.

Vincent turned to Catie. "I'll be back in a few hours." Then he disappeared down the hallway.

"You want to watch television or something?" Catie asked. "It's going to be a long day. I've got an appointment in an hour, otherwise, I'd be watching with you."

"I'm fine with whatever."

We watched the opening ten minutes of different shows until we found one we both liked. Once we settled into it, Catie hovered over paperwork, and I pretended to be happy that I was out of the basement. I mean, I *was* happy, but it reminded me of my situation. I wasn't supposed to like any of this. I was supposed to be investigating Vincent. Whatever that meant.

Halfway into a new episode, footsteps pounded in the entrance lobby. Catie peeked down the corridor, then her face flushed red, her jaw tight. "Stay in here," she whispered. But having lived with an overprotective mother and a curiosity streak wider than a valley, I pressed open the door slowly. Andrew stood in the hallway, his thumbs in his belt loops. The two of them spoke.

Relief swelled through me, followed by an overwhelming sense of terror. I didn't know what to do. So I stood there waiting, ripping holes into my pants. Sweat beaded on my forehead.

Finally, Catie went to another room to get something, and I raced down the hallway.

"Andrew," I said. I threw my arms around him, and he patted my back. But it wasn't comforting. It felt off.

"How are you, Miss Kora?" he whispered. "Are you all right?"

I peered into his blue eyes, trying to find the safety I needed. He stroked my back, giving me reassurance. "Take me home," I said. "We don't need to make a scene. We can leave now—"

"I came to check on you, darling. Make sure you're alright."

"Check on me?" Did that mean he was leaving?

"You find anything out about Erickson?"

He wasn't checking on me. He was making sure I was still doing my job. "No," I said, my stomach dropping to the ground. "Nothing. But will you please get me out of here?"

He grinned. "Don't you worry your little head," he rubbed his knuckles into my hair, "I'll send help as soon as I can. We just don't have the resources right now. But until then, remember, you have *got* to investigate Erickson. Use your time wisely."

"You're leaving me here?" my voice thick with fear.

"Miss Kora, get this right. I am assigning you a task to take care of. It is of the utmost importance." He straightened, adjusting his shirt as if I had dirtied it somehow. "I was checking his files, and you know his brother died exactly like these Echo victims?"

I squinted my eyes. "Was Echo even around back then?"

"Darling." He gave a deep sigh, shaking his head. Had I said something wrong? "Drugs in their system. Unexplained wounds. It all adds up." He grabbed my hand and squeezed it. "People are dying, Miss Kora."

His hand was sticky and cold. It gave me chills.

"You think he killed his own brother?" I asked. "Then why isn't he in jail?"

"Trust me, if it were that simple, he would be." He scoffed to himself. "But you can change that right now. A man like Vincent is wrong in the head. We need to lock him up, put him in his place, before it is too late." Catie's footsteps reverberated down the hall. He grabbed my shoulder and gave me a stern expression. "You can do this, Miss Kora. I believe in you." I sucked in a breath. "For Nyla."

Nyla.

I ran back and quickly closed Catie's office door behind me.

Their voices were faint through the walls, but I could still hear them.

"You have not seen or heard from her, then?" Andrew asked.

"Not at all."

"Mind if I check here again later when Erickson is around?" I imagined Catie shook her head. How could she tell an officer 'no'? "Perhaps we can keep this visit between us, Miss Catie. I would hate for you to obstruct our investigation."

My stomach turned, though I didn't know why. He was trying to do his job, but why did it feel wrong?

Eventually, Catie returned and shuffled behind her desk.

"What did I miss?" she asked.

I blinked rapidly. She meant the television. I hadn't seen a single thing.

"Not much," I said.

Catie lifted a brow at me, knowing that I had been up to something. "You okay, there?" she asked. I shrugged, not really sure what to say. "Okay. Spill." She turned off the television and swiveled her chair to me. "What's that face for?"

"I just—" I paused. What could I say without letting her know I had spoken to Andrew? Could I tell her I was supposed to investigate her boss? I couldn't. Instead, I word-vomited the one thing that had been on my mind since he had left the basement the night before. "I don't even know who Vincent is. What he wants. Why he's—" I stopped again, unsure of how to word it, "—why he's helping me." I tucked the short hairs behind my ears, then crossed my arms. "Some days, it's like he can't stand me at all. And other times, I don't know what to do to get him to leave me alone."

She tapped her fingers together, squinting at me. "You have a crush on him?"

I gawked at her. "Absolutely not."

"Uh-huh," she nodded slowly.

My skin flushed red. "It's nothing like that. I just don't understand him."

She tapped a pen to her temple, turning back to the paperwork. After a few minutes passed, she turned back to me: "You've known Vincent for a long time, right?"

I blinked. How had she gotten that impression? Technically, we had only gotten to know each other recently, but it had always felt like I had known him for much longer. I never thought of him as a stalker, but as a guardian. A shadow watching over me.

But how did you explain that to someone without sounding crazy?

"Sure," I said.

"Go to his art studio." She pointed in the house's direction. "That'll clear up any doubts."

"What's in his art studio?"

She smiled. "You'll find your answers there."

"Answers to what?" I raised my voice. My toes curled, and Catie lifted her hands defensively.

"Calm down, now. See it for yourself," she laughed. "I'll be here."

The base of my neck tingled. "You're going to let me go without you?"

"What are you going to do? Run away?"

I wasn't sure if she was joking, or if she knew Vincent had a tracking chip in my arm. But either way, I wasn't going to miss the opportunity.

On the trail, the dogs joined me, but when I got to the studio, the dogs stopped in the hallway, as if they were obeying a rule not to go inside. It was dark in there, so I turned on the light: a single lamp in the corner, dimmed by a shade. Every inch of the wall and ceiling was covered in canvases and thick pieces of paper with black, gray, and blue images of a woman, with round eyes and plush lips. A slim neck. A pointed chin. A dangling arm holding a cheek. Eyelids that were heavy with dread, gazing out a window. On her knees with her wrists behind my back, her head bowed. There was even a black-and-white photograph of the same woman sitting on her bed, staring at the door to her room. I didn't remember that night. Was I upset at something my mother had said?

All of those paintings, all of those pictures, were of me.

There was pain and emotion in every painting, and while it looked like they were mine, I knew they were Vincent's feelings, his emotions bubbling to the surface, being channeled through his art of me. It was like seeing behind the curtain for the first time, understanding how much he truly thought about me. Like an obsession. Like a curse.

My mother had a fixation with me like that. But this was different. This was lust. This was greed. This was—

Like he cared.

My eyes fluttered to the ground. Did Vincent actually care about me? My eyes locked on a piece of paper face-down on the floor. I picked it up: two eyes hid behind a divided window, peering out, black smoke swirling from inside, as if the darkness had always been there, lurking.

My eyes.

A fiery sensation crawled in my belly, a tenderness that happened frequently now. Vincent was my captor. He had burned my parents' home. He might have killed my best friend.

But none of that sat right with me. Vincent didn't think of himself as an abductor, but as a savior. Whether or not I disagreed, didn't matter. Because when I was here, I had more freedom than I had ever had. I had felt things I didn't know existed. I wasn't chained down to an empty dream. I could have felt this all along. The joys and terrors, all the wonders of life. But I only found that once I met him.

And maybe there was comfort in that, even if it came with pain. Even if you could never untangle love from how it ruined you. Maybe someone like me could find that with someone like Vincent.

I shook away the thoughts. Vincent wasn't in love with me. Obsessed, maybe. Fixated. Infatuated? Yes. But whatever this was, it wasn't love. Because love didn't steal you from your bedroom and light your house on fire. Love was where you protected someone from the world outside, from their own worst demons, where you made sure that their pain never reached the surface.

But what was pain, really? Especially when it called to me, deep down. When I liked it. Wasn't the only true opposite of love, apathy, anyway? Numbness. And what if burning someone's house meant you were protecting them, somehow?

None of it made sense.

I pressed the painting of my eyes in the divided window against my chest, then I slid it underneath the door to the basement, keeping it for later. I walked back to the funeral home. My mind buzzed with these thoughts all day, and when Vincent finally came back, it seemed like so much had changed since I had seen him last. But nothing had happened. This part of Vincent had always been there.

When he escorted me back to the basement, I kicked his painting to the side so he wouldn't see it, then I snapped around to face him before he closed the doors.

"Tell me about yourself," I said

"Why?" he asked.

"I'm curious!" I squealed. My entire body vibrated with adrenaline, unable to choose between fear and confusion and desire. I was desperate for answers, to do the right thing, because I knew that's what I was supposed to do. Be the good girl. Help the police. Go home to my mother. Take care of her, like she had taken care of me.

I forced the words out of my mouth: "Come on. We ought to know each other if we'll be together for a while." I laughed, but Vincent just stared at me. I cleared my throat, then pressed on: "What's your favorite color?"

He glared at me.

"Your favorite food?" He grunted. "Favorite part of the day?" He scowled at me. "Tell me everything." I tilted my head, waiting for an answer, but his eyes were hard. "No? Then tell me anything. Anything at all."

"I hate surveys."

I raised my brows. "That doesn't count. And this isn't a survey or a quiz." He was silent. I breathed through my nose. "You must really hate talking about yourself." He took another step toward the door. I grabbed his arm. "What if I asked about your art?"

"Don't push your luck, flower."

I blushed at that nickname, my eyes fluttering down to his

chest, imagining his weight crushing against me. I started again, filled with a renewed sense of purpose. This was my investigation, wasn't it? Get to know him. Prove one way, or another, that he is or isn't guilty.

"My favorite color is green," I said.

"Let me guess—because of plants."

"Am I that cliché?"

A small smirk crossed his lips. *Finally.* I didn't even mind that he was making fun of me.

"My favorite food is yogurt," I said.

The smirk widened into a grin. "So you throw it on the floor."

"I mean, I cleaned it up." I smiled, then lifted my shoulders and knocked into him playfully. "My favorite time of the day used to be the morning, but it's not anymore." He waited for an explanation, but how could I tell him that once the morning came, he would be off to work and I would be back in the basement, without him? I didn't know if it was about the freedom that he gave me, or if I preferred night because it meant him. A man who may have killed his brother. Who may have killed my best friend. A man who had shown me more about myself than I had ever known.

"Mornings suck," he said, the smile gone from his face. Like he knew what I meant. Like he felt the same way too.

Chapter 18

Vincent

The next day, Kora knocked on the basement door earlier than usual. My pulse quickened. I took a deep breath, then opened the door and glared down my nose at her. Wearing a light sweater that hung over her shoulders, tight leggings, and fluffy socks over her feet, she was completely covered, and all I wanted to do was undress her. To kiss every inch of her body.

I clenched my jaw tight.

"Yes?" I asked, my tone harsh.

"Can I stay up here for a while?"

I balled my fists, then relaxed my fingers and stepped to the side. It was Saturday, and for once, I wasn't needed. Kora went around me, her footsteps like the taps of a butterfly's legs on a petal. The sunlight came in through the glass window on the front door.

"It's daytime," she said, grinning. "I was right."

"Congratulations. You can tell time."

She pressed a finger to her forehead. "By instinct." She rubbed her arm where the chip was, then wandered through the house. I went back to the studio and opened my phone, turning to the tracking app, the red light flickering around the blueprint. I angled my chair and easel so that she couldn't see my latest piece.

On the canvas, Kora was wrapped in plastic, her body squished, her mouth and pussy dripping with come.

Kora knocked on the door. "Vincent?"

I blocked the view of the canvas. "What?"

"Did you murder the Echo victims?"

I moved my head back slightly, surprised at her words. It was bold of her. Did I seem like someone who would stab a body and let a drug take the blame?

"If I murdered someone, you would know," I said.

She studied me, searching my eyes. "I thought so."

"What made you ask that?"

She dragged her fingertips across the doorframe. "I don't know. I figured I should ask." She looked up. "Can I come in?"

"Let's go outside."

I put a hand in front of me, and she stepped ahead, going to the front door to follow me to Quiet Meadows like before. But this time, I led her to the backyard. A pomegranate tree shimmered in the distance, and the fir trees stretched up in front of it. A firepit was empty to the side of the yard, and a deep freezer hummed against the house. It was a small patch of grass, pressed against the base of the mountain. Kora ripped off her socks, wiggling her toes in the spiky green blades. Sulfur from the fissures mixed with the woody plants, but Kora sucked in a long breath of fresh air as if it was all the same: rotten eggs, wind, or forest. She closed her eyes as she tilted her head toward the sunlight, basking in its glow, reminding me of the first time we met, on the viewpoint. My heart thumped hard in my chest, and the dogs circled around her, barking, sharing in that same bliss. Everything seemed like it could stretch on for a millennium right then. With my eyes on her, I forgot to breathe.

She turned and smiled at me. My heart stopped.

What was wrong with me?

"It's sunlight," I barked, louder than I had expected. "Not a fucking miracle," I muttered.

"I haven't seen or felt sunlight in who knows how long," she said. She motioned at the sun. "You should try it." I crossed my arms, but she came forward and pulled my hand. "It won't hurt you." I groaned, but let her yank me forward. "Isn't it beautiful?" The light fell on my skin and my entire body radiated with fire, but my eyes were on her, twirling in the sunshine.

"Yes," I said.

Her gaze found mine, and still, that smile painted her lips. A question formed on her face, pinching her thick eyebrows together.

"What is it?" she asked.

There was so much I wanted to tell her. To show her the world. Parts that she could never know. So much that she had shown *me*, proving that there was a lot that I didn't understand either.

But I couldn't.

I went past her and sat down on the wooden bench. She plopped down beside me, sighing with satisfaction. Bernie brought over a ball, and Ulysses whined at us, while Sarah barked instructions to them. Kora threw the ball, then the three of them rolled in the grass.

"There are two things you should know about me," I said abruptly. Kora faced me, her lips pressed together, waiting. "My parents died when I was young. And my brother died a few years ago." Her shoulders lifted in solace but I shook my head. "They say there are five stages of grief, but that's wrong. There's more than that. When you lose someone, your whole mind breaks loose. You show your worst, parts of yourself that you didn't know existed. Like a part of you is missing. A gaping hole where you'd rather feel *anything* there, than nothing at all."

She stared at me, her green eyes piercing and clear.

"I had no idea," she said.

I sighed. "I'm trying to say that I know what it feels like. With Nyla."

"How did your brother die?" She flushed at those words, then looked away. "Wow. Sorry. That was insensitive of me."

"It's not a big deal. It's been years now."

"What happened to him, then?"

I could have told her what the coroner's report said and left it at that. *Suicide.* But it wasn't that simple, and I had no compulsion to explain myself.

"Honestly, I'm not sure."

"Do you have anyone else?"

I forced a laugh; she could figure out the answer on her own. "Death of a loved one can make you do crazy things," I said, staring into her eyes. I wasn't sure what I was talking about anymore. Sometimes, I wasn't even sure that *I* understood what love was, but I knew that the thought of killing Kora did something to me now. Made me feel insane. Unhinged. Not myself.

She squinted, tilting her body toward me. "And you said there are two things?"

I rubbed my forehead, piecing together the words. "Destruction. Transformation. Reaction. Whatever you want to call it: ruining things makes my blood pump."

Her lips opened, her voice quiet: "Would you ever kill someone?"

I couldn't help but smile. She was so innocent sometimes.

"Yes."

She swallowed, her eyes focused on my lips. Before I could do anything stupid, like fucking kiss her, I excused myself, going back inside. I splashed water on my face, cursing myself for saying all of that unnecessary crap. When I returned, the bench was empty. I glanced down the hallway; the door to the studio was open.

Inside, Kora was in the middle of the room, looking around. My gut twisted and my shoulders tensed, but she gazed at me with that same courage that always simmered below the surface. The part of her she kept hidden like she had been taught to.

Her voice was breathless: "How long have you been painting me?"

Years.

"A long time," I said.

Her eyes met mine. "Why me?"

Could I tell her I had been hypnotized by her mix of innocence and darkness since the first time I saw her? That she drove me insane, thinking of the ways I wanted to torture her, to use her, to make her into my art, to literally paint her body on my walls?

That she was an obsession that had led me down a path of mistakes and ruin and lack of thought, and now I was here, seeing the woman who was underneath all of that? The woman who relished in life, even when she was swallowed underneath all of those walls and barriers. Even when she was locked in a cage, by me.

"You fascinate me," I said in a low voice. "Nyla was your first experience with real pain. I've never met someone so protected."

And there was a chance that Kora would never have that level of pain again. I didn't know whether I wanted to force her to experience more of that, or to save her from it. She gave me a sad smile, then her chin fell to the floor.

"I'm not the kind of person who can deal with stuff like that. Regularly, I mean." She forced a laugh. "Feeling. Pain. Anything hard like that."

With the back of my finger, I lifted her chin, making her eyes meet mine.

"You are stronger than you know, Kora Nova," I said. "Think of everything you've been through. Your mother sheltered you your entire life. And then your best friend died. Your house burned down. You were ripped from your home. You had no experience with anything difficult, and now you're here." I narrowed my eyes. "I beat you, nearly tore the skin off of your nipples, suffocated you even, and you're still here, still alive. Still thriving."

She blushed, and I wanted to pull her into my arms and hold her tight, to never let her go.

But I did nothing.

"You really think that?" she whispered.

"Stop questioning it." I grabbed her arms. "Feel it here." I pointed to her chest. "You, Kora. You've endured so much."

That flush spread across her face which she tried hard to suppress, but she couldn't help it. She smiled. And that smile filled me. I enjoyed seeing her like this, figuring out what else I hadn't expected of her. What else she could teach me. What we could learn about each other.

I turned away, shaking my head. None of that mattered. I wasn't supposed to feel anything for her.

But perhaps this was part of the plan. Building her up so I could watch her fall.

"You know what?" she asked, grabbing my hand. "I've got an idea." She pulled me into the kitchen. "Hear me out." She held my hands and the electricity of her touch shot to my shoulders, tensing in my chest. "You've got a fridge full of food, right? One of us will be blindfolded, and the other will feed the person. So it's not about the way it looks, but about the way it feels."

I huffed out a breath. "Sensory play."

"I call it being in the moment," she grinned. "It's worth a try."

Before I could convince myself to lock her in the basement for the last time, I went to my bedroom and found a sash that would work as a blindfold.

"Me or you?" she asked.

"Is that a real question?"

She shrugged, then sat down and lifted her hair, the elegant curve of her neck exposed. I tied the sash over her eyes, my fingers touching her skin, and a layer of goosebumps erupted all over her shoulders. *Damn it.* I wanted to bite her neck.

Instead, I went through the fridge and found a few items, stacking them up on the table in front of us. I lifted a cold piece of pizza to her mouth.

"Hmm," she hummed to herself, chewing the slice. "Flatbread. With mozzarella and arugula?"

"Pizza."

"*Cold* pizza." She sniffled. "My mother always made me heat it up."

I stiffened, then forced myself to relax. Shea was far away. It was just us right then. Even the dogs were out in the backyard, roaming around. I opened a plastic container full of fleshy red seeds.

"Stick out your tongue," I said.

And like a timid creature, she stuck it out. I placed a seed in her mouth, my mouth salivating at the sight of the decadent red on her plush tongue.

"Pomegranate," she hummed. "Hmm. It's not as bad as before. I never thought I'd acquire a taste for it." I chuckled and a smile spread across her face. "I found some in the basement when I first got here."

"I was hoping you would," I said.

Next, I dipped the spoon into a container, taking out some plain yogurt. When she licked it off, she moaned in pleasure, and my cock twitched against my thigh. I grit my teeth. What was with this woman? It was yogurt. Nothing special.

"That's so good," she said. "What brand?"

"No brand."

"What do you mean?"

"I made it myself."

"Now you're messing with me."

I stared at those lips, then dipped my finger in the yogurt and dragged it across her bottom lip, entranced as her tongue licked the white substance up. I couldn't think straight. I wanted to do something for her. A gift that would be completely hers. Something that would make her more at home here. Even if it wasn't much—even if it would never be enough, the only thing I could, right then, was try.

"You seriously make your own yogurt?" Her voice was silk against my ears.

"Why wouldn't I?"

She shrank down, and that made my heart pound. "Because, well—"

I pressed my mouth to hers, grabbing her face in my hands, squeezing her tight. At first, her body tensed, then she relaxed, melting into my touch. My tongue searched for hers, vying for her attention, and finally, she pressed her tongue against mine. It was a devastating kiss, driven by impulse and need for what I knew would never be mine. Kora was the light of this world, and I was trapped in the darkness, where dim flames lit the night and left ash on our skin. And that's where I would always stay.

But for that small moment, with her lips against mine, she sucked in my shadows, and I breathed out her glow.

Chapter 19

Kora

His lips were brutal, claiming me, making me shake. His fingers twisted into my hair, embracing me, and the sash fell down from my eyes, and I studied him. The laugh lines around his face. His weathered skin. The scars reaching up around his neck. The stubble on his chin and cheeks. His black eyes. Vincent was kissing me like he worshipped me, like he wanted to possess me to my very core.

When he broke the kiss, his gaze was glossy, seeing deeper than he meant to. He blinked, and I shied away, wrapping my arms around myself.

"I have something I need to do," he said, breathless. He straightened, then held out a hand.

I took his grip, but as soon as we stood, I let go of it. We were heading back to the basement, and I hated that he was leaving me again. Outside of the door, he grabbed my shoulders, bringing me closer to him, and he kissed my forehead, the bristles on his chin and upper lip rubbing against my skin.

"I'll be back soon," he said.

"Promise?" I asked. He nodded, then locked the door behind me.

Once I went to the bottom floor, my heart sank. I missed my mother. I missed my father. I missed Poppies & Wheat. And while

I would never see Nyla again, I knew I wanted to see my parents. One day.

And I knew that there was an unexplainable urge inside of me to stay here, with Vincent.

Hours passed. I tried sleeping, but I was restless, so I roamed that bottom floor endlessly. When Vincent finally entered the room, his face was cast in that same hopeful stare as before, but he looked as if he had showered and groomed his facial hair, the scent of pine and wood clinging to his skin.

He held out a hand, then smiled. It was the first time I had ever seen him smile when he wasn't mocking me. I blushed, the heat rippling through my body, then let him lead me upstairs, down the hallway, to one of the rooms that I had never been inside of before. He put the key in the doorknob, unlocking it, then turned to me.

"I'm going to cover your eyes," he said. "You'll open the door when you're ready."

Ready for what? "Okay," I said.

"You trust me?"

His eyes were open and yearning, as if his entire world was me. What could I say? He had done so many horrible things to me, and yet I had this feeling that I knew who he truly was.

I nodded. That smile burst across his face again, and I swear I could have melted right there. His warm hands covered my eyes and I sucked in a deep breath, waiting.

"It's not much," he said.

"What is it?"

I turned the knob and opened the door. We stepped forward together, and once we were inside, he let go.

A giant window was open, revealing a blue-lit mountainside. Every surface was covered in green leaves and flowers, tiny lights strung throughout the room. The starred leaves of ivy stretched across the walls. The droplet petals of hydrangeas, blue blurring into white. Roses brighter than what was natural. Daisies that shivered in the breeze. The graceful clusters of lavender. The threaded edges of a lily, fraying at the ends. And though the window let in the cool air, every plant in the room was synthetic.

Here, in this room Vincent had made for me, nothing would ever die.

A daffodil was in the middle of the room, just like the one I had found in the field when I had been searching for answers, and found Vincent instead.

They symbolize rebirth and spring, he had said.

And I felt like I was being born again. I didn't feel like myself anymore, but someone new. More than I had once been.

"Do you like it?" he asked.

I sank down to my knees and I laid down in the blanket of leaves, vines, and blossoms. He stood straighter, looking down at me.

"It's beautiful," I whispered. When he didn't move, I asked in a quieter voice, "Could you lay with me? Please?"

He didn't move. A tingling sensation swept across my neck and cheeks, and I tried hard to force down the embarrassment, the rejection, but I told myself that this was real. Even if he said 'no,' whatever happened—*this*—everything he had made for me in here, was real. And it was mine.

Finally, he kneeled down, then laid beside me, our arms and legs touching. The ceiling was covered in leafy green foliage, the tiny star lights poking between the vines, the wires shining in the empty spaces between the artificial life. It was strange, and beautiful, like Vincent had wanted to steal the beauty from the world and wrap it up into a place where it would always be mine, forever.

"No one has ever done anything like this for me before," I said.

I held my breath, expecting him to say that I simply needed to experience more of the world, but he said nothing. He propped himself, leaning on his arm, then he cupped my head, holding me like he wanted to keep me safe.

"Kora," he said.

I opened my eyes, my stomach clenching with knots. A warm fire burned in my belly. I was melting with need.

"Vincent," I whispered.

He kissed me, slow and passionate, searching deeply within me this time, waiting to see where I would lead him. And when I kissed back, letting my lips and tongue dance with his, he pressed into me, leaning on top of my body. His cock was hard, pressing into my legs, and I moved my hips forward, trying to tell him what I was too nervous to say. *Thank you, for everything. For this.*

I lifted my back, letting him pull the shirt over my head, unsnapping the bra, sliding it off of my arms. I reached for his shirt but he took my wrists, gently pressing them down as he kissed my neck, my chest, traveling to my navel, then farther down between my legs. He stared down at me, then he slid off my pants, leaving my underwear on. His eyes were heavy with lust, and he breathed onto my panties, his hot breath tickling my skin, making me shiver. Then he pulled the fabric to the side and licked me there until I twitched against him. He slid my underwear off of my hips and began unbuttoning his shirt. When that proved to take too long, he ripped off the rest of the buttons, yanking his jeans and boxers down over his legs. Muscular and thick, covered in masculine hair like a forest, the scars on his chest and arms and back, creeping up his neck, marks that I had never seen in full: thick white lines danced around his body like thorns. So many thorns.

He kneeled before me, his gaze full of desire.

"I've never met anyone like you before," he said. And though I knew he was a grown man, someone who had experienced far more than I ever had, I held this belief that everything he was saying was real.

He held my hips and legs, moving me until I was level with his cock. I held my breath. He pressed in and I tensed up, the pain seizing me, tightening every muscle. My face scrunched, and once it dissipated, I waited for him, but he didn't move. He stared into my eyes, reading me.

"Take me," I whispered. But he was still. Waiting for me. "I'm yours."

With those words, he plunged in, the pain rushing to my head, but he held me there, waiting for my muscles to relax. His face was expressionless as a statue, and yet I knew that there was nothing icy about him. Vincent was consumed by death, but this?

Surrounded by fake plants, by what he *could* control, by what he could make for me—this was life. This was the joy and the pain of living, of sacrificing his own needs to be safe. Of risking himself for what he truly wanted.

I relaxed my jaw, my eyes locked with Vincent's, and I nodded. He moved my legs so that my feet rested on his shoulders, and he moved me back and forth over his length. He licked his thumb, rubbing it over my clit. My face heated and my body clenched but Vincent never blinked. He was too focused on me, too consumed, as if he didn't want to miss a single breath. My breathing quickened, and when his fingertips brushed my legs, light-headedness fluttered through me, making me dizzy, like the world was spinning even though we were both grounded, both held down inside of that room. My room. My hands and legs ached to bring him closer, so I wrapped around him until he was completely pressed against me. His breathing was ragged, and his skin rubbed against my clit, making me sink under a building heat. And when that frenzy of pleasure became too much, Vincent didn't stop. He stared into my eyes, then he kissed me hard, with fever, with more passion than I had ever felt. My body thrummed and tensed; his cock pulsing into me, and we battled forth until I finally surrendered to him like I did every single time. As those waves crashed through me, I watched pleasure decimate him too. That's when it connected: this was a temple for me, Vincent's queen, his flower that could give him life when everything else was dead and gone. My breathing slowed as those words hung in my brain: this was a shrine to his last hope.

And that didn't feel wrong anymore.

Chapter 20

Vincent

Before the sun rose, I scooped Kora into my arms and brought her into the basement. Exhausted from the night, she barely stirred when I laid her on the couch. I tucked her inside of a blanket, then kissed her forehead.

Everything should have been perfect. But as I left the basement, the truth nagged me: all of this was still a cage, a way to keep Kora happy inside. I truly believed that I was helping her escape from a numbness that was holding her captive.

But that didn't mean that this was any better.

Once I entered Quiet Meadows, Catie handed me a stack of papers I had forgotten the previous week. Just then, the door to the front of the funeral home opened, and the clack of boots ricocheted down the hallway.

"The wake doesn't begin until this afternoon," I said.

"It's too early, even for the family," Catie said, raising her brow.

"Always a pleasure to see you, Miss Catie," Officer Andrew's voice called down the hallway. I clenched my jaw. Andrew needed to get a life. "Is Erickson in, by chance?"

I went past Catie and stood in front of Andrew. "How can I help you, Officer?" I asked. "I believe Regina James is too old to be an Echo victim."

"You're right. But she's not why I'm here." He tipped his imaginary hat, then stuck his thumbs in his belt loops, his gun visible to his side. "I'm here regarding Miss Kora Nova. Has she been around these parts lately?"

Blood thrummed in my veins. Catie flinched beside me, the words itching to come out of her. I held onto the hope that she had enough loyalty to me to withhold the answer.

"I hear she ran away from home," I said plainly.

"Doesn't appear so. Her mother says she was kidnapped."

"You'd have to be a child to be kidnapped," I corrected. "Kora is an adult." Whether or not her parents believed that.

"You two are on a first-name basis, then?" Andrew forced a smile. "You are correct, though, Erickson. Always a clever man. *Abducted*, then." Andrew turned his attention behind me. "What about you, Miss Catie? Have you seen or heard of Miss Kora in these parts?"

"Kora?" she asked, her voice rattled. "Who's that?"

Andrew pulled out a picture from his pocket. In the photograph, his arm was around Kora, her shoulders shrinking underneath him. That bastard knew she was uncomfortable in that picture, the fucking prick. My jaw ticked.

"You might recognize her. Her mother, Miss Shea, has been calling every news station to find her daughter. Here's the interesting part, though: one of the last places she was seen, was here. At your fine establishment." He tilted his chin at me.

"Was she attending one of the Echo victim's funerals?" Catie asked.

"Yes, ma'am. Nyla Nerissa, her best friend." He crossed his arms. "I knew Miss Kora well. And I am sure you might have heard, but they found Echo in the Nova house. Seems that Miss Kora could have been murdered. Or—" Andrew faced me, "—someone thought it would be a fine idea to steal the girl away from her bed while she slept."

"Or, she found an opportunity to run away," I said. "If I'm remembering correctly, you and her father were the only men she was ever allowed to speak to." I shook my head. "It's a shame that she didn't tell you anything before she left."

He narrowed his eyes at me. "Precisely, Erickson. And that's why I have always had the urge to protect someone as—" he paused, thinking of the word, "—as *delicate* as Miss Kora."

She might have been delicate, but she was more powerful than he could imagine.

"You seem to be awfully interested in Kora," I said.

"It is my job. And my duty as an officer. Cut the bullshit, Erickson." He sneered. "I know you've got her."

I smiled at him. This was fun. "I have no idea of what you're talking about."

"Then you don't mind if I look around?"

I spread my hand out before him. "Look away, Officer." I had nothing to hide.

He strolled through the funeral home, whistling. The break room. The crematory. He went into Catie's office, then mine. Next, he knocked on Lee's locked door.

"Is this where you keep her?"

I unlocked Lee's office, and he glanced inside, satisfied. Finally, he checked the viewing room.

He had found nothing. His jaw clenched tighter, and he stared at me.

"I know more than you think, Erickson," he said. "And I suggest, if you want what's best for you, then you let Kora go and stop us from adding another charge to the list we're accumulating for you. Think of it this way." He smiled. "A warning. Friend to a friend."

I didn't bat an eye. "Warnings only matter when concern is needed."

"And you should be concerned. We're coming for you."

Andrew tilted his imaginary hat to Catie, then smiled with his pearly whites. "Have a good day, Miss Catie. Say hello to Miss Kora for me."

As soon as he stepped into the sunlight, Catie turned to me.

"What did he mean, *another charge?* What's going on?"

I pinched my mouth shut. "How should I know? He's full of shit, like the rest of them."

"I need to tell you something, Vincent."

I ignored her, heading back to the crematory room. Inside of the doorway, her posture stiffened, and I rubbed my forehead. "What is it now?"

"I went by Poppies & Wheat."

I stilled. "What?"

"I wanted to check on Shea. The flower orders haven't been fulfilled—we've been calling the grocery store instead, and while most of the families are fine with it, some are annoyed, and I figured I should check on her. She's a mess." Her shoulders tensed, and she swallowed hard. "I don't know what kind of mother she was in the past, but she won't even leave her bedroom. She barely eats. The only time she leaves is when there is a possibility that her daughter might be out there." Her hand fluttered to her ears. "Isn't there a way you can help Kora, and make sure her mother isn't torn apart like that?"

I tipped my head back, my chest expanded. "The Novas aren't so perfect after all."

She scowled. "You're acting like that makes you happy," she snapped.

I shrugged. "If she wasn't such a controlling mother, maybe Kora wouldn't have left."

The loosely curled mohawk on top of Catie's head shimmering in the light. "I don't know what's going on with you lately," she crossed her arms. "This fascination you have with Kora. Why she never leaves. Why you feel the need to keep her here. But I do know that Shea needs my help, and I heard someone screaming the night of Nyla's funeral."

I looked down at my watch, dismissive. "You were hearing things. Seeing things. It was dark."

"You know that's not true."

I smiled, finally looking back up at her. "Tell me what you think you know, then."

She narrowed her eyes. *You are an asshole*, she seemed to say. "I would never rat you out," she said quietly, "But I will help Shea."

She turned toward the door, and I shook my head. "Remember that if I get convicted, this place will go under. You won't have a job to come back to."

"I'm aware. But this job has always been about helping people who are suffering. And Shea? She's *not* okay," she said. I smiled. Good. That was what was *supposed* to happen. "I'm going to finish the wake, and when I'm done, I'm going to help Shea search for her daughter. Her *only* daughter."

"Do what you want." I wasn't going to stop her.

She stormed out of the door.

Once the day was finished, I waited an extra three hours before I went back to the house. I don't know why. A dull pain inside of me lingered, warning me that whatever it was, I wasn't going to like it. Before Kora had the chance to knock, I let myself into the basement, but I sat in the loft, trying to gather myself. What did I want to accomplish with her now? She was supposed to be nothing. A plaything. An innocent woman I could break apart. Her life, *her happiness*, was never supposed to mean a thing to me.

"Vincent?" Kora said, stepping onto the loft. I slid over on the couch so that she could join me. "I thought you were up here."

Her body was warm beside me, but I was cold. Kora was my spark, the fire I needed to help me see through the darkness. The only way I could make this all go away, was to kill her, like I had always planned. And I had to do it right now. I had a gun in my holster, a knife in my pocket, a device that would release toxins at the push of a button. And yet now, *now* that I had seen how brightly her flame could burn, I had no desire to extinguish it.

And that enraged me.

"Why did you come here?" I asked. Anger rang through my tone, but I didn't care. I wanted her to be scared. Like she should have always been.

"What?"

"Why did you come here?"

"I heard the door, and you didn't come down." Her eyes flicked to the ground and she rubbed her hands down her pants. "So I came up."

It was a simple response, like she could never hate me for anything, and yet we both knew the reality. I *had* broken her, transformed her until she was nothing like her old self, and now we were here, dancing around what we knew would haunt us for the rest of our lives.

"Remember when I asked what you wanted out of life?" I asked, softening my voice. I hated myself for it, but I couldn't stop it. "Have you thought about that?"

She cleared her throat, giving a high-pitched laugh. I didn't relax my gaze. I wanted her to feel it, to know my truth.

"I've always wanted to run my own greenhouse," she finally said. She waited for my reaction, but I gave none. "That way, I can take care of the kinds of plants I love all year long. I would never have to worry about seasons or anything like that. I could be on my own and still work with my mother. Partner with her. Something like that."

A greenhouse would give her autonomy, a place to focus her passions, but were plants her passion because she had never seen the world? Never given anything else a chance?

"Don't you want freedom?" I asked. "Freedom to do what you want. To explore. To try everything. Without your mother?"

Without me?

"It'd be nice to do some things by myself," she shrugged with a smile, "but I miss her."

I wanted to rip off her head and shake her until she made sense. "There is more to life than pleasing your mother," I snarled. "She never let you do anything."

"She was only trying to protect me. Like you are."

My heart stilled. Silence overcame us. The difference between Shea and I was that I had always planned to get rid of Kora. I was never supposed to protect her.

But I had.

The best option was to burn Kora. Bury the ashes. Cover her up with another person's body, so that there was no way they could trace her back to me. And there weren't any more reasons to keep her alive. I had already destroyed her false sense of security, of safety, of love. I could crush her one last time, throw her into the retort, and watch her burn.

And if I needed to, I could do the same thing to Catie.

But I didn't want to kill anyone. Especially not Kora. I wanted to run away this time, to find a safe place for us to survive.

But Kora deserved more than survival. She deserved the fucking world.

Some stupid sensation in my chest made it feel like Kora was living inside of me, like she had control of me. But Kora wasn't mine, and she never would be. She was breakable. A way to watch a family fall apart. To make sure that nothing was ever pure for *anyone.* Not for me. Not for the Novas. Not for Kora.

My only hope, at this point, was that Kora would tell the authorities—including her father—the truth. That I never once hurt her. That I saved her from a life of nothing. That I showed her how to breathe again.

Until then, I had to tell her the truth. What she did with that, would be her choice.

Chapter 21

Kora

Vincent leaned back into the couch and rubbed his eyes. Something was clearly bothering him.

"Do you want to talk about it?" I asked.

He swallowed, then offered me his hand. "I want to show you something."

They were almost the same words he had used before taking me to the garden room he had created for me, but this time, the tone felt off. Like this was something he didn't actually *want* to show me.

"This isn't like before," I whispered, "Is it?"

His eyes flicked down, then returned to me. He waited, his mouth silent, but his eyes begged me to understand. To hear the words he couldn't say.

It was dark again. The new moon was haunting, almost like it was whispering secrets to us. Vincent led me to the cemetery, his steps heavy. But instead of going to the main plots that were open to the public, he led me to the back, around one of the mausoleums. Behind a row of untouched candles, there was a rectangular hole, ready for a casket. The walls of the hole were smoothed as if Vincent had come here to touch it up recently. A daffodil was engraved on the tombstone, the strokes similar to what I had seen in his studio. The inscription read: *Here Lies My Flower.*

My muscles tensed. Dizziness filled me, like the world was tilting.

"What is this?" I asked.

"It's yours," he said, as if it was as simple as a lost sweater.

Did my mother think that I was dead? But that couldn't be it —my mother would never give up on me. My thoughts wandered to Vincent. Had he known that I would need a plot? Unless—

No. I refused to let that thought surface.

"Don't worry," he said, reading my mind. "Your mother is determined to find you."

But she still hadn't found me. Because Vincent was even more determined to keep me here, than Shea was to find me.

"Then what's this about?" I asked, gesturing at the tombstone. "It's frightening to see a grave that's clearly mine."

He rubbed the back of his neck. "It doesn't say your name."

My cheeks flushed red and I grit my teeth. "Come on, Vincent," I said. "I may be inexperienced. But I'm not stupid. How many people call someone their 'flower'?" A wave of heat surged through me at those words. I couldn't deny it anymore. *He* was the only one who called me that. *He* was the only one who had ever given me that nickname before.

He had made the grave for me.

I sank down to my knees, running my fingers over the headstone. Even with the rough texture under my fingers, none of it felt real.

"Why?" I whispered.

He sat down on the other side of the hole, putting the distance between us, like he knew I needed that protective barrier.

"Three years ago now, my brother died, leaving me alone. My parents. My brother. Even my uncle was gone. And I hated myself for out-living them. Hated that for some fucked up reason, *I* had survived. The kid who wanted to destroy everything. The man who could only connect with someone after they were dead."

A cold sweat broke out all over me. "What had happened?"

"Then on Halloween," he continued, "I saw this family. They were perfect. Happy. Enjoying their life. And they had this innocent daughter. Despite being prominent members of the community, I had never seen the daughter before. They were actually able to protect her from everything. It seemed like nothing could touch them, and I didn't understand it. Why could they have everything, when I was left with nothing? Why did I have to suffer, while they thrived?"

My heart plummeted, full of dread.

"And I wanted to watch them fall apart."

Chills ran over my arms, an ache tingling in my chest. His eyes darkened, and for once, I couldn't see any starlight inside of them. They were completely empty.

"Then I met the daughter. She was beautiful, like a rose cut fresh from the stem." He jerked his angular jaw to the side, facing forward. "And I knew what she could be, what she was capable of, if someone let her. And some fucked up part of her pulled her to me too, though neither of us could explain it." He turned to me again, his face cold and haunting. "Like everything in my life, since the moment I was born, had led me to her."

The hairs on my arms and legs stood on end. The back of my neck burned with heat. I remembered that night so clearly. Standing on the viewpoint, gazing up at his dirt-covered face.

"I thought to myself that ripping her from her cage would save her life. Her mother hadn't let her experience anything, so why couldn't I give her release from her numb existence? In the only way that I knew how."

A twisted, sick sensation swirled inside of me. "But what does that mean?" I trembled.

His hands curled into fists. "I wanted to break you down so that you would never resemble what your parents had wanted so badly to protect. I wanted to use your body to make art that I knew, a good woman like your mother, would never approve of. And when that was all done, I wanted to bury you in this hole."

Everything inside of me shifted. A ringing blared in my ears, and the world went blurry like I was drifting, floating on the wind, like none of this was real.

He leaned over the hole, catching me from falling.

"Kora?" he asked.

The ringing stopped. I stared at him.

Was he telling the truth?

"That was three years ago," I said. "And you followed me. Stalked me for years. Waiting until the right moment."

His stare lacked warmth. "I had made a promise to myself."

I held my chin high. "You've always wanted to hurt me."

"Pain comes in different forms," he said, his voice measured like it always was. "If you only experience the absence of it, of all feelings, then how could you know I wanted to hurt you? You're not the little girl your parents think you are."

"Then what am I?" He searched me, but I knew he would never find that answer because he didn't see me as anything more than a girl too. A toy he could break. "We did nothing to you," I whimpered. "It's like you're out for revenge for something that never had anything to do with you."

He lowered his eyes, his jaw set. "It was never about revenge."

"No," I shook my head, "just your own messed up version of justice."

Vincent didn't move. I tried to understand, to make sense of it all. But I couldn't. Had he been thinking about killing me this entire time?

Why had I let myself believe I was safe with him?

"Did you kill your brother?" I asked. His forehead scrunched and his eyes hardened. "Answer me, Vincent. Did you kill your brother?"

"You don't know what you're talking about," he muttered, peering down at me. I had no idea what to say. He wanted to destroy our family, simply because all of *his* family had died?

A man like Vincent is wrong in the head, Andrew had said. Now, it seemed so true. Maybe there was something seriously wrong with him.

As we went back through the graves to the main part of the cemetery, we passed some empty rectangular holes, like the one that had been dug for me. Lined up. Waiting to be filled.

"What's this?" I asked.

"The Echo deaths," he said. "They come at a steady pace, so I figured I'd plan ahead. Be ready for them." Was he anticipating them because he *knew* when those waves were coming?

"Have you picked up their bodies yet?" I asked.

"They're coming."

My stomach dropped, but I held it together. Because I knew I had to do something. Everything seemed to indicate that he no longer wanted to kill me, but that meant that I had to work *now*. He could change his mind at any minute, and I had to help. Because if he had killed Nyla, then I—

But he hadn't killed Nyla. He had just wanted to kill *me*.

We continued walking and it all passed so quickly. Like we were watching ourselves in a dream. Then, inside of the house, he turned to me.

"You can stay up here for a while," he said. "But I need to clear my head. Do some art." He nodded toward his studio. "You inspire me."

"Maybe I'll go to the basement," I said. It seemed safer there when I would at least be able to hear that he was coming. His brows furrowed, but he said nothing. As we went down the hallway and he headed to the studio, I followed him. On the pencil bank of the easel, sat a bright green pill broken in half, like a burst of life in the room's darkness. Three wavy lines on top. Was that Echo?

"On second thought," I asked, not sure what the hell I was doing, "Can we go to the funeral home? I think I forgot something there. In Catie's office."

He led me in complete silence to the funeral home. Our footsteps vibrated in the empty building. Right outside of her office, I turned to him and held my breath. "Can you get me a snack from the break room?" I asked. "I'm starving."

He cocked his head to the side, his lips pursed together. "Okay," he said.

Once he was in the hallway, I immediately dialed Andrew, my heart pounding so hard that it thumped in my ears.

"Officer Andrew," he said.

"Andrew," I said.

"Miss Kora? Have you found anything yet?"

I didn't think Vincent could be the Echo Killer. *But what if he was?* That had to be why he had that unexplained pill in his studio.

The truth was that he had never hurt me. Not like that. And even if he had, he had done it in a way that had made the pain *mine.*

But was that another lie he was feeding me?

I honestly didn't know where he was during the day, or the nights when he left me in the basement.

Who was Vincent, really?

"Miss Kora? Are you there?" Andrew asked. "Is Vincent the Echo Killer?"

I could say the one truth that I knew.

"I don't know who burned the house," I whispered, "but Vincent was there. He saved me from the fire. But he didn't abduct me, Andrew. You've got to believe me on this." My head throbbed, and I swear the seconds ticked by slower, the air leaking out of my lungs. "Please."

Silence lingered between us, the chirps of the police department's bullpen trickling through the line. The microwave beeped in the break room. I was out of time.

"Give me something I want to hear," he said, his voice cold.

My fingers raced, tapping against the phone. "There are extra graves. Like he knows they're coming." I looked around frantically, trying to think. "And I found a green pill in his studio. Half a pill."

"A green pill, huh?"

"Yes!"

"Can you get to the funeral home tomorrow, during the day? I can make a surprise visit with your daddy. But we need you to be there. Use the element of surprise. All of that."

I swallowed. "I'll do my best."

"Good." His chair squeaked. "I promise, I'll help you, Miss Kora. We will ensure that Erickson pays for what he's done."

I wanted to remind him that the only thing Vincent had done was rescue me from a burning house, but footsteps thudded through the hall, so I hung up.

Those words should have comforted me, but my skin was itchy, my throat tight. Vincent appeared in the doorframe and I swallowed. I pulled at the collar of my shirt.

He lifted the microwave dinner on the plate. My stomach churned. "On second thought," I said quietly, "Could I save it for later? I'm not feeling great."

"Let's get you to bed," he said.

He put a protective arm around me, shielding me across the threshold and back to his house. Like he wanted to help me. To make sure I wasn't sick.

What had I done?

Chapter 22

Kora

I made up an excuse to be by myself; I was feeling fine, but I needed sleep. A few hours later, Vincent burst through the door. His footsteps sounded different from usual, like he could barely pick up his feet. The metal stairs rattled with his gait.

Before I could open my mouth, he said, "If anyone asked you about us, would you tell them the truth?"

I titled my head. "I always tell the truth."

"So what happened that first night?" he asked, then grabbed my shoulders, staring into my eyes. "With the fire. From *your* eyes." I opened my mouth to speak, but he kept going: "I saved you from that fire, Kora. If I hadn't taken you from that room, you would have died."

I studied Vincent's face, the bleary eyes, the hard creases around his mouth, the tension in his brow. He let go of me, then rubbed the back of his neck.

But I deserved to know the truth.

"Did you start the fire that burned down my house, Vincent?" I asked. His eyes met mine, and the flames burned inside of him. I raised my voice: "Did you?"

"It was never *your* house."

I pinched my lips shut and he glared down at me. I stared into those dark irises, seeing the vastness that ran deep within him, that he had filled for so long with his compulsive need for destruction. With his hatred.

"You burned down our house," I said. His jaw ticked. And I knew, then, that it was the truth. "But you're right. I would have died in that fire if it wasn't for you."

"No one died," he said, his tone stern. *I didn't kill your mother.* But somehow, I had this feeling that if she had died in the process, he wouldn't have cared.

He went to the stairs, then stopped and turned toward me before ascending. "I've done so much for you," he said, his voice a low growl. "They would have let you grow and die in that house. No matter how fucked up this world may seem, that isn't any way to live."

I let out a slow, even breath. "I know." But that didn't change the fact that he had ripped me from my life.

His steps pounded up the metal staircase like thunder.

"Vincent," I shouted. At the top of the stairs, he turned toward me. "Could I stay with you at the funeral home tomorrow?" I asked. "I'll stay in the office. I just—" What was my excuse? "—I just need a break from here."

He stared down at me, then slammed the door shut without a word.

My heart raced for several minutes after he left. I had to calm myself down. Everything would happen tomorrow, and for now, all I had to do was make it through the night.

So why was I restless?

In the morning, I couldn't eat the yogurt he had gotten for me. I had no appetite. Then, in Quiet Meadows, Catie opened her mouth to speak to us, but Vincent lifted a hand, and she stayed silent. He pointed to the chair next to his desk and barked out an order to me, "Stay here."

He stomped to the crematory room, and I stared at the office wall, wondering when my dad and Andrew would show up. It could be hours. My stomach churned and my palms were wet with sweat. I had to figure out a way to make sure that Vincent let me stay for as long as possible.

Then what would I do?

Technically, *yes*, Vincent deserved to go to jail. But my heart wouldn't let those words sit in my chest. He was different. He did bad things for reasons he thought were right.

I couldn't figure out if that made it okay.

I dug through his desk drawers and filing cabinet, trying to find something that would explain the truth underneath it all. If I found evidence that proved that he was as bad as Andrew said he was, then by doing this, I *was* doing the right thing. But I didn't find anything. Paperwork. A loose brush. A tube of acrylic paint.

An hour later, Catie opened the door, glancing down the hallway as she did.

"I'm going to your mother's hotel," she said quietly. "Come with me."

I had the chance. I could go *now*. But that felt wrong too.

"Get up," she said. "I can take you to your mother. Everything will be fine."

But I didn't *want* to go to my mother's. Being with her wouldn't fix anything. In fact, it might make it worse.

"Kora?" Catie asked. Finally, I looked her in the eyes. She stared at me, waiting. "Are you coming?"

I didn't say anything.

"Go through the back door," she said, "I'm parked to the side of the building. I'll wait five minutes. But after that, I have to go."

She left the door and argued with Vincent in the crematory before heading out. The clock above Vincent's desk ticked by. But I couldn't move. I couldn't make myself go back to that life yet.

So why had I called Andrew?

In the distance, an engine started. I tucked hair behind my ear, biting my bottom lip. I knew what had happened; I had panicked. I had called Andrew because it was the right thing to do. Because I had to do it. Vincent was a bad man, someone who deserved to be in jail.

But I couldn't seem to accept that.

I needed to fix this.

My stomach leaped into my throat as I burst through the door, finding him in the lobby, speaking to an older couple in a quiet voice, his head bowed. All three of them startled, turning toward me. Tears formed in my eyes.

"Vincent," I said.

"What is it?" he asked.

We locked eyes, and for that moment, I thought about his future. The funeral home. His house. His studio. His dogs. I was forcing him to leave all of that behind.

Just like he had forced me.

The door to the lobby opened with a loud smack. The impressive thuds of hard boots crashed in the lobby. I ran back into the office. Familiar voices reverberated down the hallway.

"Good to see you, Erickson," my father, Sheriff Mike, bellowed. "We got an interesting tip that the Echo Killer might have left some evidence here."

"Mind if we look?" Andrew asked.

"I've got nothing to hide," Vincent said.

"Look in the cemetery, then," my father said to Andrew.

My heart pounded in my chest as I watched from the office door. Sheriff Mike made small talk with the couple Vincent had been helping, talking about his campaign and how much he missed me. They bowed their heads solemnly.

Andrew emerged from the back door.

"Three empty graves, Sheriff. Like he was planning on burying people soon."

"I run a funeral home," Vincent said under his breath.

"How many bodies are you burying today?" Sheriff Mike asked. He smacked Vincent on the back. "Busy day, huh? But it doesn't look like many people are here for the service."

"It seems that you're anticipating the deaths," Andrew said.

Vincent shook his head. "That's not evidence."

"But this is," Andrew said. He lifted a small bag out of his pocket, with a little green pill. "Took the liberty of going through your office. This little pill right here is responsible for a lot of deaths."

"One way or another, we're going to bring down the Echo Killer," my father added, a gleam in his eye.

But I had been in Vincent's office all morning. Andrew hadn't been in there yet. And I hadn't seen any strange pills in his office. I had checked! All he had were random papers and art supplies.

What was this?

"You remember I told you I saw him at 52 Peaks," Andrew said to my father.

"*You* were at 52 Peaks," Vincent growled.

"I told you I was working for the sheriff."

My father hung his chin low. "I have enough reasons to believe that you're our primary suspect for the Echo murders."

"You have got to be kidding me," Vincent said. "There isn't any proof."

The urge to help him fought with my desire to run away, to forget all about this—my parents, this place, even Vincent—to run away and never come back. To not feel any of it. I erupted from the office, not knowing what to do.

Andrew's eyes immediately fell on me. "Miss Kora!" he shouted. "You're all right!"

But his words were false. He had known I was here for a long time. And now, he was acting grateful that I was alive.

My father ran toward me and put his arms around me, his embrace hollow. "You've been here this whole time?" he asked. He released me and shot an icy glare at Vincent. "You were hiding my daughter?"

"Tell them the truth," Vincent said, staring at me. "Those nights when the victims died? I was with Kora." He nodded at me. "Tell them what happened, Kora. I was always with you."

Some of that was true, but there was so much that was left unaccounted for. And while I didn't think he would kill that many people, I knew he had wanted to kill one.

Me.

Vincent turned back to my father. "You don't have enough evidence to lock me up for the Echo deaths and you know it, Sheriff," he growled.

"You're right," he said, crossing his arms, "But I do have enough to put you in jail for what you did to Kora."

Andrew removed his handcuffs, moving toward Vincent. "You're under arrest for the abduction of Kora Nova—"

167

"Tell them, Kora!" Vincent demanded. I stared into Vincent's eyes, seeing the anger in his soul, everything boiling up inside of him, focused on me. He had wanted to kill me, but I was still there, and I knew that there was something inside of him that burned brighter than his taste for violence. Shallow breaths coursed through me, my heart palpitated in my chest, spots darting my vision. My stomach churned.

Andrew put cuffs around Vincent's wrists. I opened my mouth to speak, but vomit ripped through me, spilling on the floor. My throat burned and my eyes watered. I wiped my mouth on the back of my wrist.

Vincent let out a guttural roar, his black eyes pinned me in place.

But the words still wouldn't come out.

Part Two

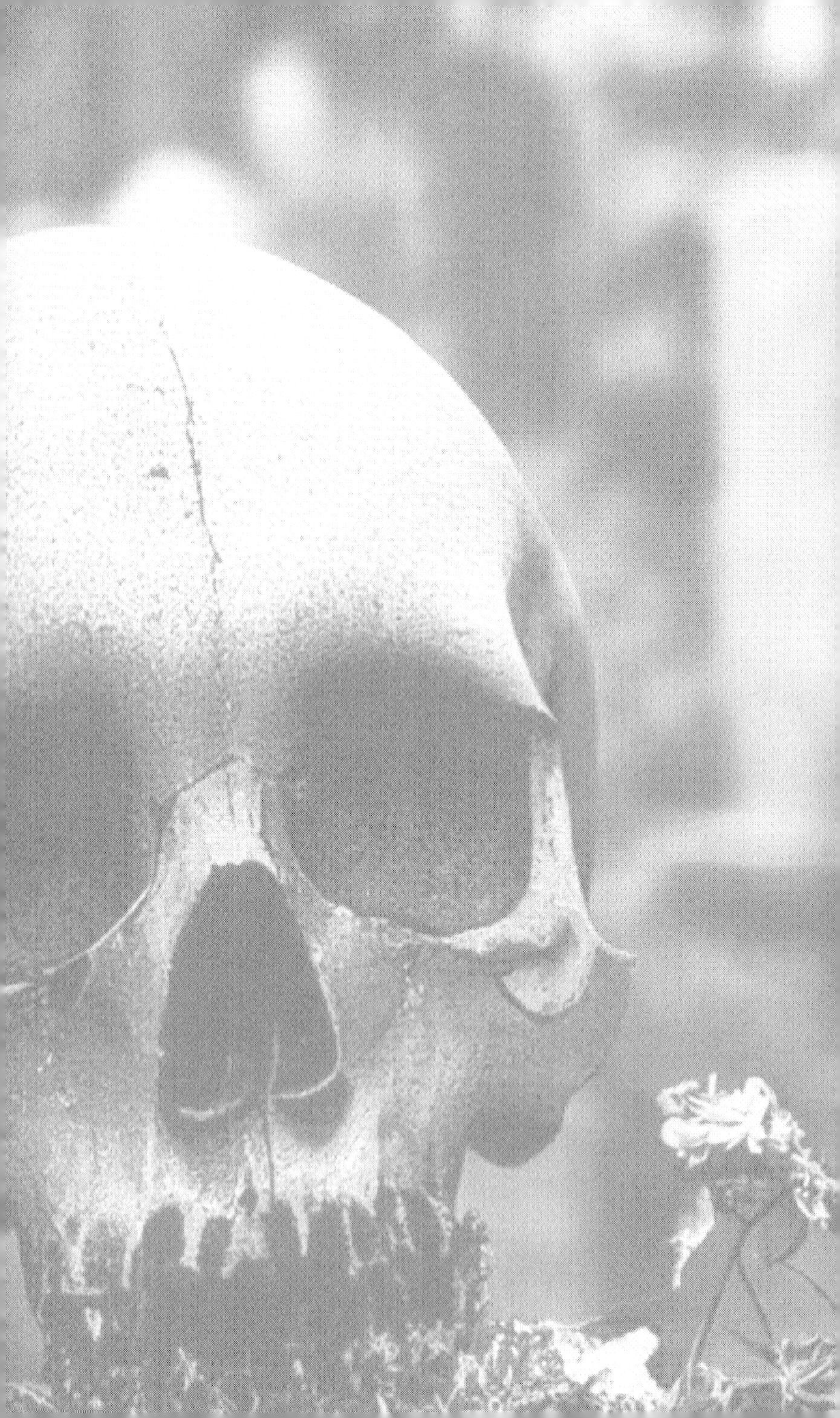

Chapter 23

Vincent

three years earlier

A LOW BUZZING CAME FROM INSIDE THE BREAK ROOM. I KNOCKED on the doorframe and waited. It had been my idea to give her the job, but only because my brother was supposed to be around to deal with her. Instead, I had to keep asking her to cover funeral directing.

It was just me. Picking up the pieces.

A grunt erupted from the occupant, followed by a mumbled, "Come in." The new employee held an electric shaver in her hand, long strands of dyed-gray hair spread across the floor. The side of her head looked like a lawnmower had destroyed it. A round table was shoved against the wall, and a sleeping bag was stuffed in the corner by the window. The bag of toiletries I had put together from my uncle's old things rested on the countertop. It wasn't much, but it was better than sleeping in the mausoleum.

"Can you cover tomorrow too?" I asked. Her pinched face softened, realizing I wasn't there to reprimand her. She slid the buzzer onto the countertop and waited. While she was good with the families, she was hesitant around me. Understandably so. I was her boss.

"Your brother is still gone?" she asked.

I didn't know when he was coming back. "You'll get your overtime," I said. "And the bookkeeper will be in. She'll help—"

A vibration rumbled through the ground, the bass of progressive metal music blasting through the building. The employee looked at me, raising her brow. I turned in the direction of the house.

So Justin had finally decided to show up, then.

"Excuse me," I said. I closed the break room door behind me, then stomped through the building and the cemetery, toward the house. The melody shook the ground. Apparently, he was enjoying his time off work. I clenched my fists, then opened the front door.

The music crashed into me, but otherwise, the house was empty. I glanced in the backyard; the dogs were out back, avoiding the racket. I turned off the stereo, an eerie silence falling over the house. My boots fell heavy on the floors as I searched for him, but every room was closed off. A light came from the gap at the bottom of the bathroom door.

I wasn't one to interrupt someone's privacy, but for all I knew, he was passed out with his head in the toilet after a bender. We had done that a lot when we were younger.

"Where were you?" I asked. No answer. I cleared my throat. "You in there?"

"Yep."

Not passed out, but just as irritating. "You can hear that shit from the funeral home."

"Not anymore."

I shook my head, then continued down the hallway. But something stopped me. This wasn't like him; he was full of smart-ass comments and had given up too easily. I checked his room: everything was in its place. There wasn't even a dirty shirt in the hamper. But a single piece of paper caught my eye, perfectly folded in the trash bin, as if he knew he might have to dig it out later. A pamphlet. I fished it out and opened it: *What Your Prognosis Means,* followed by more information. But one line stood out to me.

It was the same disease that our mother had died from.

I swung the bathroom door open. Muggy air enveloped me. Justin laid in the bathtub, the water steaming, his eyelids drooping. I lifted the sheet of paper.

"What's this?" I asked.

"What does it look like?"

So it was what I thought, then. I scowled. "When were you going to tell me?"

"I wasn't."

The paper crinkled in my hands. "When did you get this?"

"About a week ago."

"And you're showing up now?"

He lifted his shoulders, then slumped down, sinking until his chin was in the water. A full syringe laid on the side of the tub. I backtracked, opening the closed door of the studio: the floorboard was removed. Vials and pills and more crap we used to keep away from our uncle were spread out on the floor. I hadn't touched any of it in a long time. And Justin? He had been off of it longer than I had.

So he was self-medicating, then. Not my problem. At least, not right now. I went back to the bathroom.

"What's the plan?" I asked.

His pupils were dilated, his breathing slow. "What do you mean?"

"When do you start treatment?" I pointed in the direction of the funeral home. "We hired that new employee. And in a few weeks, we can give her a raise. Or—" I shrugged, "—increase hourly service costs to cover the medical bills."

He leaned his head to the side and let out a long breath.

"So?" I asked.

"Don't care, really."

Fine. I could figure this out myself. "She needs the money. So we'll—"

He sat up, wobbling from side to side like the energy had rushed to his head. "Have you forgotten what it was like? Watching Mom die?" He forced a laugh. "How it destroyed us? I'm not going through that. And I'm not going to make *you* go through that." A sigh whined through his lips. "And you sure as fuck aren't going to make me."

I narrowed my eyes. He acted like he was destined for the same fate as our mother, when he hadn't even tried to do anything to stop it.

"It's been twenty-five years," I said. "There have to be better treatments available—"

"Not enough."

"How do you know?"

"What do you think I've been doing for the last week?" He grimaced, folding his arms across his chest. He pressed his lips into a thin line. "I'm not going through that."

"You don't know what would happen."

He gave me a hard smile. "Are you that stubborn?"

I clenched my fists, biting my jaw so hard that my teeth crunched in my ears. "You can't give up."

"It's my fucking life."

"And mine too," I shouted. "What you do affects me. You're not going to do this. You can't. You're about to—"

"What?" Justin shook his head. "I'm about to do *what?* You have the new employee. Make her do the people work." His gaze flicked upward, avoiding my eyes. "Trust me. We both know it'll be better when I'm gone."

I wanted to punch him in the face for suggesting that. "You don't know what you're saying."

"You don't need me. You haven't in years."

A dull pain grew in my chest. We hadn't been close since before our mother got sick, but the reason I didn't need him like that was because he had always looked after me. We stood by each other, even when we were stupid idiots. Disappearing for weeks. Getting arrested. Shooting up when we should have been working.

Like now.

"It's not about needing someone, and you know it," I said. He rolled his eyes. "Give it some time. You know that—"

He put the syringe in the crook of his elbow and pushed on the plunger.

"The fuck are you doing?" I asked.

Another syringe caught my eye, tossed behind the toilet. This was his second hit. He was going to overdose.

I smacked the syringe away, but he was already halfway there. Rage flushed my skin, throbbing in my ears. I was back in our parents' bedroom, watching as Dad put the gun to his temple, his body slumping over Mom's blue-green flesh. Helplessness crawled up inside of me. None of it seemed real then. And it didn't seem real now.

Justin's eyes were bottomless pits staring back at me. He smiled.

My heart palpitated. Spots crowded my vision, covering him. We weren't supposed to go out like this. I was never going to let that happen.

It wasn't up to him.

My own fucking brother.

I ran to my closet, getting the canvas bag from the top shelf, then pulled out the pistol. I brought it to the bathroom, loading the gun as I walked. My heart drummed in my chest with each step, and I opened the door.

His eyes were glazed over, cast in front of him. His chest exhaled, and he settled deeper into the water. He wouldn't feel a thing.

He wasn't going to leave me. Like they left us.

But not without misery. I lifted the gun. Pulled the trigger.

The bullet went through his temple. He fell back, slumping in the water, a sinking ship. But that wasn't enough. I rushed to the medicine cabinet and found my straight razor, then reached into the water, ramming it into his arm, slicing down toward his wrist. Red swirled in the tub. I smashed my fists into his chest, holding him under, then stabbed the razor into the other arm, going as deep as I could until the muscles, veins, and tendons caught on the blade. The water sloshed over the sides of the tub, spilling on the ground.

His face was blank. Emotionless. *Empty.*

I held my breath. Then I brought the blade down again, and again, until his chest was battered with punctures and my whole body buzzed with heat, soaked with water and blood.

The razor dropped from my palm, clinking on the floor. The *tap tap tap* on the tile interrupted my thoughts. I looked down; my palm was bleeding. I must have squeezed the blade too tightly. I slid onto the floor, the bathwater soaking the bottom of my pants, my eyes burning, warm blood covering my arms and chest. The air conditioning kicked on, blasting from the vents. I shuddered, but my breaths came out even and slow. I wiped the back of my hand on my face; I was drenched.

Justin floated in the tub behind me.

Was it an overdose? The bullet? The loss of blood? Drowning?

He was going to leave anyway.

I should have felt something. Should have felt guilty. Afraid. Angry. But my mind fixated on the razor. On the gun.

I wiped them off, then I soaped the blade, ran it through the water, and wiped the edges until it was clean and smooth. Next, I used a cloth to wipe my fingerprints from the gun. Once the evidence was gone, I used a towel to bring both of them to the tub. I pressed the pistol into Justin's hand. I put the blade in his other palm, wrapping his fingers around it. I would have to burn my clothes in the firepit soon.

I kneeled at the side of the tub, my eyes half-lidded. The steam rose from the water. I wiped my wet face on my hands again as the events kept replaying in my head: he hadn't even moved; he had just stopped. There was no response, and there never would be again.

But it didn't give me any closure.

I should have watched him burn.

Kora

a few days later

Steam danced above a cup waiting on the table for me. I lifted a brow; that hadn't happened in ages, just like the outfit laid on my bed. Shea, my mother, was standing at the kitchen sink, looking out our window at the rose bushes blooming in the backyard. Her hair was twisted into a bun for the first time in ages. Before she could make a comment about my long, low ponytail, I quickly copied her hairstyle.

"Morning, sweetheart!" she said, picking up where we left off. Her honeysuckle perfume filled the air; I scrunched my nose, then straightened. "You look adorable!" It was like the last six months had never happened, but I wasn't going to complain about that. I was wearing the same black dress as her. It had a high waist and a shiny orange sash, three-quarter sleeves, with lace covering the bodice and arms. I had opted for black flats, instead of the orange heels, like she was wearing, but luckily, she hadn't noticed yet. "I knew we'd look perfect in it."

She loved playing up the mother/daughter image. I had learned a long time ago not to make a big deal out of it. Pick your battles wisely.

"Did you sleep well?" she asked.

I blinked at her, my skin tingling with discomfort.

"Yes," I finally said. It was a lie, but I wasn't going to risk upsetting her. I hadn't been able to sleep in ages.

She flicked a thumb at the backyard. "Are those rose bushes new?" I nodded, though whether or not they were *actually* new was debatable. I had planted them two months ago. I admit I had taken advantage of her lack of interest lately; she had never allowed me to garden by myself before. "They're beautiful."

I smiled. "Thanks."

"Be careful with them, you know?" she said. "They're not as easy to take care of as you'd think."

My stomach twisted. They had survived the last two months fine, but there was a chance she would remove them anyway.

"I'll be careful," I said.

Shea hummed along to the radio as we drove to work. I tapped my fingers against my legs. Despite the fact that the dismissive comments were back, I welcomed her return. And yet, I didn't understand this sudden shift. For the last few months, we had been driving to the flower shop in silence, where I'd scrounge my breakfast to-go from the pantry, while my mother skipped her own. She saved her energy for the shop, where she kept an even smile on her face until we closed, then it was back to silence again. At night, I left her dinner on the vacant side of the bed, where it cooled, undisturbed.

It was like a switch had been flipped, and now she was back.

Pumpkins lined the shops downtown. My cartoonish, but cute monster scowled outside of our entrance door. I turned off the electric candle.

"That's cute, sweetheart, but it doesn't match our image," Shea said, bopping my nose. "I don't want our customers to associate our flowers with something spooky."

It was more cute than spooky, and we had already had it out for a few days. She was going to reject it *on* Halloween?

"You might find some new customers," I argued. "Some people really like Halloween."

"They like the candy." She winked, then fluttered inside, pulling a small bowl of chocolates from under the register, putting it on display. "Get the other pumpkin and carve the rose. They always like that."

I let it go. It was just a pumpkin. I didn't need to hold my ground for something like that. But when it came to things that mattered, I had to stand up for myself. I was eighteen now, and I had already applied and been pre-selected for a scholarship at the University of Dixon on the West Coast. All I had to do was accept.

That evening, we met Sheriff Mike at a charity event for a photo opportunity. He was my father, but he was rarely home, and when he was, his moods fluctuated so wildly that I stayed out of his way. But I smiled at the cameras anyway, happy for the chance to be out in public for once. Afterward, we walked to Nectar Latte, grabbing a tea for me and coffee for my parents, then headed back to Poppies & Wheat. My mother talked idly at my father, who nodded along with her.

Everything seemed at peace for once. It was now or never.

"There's something I wanted to ask you two about," I said, interrupting them.

"Oh?" Shea asked.

Sheriff Mike opened the door to the shop. We went inside. My mother found her place behind the counter and started rifling through the supplies. The latest assistant manager buzzed out of the way.

"What's the weather like in California this time of year?" I asked.

Shea tilted her head at me. "Why do you ask?"

"Could I wear this over there for Halloween?"

"That's silly," she smiled brightly. "Why would you need to wear that dress over there?"

"I got this letter." I ran to the storeroom and grabbed the envelope from my cubby. "I was pre-selected for a scholarship. And I got an early acceptance—"

"You applied for college," she interrupted, her jaw dropped. "When?"

Her eyes were weary, her jaw loose, like I had betrayed her. My stomach dropped to my toes. Sheriff Mike's posture stiffened.

"Last month," I said.

Her chin darted away as if she couldn't stand to look at me. Then she dashed to the storeroom, busying herself with organizing the ribbons.

"Mom," I said. "It would only take one plane ride. It's not that far."

She ignored my words. Sheriff Mike sighed deeply, his shadow hovering.

"I would only need a little bit of financial aid. Maybe a thousand or two. That scholarship is—" the excitement welled up inside of me, my words coming out faster, "—*really* big."

She went past me, practically knocking me out of the doorway.

"Mom?"

"It's not about the money," she said. She opened one of the display coolers, then slammed it shut.

"They have a great program for floriculture and agriculture, and I really, *really* think it would be good for me."

She pinched her lips together. "I'm sure you can take online classes."

"There's an idea," Sheriff Mike said.

I shook my head at my father. "I told you, it's not the same." I turned back to my mother. "With floriculture, you need in-person learning. Labs and stuff. Greenhouses, the climate, the soil—"

"How did you even get into a college like that with a GED?" she asked. "Surely, they would have highly competitive applicants more suited than you, a homeschooled child from Punica." My cheeks flushed with heat. Yeah, I hadn't graduated from a high school like my peers. But it helped that my father did his best to get my application into the right hands. But if I said any of that, I would risk revealing him. His brows furrowed; he didn't want me to say anything. "So why did they pick you?" Shea continued. "What did you *do*, exactly?"

I flicked my eyes back and forth across hers, my skin hot. "I don't know," I said. "But they chose me. And I want to go." I clenched my jaw. "I *need* to go."

"Don't be ridiculous, Kora." My breath caught in my throat; she rarely used my name like that. "Without you, I'd have to hire another worker. And right now, that's all I can afford; one assistant manager, plus the two of us. But how's this? I'll fire the current assistant manager and I'll get someone around your age. A friend for you. How's that?"

"Miss Shea?" the assistant manager asked.

"Not now," my mother said, waving her hand.

But I didn't want a friend. I wanted my own life.

"It's a once-in-a-lifetime opportunity," I said.

"I don't even understand *how* you applied," she said. "Can you explain how you went behind my back?"

If I told her the truth, she would be devastated, and Sheriff Mike would never forgive me.

"I want to go to college," I said.

She turned around slowly. Silence filled the space between us. Then she whispered, "I can't deal with this right now." She went to the back patio. I followed her, but before I reached the door, the assistant manager grabbed my arm.

"Give her a minute," she said. "She needs time to cool off."

Cool off? I shook my head. "She's my mother."

Shea sat against the wall, staring out at the trees stretching up behind the shop. The shadows made her eyes look like water-filled caves. Exhaustion riddled her face.

"You're the most precious flower we have," she murmured. I hated when she said that, but right then, at those words, pain prickled the back of my throat. "I don't know what I'd do without you."

"You have Dad," I said.

"You know that's not true."

We stayed in silence like that, the trickles of laughter from store-front trick-or-treaters filling the air. Even if Sheriff Mike was technically around, it had been the two of us for so long, and we knew it might always be like that. My mother needed someone to look after her, and that was never going to be my father. But still, I had hoped for something else. A life where she could find her way, and I could find mine.

A child cackled, imitating a witch, and a twinge of anger fluttered through me. I had never been trick-or-treating before. My mother thought it was dangerous. But there were children a few yards from us, most of which were *more* than a decade younger than me, free to go about as they pleased.

Sheriff Mike came to the back patio and mouthed: *Go inside.*

So I did. I bit my fingers and waited while my father talked to my mother. I hoped—no, I *begged* the universe that he would be able to convince her. To show her why college was good for me. After all, *he* had been the one who had gotten me the applications in the first place. If anyone could help her find the reason, it would be her husband.

The back door opened. I lifted my shoulders, holding my breath. My father closed the door, sealing my mother off. He grimaced, his posture stiffer than ever.

But I couldn't give up yet.

"How did it go?" I asked. He walked past me. "Did she say anything?"

"What do you think?"

His tone was cold. I froze in place. "Are you mad at me?" He glared, and I shifted my weight. "But you helped me apply?"

"I want you out of the house." His chin hung low. "You know she uses you to control me? Reminds me of the family man I'm supposed to be." He beat his fists into the countertop. "I never wanted this. But you, going to college? Then I wouldn't have to deal with it anymore." He waved a hand in front of him. "But that's not going to happen now, is it?"

I shook my head, my heart sinking.

"Stop the fucking whining. You're lucky to be alive, you know that?" he muttered. "I told Shea to get rid of you. But she said I needed you for the election, or she'd tell the press I refused to marry her." Tears welled up inside of me. I was going to break. Sheriff Mike was never good at family, but this? Was he being serious? That he didn't want me to exist? His jaw pressed into a hard line. "You act like you've got the worst life, but you have a home. A sheriff for a father. A mother who is obsessed with you. And you'd rather push her into another episode, make everyone else deal with the fallout. Why can't you be grateful?"

My throat ached and the tears streamed down in angry bursts. I clutched my stomach, my guts twisting, threatening to erupt.

Was it my fault?

"You're just saying that," I sniffled, trying to keep my words steady, trying to convince myself that it was the truth. That he was only angry. That it was hard to know what to do with our family.

I rested a hand on the counter, balancing myself. I needed fresh air; I was going to be sick.

"Help me," he mumbled to himself, running a hand over his face in exasperation. "Don't vomit all over the place again. Take those sniveling emotions, bottle them up, and act like a fucking grown-up for once."

I crossed my arms over my chest, the sobbing finally unleashing. In his eyes, tears were fine. As long as I didn't get sick.

"You wonder why she babies you? Why she's afraid to let you out of her sight? Because of this." He threw a hand up and I shrank down. "You're eighteen years old. You're a fucking embarrassment."

I trembled, my jaw shaking. He tossed his head to the side,

then picked up a daffodil with browned edges, one we had unpacked that morning.

"Our precious little flower," he said, mimicking my mother's words. "Worse than this." He crushed the petals in his hand. My heart pulsed. It was true that we couldn't sell it, but it didn't need to be discarded like that.

"I need air," I managed to say. "I'm going to be sick. I need—"

"Then go," Sheriff Mike shouted. He threw a hand at the door. "Leave! Get out!"

He bared his teeth. The tension inside of me built into a heaviness that settled on my shoulders, sinking down to my stomach. He wasn't going to stop me. He actually wanted me to leave.

So I ran.

The door closed behind me, the jingling bell mixing with the laughter of children. The night air hit my face, cooling the tears on my cheeks. I barrelled across the street to the viewpoint looking over the stream, banging my hands into the railing. A full moon hovered over the water, judging me.

But no one followed me. I was alone.

A shadow shifted to the side. A man, taller than me, rubbed a hand across his chin, smearing the dirt on his face. He had broad shoulders, thick arms, and bulbous white scars twisting over his arms and neck, tinted purple in the night. Mud was caked in his fingernails, as if he had been crawling in the woods for days, barely surviving. I had never been this close to a strange man before. I had seen men from the cracked door of the storeroom, but I had only been this close to my father and my childhood friend, Andrew. This stranger fascinated me. He was raw and masculine. He stepped forward, locked eyes with mine, holding me still. My stomach strained, electric nerves circulating inside of me.

I swallowed, unsure of what to say. But he was waiting. Maybe I was supposed to speak first.

"Is that your costume?" I asked, motioning to the dirt on his skin. He looked too old for Halloween, but I didn't know what else to say.

"I was working." His voice was rough and cold, like a winter night.

"What do you do?"

"I dig graves."

I wrapped my arms around myself. Graves? That explained the dirt on his skin. A flash of heat covered me from head to toe, then disappeared.

"I didn't know they still dug graves by hand," I said.

"Most don't."

I bit my lip, trying to keep myself together. I glanced back at Poppies & Wheat; the *Closed!* sign was in the window now, but the lights were still on. My stomach clenched. When I turned back, the man's eyes were still roaming me, unrelenting. My cheeks flamed, and my head pulsed with pain. I cringed. It was all of this stupid hair. I pulled out the ties and pins, letting my hair shake down my back.

"Maybe I should just cut it all off," I muttered.

"That will show them," he said, a hint of laughter in his voice, like he was mocking me. What was his problem?

But I realized something then: the sadness was there, but it seemed lighter than before. And I could actually move without being afraid of getting sick.

"What's your name?" he asked.

"Kora." I tucked a lock of hair behind my ear. He seemed trustworthy, though I had no idea why—only pure instinct. "Kora Nova. My mother owns the flower shop. You might know my father—he's the sheriff?" My words were so fast, I sounded desperate. I scrunched my eyes closed. *He didn't ask about your family history, stupid,* I told myself. *No one cares.*

But he was the only person who wasn't treating me like a child right then.

"What's your name?" I asked.

The door to the shop opened and closed. My father spoke into his radio, then headed to his squad car parked down the street. I shook my head. Even when your family was falling apart, duty always came first. At least he was reliable.

Once my father was gone, the strange man turned back to me.

"Why were you crying?" he asked.

"My parents." I must have seemed like such a baby right then, but maybe that was the point. Maybe at eighteen, I *was* still a child in their eyes, and that was the problem. Like my father had said. But how could I grow up if they never let me go?

"They won't let me go anywhere," I continued. "This," I slapped my hands onto the railing, "*This* is the first time I've ever been truly left alone. Why did I think they would let me go to college? I'm just their precious little flower." I closed my fists, my nails digging into my palms. "But you don't help a flower grow by blocking out the sunlight."

He stared at me, then moved his body so that his entire focus was on me, completely enraptured. My knees were weak, my cheeks burning, but his gaze still magnified closer. As if he knew he had a hold on me.

"Your life isn't over because you can't go to college," he said. "You're—what, eighteen? Your life has barely begun."

That's what they always said. That there were more years. That this wasn't the end. But that never seemed like a good enough reason to keep going. To try harder. To do more. I had to bottle it up. Had to be the daughter they wanted. The child my mother needed.

Because I would never be enough.

"It's not just that," my voice quivered. I squeezed the railing. My breathing hitched and I shielded my body from him. My father's words blasted in my mind: why couldn't I be grateful? Why couldn't I be happy with what I had? Sheriff Mike was right. I had everything, and I would live and die here like my mother wanted me to. I hated that. My body trembled as the realization came to the surface: "No matter what I do, I'm stuck here."

"And you always will be," he said. Finally, his eyes left me, glancing at the moon over the water. In a softer voice, he added, "This world traps all of us."

The tears stopped. I had this instinct that he was trying to make me feel better somehow, by showing the reality of the situation. No one was ever satisfied. We were all stuck here. Even him.

The man came closer and locked eyes with me. His eyes were

black, the moon shining in them like flecks of gold. Earth and ripe sweat floated in the air. He needed a shower, but I didn't mind his scent, because it seemed real. More real than the perfume my mother used in the morning. More real than the way my father's uniform constantly smelled freshly laundered, as if nothing bad ever happened during his shift.

Because this man, covered in dirt and sweat, *was* real.

The man grabbed my chin. My skin tingled, my body instantly flushing, my heart thumping in my chest. It seemed so intimate. His eyes shined like rocks at the bottom of a well, beautiful and haunting, like he could see so much more than I exposed.

And I wanted him to see it all.

"One day, you'll wake up and you'll realize none of this matters," he said, his eyes searching mine, his grip on my chin firm. "Your dreams. Your failures. These tears." He dragged his fingertip along my cheek, painting me in my own sorrow. "None of this will matter." He leaned in, our faces close. "I promise."

His words laid on my lips, as if I could taste them. "Who are you?" I asked.

"I'm no one." He cupped the back of my head, his fingers tangling in my hair, and kissed my forehead, dirt smudging me. Then he turned away, walking down the sidewalk, his boots heavy on the cement.

I stood on the viewpoint, watching his shadow disappear, until it was like he had never existed at all. A group of costumed children knocked into my sides, but I was hypnotized, unable to comprehend what had just happened. A stranger had kissed my forehead. A man. A stranger. He hadn't tried to hurt me like my mother had sworn they would all do. But he had spoken to me like I was his equal. He had even tried to cheer me up.

And for a few seconds, I wasn't thinking about my parents, or college, or my sick stomach.

It was all him.

I had to remember his words. These feelings with my mother, with my father, of wanting what I couldn't have—he was right; none of it mattered. The only thing that was truly important was making sure that I did right with what I had. And if that meant taking a few more years to find a solution where I could do what I wanted, and still make my family proud, then that's what I would do. My father might have been a neglectful jerk, and my mother might have been obsessive to the point of insanity, but they were still *my* family. So I could bottle these emotions and do something useful for once. I could take that man's words to heart and *move on*. Because tears were never useful. But living was.

I ran a hand across my forehead. Dirt smeared my fingertips, proof that he was real.

There were questions I wanted to ask him. So many questions.

I wanted him to teach me exactly what he meant.

Chapter 24

Kora

present

Vincent's coal-black eyes threatened me. Everything went quiet in the lobby of Quiet Meadows. I had wanted to be free more than anything for so long, and I kept telling myself that now, I finally was. But a sudden coldness expanded in the center of my rib cage, bursting out. Was this really happening?

"You're under arrest for the abduction of Kora Nova—" Andrew said.

"Tell them, Kora!" Vincent shouted.

Everything spewed out of me, landing on the floor. My father patted my back, mumbling nice words, but he hated when this happened. I wiped my mouth on the back of my hand. Everything felt wrong.

So why couldn't I stop it?

"Are you all right?" the older man asked.

His wife grabbed his arm. "Yes, dear. Are you—"

"She's fine," my father said.

"You have the right to remain silent," Andrew continued. "Anything you say may be used against you in a court of law."

"That's right, you sonofabitch," my father muttered. "No one hurts the Novas."

But Vincent hadn't hurt me. Not like that. But my father didn't care.

"Kora!" Vincent howled. "Tell them!"

One day, you'll wake up and you'll realize none of this matters.

Those words seemed so real now, like I finally understood what he meant. College. The greenhouse. This idea of freedom. There were bigger things at play. Things that mattered. And everything that I had thought ruled my world, never actually did.

"Kora!" Vincent shouted.

Once the older couple left, Andrew handed off Vincent to my father, then put his arm around my shoulder. His embrace was full of dead weight. I shrank underneath him. Vincent glared daggers as Andrew waggled his fingers.

"The county will be happy to hear about this," Andrew said. "The Echo Killer finally in jail, and our good ol' Sheriff saved the day once again."

My face turned pale. "You don't really believe that Vincent killed those people, do you?"

Andrew smiled, proud of himself. "I believe that there are some suspicious circumstances with Erickson. And when it comes time to put him under the court of law, he will pay with a swift hand for the crimes he has committed." My limbs were weak. I understood that Vincent had done something wrong, but the murders too? That wasn't fair. "It sounds like you don't believe that to be the case, Miss Kora."

"I don't know what to believe." The words were dry on my tongue; it took everything in my power to admit that. Had I put an innocent man in jail?

Was he ever innocent?

Andrew tilted his head, studying me. "He kidnapped you, Miss Kora."

I narrowed my eyes. "I'm not a kid."

"Well," he nodded, "You've always been in your mother and father's care, up until this point. Am I correct?"

I seethed at him. For one thing, my father had almost nothing to do with my upbringing, and why would he rub my mother's helicopter spirit in my face like that? I had thought he understood me. That we were friends.

"What are you saying?" I asked.

He lifted his hands, holding back a laugh. "Nothing, Miss Kora. Nothing at all. There you go, worrying your little heart." He winked at me.

I turned away. My father slammed the back door of the squad car. I bit my tongue. Andrew squeezed my shoulder. "I'll take you to the flower shop."

"I can walk," I said quickly. I didn't want his help.

"Your mother would have my corpse for supper if I let you walk there all by yourself," he said. My body flushed with heat, my fingers wrapped tight, but I swallowed it down. None of this mattered; I had to remember that. I had to be strong. Had to think straight. Couldn't let these emotions get the best of me. Not when I needed to focus on what was coming.

At Poppies & Wheat, Andrew escorted me to the front door, then knocked on the glass so hard that it rattled the windows. I steadied myself; I couldn't let myself throw up again.

"What's wrong, Miss Kora?" he asked quietly.

I wanted to answer, but he would never understand. To Andrew, justice had been served, and now it was time to deliver the princess back to the queen.

But to me, it was another cage.

"I don't know what I'm doing," I admitted.

"None of us do," he said. "But think of your mother." He rubbed a thumb over my cheek, and my skin prickled with knives. "She's been lost without you. All of us have." He pressed his lips together. "I've missed you."

Saliva gathered in my mouth. He had known exactly where I was for a long time. He had even told me to stay there, that it was my duty to find evidence against Vincent. How could he claim that he missed me?

Catie's familiar poofy mohawk filled the glass walls.

"Andrew," she said curtly. She turned to me, giving me the same cold stare. "Kora." She forced a smile. "So good to see that you're finally back."

She gave me a sharp hug, one that was stiff and uninviting. My body ached all over. "I'll take it from here, Officer," Catie said, then pulled me inside. She closed the door behind us. The sweet stench of decay and rot filled the air. Fruit flies darted around my head; I swatted them away. Petals and leaves littered the ground, the limp remains of bouquets dangling out of stale buckets. I wrapped my hands around my stomach. This was worse that it had been.

"I tried to clean," Catie whispered. "But your mother wouldn't let me. She said I was going to jinx your return."

"Andrew?" a hoarse voice called through the shop. "Andrew? Is that you?"

"Mom!"

A sudden warmth surged through me, tears welling in my eyes, but I held them back. Even with how much I didn't understand why Shea raised me the way she did, there was still so much comfort in seeing her. She might have had her reasons mixed up, but she had always wanted me. She swiveled around, knocking an elbow into a vase, the shards crashing around her. Her jaw dropped, her eyes wide and fatigued.

I stepped over the glass and hugged her.

"You're here," she said, her voice lost and confused. I squeezed my arms around her, but she didn't move.

"I am here."

Finally, she embraced me, but her shoulders shook, and soon, her wails were so loud that I cringed. She pulled back, then looked down at me, to assess the damage. The rings around her eyes were like a drained moat.

"What happened?" she asked. Then she blinked, staring at my shoulders. "What happened to your beautiful hair?"

I absent-mindedly stroked my shoulder-length locks. "It's a long story."

She quickly moved on: "Where did you go? Who stole you from me?"

"Yeah, Kora," Catie asked, an edge to her voice. "Tell us. What happened, exactly?"

Catie grit her teeth, a false smile on her face, judging me, daring me to say what had really happened, warning me to leave Vincent out of it. But a fist banged on the door. The three of us jumped, turning toward the entrance. Sheriff Mike put his key in the door. He beamed at me, then wrapped an arm around my mother's shoulders. She sunk into his side.

"She's finally home," he whispered, a tear in his eye. He pulled me into his arm. "Our baby is finally home." But those words were so empty. The back of my throat itched. Had he been happy that I was finally gone?

"We took care of Erickson," Sheriff Mike said, turning to my mother.

"Erickson?" Shea asked. "From the funeral home? What did he do?"

"Now's your chance," Catie said.

Shea turned to me. "Chance for what?" she asked. Her face turned between Catie and me, then back to my father. She went to the door, locking it again. "What happened with Erickson?"

"He's at the station," my father said. "Being processed, then moved to holding cells."

"For what?"

"He abducted Kora." Sheriff Mike lowered his head like he had done on the television to deliver bad news so many times before. "I'm sorry, Shea. I should have known."

"But he was—he was—" Her whole body trembled. She shook her head frantically.

"It's okay," I whispered, holding my mother's hand. "I'm here. I'm okay."

Her eyes were glossy with tears. "He didn't hurt you, did he?"

She gripped my shoulders until her knuckles turned white. The pain intensified at the back of my throat like it was my fault that he hadn't hurt me. Because at least if he had, I would have something to show for it. But every time he had hurt me, I had *liked* it. Wanted more of it. And that made me a consenting participant, didn't it?

"No," I said quietly, averting my eyes. "He never laid a hand on me." Not like that.

She let go of me and wobbled, catching herself on a display table as she straightened.

"As long as you're okay now," she said.

We stayed like that for a while. My mother sobbed silently, holding me, while my father wrapped his arms around the two of us. I used to think their touch was burdensome, especially my mother; she held me like I would disappear. But now it was like I wasn't there. Like everything we had once been was already gone.

My mother wiped her nose on the back of her sleeve. I turned to her.

"My stuff is there," I said. "My clothes."

"You brought clothes with you?" she asked.

It wasn't like that, but the details wouldn't make sense. "I want to go get them, if that's okay," I said.

Mike widened his stance. "I'll go and check it out. It'll give me an opportunity to make sure there's nothing else that criminal is hiding."

"I'll go with you," I interjected. I made myself say it before I could stop; I had to keep a close eye on my father when it came to Vincent's house. "I spent so much time there. I know where my stuff is."

"I'm not letting you go back there," Shea said.

My arms flexed impulsively. "Vincent is in jail. He's not going to hurt me."

"I don't want you there," she said, punctuating her words, her voice resolute.

"I'll go with Mike," Catie offered. "I used to house-sit for Vincent occasionally. I'll find her stuff. Do you know where he kept the key for your room?" She glared at me, daring me to answer. To show how close I had gotten to him. I shook my head.

"Why would she know that?" my mother asked. "He held her hostage."

"I'll find it then," Catie said, shrugging. "But you can answer your mother."

There was so much more that Catie was holding back. That she hated me for not speaking up about Vincent. Shea turned to me, doe-eyed.

But what could I say? They had found extra graves. He had Echo in his studio and in his office. I couldn't vouch for him every hour of the day, could I?

Punica had only one hotel on the edge of town, off of Willow Highway. My father's radio filled the car, my mother's sniffling interrupted it. She squeezed my hand, snot caked in layers on her face. But a dullness overtook me as if I was filled from head to toe with sand.

After walking us to the hotel room, my father left for work and I readied a bath for my mother. She asked me to leave the door open so that we could talk, but she didn't speak the entire time. She just wanted to keep an eye on me.

A few minutes later, a polite hand knocked on the door. Shea stumbled out of the bathtub, dripping all over the carpet.

"Let me get that," she said.

"Come on, Mom," I said, forcing a laugh. "You're wet. Let me."

She smacked an arm against my chest, then threw on a robe and opened the door. Two plastic bags laid on the floor.

I grabbed them from Shea's hands before she could look inside. If I couldn't answer a door by myself, then at the very least, I could go through bags of clothing in peace. Leggings. Shirts. Underwear. An unscented bar of soap. My toothbrush, the bristles bent and worn. A hard piece of thick paper stuck between the clothing. I turned my back to Shea, making sure she couldn't see any of it, but she was too exhausted to care. I carefully peeled back the layers: my charcoaled eyes behind the divided window.

"Where did you get that?" Shea asked. I startled, shoving the paper under the clothes.

"What?"

"That ring." She pointed to my hand.

Nyla's ring. The black gem shined back at me, catching the light. It reminded me of Vincent's eyes. I hadn't taken it off since Vincent had given it to me.

"It was Nyla's," I said.

"Oh." She turned off the television and laid down. "Get some rest, sweetheart. You've been through so much lately."

I had been through a lot of things, but I had clearly rested more than my mother. She was the one who needed sleep.

"Please," she said, her voice weak. She was scared to sleep, then. She didn't want me to leave while she was unconscious.

"Just a second," I said. "I've got to brush my teeth."

I went to the bathroom, clutching the bags under my arms, and when I was behind the door, I pulled out that thick paper. I stared at the painting. The haunted expression on my face, peering straight into Vincent's soul. It reminded me of how he had kissed my forehead like he was bestowing a gift upon me. *I promise*, he had said. *None of this will matter.*

And he was right. Everything I had cared so much about then was insignificant now.

Chapter 25

Vincent

A full day had passed in the holding cell. A musty scent permeated the air and the lights flickered overhead. A bench rested along the back of each cage; three cells side by side, with thick metal bars and fencing between them. Sheriff Mike dragged the police baton against the bars, each bang clattering between the cement walls.

"You piece of trash," he said under his breath. "You know how much time this has cost me? And publicity?" He rubbed his forehead. "Since when does the daughter of the sheriff get kidnapped? It could have cost me the election."

"And your daughter," I said.

He lifted his head at me, finally making eye contact. "What was that?"

"Your daughter," I added with a sharpness to my tone. "You could have lost your daughter. Or were you too busy to remember that you have a family?"

He beat the baton into the bars, shaking the cell. His bloodshot eyes bulged out of his head.

"I am doing what's right," he howled. "My work protects my family."

A smile crept onto my lips; there was no need for me to prove that he was lying to himself because he *knew* it. He didn't care about his wife or his daughter, only that they made him look like a family man. And because he had been obsessing over the Echo Killer, he had been gone the night I had taken Kora. That should have been the wake-up call, but it wasn't. He was more pathetic than ever.

"You haven't got shit on me," I said.

"There was Echo in your office, extra graves, and my daughter. You want me to spell it out for you?" He holstered his baton, then put his hands on his hips. "All right. Let's pretend for a second that you *didn't* abduct my daughter, then yeah, you're right. The graves and the Echo by themselves don't prove anything besides the fact that you're a drug addict necrophiliac, which," he laughed, "we already knew." A sneer crawled across his face. "But I'm still the sheriff of Acheron County. And if that means keeping a man locked up in order to ensure that the people of my county are safe, then I am positive that the citizens will support me."

He found a place against the wall and leaned back. I kept my gaze fixed on him.

"It's convenient that it came together right before the election, isn't it?" I said. "Who knows what would have happened if you actually had to work when you needed last-minute campaigning?"

He snarled. "You want to say that louder?"

I stood up, grabbing the bars, and put my face between them.

"Your voters might be too dumb to notice what's going on, but I see through you, Mike. You're nothing but a con artist."

"Are you accusing me of a crime?" He took heavy steps forward, broadening his shoulders. "Need I remind you that Kora is my only child? My *only* daughter. And you took her from my home." His eyes were cold, but I didn't back down. I didn't have anything to lose anymore. I knew the truth; he was never home.

"All hail Sheriff Mike, the savior of Acheron County," I said.

"You took my daughter."

"I did a lot more than take your daughter, you sorry fuck."

He rammed a hand through the bars, punching me in the gut, the ache dull and penetrating. I clutched my stomach, the pain shooting to my head, and I laughed.

"Finally, the sheriff emotes like he actually cares." I clapped as loudly as I could. "Here goes the award for best actor in Acheron County."

A flat expression filled his face. He fixed the cuffs of his uniform, shoving down everything that he wanted to do to me.

"It's a good thing you're here, Erickson," he snickered. "You might not make it through the night if you were out there. The Echo Killer is still out there, after all."

I bared my teeth. He was flaunting it in my face. "You know who the real killer is, then."

"Of course I do," he said, patting my knuckles clutching the bars, "It's you."

"Erickson," another officer called. "You've got a visitor."

"I'm off," Sheriff Mike said. He knocked his hand into the bars. "Good luck getting out."

"Eat a dick," I growled.

Catie walked in, running a hand through the barrel-curls at the top of her head. Sheriff Mike strutted down the hall. Catie flattened herself to the side of him.

"Good to see you, Sheriff," she said, shaking his hand.

"Likewise. Are you here to talk business with your undertaker?"

"Gotta figure out what the boss wants." She nodded in my direction. "I'll see you around."

Sheriff Mike strode down the hall with his head held high, and Catie sheepishly went around him, then dusted herself off. A gnawing sensation crawled in my stomach. I wanted to get out now, but I had this instinct that something was in my way. What was Catie coming to tell me?

"How's Quiet Meadows?" I asked.

"Fine," she said, huffing out a breath. She leaned on one hip. "I'll have you know I embalmed all on my own yesterday. And Lee has been working in the office to help with sales and coordinating."

"You got Lee to come out?" I asked. Lee rarely left her home or office. At times, she was more reclusive than I was.

"Desperate times call for desperate measures," Catie said.

I could understand that. "I owe you both. Now, please," the

aggravation leaked into my voice, "Get me the hell out of here."

She gritted her teeth, holding her words. "I can't," she finally said.

"What do you mean, you can't?"

"The judge set the bail too high."

My chest tightened. "How high is that?"

"Two hundred fifty thousand."

I slammed my fists into the bars and cursed under my breath. I waited for her to say it was a joke, but she shook her head. "Two hundred and fifty thousand?" I repeated.

"Sheriff Mike convinced him that you're our biggest threat to the area, and the judge ate it right up. I'm sure he's in the sheriff's pocket too." She crossed her arms. "And I've got more bad news for you."

I clenched my fists. What could be worse than that?

"The Echo murders stopped once you were arrested." She put a hand up to her brow. "So they're saying that you definitely did it."

That wasn't possible. "But you were embalming yesterday."

"Natural causes," she said, cringing at the words. The first time in ages that she had been reluctant to announce a death like that.

I clenched my jaw. None of this made sense.

"That means that the killer *knows* that I'm arrested," I said. "It's a cover."

"There wasn't anything on the news about new victims this morning, and now they're saying they've got the main suspect under arrest. I haven't gotten any calls yet either."

My chin dropped. "You know I didn't do it." She gave me a sympathetic look. "Find that killer," I ordered.

"I'm not a detective." She rolled her eyes. "I'm a funeral director."

I gripped my fists. "And there's not going to *be* a funeral home if I don't get out of here."

"Your visiting time is up," an officer called down the hallway. He motioned for her to move.

"I'll be back," Catie said.

I stood against the bars, looking down that damp hallway into the bright office. Andrew waltzed into view, then smirked down at the holding cells, his eyes locked with mine. I hated him with a fiery rage.

"How are ya, Erickson?" he asked, his smile wide.

I imagined his neck snapping in my bare hands, his flesh easing apart with my knife. With my access to the crematory retorts, he'd be gone in a few hours, and there'd be nothing left but some bones to pulverize.

"Fuck you," I hissed.

"Always a pleasure," he said, tipping his imaginary hat as he walked back to join the bullpen.

The clock ticked by. I paced the cell. Would anyone else come? Would Kora help me? But why would she come? She had chosen her path. Left me behind. I went over the ways I could torture her: suffocation, drowning, my knife, a gun, a fire. And each time, I pictured her beautiful corpse lying there at my feet.

Which was easy to imagine until I saw her in person. She pulled hair behind her ear, showing off those big green eyes, sparkling under the fluorescent lights. Andrew said something, and she laughed. My stomach hardened with nerves.

"Kora," I said, my voice low. She was across the office; I could barely see the details in her face, but I knew it was her. I had been hunting her for so long. I could always spot her in a crowded room.

"Kora," I said again. Sheriff Mike brought a bottle of water to her, and Shea put an arm around her daughter. Kora's eyes were half-lidded, her shoulders loose.

"Flower," I said.

Kora instantly straightened, her hand grazing the back of her neck as if I was breathing there. Then she turned toward the darkness leading to me. Her eyes locked on mine, and still, she said nothing. She must have come here to press charges. So that they could lock me up forever.

Everything inside of me boiled up, threatening to incinerate me. If the day came, I would push her into that grave and watch her die.

Chapter 26

Kora

Inside the police station, processing my statement didn't take long since my father had prepared one for me. It was vague, stating that I had been abducted, and while I had said I would sign it over the phone, I couldn't put the pen to the paper now.

"You take it home," Andrew said, putting an arm around my back. "Think it over. It's a lot to take in. Trust me," he gave a sad smile, "We all get it."

"You've been through so much," Shea said. "It's understandable that you'd want to take time with it."

"Or I can write my own," I said.

"That's not necessary," Sheriff Mike said. "Mine is perfectly functional. And besides, it..."

I zoned out, forcing myself to smile and laugh so that my mother would feel safe. So that everyone would leave me alone. So that I could go home, back to that hotel room, and bottle everything up inside of me again. So I could go back to being empty. To forgetting him.

Flower.

The hairs on the back of my neck lifted. I glanced at the hallway that led to the jail. Vincent stood in the center of one of the cells, his gaze locked on me, hatred growing in his eyes. Chills ran down my back.

I shouldn't have cared about Vincent. I listed the things I knew: he *might* have been involved in his brother's death; he *might* have burned my parents' house; and he had, in fact, *definitely* abducted me; but he had also *saved* me from death. But there was no way that he could deny that he had wanted to murder me. I had seen the grave. Nearly been shoved inside of the crematory. Ran my fingertips over the daffodil engraved on my headstone: *Here Lies My Flower.*

He had been that close to killing me before; why wouldn't he kill Nyla too?

———

The next morning, the air was infused with burnt coffee. I wrinkled my nose, but when I realized what it was—that my mother was out of bed—I darted up. I glanced around. Where was the outfit she had laid out for me? She sat at the edge of the cushioned chair, a styrofoam cup in her hand. Her hair was shoulder-length, curled in. The same length as mine.

"You're awake," she said, her voice pleased. "Good morning, sweetheart."

I tilted my head, rubbing my eyes. "You're…" I looked around. What had changed since I had gone to sleep? "You're up?"

"It's a new day," she said, her smile sparkling white. She got another styrofoam cup from the dresser. "You take cream and sugar with your tea, don't you?" I didn't, but I didn't say anything. She was trying, and she had slid right back into our old routine like I had never left. Like nothing had happened. Like she had always had short hair.

She was as numb as I was supposed to be.

I lifted the cup to my nose. "Smells good," I said. "Did you get it in the lobby?"

"In the room." She motioned to the pod machine. I guessed I had slept through it. I motioned at her cup.

"Is the coffee any good?"

"Don't know," she said. "Haven't tried it yet."

I raised a brow. "But you've been here since the house fire, right?"

"Haven't wanted any."

The flower shop had been in a horrible state. It made sense that Shea wouldn't bother with coffee. I took a sip, and though it tasted a little sweet, I smiled at her.

"Thank you," I said.

She beamed at me. "I'm so glad you're home."

Home was a bittersweet word. The hotel obviously wasn't our home, but to Shea, home was a state of being. Home meant that I, her only child, was close to her. It meant safety. And while I didn't feel the same way, it was all she had. In some ways, it was all I had, too.

My safe place didn't exist anymore. Not really.

But had I ever really been safe?

As Shea took a shower, I turned on the television, flipping through the channels. I was never allowed to cable surf at home; Shea was the one who chose what we watched—but she didn't seem to notice. It was as if those little things—controlling what shows I watched, how I dressed, who I spoke to—weren't problems anymore. As long as I was simply there.

I stopped on a reporter's image, her face filling the screen.

Sheriff Mike arrested the main suspect for the Echo murders, she said. *At the time, the suspect's name has not been released. The arrest interfered with the sheriff's latest charity event to donate to Punica Little League, but his supporters are relieved, knowing that he brought peace to Acheron County once again. The same suspect is the abductor of his daughter, Kora Nova, who went missing after the Sheriff's house was decimated in a fire. She's been brought back to her mother, and though Mrs. Nova has refused to comment, the sheriff says that the family is happily reunited.*

I scrunched my forehead. Why hadn't I been interviewed myself? Had my mother and father not allowed it?

My father flashed on the screen. *Our people can sleep comfortably tonight,* he said, *and that's all you can ask.* He rubbed a hand through his hair. *Family means everything, and here in Acheron County, we are all family. We have to serve each other.*

At first, I rolled my eyes in annoyance. My father had never wanted a family and had made that perfectly clear. He only wanted power. But then something made me stop: There was no way that Vincent had committed those murders. It wasn't possible. And it's not like I wanted to save Vincent, but—

Maybe I did.

If Vincent had helped me to realize what freedom was—even if it was a false sense of freedom—then maybe it was my job to help him. He might have deserved a lot of things, but years in prison for a crime he didn't commit, didn't seem fair.

And I wanted this guilt in my stomach to go away. I needed to do something.

Shea returned to the room with a towel wrapped around her head and fresh clothes on. She stood in front of the sink, rubbing cream on her cheeks.

"I want to visit Dad," I said. She continued smoothing her face. "At work."

"Is this about your statement?" she asked. "We visited him yesterday. I don't think he'll have time for us."

Those words made me crumble internally. Even Shea knew that he rarely had time for us.

"I want to try," I said.

She breathed steadily, trying to concentrate. Her hands shook in the mirror. Once the cream was blended in, she turned to me.

"You just want to see your father?" she asked.

Did she think I wanted to sneak out or something? "Maybe I can go see him by myself," I tried.

Her eyelids fluttered, but then she smiled, her teeth clenched.

"I agree. That's a fantastic idea."

The word 'fantastic' sounded strange coming from her mouth, but I couldn't help myself from being excited.

"Really?"

"You need more responsibility. If that means going to the police station and visiting your father, then why not?" She shrugged her shoulders. "Besides, you're going to be the new assistant manager once we open the store back up."

"Assistant manager?" I repeated. "You realize that means I have to talk with customers, right?"

Despite the cream, her skin turned blotchy, but she smiled anyway and stroked my arm. We both knew that I could have done Nyla's job ages ago, but my mother never wanted me to. Never wanted me to have contact with anyone else.

"You're ready," she said quietly. "I hired a new girl. Same age as you." She turned back to the mirror, grabbing a palette of eye shadows. "I've been putting off her start date though. We'll open back up tomorrow. And we can browse that catalog again, see if there are any more potted plants you want."

"For the house?" I shook my head; we didn't have a house anymore. "The hotel? The shop?"

"For wherever you want."

I blinked at her. How in the world had she been so distraught yesterday and the day before, but today, it was like I had never left? Like she suddenly trusted me? Why was she giving me the ability to go out by myself *now?*

"Sweetheart?" she asked.

I forced a smile on my face. "Yes," I said, "that sounds—"

"Perfect!" she finished for me. And there was no other word to describe it. Things were practically perfect. If you had put us into our old home, our lives would have been better than ever at that moment. My mother was letting me go out.

On my own.

It seemed too good to be true.

"Well, go on," she said, pride bubbling up inside her as she shooed me away. "Get ready for the station."

Anticipation bubbled inside of me, making my fingers flutter. I imagine that this is what it would have been like if she had taken me to school on my first day of kindergarten, but I had never had that experience. Still, I took a shower; the lighting was brighter than it had been in Vincent's basement, but when I opened the body gel provided by the hotel, I flinched. It reeked of fruit punch. It was such a simple choice—the type of soap to use—and yet, I stopped.

I reached out of the stall, grabbing the bar of soap from the counter, the same one Vincent had left for me to use in the basement. It was plain, forcing my body to smell like it naturally did, but the lather was clean, and I tried not to think about why I had chosen a plain bar of soap over the perfumed body gel.

I stepped out of the shower and my mother smiled. Several outfits were laid on the bed, though all of them seemed younger. *Different.* And there were no doubles—none of the outfits were the dress Shea was wearing herself.

"I had some time to go shopping," she said. She must have spent those days when I was gone, dreaming of the day when I would return. Buying stuff for me so that I would know that she had never stopped trying. That she had never given up on me.

And it made me sad.

I picked up a flowery loose blouse. It was easier to accept it. "Thank you," I said.

"I got you something else," she said. I raised a brow, and she grinned. "Well, two things actually." She went to the nightstand and pulled out a manilla folder, then opened it to the first page. *Letter of Intent for Purchase of Commercial Property, Lot 246.* I skimmed over the rest, not making sense of it.

"What's this?" I asked.

"It's for the lot." She took the folder, placing it inside the nightstand again. "It's not ours yet, but if everything goes according to plan, it will be soon."

My heart thumped in my chest. Was I supposed to know what she was talking about? "What lot?"

She crooked her head to the side. "The wildflower lot by Poppies & Wheat? The one you wanted to replace with a greenhouse?"

"Oh!" I smacked a hand to my face. My cheeks flushed. I had been so out of it since returning from Vincent's. "You're going to expand?"

"No, sweetheart," she laughed. "Andrew and I both agreed that you need something for yourself."

I wiped my palms on my legs. "What does Andrew have to do with this?"

"I always thought that the greenhouse proposal was an interesting idea," she said, a smirk on her lips. I clenched my teeth together. That wasn't how I remembered it. She dropped her eyes, her chin quivering. "I'm sorry that it took me so long to realize it." She was apologizing too? Was I dreaming? "Even if it's owned by Andrew, it'll be yours, sweetheart."

My heart sank. Owned by Andrew? That was the catch.

"Can't I own it by myself?" I asked.

"At your age, with your lack of background? No, sweetheart, not yet. But eventually, he can transfer everything over once you two come to an agreement."

The room spun around me. I should have been grateful. Should have been jumping for joy. But Andrew had proved that my life was secondary to his career goals. Would he be fair when it came time to discuss something like transferring the business to me? And what about the 'conditions' he had asked my mother about before everything had happened?

"What about the marriage?" I asked. "The wedding? I don't want—"

"Oh, hush." She shook her head. "Don't worry about that right now. Let's focus on figuring out the bill of sale first." She squeezed my hands. "And I've got something else!" She pulled an object from her purse: a brand new smartphone.

A phone.

"I know, I know," my mother giggled, "I swore I'd never let you have a phone, but," her voice cracked, and she closed her eyes, holding back tears. When she opened them again, her eyes were glossy, but she was still smiling. "I talked to your father about it. He said that if you had a phone on you, we might have been able to track you better. Or at least see who you had been in contact with. But because you didn't have a phone, we didn't know where to start." The tears finally fell down her cheeks. I put my hands on her shoulders.

"Mom," I said quietly. "A cell phone wouldn't have saved me."

"I know," she sighed. "But what if it could have helped? What if it's my fault that you were gone for so long?"

The woman who had seemed like the anchor that held our small family down, seemed so frail right then. My throat ached seeing her like that.

"Please, Kora," she started again, "Forgive me." She forced

the tears down, then grabbed my hands, squeezing my fingers. "I realized maybe I can't control the world anymore. Maybe you need more ways to help yourself."

I wasn't sure what to say. She really believed that, but I knew that part of it may have been to protect herself from losing me again. But that didn't matter either. None of it mattered.

I hugged her.

"I love you," she murmured.

"I love you too, Mom."

She handed me my purse. "Call me when you get there."

"Of course."

I walked out of the room, gently closing the door behind me. And for the first time in my life, there was no one there besides me.

Punica was a small town, so I was able to ask the concierge how to walk to the police station. It was a sunny day and the warmth soothed me. I had missed it. For a second, I closed my eyes, letting the rays rest on my cheeks, thinking of Sarah, Bernie, and Ulysses barking at my feet. Then Vincent's gaze consuming me. I shook my head, pushing those thoughts away. I swallowed the pain in the back of my throat and forced myself to think of my mother, one of the only important people in my life. As screwed up as she might have been, she was obsessed with my safety. Even if it hurt her, she would always love and protect me.

But then my mind was back inside of Vincent's studio, surrounded by those paintings of *me*. My body tangled in rope. Bowing before him. Lying on my back, my hands folded on my stomach, ready for a casket.

He was like that too, wasn't he? *Obsessed with me.* Maybe I wasn't safe with him like I was with my mother, but I was still alive.

But was that love? I wasn't sure anymore.

The clerk told me the sheriff would be right out. And because the clerk was on the phone with her head buried in the computer, no one noticed when I walked past the front desk. I cautiously made my way toward that hallway for the holding cells. I don't know why. I hadn't planned to see him, just my father.

"You're already bored with your ivory tower?" Vincent asked, his voice loud and aggressive. His eyes were sunken, his skin oily. "But you're too scared to let go of your easy little life." He shook his head, disgusted with me. "You're weak."

I came closer, drawn to him. Those words meant nothing. And yet, a part of me knew that what he said was true. I was closer than I had ever been to getting what I thought I wanted. I was supposed to be content.

But he was right. I felt empty. Weak.

His lips turned. "You're happy with being numb. Never going after anything you want."

I shook my head. Even after everything he had done, he had the nerve to ridicule me. When he was the one who deserved cruelty.

But there was so much that he didn't know about me. And I wasn't going to give him the satisfaction of why I was there. Not yet. I stared into his dark eyes.

"You're wrong about me," I said.

He blinked, and I put my hands on the bars, looking up at him, unafraid. He opened his mouth to speak.

"There you are!" my father shouted. "Is he giving you trouble?"

As I whipped around to face Sheriff Mike, my ring knocked into the metal, the loud bang vibrating through me. I flushed with heat and forced myself to smile.

"It's fine, Dad," I said. "Really."

"Good," Sheriff Mike said. He patted my shoulder, bringing me out of the hallway. Vincent's glare seared into my back. "I'm glad you're smiling again," he said. My mouth was awkward and unnatural, but I smiled anyway because that's what was expected of me. He needed me to be strong, like his image. "Now, I know you came all the way down here, but I've got a matter to take care of for the campaign. Perhaps we can talk later?" he said. "Make an appointment?"

At least he was brushing me off in a nice way for once. A few of the officers were looking at us. He couldn't be his usual self. I rubbed my ring, staring at the black gem. I was having trouble remembering why I wanted to help Vincent in the first place.

"Sure," I said. "That's fine."

Chapter 27

Kora

The next day, my mother wanted to start touring rental houses. If we were lucky, the construction repairs on our home would be done in a few months, though it was likely that it would take much longer. Most of the damage was so bad that they would have to start from scratch. Insurance was paying for the hotel for the time being, but now that I was back in the picture, my mother was ready to talk about a long-term arrangement.

"What do you think?" she asked. She pointed at the yellow front door of a rental house. A white picket fence surrounded the yard with butterfly decorations on the front porch. A dragonfly darted across the turf, zipping by to another yard with green grass. Everything about the rental house was manufactured. The green plastic grass blades would never need to be watered. There wasn't a garden in sight. Even the insects were metal decorations. But a dry spot of grass would never disappoint the people who moved in there. It symbolized the perfect family.

"It's beautiful," I said, my voice drifting away.

"I knew you'd like it," she said, her smile beaming. I grit my teeth, but I wasn't going to argue. It was three bedrooms and the price seemed fair. It would do.

In the car, I looked out the window. Flags decorated driveways. A child hopscotched on the sidewalk. We were in Rose

Garden Neighborhood, the same community as our house, but the other two rentals were in different areas. I didn't want to see them. My energy was gone.

"What is it?" Shea asked. "You're quieter than usual."

I spun my ring around my finger. "I'm just tired."

"As you should be." She spun the wheel, taking the next turn. "You've been through a lot lately. I'm not surprised that you're exhausted."

I kept my head forward but gave her a sidelong glance, unsure of how to take her words. She had been kinder than usual lately. I hated that the fear of my death had inspired her to be more tender, but in the end, this was just how things were now.

"Cheer up," Shea said. Ah, there it was. My hands fidgeted, spinning that ring like a top. "How about this: whatever place *you* like best, we'll live there?"

I blinked. Was she serious? As in, *I* would have the final say? "Really?"

"Of course, sweetheart."

A slight burst of energy cracked through me. "Okay," I said. "That'd be nice." After a few seconds went by, I blurted out, "Why don't we pick that first one, then?"

"Oh?"

"You liked it. I liked it." It was almost the truth. I just didn't want to deal with it anymore.

"Sure," she said, her eyes forward.

An uneasy silence sifted between us. Each day brought me more autonomy, which should have comforted me, but nothing felt right. How was it that I felt more like myself with Vincent, than I did with my mother?

I pictured him in that lonely cell, his eyes dark and malevolent. No matter what had happened, no matter the crimes I *knew* he had committed, I knew Vincent wasn't the Echo Killer. And I needed to do something to make it right. Even if that meant making my parents upset.

As we turned onto the main street, I sat up and faced Shea.

"I need to talk to Sheriff Mike," I said. "*Now.*"

"We can head to the station," she said.

"Alone."

The engine rumbled, and Shea's eyes flashed with anger before returning to her cold kindness. Did she think I was hiding something from her?

"Of course," she said, her voice dry.

I wiggled my fingers, trying to stay strong in my convictions. I needed to do this; it was the only way to make things right. We pulled into the parking space, and she grabbed her sunglasses from the overhead console.

"Oh, and Kora?" she asked. "Before you go. I set up a coffee and tea date with Andrew at Nectar Latte. You know, like we used to…"

She trailed off, saving me from the words, but I knew what she meant.

Like we had done with Nyla.

"Awesome," I said, sarcasm zipping through my tone.

She crossed her arms. "You like Nectar Latte." She looked down her nose at me. "Andrew is one of your oldest friends. He's a very good catch."

She must have had no idea that Andrew had known where I was long before my father had 'found' me. I got out of the car, but before I closed the door, I leaned down.

"Really," I said, trying to seem as genuine as possible, "It'll be great to do something normal for once." That sounded right. It's something I should have been saying. It was something my mother probably wanted to hear. "I can't wait."

"Good."

As I made my way toward the entrance to the police station, I listened for the shifts in the engine to signal that Shea was leaving, but the car idled in the parking space, waiting for my return. I didn't look back. Her glare seared through those thick sunglasses, boring into me. Raging at me for keeping this from her. Angry at herself for letting me.

I held my fists at my sides, then stepped forward and opened the door to the station. Immediately, Sheriff Mike saw me and brought me into his office.

"That's right. We had an appointment today, didn't we?" he

said. "What can I do for you, Kora? Did you remember anything about your abduction?"

Even if we were blood, it was always business with him. He was a man of the law, and he liked it that way. At one time, I had thought that it was part of what made him a good person. Something to admire. But after I realized how little he actually cared for me and my mother, I stopped trying. The abduction emphasized that. I had disappeared, and yet there was no concern for me, now that I was here. I simply existed. A citizen to protect.

"About that," I said, "I need to ask you for a favor." I straightened, and he raised his brows. There was no easy way to put this, so I said it as plainly as I could: "I need you to let Vincent Erickson go."

Sheriff Mike laughed, his chest rippling with amusement. "Let him go? Are you kidding me?"

"He didn't kill those people," I said as confidently as I could. "He didn't kill Nyla." Everything inside of me was hot; I *had* to do this. I couldn't let go now. "I'm dropping the charges. There's absolutely no reason to keep him here."

"He kidnapped you," my father said.

"I told you: he was rescuing me."

"From a fire that *he* started."

"Do you have any proof that Vincent started the fire?" My father tilted his head in silence. I knew the answer. "Then why is he still here?"

"The people of Punica feel safer when he's behind bars."

"But will they actually be any safer?" I crossed my arms. Nerves fluttered in my chest, throbbing with my heartbeat, but I stayed strong. "You and I both know that the real Echo Killer is out there. And you're not using the taxpayers' resources to find the actual criminal."

He sucked in a long breath. "I see what you're saying, but I can't change what's been done. Vincent chose his path; now he has to see where it leads."

He had chosen a path that led to me. And whether or not that was a good thing was still to be decided.

By me.

And I needed to see where that path would lead me too. I was done living like this. Vincent might have had some flaws, but he didn't deserve to take the fall for crimes he hadn't committed. It killed me to think of him like that.

And then, rebellion took hold of me. Like Vincent was there, supporting me. I knew exactly what to say.

"What about your campaign?" I asked. Mike lowered his chin, his eyes narrowed. "I'm sure it wouldn't look good to your supporters if your own daughter went and told the press that you were *lying* in order to get their votes." I shrugged as nonchalantly as possible, though my mind was reeling: *What are you doing? Blackmailing a sheriff? Your own father? Are you crazy?!* But I had to get Vincent out of there. Then, we would be equal. Then, I wouldn't have this anxiety gnawing at my stomach constantly. Besides, what I was doing was minimal compared to what my father was doing to him. At least, that's what I told myself. I continued on: "What kind of sheriff lies to his own people?" I cocked my head to the side, my heart beating rapidly. "Only a corrupt sheriff."

"Kora," Sheriff Mike said. He flexed his arms at his sides. "You don't know what you're saying."

And maybe he was right, but I couldn't stop myself.

"Put him in jail for something he actually did," I argued, "Something that you actually have proof of. I'm fine with that." Mike furrowed his brows. "But this? The Echo Killer is out there, Dad. And you need to find the *real* murderer. Or I *will* go to the press."

Sheriff Mike scrutinized me. My heart thumped in my chest. Then he drummed his feet against the floor. A weak smile covered his face.

"On one condition," he said. His smile transformed into a wide grin, and my gut sank, knowing that his next words would be hard to swallow. "You have to accept the situation with Shea and me. However your mother deems fit, now, and forever." *Forever?* What was he talking about exactly? "That means being the obedient daughter we raised you to be. Being happy with your life. You are the florist's daughter, and you will take over the shop like Shea wants you to."

215

"But the greenhouse—" I started.

"Forget the greenhouse. You will no longer create problems for her, or for me." I shrunk down, but his words grew louder: "And if you so much as step out of line, Erickson goes back to jail. I don't care what he did or didn't do. You understand me?"

My cheeks flushed red. What was I supposed to do?

He smiled to himself. "And you'll start by going on a date with Andrew."

My breath caught in my throat. Andrew was like my father and mother combined, concerned with his appearance, his image, about what it meant to be a good citizen. He was the kind of man I *should* have wanted. But nothing about him seemed authentic.

And if I agreed to all of this, I would never be myself. But maybe I deserved it. If I had been as strong as Vincent thought I was, if I had spoken up that day at the funeral home while Vincent was being arrested, when that older couple was there to witness everything, maybe Vincent wouldn't be in this mess right now.

Instead, I had locked up inside of myself.

I had to do this, then. Even if it meant giving everything up.

"If you arrest him, or if *any* of your men do anything to him," I said quietly, "then the deal is off."

"Make sure he doesn't do anything illegal, then." He folded his fingers. "And not a word of this to anyone, including Vincent, or I will end you." He rested his elbows on the desk. "Are we clear?"

My heart dropped to my feet. "Yes."

"Do we have a deal, then?"

I lowered my eyes. "All right," I whispered. "We have a deal."

He held out his hand, and I shook it, my stomach sinking. "Now wipe that look off of your face and smile." I cleared my throat and obeyed. I forced out the biggest smile I could manage, like Shea taught me, nausea twisting through my gut. *Don't vomit. Don't vomit. Don't vomit,* I thought. *Don't feel. It's nothing. You feel nothing.* Sheriff Mike patted me on the back, and I stiffened. "You drive a hard bargain, Kora. I'm proud of that."

He had nothing to do with that quality. Vincent had shown

me that I needed to fight for what I wanted, and I couldn't let it go anymore. I owed Vincent that. My father straightened his button-up shirt. I gazed at the hallway leading to the holding cells.

"Can I talk to him?" I asked.

"Hell, we can let him out now."

My father was stopped by another officer, but I hurried on, trying to get to the cells before he did. I wanted a minute alone with Vincent. My stomach clenched, my muscles twitching, my mouth dry. I wanted to see Vincent, but I dreaded it too.

Inside the jail, the air seemed colder. Vincent's dark eyes seared into me, full of hatred.

"They're letting you go," I said. "My father will be here in a few minutes."

"Did that piece of shit finally realize he doesn't have anything on me?"

I crossed my arms. I hated dealing with him like this. "Can't you be happy that he's letting you go?"

"I suppose I should be grateful," he said. He leaned back, looking down his nose at me. "All my thanks to the Nova Family," he muttered. "Especially the little princess who can't do anything unless her parents give her permission."

My heart ached. He was hurt; that's why he was saying things like that.

"I know things didn't end well with your arrest," I said, "but I wanted to say goodbye." His face twisted. "You were—" I was at a loss for words, but there was no other way to put it. "You were good to me. I know that. But I have to move on. And that means doing what's right for my family." *For you*, I thought.

The seconds ticked by. Vincent let out a drawn-out breath.

"You come here to tell me that I'm free, then you end things like I'm a piece of trash you need to throw away?" He gave a dark laugh. "Now that you have your perfect life back, you can wave goodbye to everything you don't need." He pinched his brows together. "Let me tell you something, princess. There's nothing to say goodbye to."

Those words struck me, filling my chest with heaviness. "Vincent," I whispered. "I—"

"You already said your goodbyes the day you let them take me." The rage pooled behind his eyes and I forced the tears away. Did he hate me already, then?

"I'm sorry," I said.

He sneered. "If you're sorry, then go to the grave."

"What?"

"Yours." His eyes burned a hole right through me. "*Ours*," he added in a quiet voice.

I didn't know what to say. It was *ours*, the plot he had picked for me.

But I had to do what was right. And that meant letting go.

"I can't," I whispered.

He threw his chin to the side. "Fine," he said. "Go on. Live your life. Arrange your flowers. Decay in a house with a white fence that you look past and wonder why nothing ever feels like it did when we were together. Why you're so damn numb now. And you can go fuck yourself while you're at it."

My stomach hardened. How could he dismiss me like that? It wasn't like it was easy to let go, and yet he still had so much hatred inside of him. Hatred for me. My shoulders sank, but I stopped myself. This time, I forced myself to feel it. To understand that this anger was justified. Vincent *was* ungrateful. He had hurt me, and I had hurt him too, but I had gotten his freedom anyway.

But I didn't have to stand for this kind of treatment anymore. Neither did he.

"You have a second chance," I said, my voice stern. I lifted my head, my face heated with fury. His nostrils flared. I locked eyes with him. "You need to let go," I moved my hand between us, "of this hatred you have for me. This jealousy you have of my family." I leaned in closer. "No one is perfect. Not us. Not me. Not even you. Focus on your art. Follow your passion. Do something good with your life."

"That's easy for you, isn't it? All you have to do is smile pretty for your mommy and daddy and then everything falls into place like they told you it would."

Tears blurred my vision, but I wasn't going to let his words get to me.

"Goodbye, Vincent."

I turned, walking away. He laughed loudly. "Go back to your tower, princess. I'm sure your queen needs you," he laughed.

I couldn't take it anymore. Screw being the better person. I snapped back around.

"You have no idea about anything, do you?" I hissed. I sneered at him, jutting my body forward. His eyes widened. "You're so stuck inside of yourself that you don't see that I'm fighting for you." I turned to leave, but Vincent grabbed my shoulders, bringing me to the edge of the bars so that my face smashed into the metal, and he pressed our lips together. My heartbeat rattled through my body, my knees shaking, and he bit my lips as I trembled, pressing harder into my mouth, forcing me to endure his pain.

"Kora!" my father's deep voice barked down the hallway. "The hell are you doing?"

The sheriff raced toward us and Vincent immediately broke apart. Sheriff Mike shoved me away and I stumbled backward, catching myself on the wall. I wiped my lip; a drop of blood smeared my palm.

"Don't you dare lay a hand on my daughter!" my father yelled.

Vincent glared at me. Heat intensified in my lower belly, swelling into a dull ache. Mike kept shouting as more officers came, and Vincent lifted his chin, leaning against the bars, waiting for me to say something. *Anything*.

"What did he do to you?" Sheriff Mike said.

As I stared at Vincent, the weight lifted from my shoulders. I knew what would hurt him the most.

"He did nothing," I said. "Nothing at all."

Chapter 28

Vincent

By the time I was released, a headache riled through me. I needed a shower. Sarah swirled around my legs while Bernie leaped over to snatch a slobbery tennis ball, dropping it at my feet. Ulysses immediately grabbed it. I unlocked the door, going into the house.

"Yes, yes, yes," I said. "Has Catie been taking good care of you?" Sarah barked in response. A warmth flickered through me, but it dissipated quickly. My three housemates were with me again, but the house seemed bigger. Empty. Different from before.

The door to the basement was locked, but I found the key under the floorboard in the studio. The room was stale, and though her things had been scattered about before my arrest, they were gone now. Like she had never been there.

I stared at the icon for the tracking app on my phone. Then I turned off the screen. I couldn't keep doing that.

After I took a shower, exhaustion settled on my shoulders as I studied the closet, the sour scent of an unused home enveloping me. I pulled out a black button-up shirt and jeans. It's not like I had many choices.

It's not like Kora had a choice.

I shook my head and closed the buttons. The point was that

she *did* have a choice, and she had chosen to be silent when I needed her.

At least the sheriff had realized he didn't have any evidence on me.

I sighed deeply, then checked the mirror. The circles around my eyes seemed darker than before, the creases deeper too. As if a man could age a whole decade in a few days. As if betrayal that deep could ruin you.

I went through the front door, telling the dogs to stay behind. I wanted to be by myself. I didn't deserve their company. A light was on inside of the funeral home; Lee had probably left the light on in her office again. I'd turn it off later.

I sat down in the grass next to her grave. The smooth edges had frayed, a few clumps down at the bottom, likely from insects or other creatures wriggling around in the earth. My shovel was somewhere close by, but my legs and arms were unwieldy. I didn't want to move. If I let myself go back to work, I would get lost in digging graves, in fixing them, only for the sunrise to burn my skin, and to finally understand that she would never come.

So I stayed there, stuck in place. I ran my fingers over her headstone, remembering how the sunlight glowed around her as she bent down to pick up that daffodil in the flower field on Mount Punica. The stars flickered in the dark sky above me, and the cicadas called out their mating cry. The rotten scent of the volcanic fissures mixed with the floral perfume of the cemetery. I ran my palm over my nose; I rarely noticed the vents anymore, but I hadn't been here for a while.

I knew she wasn't coming. Why did I even want to see her?

A figure came toward me. I ignored it, knowing it was too tall to be her, and grabbed my shovel, heading back to the empty grave. Catie came into view, tilting her head at me.

"I thought I saw you out here," she said. I glanced over at the funeral home; the light was off now. So it was Catie then, not Lee.

"Why were you working late?" I asked.

"Boss is out of town. Had to cover for him."

I scowled, a huff of air escaping my lips. "Sounds like an ass,"

I muttered. But then I nodded to her. "Thanks." I slid the ladder into the hole.

"You're welcome," she said. "So you got out, then?"

I hated small talk. "Seems that way."

"You break out? Make a deal with Mike?" Her eyebrows scrunched together. "Oh! Was it a deal with Andrew?"

Why would Andrew help me? I jumped down into the grave, then grabbed a clump from the bottom, carefully placing it in the hole it came from, then smoothed it with the back of the shovel.

"So?" she asked.

"You have to have every detail?"

"Seeing as I'm one of your only friends, yeah, I do."

'Friend' wasn't accurate. Friendship implied that you *wanted* to be around the person, even when you weren't required to. Catie was more like family, a sister; I respected her and tolerated her presence when I had to.

But even I could admit that 'family' meant telling her *something*.

"Not enough evidence," I said. "But I saw Kora."

"Yeah? That's strange."

"Why?"

"Her mother keeps letting her out." She lifted her shoulders. "She said that she wanted to try a different parenting tactic. I guess she thinks more independence will show Kora how wrong the world is? Reverse-psychology or something?"

It didn't matter what Shea's reasons were, because the fact was that I was here, and Kora was not. She belonged in that grave. We both did.

"You better start work tomorrow," she grumbled. "I don't mind most of it. I'm not good at embalming, but I'll do it."

"Then what is it?"

"The new coroner is an asshole," she said. "Oh. My bad. *Medical examiner.*"

I laughed. She had called me that too when we first met, but that was years ago now. And this was different. There was a hint of amusement glimmering in her eyes. I tilted my head.

"I don't have the patience to tolerate him," she said.

"Fair enough."

A beat of silence passed between us. I resumed my work, fixing the walls of the site. Catie shifted her weight from one foot to the other.

"'My Flower,'" Catie read. "I've always wondered who that was for." I climbed up the ladder. "What are you doing out here, anyway?"

I shrugged. "Working."

"But you were sitting."

I pulled the ladder up and collapsed it, leaning it against a tree.

"The dogs aren't even here," she added.

She was persistent. I rubbed the back of my neck.

"I was waiting," I said.

"For?"

"Does it matter?"

"You're waiting out here, *alone*, mind you, for *something*. You just got out of jail. And you saw Kora, the woman you were keeping in your basement, right before you were released." She wrinkled her nose. "You can explain why you're moping."

I stomped through the grass. "I'm not moping," I muttered.

"Careful," she said. "You're moping is about to wake the dead."

Why I had insisted on digging Kora a burial plot when I had always planned to cremate her anyway, was lost on me. It was the act of it, I suppose. Knowing that her future lay in my domain. That she would be trapped with me here forever, without a way to leave this place behind.

We made our way to the mausoleum, and I kept my head low, trying to understand it myself. "I was waiting for Kora," I said.

For once, Catie fell silent. I took a seat on the marble bench. She sat down next to me. Her fingers flinched. She was trying to find the right words to say.

"I understand that you're hurt," she finally said.

I wasn't hurt. I was angry. I scoffed under my breath, and she rolled her eyes.

"All right, fine. You're not 'hurt,' but you are sulking."

"Are you trivializing my feelings?" I asked.

"So you *are* hurt!" She smacked my arm. "I knew it."

"You don't know shit," I said, my tone angrier than I had meant it to be. "You don't know what happened between us."

Her eyes bounced back and forth across my face, trying to get a good read on me. But I gave her nothing.

"You're right," she said. "I have no idea what you and Kora were doing together. But you've got to pull yourself together. Waiting for her to declare her love for you isn't going to happen. She's got her family now."

Behind the mausoleum, there was an empty field that would hold families one day. Like the Novas. For a moment, a bright flash of a vision filled my mind: that area filled with trees. Burial trees, like Kora had suggested.

I rubbed my forehead. She was still on my mind, even now, when I knew it was over.

"Where's the friendliness you use with the guests?" I asked, focusing my annoyance on Catie. "Do you save all of your mood-killing ammunition for me?"

"Only when you need it." She smiled. "Seriously, Vincent. She's not going to come crawling back to you."

And even though Catie was right, everything tensed inside of me.

I wasn't going to leave it up to Kora, then.

"Go home," I said. I motioned toward the funeral home. "I've got it from here."

"Got what?" She threw an arm around us. "From what I can see, you haven't got a thing to—"

"Go home, Catie," I said, more firmly this time. She blinked, trying to read me.

"Okay." She got up from the bench, then glanced to the sides. "I guess I'll see you tomorrow?" A hint of worry lingered in her voice.

"Yeah," I said. "Sure."

She walked through the cemetery back to the funeral home, where she went around to the front, finding her car. My body tensed, my blood pounding in my ears.

I opened the tracking app on my phone. A red dot flashed on

the screen in a familiar area: Rose Garden Neighborhood. I smiled to myself. It was amusing that she wouldn't move that far, even after everything that had happened. Almost like she was waiting for me.

Calmness washed over me as I turned on the engine to my car. It was like falling back into a familiar pattern, one that I looked forward to.

But this time, it would be different.

A few blocks away from the old house, the tracking app led me to a rental. Everything was fake, from the grass to the plastic fence. A perfection that only a woman like Shea Nova could appreciate.

Kora may not have gone to the grave, but if I knew Kora—if I knew anything about her—she would be on the bottom floor again.

And her window would be open for me.

I went around the side of the house, lifting the latch for the fence, then entered the back. A sliding glass door led to the living room and an empty kitchen. And to the side, another small door was closed. Next to it, an open window.

I peeked inside, seeing the hill of her hips as she faced the wall like before. A babydoll clung to her body, just like that first night. Heat crept through me. I wanted to hold her close to my chest, to never let her go, but I also wanted to wrap my hands around her throat, twisting until her neck snapped. How could she be so naïve to think that everything would be fine after what I had done to her? She would never be the same. She would be unhappy, and if that's what she wanted, then maybe she deserved to die.

The words pulsed inside of me. My lips curled and my nostrils flared. It's what I should have done the first time.

I removed the screen, then quickly hopped inside. Kora immediately stirred. I didn't care if she knew I was coming.

"Vincent?" she asked. "What are you doing? You can't—"

I pressed a hand to her mouth, pinching her nose shut. Her eyes widened, focused on me. She fell silent. I removed my hand.

"I won't let you do this to yourself," I said.

I climbed out of the window, holding her against my chest, my body raging with need and brimming with fire. The need to save her from herself. The desperate fiery urge to burn her to ashes.

I put her in the backseat of my car. "Lie down," I ordered.

"If my mother finds out, she will kill you," she said. "And if she doesn't, my father will put you back in jail. For good, this time."

I started the engine and drove. None of that mattered anymore. Not to me.

And soon, it wouldn't matter to her either.

Once we parked, I pulled her out of the backseat, holding her in my arms once again. It wasn't lost on me—carrying her like a damsel in distress—but Kora was no damsel, and she was far from a maiden. I had made sure of that.

But still, she loved looking like that was all she would ever be.

She was silent, letting me do as I pleased, but when she saw her grave coming into view, her body tensed.

"What are you doing?" she whispered.

I put her bare feet on the ground, letting her find her balance.

"Get in the grave," I said.

"No."

I cracked my neck to each side. Neither of us had time for this game anymore. I lunged for her shoulders, and she dashed off, immediately tripping over a shovel lying in her path. Her chin landed on the ground with a hard thud, and I pinned her against the grass, putting her wrists behind her back, quickly binding her limbs with the cable ties in my pockets. I carried her again, this time like a piece of luggage, ready to be tossed away.

I threw her down into the burial plot. She thrashed around.

"You don't want to do this," she whimpered. "I know you, Vincent. This isn't actually you."

"You don't know anything about me," I murmured. My whole body tightened. I tossed the ladder into the hole, then jumped down with her, my legs straddling either side of her hips, immobilizing her. I covered her mouth and nose, restricting her air, but this time, she didn't move. Her eyes were glued to me, holding still. Like none of this mattered to her anymore. Like she expected this from me. Like she would stop too.

A single tear ran down the side of her face.

I removed my hands. Her breathing returned, steady and calm. Why wasn't she afraid of me anymore?

"Vincent," she whispered.

I grabbed her throat, and finally, her bottom lip trembled, and I pressed against her, devouring her mouth like I wanted, because if this was it, if I was finally going to do it, then I was going to do whatever the hell I wanted with her. I shoved a hand into her panties and she whimpered, but her pussy lips were drenched, and I moaned, breaking from that kiss to throw my head back. I fingered her hard and rough, shoving in one finger, then another, and another, not waiting for her to get comfortable. I wanted her to feel used. The bitch writhed on my hand, bucking her hips forward, her hands bound behind her back, digging into the dirt. Another finger. My hand pressed together like a cone, stretching her out. Her muscles clenched around me and I shoved my mouth onto her again, staring into her eyes, begging her to understand why I needed this. Why I needed to have her. Why I couldn't shove my dick inside of her. Because if I did, I knew that would be the last of my resolve. I'd give it all up for her.

She jerked to the side, gasping for air. I growled under my breath.

"We're supposed to meet Andrew in the morning," she said, her voice shaking.

My heart stopped. "Andrew?"

"My parents want me to date him," she stammered. "And if I'm not ready, my mother will figure it out. She *will* find us." She shook the loose hairs from her eyes. *Us?* "And when that happens, I won't be able to help you this time."

I exhaled sharply. What was she talking about? "Help me?" I asked.

She nodded, and I stopped. That was how I had gotten out of jail, wasn't it? Because of Kora. Because she had been there, right before her father released me.

I had been too full of anger to see it.

"Let me go," she whispered. "I still have enough time to get home before my mother finds out. But if I don't, my father will put you back in jail. It's part of the deal." She gritted her teeth together, chattering. "Please, Vincent. Don't let this go to waste."

The stars and the moon sparkled like white beads in her eyes. No one had asked her to save me. She had done it for herself. Put herself in a predicament where she was still her parents' pawn, but at least I was free. I knew her mother would never physically hurt Kora, but I didn't trust the sheriff to protect her, especially not when it came to Andrew.

But this wasn't about me. It was always about Kora. I was just too blind to see it. And that meant forgetting about what I wanted for a second.

She wanted to go back. Everything inside of me vanished.

I climbed out of the pit. Numb to my core, I ran back to the house, the dogs following close behind me, and grabbed the canvas bag out of my closet. Once I was in the grave again, I cut her cable ties, and when she stood, rubbing her wrists, the sides of her body were covered in dirt. I dropped the canvas bag on the ground.

"Take it," I said. She pulled it closer, and when she looked inside, her lips quivered. "If I can't help you," I started to say, but then I stopped.

It had never been about helping her. But now it was.

I went up the ladder. She didn't follow me.

"Catie will pick you up," I said.

And then I left.

Chapter 29

Kora

In the car, I kept the canvas bag on my lap. Catie focused on the road. Traffic was quiet, as I assume it usually was at this hour. Dirt was caked into my fingernails.

What had just happened?

Vincent had taken me again, but this time, he had a look in his eyes like he was actually going to kill me. But then he gave me a gun. Was that protection from him?

We pulled into Rose Garden Neighborhood. As soon as the white fence came into view, my stomach turned. I would always be looking out from behind one fence or another. Vincent always seemed to know that, didn't he?

Catie and I waited for a moment. Finally, I opened the car door.

"You know you could come to me if you needed help, right?" she asked. "If your mom asks, you can say you snuck out with me."

"Thank you," I said.

She smiled. "Good luck."

I went around the side of the house like Vincent had. Everything was quiet. I had never thought I would sneak back *into* a house to pretend like I had never left. It was eerie and still.

I sat on my bed, then opened the canvas bag. The pistol was

small, but weighty, like a full vase. I put my hand around the grip. Had Vincent ever used it?

A chill ran through me. He thought I was in danger, then. Whether it was from him or from someone else, he wanted me to have this.

The floor creaked above me; my mother was coming down the stairs. I quickly wrapped the gun in the bag and shoved it under the bed.

The door swung open. Shea stood there in her pink robe, her arms wrapped around herself.

"You're here. Good," she said, still half-asleep. "I thought I heard something."

"No. Just me," I smiled, casually pushing my feet against the bag so that it went further under the bed. I crossed my fingers that she didn't have her contacts in, that she was too sleepy to see the dirt on my pajamas. "Are you okay, Mom?"

Her eyelids fluttered at the word 'Mom.' "Of course," she said. "As long as you are." She turned to leave, but then she swung back around to me. "Why are you awake?"

"Couldn't sleep." I grabbed a book off of my nightstand. "Reading."

Her eyes flicked over to the open window. "What happened to your screen?"

"I took it off." I chewed on my lip. "It reminds me more of home this way."

Her eyes filled with tears. She closed the door behind her and I let out a sigh.

Why had I covered for Vincent?

I laid on my back, zoning out at the blank ceiling. I imagined dried flowers were pinned to the walls, as if they were painted in shades of pastel and creams, like my old bedroom.

But when I closed my eyes, I dreamed of that room in Vincent's house, where every available space was taken up with flowers—synthetic, yes, but not dried or dead. Perpetually in bloom. We had been surrounded by everything fake, and yet he made it seem more real than anything I had ever experienced.

More real than this rental's turfed front lawn. More real than the dried flowers on my old bedroom walls.

Had the plants in my old bedroom window burned like the rest of the house? If the house hadn't burned, would Shea have watered them?

It was a stupid question about a past that wasn't real. All I had, right now, was the canvas bag, and Vincent's warning.

In the morning, the warm tea trickled down my throat. Everything inside of Nectar Latte was muffled and blurry, and I felt empty without that canvas bag in my arms, but I smiled anyway, like I was supposed to. Shea put her hand on my back, bringing me forward, closer to Andrew, and he tipped his imaginary hat and winked at me, then rubbed the back of his hand on my arm. I nodded, pretending to follow along, but instead, I thought about Vincent. Where was he now, *now* that he was free? Would I have to insist on wearing fireproof pajamas to bed? Would Vincent put me in that grave for good?

"What is it, sweetheart?" my mother asked. The grin on my mother's face was pressed against her lips, permanently there. Like she expected from me. Her hand dropped from my back, but Andrew continued to stroke my arm. I flinched away, but he inched closer.

I couldn't tell her the truth.

"I thought I saw someone," I lied. I widened my smile, showing my teeth. But Shea's eyes darted around the room.

"Who did you see?" she asked.

"Miss Kora and Miss Shea, you can rest assured that if you were in any danger, I would put your safety above my own," Andrew said, putting a hand up to his heart. I grit my teeth.

"Let's go," Shea said, pulling my arm toward the door. "We should head back to the shop anyway."

At Poppies & Wheat, the new seasonal worker, Nikki, wasn't the fastest learner, but she was dedicated to doing her job as perfectly as possible every time. At first, this made her five times slower, but by the end of the day, she had gotten the hang of it. And it was like nothing had changed. The same customers. The same windows to stare out of. The same dreams to let go of. Just now, Nyla was gone, and Nikki was here.

But there were some differences. Like going with my mother on errands. Part of me thought that she truly wanted to include me, and the other part knew that it might have been her fear, that if she left me alone at the shop, I would disappear again.

One of Shea's committees was meeting at the farmer's market downtown. Booths were set up on either side of us in turquoise tents. I zoned out, looking around, taken aback by the number of people. But one booth stopped me: black and white art hung inside, a few canvases displayed on easels. Still life. Mount Punica. A portrait of a man standing by the stream near the flower shop.

"We're hosting a competition auction," a man said. He lifted his baseball cap so we could make eye contact. "Whichever piece gets the highest bid wins a gift certificate to Art Supplies & More. Auction proceeds go to the organization, We Are One Family."

I glanced back at my mother. Her eyes flicked over to me, but she continued talking to the committee. I pulled the folded paper out of my pocket. For some reason, I had kept his painting with me, afraid that my mother would find it if I left it at the rental house. Would Vincent be mad if I entered his work?

Screw it. He wanted to protect me, and I wanted to do this for him.

The man handed me a submission card. "You want to enter?"

I filled it out quickly, leaving the artist's name blank. On the title, I wrote, *Her Ashes*. I hoped Vincent would understand. At least here, in a contest, it would go to a good home where my mother wouldn't find it.

"You don't want to leave your name and number?" he asked.

I shook my head, then joined my mother, politely smiling whenever she turned to me for input. After she finished her meeting, we walked side by side, back through the farmer's market. She never once glanced at the black and white art booth.

"There's a wildflower I was curious about adding to our seasonal bouquet," I said, as nonchalantly as I could manage. "I hear they have it on Mount Punica." Shea didn't say anything, so I continued on: "I was thinking we could look for it together."

"Oh?" She tilted her head. "Which flower?"

I paused, biting my lip. "The narcissus."

"A daffodil? We could have those delivered in perfect condition overnight if we wanted." She tossed her hair over her shoulders. "That would be a waste of time."

"It's a rare species," I muttered, but she must have known I was making it up now.

"I've never seen them on Mount Punica before."

"I have."

"Where?"

"Off of the Wild Berry Trailhead."

The realization crossed her face, twisting her nerves. She remembered who we had seen the last time we were there together.

"Why do you want to go there?" she asked.

"I told you. I want to see if they have a narcissus."

She shrugged her shoulders. "Let's go."

I perked up. "Really?"

She let out a small sigh. "I'd rather you not sneak out without me."

We were both quiet for a long time, the trees whooshing to the sides as we drove. We parked in our usual spot, then walked to the trail. She cautiously scanned the area.

"I heard they're in that grove," I said, pointing beyond her. "You check there, and I'll check the meadow?" I silently hoped she would give me as much freedom as she had been lately.

"All right," she said, her voice hesitant. "Don't talk to anyone you don't know."

The air was chilly, nipping at my bare neck. I wrapped my arms around myself, making my way toward the flower field. The bright petals shimmered in the light, and in the middle of that rainbow, the sunny daffodils sprouted up. There had only been one stem before, but now, there were more than I could count. I kneeled down, touching their stems, brushing my fingers along their petals. Even when we weren't together, he called to me through things like this.

A shadow appeared to the side, the presence like a magnet pulling at my skin. My cheeks flushed: Vincent stood between the trees, his eyes locked on mine. We stayed there for a while, both of us staring at each other, coming back to this place where we had once met. Knowing our memory lingered here.

"Kora!" Shea shouted. Vincent and I both startled. "I found a Middlemist Red. Come look!"

I turned back to Vincent, and he motioned in her direction. I got to my feet. "Coming," I said. I had to. If I didn't, she might find Vincent.

Deep green vines stretched across the path, the red flowers reaching around like a kaleidoscope. My heart skipped a beat. The Middlemist Red camellia. How long had it been here?

"I checked this place before," Shea said. "Last time we were here. And there was nothing." We both stared in awe. She shifted her weight. "Is it the mountain's soil?"

I turned back to see if Vincent was there, wanting to share this small moment of beauty. But the path was empty.

"I don't know," I said.

Chapter 30

Vincent

A few days passed in a blur of routine. When we finally had a day with no services scheduled, Catie asked for the time off, and since Lee was working remotely, that left me to manage the funeral home. Luckily, we rarely had walk-ins. I could hide in my office.

The entrance doors to the funeral home opened, the air pressure changed in my office. I finished the line in the spreadsheet, then leaned my ear toward the corridor.

"Vincent?" Kora asked, her voice wispy and full of trepidation. My jaw ticked, my body immediately going rigid. What was she doing here?

She awkwardly held a giant vase in her hands, full of pink, white, and yellow flowers, some in bloom and others still buds. "Where do I put this?" she asked.

I grabbed it from her, refusing to acknowledge the shiver that ran through her body when my hands skimmed hers. I put the vase into the empty viewing room in the back.

"For the Jeffersons tomorrow?" I asked.

"I think so."

I tilted my head. She didn't know?

"Well," I said, gesturing toward the door. "Your family must be waiting."

"You want me to leave?"

I pinched the bridge of my nose. "What do you want, Kora?"

"What do you mean?"

"You're still here," I gestured between us, "wasting my time."

"I came to drop off the bouquet."

"And you have." I crossed my arms. "Now, you can leave."

Her bottom lip quivered. She wanted to say something, but I didn't want to hear it. Didn't want to think about what it would mean if she said those words I longed to hear. Because I had saved her life, and she had saved mine. We were even. There was nothing more to say.

"I want to talk," she finally said, clenching her fists together at her sides. "I came here to talk to you."

"And your mother let you." I snickered, tilting my chin. "I hear she's lengthened the leash."

She scrunched her eyes shut, and when she opened them, she glared at me.

"You have no idea what you're talking about."

"Enlighten me."

Another moment passed, but then her shoulders sagged like she was tired of pretending. "Do you ever get the feeling like you're reliving the same day on repeat?" The windows let in diffuse light. Dust particles, little flakes of skin, hovered in the air. Decay was always around us, but especially around me. "I have more privileges. That's true. But it's always about what's acceptable. What my mother thinks is best. What's best for our image."

"I'm sure you're right at home, then."

"That's just it," she said. "I don't anymore. I miss—" She threw a hand around us. "I miss this. I miss the cemetery. The mausoleum. Playing with the dogs. Hanging out here. I miss everything." She wrapped her arms around herself. "But most of all, I miss you."

My heart pounded in my chest. Every muscle in my body tensed. Kora would be better off with her mother and father. They might not give her the life she wanted, but she would be safe. I could never guarantee that with me.

"The grass is always greener, isn't it?" I snickered, steering myself in a direction where I was angry that she could let it all go. For me. Someone who didn't deserve her in the first damned place. "Are you wondering what it would have been like if I had kept you in my cage forever?" I smirked, full of malice. "You're pathetic."

"I wish I hadn't done it."

The air squeezed from my lungs. My fingers twitched at my sides. "I don't care about what you *wish*. You did what you did. There's no changing that."

"But I'm trying," she said. "I'm trying to be there for you, even though it hurts." She shook her head. "Love is hard work. I understand that."

Love? I grit my teeth. How could she throw around a word like that? She didn't *love* me. She couldn't.

"What do you want, Kora?" I clenched my fists at my side, my tone angry. She didn't say anything, so I asked again, "What. Do. You. Want?" She looked down at her feet. All I wanted at that moment was an admission that she needed me too. But she couldn't say a thing. "Figures you can't answer for yourself," I muttered. Her shoulders sank, and I began to walk away. It was better to leave her like this, sinking down to a place where she didn't have to feel anything. Where she could make up her mind about me. Where she could move on. Without *me*. I reached for my office door.

"No," she said, her voice shaking. "You don't get to talk to me like that." I turned, staring at her. Her jaw clenched, her fingers twitching at her side. "I don't have to put up with this anymore," she said. "You, of all people, the one person I actually *like* talking to right now, *you* are better than this. If you see me—really see me, like you always claim you do—then you have to start treating me like I treat you. And I have been nothing but kind to you. *Yes*, I made a mistake. But so did you. I didn't speak up when I knew that you weren't the Echo Killer, but have you considered what *I* was going through?"

My gaze flicked to the ground. She raised her hands, her neck wiry with fury.

"You almost killed my mother. You burned down our house.

Why would it be *that* far off for me to consider that maybe you killed those people too? When I couldn't prove one way or another if you had, or hadn't?"

I balled my fists. "*You knew that I didn't,*" I bellowed. "You knew. Or you wouldn't have let me—"

I stopped. I didn't want to finish my thought. There was a fire inside of her that ignited passion inside of me. She might have been raised to be numb, to be the perfect image of innocence and light, but something had changed. She could feel things now.

And that made me want her even more.

"Let you do what, Vincent?" she asked.

I pictured her on the ground, bundled in a plastic cocoon, her mouth fogging against the thin sheet. She gasped in the air, twitching like an insect on its back. I imagined her lying down in that room, surrounded by fake flowers and vines and strings of lights. The sunlight on her skin as she spun in the grass, the scent of jasmine on her skin.

"Let you do what?" she said, louder this time. "Say it, Vincent!"

I stepped forward, coming to her. We were so close that I could see her heartbeat pulse beneath her skin. Her pupils dilated; her mouth opened. I grabbed her shoulders, pushing her down to her knees. She didn't stop me. Those big green eyes gazed up at me, waiting for my demands. The ripe scent of anticipation wafted between us. Her knees subtly moved, parting for me.

"Say what, flower?" I asked.

She bit her bottom lip, and my cock twitched. Her eyes flicked to my bulge. I grabbed a fistful of her hair, forcing her to look into my eyes. Our breaths were uneven, panting. Anyone could walk in and see us. They could run and tell her mother and father. We both knew we should stop, but neither of us wanted to.

"Say what?" I asked again, my voice quiet.

"You stole my innocence from me," she murmured. "Admit it."

"Oh, flower." I forced a finger under her chin. "We both know that you were never that innocent."

In a quick movement, I yanked her up and grabbed her by the ass, hoisting her so that she wrapped around me. A breath caught in her throat and I pushed her against the window, banging into the glass. I pressed my mouth to hers, forcing her to feel the torture. That I wanted her, but I knew that she would never be mine. She couldn't. She had told me that a flower would never grow if you hid it from the sunlight.

And I would always be forgotten in the shadows.

"Vincent," she trembled out. Her skirt pooled around her hips and I pulled her panties to the side. I dragged my fingers over her slit and a shudder rolled through me as my hands drenched with her desire. I growled into her neck. I couldn't do this to her. She didn't deserve it. She deserved more. Better.

But I wanted her and if this was our last chance, then I didn't fucking care. I wanted her to feel everything I had. I bit into her neck, digging in with my teeth. Her muscles snapped with tension underneath my canines, and she cried out. I carried her by her ass, making her wrap around me again, bringing her into the viewing room. There was no casket displayed on the bier, so I hoisted her hips onto it, then pushed her knees apart until she was spread before me. Her white cotton panties were soaked, see-through now that they were wet, and I ran my fingers over the fabric, the bumps of her hair, her swollen pink lips. I kneeled down, looking up at her. The light from the window in the ceiling cast a halo around her head, her eyes dark.

I pulled her panties swiftly off of her legs, then brought my mouth down, hungry, onto her beaded clit. I lapped and licked and tasted her, sucked in her fragrance, her primal need. She moaned loudly, calling to the empty chairs around us, as if each seat was full of ghostly followers ready to worship their queen.

My queen. My flower. My Kora.

I pressed a finger inside of her and she whimpered, grabbing the back of my head. My cock pulsed, desperate to be inside her, but I wanted her to understand what this was. Desire could consume you, ruin you, wreck you until you were nothing you thought you were, and she had done that to me, time and time again, until I was so broken that I couldn't think straight. Throwing her in a grave, displaying her on a bier: everything was about her. *Always her.* I stole her from her bedroom, kept her in a basement, locked her away, because she controlled me. I grabbed her wrists with one hand, holding them behind her lower back, and then, on my knees, I continued to lick and finger her. She twitched in my grasp, eager for her pleasure, but I held her wrists tighter, lapping her up.

No, my queen, I thought. *You don't get to control this. You may control me. You may control my entire world, but I decide when you come. I decide how this ends.*

I curled another finger inside, curving toward her center. I let go of her wrists but she kept them there, like a good girl. My good girl. I added another finger and she squirmed at the pressure, cringing at the width, and my cock twitched against my thigh, begging for release. But I pumped her harder, her juices running down her legs, drenching the bier. I brought my mouth down on her clit, flicking my tongue in circles around her, slowly, ever so slowly, until finally, her thighs quaked and she bucked—as if to say that this was too much, too much—but I shoved closer to her, pressing my fingers inside and sucking and licking deeper and deeper, until she erupted with a cry that was reckless, thrusting herself against me. My mouth was rapt with her clit, my fingers deep inside of her, enjoying every last second of her surrender, knowing that this would never last.

Once she had come down, her breathing still heavy, I stood back, admiring her. Her skin was blotchy, her eyes and lips wet, her pussy and legs tender and swollen, her makeup running. I shook my head in disgust. She was everything I wanted. Everything I could never have.

And no one would ever be worthy of Kora.

"You don't miss me," I said, hoping it hurt. Hoping it ripped her to shreds. Hoping that it tore her apart like it killed me. "You just like the way I make you feel. Sex will ruin you like that."

Her eyelids fluttered, but she was too weak to speak.

"I know these feelings are new to you," I said in a low voice,

"But never mistake lust for loyalty. They aren't the same, and they never will be."

I stepped away, pretending to type a text on my phone, while inside my heart was racing, my body pulsing, my mind screaming: *Stop her! Stop her now! Apologize, you damn idiot!* But I stayed where I was, dismissing her completely.

Finally, her footsteps clattered forward, and in my peripherals, she straightened herself. Checked her hair. Wiped her mouth. Straightened her skirt.

"You wanted this too," she said.

"I wanted to prove that you're driven by hormones, flower," I said, never lifting my eyes from my phone. "Nothing more."

"I entered your painting into a contest."

Finally, I stowed my phone and stared at her, blood pumping in my chest.

"What painting?"

"The one where I'm behind the window."

"Do you think that means something to me?" I gave a subtle grin. "You're nothing but a pretty face. Someone to paint." I threw a hand in the direction of the door. "I'll find another."

"I thought—" She tucked her hair behind her ear. "I thought that you would—"

"That by entering my art into some shitty contest, that everything would be okay?"

It might have been a nice gesture, but it did nothing for me. She just wanted me to be grateful. And I wasn't. I wouldn't let myself.

She clenched her jaw. "You care more about your art than you realize."

"And you care far too much about what other people think," I said. "Just like your mother." I turned away. "Stop thinking about other people," I let my tone come down to a mild, disinterested manner: "Stop obsessing over me."

Start thinking about yourself.

"If I'm obsessed," she said, her voice quivering, "then you are *consumed* by me."

"All I wanted—" I hated myself for these words, but I had to say them. Had to push her away. "All I wanted was to show you how easy it was for me to lick your pussy." I sneered in disgust. "I wanted to get you off. Virgins always turn into sluts for their first. You're just an easy fuck."

The tears hung in her eyes. Then she burst through the front doors, disappearing into the sunlight.

Chapter 31

Vincent

The next day, I drove to remove another Echo victim: a twenty-two-year-old, this time with long black hair, and green eyes, like Kora's, already flattening to discs. Her face was sprinkled with glass.

Andrew crossed his arms. "Where were you last night between eight and midnight?"

"At Quiet Meadows," I said.

"Can anyone vouch for you?"

Luckily, Lee had come in late to finish processing some invoices. "My bookkeeper."

"I'll have one of my team contact her." He lifted his chin in the air. "I hope it's airtight. Because I need one good reason. That's all it takes, and you're back in jail."

"Good luck with that." I pressed the trolley against the back of the truck until the retractable wheels collapsed underneath it.

Once the night hit, I went straight to 52 Peaks. Every emotion stirred inside of me, and I needed to do something, since sitting around always led my thoughts back to her, and I couldn't let myself do that anymore. Or maybe it was because I needed to know *who* was doing this so that I could make sure that Kora was never targeted.

The club was nearly empty. A few people danced in the

middle of the floor and each of the small, circular bars had a bartender, but none of them had any customers waiting for drinks. I took a seat at the first bar. The bartender put his cleaning rag underneath the countertop.

"What can I help you with?"

"I'm looking for someone," I said. "Mid-twenties. Wears a flat cap? He gave me something a while back."

"You mean Deacon?" he asked. That sounded right. I nodded. "Sorry, man. Echo Killer got him."

My jaw clenched. "Where is everyone getting the Echo then?" I muttered.

"Shut up, man," he said, his eyes widening. "You can't ask that out in the open."

"Who is giving it to them?" I asked again. "You?"

He scowled at me. "I wouldn't kill my own income."

It was the same sentiment that Deacon had used months ago, but now he was dead too. How long would Shea be able to keep Kora safe? I had to do something.

The fact that I had once considered teaming up with the Echo Killer made me see red. And for once, I was glad that Kora's mother was overprotective. As long as Shea could help it, Kora would never be one of those victims.

And I could take care of the Echo Killer myself.

A few cars were in the parking lot. I wasn't a detective, but I knew when something wasn't right, and at that moment, everything seemed calm. As if the Echo Killer was asleep.

In my car, I pulled onto the road, heading down the two-lane highway to Punica. The evergreen trees shadowed the asphalt. I blazed down, going seventy, when a raised truck with a camper top hit the gas, coming directly from a side road, pulling out in front of me. I slammed on the brakes, punching the horn. The truck's windows were tinted, country music blaring from the metal can, rattling the body.

I raised my fist at the driver. "Asshole," I muttered.

Once the truck had passed, I started driving again. I drove slower, letting the adrenaline course through me until I returned to normal. My thoughts drifted over Kora and that contest. What purpose did it serve her to enter my work? Especially since she knew I didn't care about that kind of stuff. But she had even come to tell me about it. To tell me she missed me, even if she didn't know what that meant. Kora trusted me more than I deserved, and that infuriated me. That she *believed* in me. More than I believed in myself. She was either stupid or a fucking blessing.

I shifted my hands on the steering wheel. Her voice rang in my head: *You have to start treating me like I treat you.* And she was right. I needed to do better. I needed to get my shit together. To stop throwing myself a pity party because the woman I loved deserved better than me.

Loved.

I loved her, didn't I?

I hated that. What did it mean to love Kora when she had *left* me, only to come back to fix everything she could?

Two headlights appeared in the rearview mirror, the high beams bright. I flicked the angle, then leaned to the side mirror. It was that same truck: the raised wheels, the faded yellow and white paint, the same loud country music. I couldn't see the driver through the tinted windows.

I lowered my window and motioned for the truck to go around me. Guitar blasted from the speakers as the car sped up, and laughter trickled over the music. The truck rammed into the back of my car, lurching it forward.

"The fuck?" I yelled. My blood boiled. I sped up as much as I could, but the truck raced along with me. I whipped my car around, nearly rolling it in the process, barreling down the other side of the road, but the truck did the same. Who was this person and why were they chasing me?

I flipped around again, speeding up as quickly as possible, and when I was sure I had a good distance, I slowed down, flipping around again. But the truck sped up, his engine revving, and as the headlights neared, I knew it was over.

The metal crunched and hurled my car forward into a tree. The glass shattered. The airbag deployed, knocking the wind out of me. A bassy voice from the truck's radio echoed through the night. My whole body pulsed with adrenaline and pain shot through my bones. My head pounded. I punched at the airbag, making it deflate, then I fumbled for the dashboard. I kept a handgun in there. My head throbbed, my balance off; I couldn't seem to pull open the glove box.

The truck's door opened, and two feet crunched on the asphalt. Finally, I unlocked my seatbelt and leaned over, grabbing the handle for the glove box. The shadow appeared in the side mirror.

I leaned over to grab the gun, but as I pulled back the hammer, I remembered the gun wasn't loaded. The bullets were locked in a small case in the back of the glove box, but sometimes I moved them. Where were they now? I grabbed my phone, dialing emergency services.

"Nine-one-one operator. What's your emergency?"

"Sheriff Mike," I said. "Get Mike to Willow Highway."

"Sir?"

"There's been attempted murder," I said. The footsteps came closer. "Someone attacked me with their car. A truck—"

A fist landed on the back of my head. I dropped the phone to the ground.

"Hello? Sir?" the operator said. "Are you there?"

The truck driver cracked his knuckles. "Erickson," a familiar voice said. I turned around, holding my forehead. Luminescent white hair flared around the sides of his face.

"You're back at the crime scene," Andrew said. "The murderer always returns. It's textbook, really."

I scowled at him. "You're back here too."

"Now," he started again, ignoring me, "they won't find Echo in your system." He dropped a plastic baggie full of green powder on my car. "But they will find it on you. And a drunk driver is still driving under the influence, according to the law."

I hadn't taken a single sip. "No one is going to be fooled by this," I said.

Andrew chuckled. "They don't have to be."

A crowbar smacked into my side, knocking me down into the seat. As he bashed me with the metal bar, I hid the unloaded gun under my arms, waiting for the right moment to use it like a hammer. He took an ice pick from his back pocket, raising it up.

"Guess I'll have to find a new fuckup to blame these deaths on," he said. And right as he went to puncture my chest with the ice pick, I smacked the back of my gun into his hand, knocking the tool out of his grip, then I quickly brought the gun down on his nose. He ripped away, clutching his palm to his chest, cursing to himself, and I fumbled through the glove box. Where were the bullets?

Sirens blared in the distance like a soft chorus. Andrew glanced at the noise, then turned back to me. "Nice one, Erickson," he said. Then he rammed the crowbar into my head, and my world turned black.

Chapter 32

Kora

In the morning, Nikki stumbled with the bleach on the back patio, while I cut ribbons for a slew of back orders in the storeroom. The phone rang, and Nikki ran to it.

"I can get that," I said.

"I will," she said, with a big smile on her face. She took the message and then went back to her task. If a woman came in, she let me handle the sales, but if it was a man? She nonchalantly closed the door to the storeroom, pretending like she didn't know what she was doing.

My mother must have instructed her on that before she left. It had been like that since we had opened. Shea must have been having second thoughts about giving me more 'responsibility.'

A shadow flickered in front of the windows. I leaned past the doorway to see a woman in a black blazer with a magenta scarf fixed around her neck, the sides of her head shaved. Catie. Before Nikki could lock me in that room, I burst through the door and ran toward Catie, throwing my arms around her.

"Wow," Catie said. "You *are* alive. I've been trying to call you all morning."

"Our phones have been busy," I said.

"Yeah, and your new girl kept telling me you were unavailable." Catie gave her a sideways glance.

Nikki shied away. "Just doing my job."

"Don't worry," Catie said. "I know it's Shea. Not you." She turned to me. "Figured it was better if I came and told you in person anyway." She bowed her head to mine. "Vincent is in the hospital."

My heart stopped, my stomach sinking to the ground. "What?"

"He was in a car accident. Drunk driving or something."

I patted my hands against my sides in a rapid movement. "But he's not that kind of person. Why would he be drinking and driving?"

"He might have been on his way back from 52 Peaks. Possibly drugged?"

"Echo?" I asked.

She shrugged. "Some hallucinogenic, I guess. Apparently, he 'saw' things."

Even *that* wasn't like Vincent. I figured he had done drugs in his younger years, but times had changed. None of that would have interested him now.

Would it?

"He's at Punica General Hospital?" I asked. Catie nodded. I went to the storeroom and grabbed my purse. "Let's go."

Nikki grabbed my shoulder. "Your mother would never let me—"

I pushed her off. "Tell her I ran." I turned to Catie. "You've got a car?" She beeped her car fob. "All right. Let's—"

The front door opened, Shea stopping us in our tracks. She placed her hands on her hips, her eyes seething as she looked down her nose at the two of us.

"Shea!" Catie said, pretending to be happily surprised. "We were on our way—"

"On your way *where*, Kora?" Shea asked.

What was the big deal if I went to the hospital to see my friend? All right. Maybe he wasn't a friend after the things he had said. But if someone I cared about was hurt, then I needed to make sure that they were okay. I had to be strong.

"Punica General Hospital," I said. I straightened my shoulders. "My friend is there and I wanted to make sure he's okay."

"*He?*" Shea asked. "Is Andrew hurt?"

I glanced over my shoulder at Catie. She bowed her head, encouraging me, and I turned back to face my mother. "Vincent Erickson," I said.

Shea's jaw strained, her neck rigid. She turned to Nikki. "And you were going to *let* her?"

"I—"

"I was going to go with or without her permission," I said, trying to save Nikki. "If you could please step aside, Shea. My friend needs me."

Shea lowered her head to mine. "Will I have to lock you in the storeroom to get you to stay?"

I searched her eyes, trying to see if she had any sympathy for me. But she was completely cold, like nothing I would do would change her mind. "Yes," I said. "If you don't let me see him, I won't let it go until you do." Shea closed her eyes. "He's my friend, Shea. And he's in trouble. I need to see him."

Shea shook her head, then straightened again, opening her eyes. "Fine. *We* will visit him, then," she said, "but you will *not* speak to him. He might say something to you; I can't stop him from that. But you will not have a conversation with him. Understood?"

I nodded; I could compromise.

By the time we got to the hospital, Shea had already figured out which ward and room he was in. A thin sheet hung from a bar, blocking the view inside.

Sheriff Mike leaned on the counter. "It's not good," he said to Shea.

"Is he hurt?" she asked.

"Physically, he's stabilized, but something happened." He shook his head. "He's not himself."

I stayed silent. My mother always had better leverage when it came to my father. I was glad she was taking an active interest in me. Maybe she wasn't *all* bad.

"What do you mean?" Shea asked.

"He's talking like he had a vision." Sheriff Mike drew circles in the air by his ears. "Says he *saw* the Echo Killer."

"Did he?" Shea asked. Shock waved through me; did she actually believe him?

My father laughed, his firm belly jiggling. "Of course not. The Echo Killer isn't going to show himself to a civilian and let the civilian *live*. That would be suicidal!" He sighed deeply, satisfied with the amusement. "Erickson likely fell asleep at the wheel, and his dreams seemed real to him. Who knows?"

But something wasn't right. Vincent drunk driving, falling asleep at the wheel, hallucinating? All of it was possible. And he seemed impulsive enough to get himself into trouble. But would he do that?

"Vincent hasn't done drugs in years. Even quit alcohol after his brother's death," Catie said. A warmth swelled in my stomach; at least the two of us knew that if *anything*, he was drugged. I was glad she was with us.

"Can I see him?" I asked. Everyone turned to me, surprised that I would speak. I said it louder. "Please. I want to see him." I turned to my mother. "I won't speak to him. I promise."

Shea turned to Sheriff Mike. Inside the room, the bed creaked with Vincent's movement.

Sheriff Mike turned to me. "If it's all right with your mother."

Shea nodded, and the three of them watched as I stepped closer to the room. A nurse motioned me inside. I slipped around the curtains. Vincent lay there, a deep black and blue bruise on his face, puffy and swollen. Knicks of red dashed over his skin, sprinkling across his body. His eyes were closed, his lips open and chapped. I put a hand on his wrist, hoping to comfort him. His eyes fluttered awake, instantly locked on mine, and he thrust himself forward.

"Kora," he said, his voice louder than I expected. I stepped back. "You've got to believe me." He got out of bed, the IVs in his arms dragging the equipment to the floor in a loud crash. A commotion of staff rushed over. "Don't trust anything they say—"

Shea put her hands on my ears, pulling me back, while the nurses surrounded him. My whole body was hot, my pulse racing.

"Don't trust them, Kora! You're not safe!" Vincent shouted.

What was he afraid of?

Andrew appeared at my side. "Miss Shea," he said, "Miss Kora." He turned to me, his smile gleaming. My lips flinched, but then I forced a smile.

"We were lucky my boy, Andrew, was there," Sheriff Mike said, slamming his palm into Andrew's back. "If it weren't for him, Vincent would be dead right now."

Andrew smiled. "Doing my job, sir," he said, winking. "Like you taught me."

"You were the officer who helped him?" I asked. "You saved him?" I was hopeful, but it didn't sound right.

"Just because I dislike him does not mean I'm going to disregard my duties as an officer," he said. "I hope you do take me for more than that, Miss Kora."

"You know, there's another reason he's here," Shea beamed. She smiled up at Andrew and my father, then turned to me. "Do you have plans tonight?"

I raised a brow. "Is it prom season or something?"

"I set you up on your first date!" she exclaimed. "With real husband material. Like your father. Aren't you excited?"

My heart raced in my chest. "Who are you talking about?"

"Andrew Pompino," she said proudly. She patted his shoulder. "Isn't it wonderful?"

"Aww, shucks, Miss Shea," he said. "But trust me, I'm looking forward to it, Miss Kora."

If Nyla were here, she would have been overjoyed for me. She'd even offer to switch places and would remind me of the qualities that made Andrew the perfect catch. But all I could see when I looked at him was the day he told me that I should investigate Vincent for the good of the town. How he had chosen his work instincts over my safety.

It's like he knew more than he let on.

"Don't forget our agreement," Sheriff Mike said.

My father was right. A flash of heat rumbled through my body. "A date," I said. I swallowed hard. "I'm looking forward to it too."

"You could use the time to discuss the greenhouse," she said. I had almost forgotten about that. I had so much on my mind lately; I was surprised my mother had remembered for me. But I knew that if it was just Andrew and me talking, I would probably be able to say more of what I wanted when it came to the business. Even if he had been weird when it came to the abduction, he had always been kind to me before that. There was a chance he could be reasonable now. "And you can go out wherever you two want. My treat. Who knows what could happen," Shea said.

"A date. How exciting!" Catie said through her teeth.

"I know!" my mother squealed.

"The night is ours," Andrew said, winking and pointing finger guns at me. His hand was bruised, parts of it nearly matching his uniform.

"What happened to your hand?" I asked.

Shea glanced too. "That looks like it hurts. Terrible, really," she said.

"You get into a fight?" Catie asked.

"You know Andrew," Sheriff Mike laughed, putting an arm around my mother. "He's an overachiever."

"I was helping my neighbor out. Hammer fell on my hand," Andrew said. "Really, it was a clumsy affair, but no harm done. She apologized."

The bruise was dark enough for that, but something didn't sit right with me. When did he have time to help a neighbor, if he had just been on duty, saving Vincent from a car crash?

Andrew bowed his head at me. "What time works best for you?"

An idea crossed my mind. It was a date, for just the two of us? That meant that we could go by ourselves, and I could leave early, then use that time to see Vincent *by myself*, when I wasn't surrounded by others, people that I wasn't sure I trusted anymore.

"How about six?" I asked.

He grinned. "Well, of course."

Chapter 33

Vincent

A PARADE OF DOCTORS AND NURSES SURROUNDED ME. MY HEAD throbbed and my skin stung with every touch. But I held onto the fact that Kora had been there. She had wanted to check on me.

The nurse checked my vitals, then let in a visitor. My heart squeezed in anticipation until I saw it was Catie. I was happy to see her—a familiar face—but she wasn't Kora.

"Good news and bad news," she said. I motioned for her to get on with it. "The good news? They're going to discharge you soon."

I could handle that. "And?"

"The bad news is that they're saying you were drugged."

I gently rubbed my forehead. I hadn't had anything to drink. How could I have been drugged? "I told them that Andrew sprinkled that shit on my car, then attacked me."

"Supposedly, one of the symptoms of the new batch of Echo is hallucinations."

I leaned forward. "Supposedly?"

She lifted her shoulders. "I don't know. They're being hush-hush about it, but to me, it sounds like crap."

A wave of relief ran through me. At least Catie was on my side. "And Andrew? What about him?"

"He was on duty; plain-clothes officer, something like that. But yeah, you were right that he was the first man on the scene." She wiped her mouth on the back of her hand. "Of course, that's why they think you were doped with the new line of Echo."

"They're trying to spin the attack as a figment of my imagination?"

Catie leaned in closer to me. "I believe you," she said carefully. "But you have to be very careful with how you handle the next couple of days." She made sure there were no other nurses or hospital staff near us, then whispered: "Kora can't get you out a second time."

I clenched my fists, the IVs shifting in my veins. "This is bullshit."

"I told them I hadn't seen you drink since your brother." I grit my teeth. It had been a long damn time. "You haven't done anything since then, right?"

I paused, thinking it over.

"Right?" she asked.

I lifted my chin. I had taken that half of an Echo pill right before wrapping Kora in plastic. But it had done nothing to me.

"How long does Echo stay in your system?" I asked.

Catie narrowed her eyes at me. "Fucking hell, Vincent. You can't be serious?"

I shrugged. "It didn't do anything."

She rubbed her forehead. "For your sake, I hope it doesn't last." She tapped her fingers on the side of her head. "I would play their game. Pretend like those accusations aren't serious. That you *were* hallucinating about Andrew. Then, when you're out of here, try to get all the evidence you can and bring it to court."

"And what if the judge is in their pocket too, like we thought before?"

Her eyes flicked to the ground, then back up to me. "I don't know," she said. "But you have to be careful. *We* have to be careful."

How was I supposed to find evidence against a cop? There was a good chance that one of the reasons none of the Echo deaths had been linked to Andrew was because he *knew* how to hide evidence. My stomach sank, then Kora's face filled my mind.

"What about Kora?" I asked.

"What about her?"

"Andrew. She—" The fact that the only two men allowed in her life were Mike and Andrew, made me sick. "Mike wants Kora to date Andrew." Adrenaline shot through me. "We have to stop—"

"Stop thinking about her for a second," Catie hissed. "She can't help you anymore. I'm not even sure I can. And you need to keep your voice down."

"She's in danger," I said, leveling my tone. Catie chewed on her lip, staring at me. "Where's my phone?" Catie handed me hers. I scrolled through her contacts until I found Kora.

"Hello?" Kora answered. My heart stopped, my chest tingling: she was safe. "Catie? Is Vincent okay?" A warmth washed over me.

"Kora," I said. A small intake of breath crackled through the speaker. "You need to listen carefully."

"Oh, *Catie*," she said, her voice distracted and awkward. She must have been putting on an act for someone else. "Right now isn't a good time."

And I didn't have time to argue about when would be a good time to call her back.

"Andrew is dangerous," I said. Catie's head popped up to remind me that I was supposed to stay quiet about this. But I didn't care. I had to warn Kora. "Andrew Pompino *is* the Echo Killer. It's a setup. The whole thing is a hoax."

"What are you talking about?"

"For the reelection." I paused, trying to figure out what I could say. "The ice pick. The truck. He was right by 52 Peaks. Every single time. Everything points to him."

The line was quiet. Catie shifted uncomfortably on the other side of the room.

"Vincent?" Kora whispered. "Are you okay?"

Was I okay? That's what she wanted to ask? My head pounded, my body was bruised to shit, I was half-dead, and a dangerous, corrupt cop was constantly around the woman I loved. A woman who was more concerned with *my* health than she was with her own safety.

"I know I screwed up," I said, "but Andrew is not the man you think he is. You've got to believe me."

A noise rippled in the background. Footsteps. Then an older woman's voice.

"I have to go," Kora said.

"Kora! Wait—"

The line went dead. I stared at the screen, her number blinking. Then I clicked it off, handing it back to Catie. "I need to get out of here," I muttered.

"Soon," Catie said. She looked over her shoulder. "I'll make sure they're checking on you."

After Catie left, a doctor came and checked the computer.

"Everything looks good. But we're still waiting for one test result," he said. He gave a wide smile. "After that, you're free to leave."

My chest tightened. "What test?"

He tapped his chin. "Let me see if I can get someone from the lab." He dialed a department on the phone, speaking in a quiet voice, then hung up. "Another doctor will be in to deliver your results. After that, just check with the front desk on your way out."

I took a deep breath. Everything sounded routine so far. "All right," I said. But I stopped over those words: *free to leave*. Not discharged, but free, like there was something still lurking there, waiting to imprison me.

A few minutes later, tactical boots tapped against the floor. Sheriff Mike put his hands on his hips, his full uniform on, a sullen expression on his face.

"Erickson," he said, fake concern lacing his tone. "How are you?"

"Considering last night," I muttered, lifting a bruised hand, "All is well."

"I came to talk to you about that." He lowered his head. "You mentioned another car. A truck, was it? A truck that had purposefully crashed into your vehicle?"

I didn't even want to think about the state of my car right then. "Yeah."

"Did you say who was driving it?"

I thought about what Catie had said. "No," I said. I plastered a smile on my face. "I'm afraid I was knocked out."

Sheriff Mike folded his fingers in front of himself. "Good," he said. Then he removed a sheet of paper from his pocket. "Did they tell you what these test results say?"

My heart rate increased. Sheriff Mike was bringing the test results? "They didn't."

"This document says you were on Echo last night. In fact, there were so many illegal substances in your system, interacting with one another, that it's very like that you saw things. Things you didn't actually see. Like Andrew, my captain."

I clenched my jaw. "What about him?"

"Now, he *was* on the scene. But he didn't attack you. That was —" Mike lifted his shoulders, "—in your mind. All of it."

Spots blurred my vision. I couldn't hold it back anymore. "I wasn't drugged and you know it."

"That's not what your doctor will say." A small grin formed on his lips. "Now, I don't *have* to release these results. We can keep it between you and me. Or I can release them. Destroy your credibility. I can bring in a new funeral operation to replace yours. I can make sure that you never service another funeral in Acheron County again."

I narrowed my eyes. He was pulling out all the stops for this? What was he hiding?

"You wouldn't," I said.

"And I won't, *if* you fall back in line. Let the election come and go. *Then* we can talk about your accusations. Any suspect is a valuable suspect; I can get behind that." He tilted his chin. "You can wait a little while longer, can't you, Erickson?"

"You realize Andrew *is* a suspect, then?"

"I realize that not everything you say is complete nonsense." He straightened. "But as far as we both know, the real Echo Killer is out there. And I would hate for us to get distracted from the prize when we're so close to another victory."

I sneered, bile rising in my throat. He only cared about the election.

"I do want to warn you." He glanced around, avoiding my eyes. "I know you have a thing for my daughter, and she has some need to support you. But I've set up my daughter with Andrew. He might have been in the wrong place at the wrong time with you last night, but he's a good kid, and I trust him with my family. You, on the other hand? You will *not* speak to my daughter," his jaw strained, "or I will kill you myself."

Would he? "You're threatening a civilian," I said, a smile on my face. He was breaking too, then.

"Nonsense," he said, adjusting his shirt. "I'm protecting my family. That's how the media will spin it. And I will not let you ruin this for me." He held out his hand. "Do we have an understanding?"

I understood his dilemma. Kora must have had something on him and had bargained for my freedom from prison, and that's why he was willing to bargain with me now. But I could ruin his campaign if I told anyone that Andrew was part of the Echo deaths. And if that meant giving up Quiet Meadows? Then I didn't care. It was a job; there would be others.

But I did care about Kora. And I knew that if I wanted to help her, I had to stay in the shadows and figure out Andrew and Mike's next moves. If I said something now, they would only reel her in closer to their traps.

I shook the sheriff's hand, gripping hard. He stood back. "I'll tell the doctor you're ready for release."

Chapter 34

KORA

At six o'clock sharp, Andrew rang the doorbell. Out of the two outfits my mother had selected for me, I had picked a light pink dress with a lace bodice, half-sleeves, and a tiered skirt with flowing layers. Add wings, and I'd be a real-life fairy princess. Andrew's eyes widened. His hands fell, his fist wrapped around a bouquet of red roses, the tip of one of the buds browning. The floral paper crunched in his hands.

"Miss Kora," he said. "You look—"

"Like a princess," Shea called out from behind me. She stuck out her hands like she was presenting me to the highest bidder. "Doesn't she look amazing?"

"Better than that, Miss Shea," Andrew said. "She looks beautiful."

I stared down at my feet. I didn't *feel* beautiful. I felt like a fraud. All I wanted were the leggings and hoodies I had gotten used to in Vincent's basement.

"Aww, Miss Kora," Andrew said, grabbing my chin. My scalp prickled with heat, the hair on the back of my neck standing on end. "Why do you have that look on your pretty little face?"

"This is her first date, you know," Shea said. She pinched my cheek and I grimaced. What was with the two of them? "She's nervous, you know? The usual butterflies of first love. She's lucky she's going out with such a gentleman."

"It's my honor," he said. He bowed, then squeezed my arm. "Don't be so nervous around me." He grinned. "I promise, I'll take good care of you. I won't bite."

His eyes were blue and crystal clear, and yet I thought about the canvas bag under my bed. Maybe it wouldn't be such a bad idea to keep the gun with me.

No... That was ridiculous. Andrew might have been a threat to Vincent, but with me? He couldn't do anything. He was too close to my parents.

He couldn't be the Echo Killer. Why would he kill those people? What purpose would it serve?

"Where did you get these?" Shea asked, taking the bouquet from his hand. "You certainly didn't get them from Poppies & Wheat. They're already wilting."

"I got it from the grocery store." He smacked his forehead. "It completely slipped my mind that the two of you worked in a flower shop. I just knew I had to get something to impress my date. It's been one hell of a week."

"Well," Shea squealed, "Let this be the cherry on top."

The two of them turned to me, waiting for my reaction. Had they finally realized that I hadn't spoken a word since Andrew had arrived? I took a deep breath. All I had to do was get through this date, then make up an excuse to go home early, and instead, go to Vincent's house.

"To the cherry on top," I said.

The two of them cheered, then Andrew escorted me down the driveway. "I like that fence," he said. "It fits your family."

I'm sure he meant the picturesque nature of the white picket fence, but it was a cage to me.

"Thanks," I said.

Andrew opened the passenger door, letting me in and closing it behind me. It was a black sedan, a fairly unremarkable car, but it was clean, and there wasn't a dent in sight. Maybe Vincent had been seeing things.

The restaurant's dim lighting added mystique to the roses

painted on the walls. Fake vines draped down the sides of the indoor trellises. I imagined being inside of that garden room in Vincent's house again. The flowers and tiny lights, all of it for me. *It's not much,* Vincent had said. But it was more than anyone had ever done for me.

I shook my head. Andrew had gotten me a bouquet. That was something. And my father had told my mother that Vincent's test results showed he had been under the influence of so many drugs, it was a miracle that he was still alive. He had seen things. Andrew had nothing to do with his car wreck.

But still, that explanation didn't seem exactly right. It seemed…*uneven* somehow.

"How you have been, Miss Kora?" Andrew asked. "I know you've been through a hell of a lot lately."

I studied Andrew. He was so at peace with everything as if right and wrong were as easy as the difference between apples and oranges. A glimmer of light caught his face, a patch of skin powdered on the surface.

"It's fine," I said, staring at the powder. "As best can be expected with my mother."

His brows pulled down, focusing on me. "She had a very hard time without you."

"Are you wearing makeup?"

He sucked in a breath, stretching his arms out to the side. "Caught me. Got into a little tiff with one of the inmates. You know how it can be on the job. I'm sure you've seen it with your daddy." Vincent had never hidden his black eye, and yet Andrew couldn't handle jeopardizing his image, even if it was a simple shiner he had earned on the job. "But save your worrying about me, Miss Kora. I'm *always* ready and willing to protect and serve, especially for your safety."

My mind flashed to the phone call from inside of the funeral home: *You are a strong, brave girl, Miss Kora. And you have a rare opportunity. You can look into him.* Either he didn't believe that Vincent was actually a danger to me, *or* he was lying that he wanted to protect me.

I forced myself to lift the menu. "Shall we?"

Once the server brought our meals, I held up my fork. "How did you convince my mother to agree to the greenhouse?"

He grinned. "We want what's best for you."

"And you agree to transfer ownership to me?"

"Eventually," he said, stabbing his fork into a chunk of steak. "Of course, that's depending on how things work out."

"Work out?"

"I'm sure we can come to an agreement. We can discuss that later on when it's ready to be finalized."

I opened my mouth to disagree, but he started making small talk, distracting me, but still, the lingering sense of dread never left me. I didn't have a choice about the date, or my clothes, really, or what I did with my time. I could be locked in a madman's basement, and I would still have more freedom than on a date with a cop.

Outside, the night had begun to darken. Andrew offered me his hand, and I took it, even though my stomach turned. I looked up at the sky. In the middle of town, the lampposts were so bright, you couldn't see the stars. And for a brief second, I wished I were in that garden room, where the stars might have been fake, but they shined for me, and the person who made them was real.

"Do you know if Vincent is still at the hospital?" I asked.

Andrew jerked his chin, but he straightened quickly. "Why do you ask?"

"I just get," I tried to find the word that would pass me off as innocent, "I get nervous. That's all."

"Ahh, Miss Kora," he playfully knocked into my shoulder. "Don't be nervous. I'll protect you."

"But is he in the hospital?"

Andrew stopped and took both of my hands in his, peering down at me. Those blue eyes were like soulless vultures, like he was the kind of man to pick rotting flesh off of a corpse.

"I'm afraid that yes, he has been discharged, Miss Kora," he said. "Was discharged this afternoon." His voice turned low: "None of that should bother you though, darling. You're here with me."

He leaned down, his eyes closed, and when he opened his

mouth to reach my lips, I turned, making him kiss my cheek. He pulled back, and I pushed his hands away, not realizing what I was doing until a scowl twisted his face.

"You do know what a kiss is, right?" he asked. "I know you're sheltered, but generally speaking, it is customary for the man to kiss the woman after he deems it a successful engagement."

My stomach dropped. What about what I wanted?

"You're great, Andrew," I said quietly, "but I'm not ready for that. I'm not ready for any of this, actually." I pulled my hands away, hugging myself. "This was my mother's idea. Not mine."

His mouth pinched shut. Then he said, "I do understand that. But your mother knows what's best. You know that, right?"

My mother knew what would make our family look good.

"I'm not sure *why* my mother thought going on my first date *right now* was a good idea," I mumbled.

"Because she knows I'll take care of you."

He pulled me into his arms, and I pushed him away, forcefully, this time.

"Don't," I said. "Not yet," I added quickly, as if that could make the rejection less painful. "I'm not ready."

"You don't have a choice," he muttered. He gripped my hand, but I took my purse and smacked it across his face. A streak of makeup rubbed off, making his skin patchy with bluish-green bruises. His jaw clenched. A few people turned to us.

"Is that Captain Pompino?" one of them asked.

"Why did she slap Andrew? Isn't that—"

"That missing girl. The one the mortician kidnapped!"

Andrew turned to me, snapping his teeth. "You can pretend to be the strong girl who survived her suffering and became a better woman for it. But I can see right through you, darling." He lowered his voice, "You're a weak girl, Kora. And you need someone like me to protect you."

I glared at him, my eyes shifting across his face.

"You're wrong about me," I hissed.

He ignored me and continued on: "One day, I'm going to make you my wife." He tipped his imaginary hat. "Whether you like it or not. Because believe me, your mother does. And your daddy has no choice. We're the ones who control you."

I clutched my purse to my chest, then walked down the sidewalk. My heart pounded, my skin buzzing with energy. I couldn't stand to be around him anymore.

"Where are you going?" he asked.

"Leave me alone," I shouted. "Or I'll—I'll—"

"What are you going to do?" he laughed. "Call the police?"

Vincent

As soon as Sheriff Mike mentioned setting up his daughter with Andrew, I started imagining his torture and eventual death. The longer he was kept alive through his agony, the more I would enjoy it. Transforming that cocky smirk into a pained wail. Plunging the knife into his heart, the look on his face as he fell into a grave, knowing that no one was coming to save him.

I doubted Kora would be able to forgive me for taking her childhood friend's life. But if it meant Kora was safe, it would be worth it. In my mind, *we* didn't matter; *she* did.

I searched the town for her car and his, but I found nothing. After aimlessly driving, I wound up in Rose Garden Neighborhood, drifting between the houses. Between the perfect homes was a soot-covered spot, the beams still standing, with charred streaks going down the remnants. Like black paint spilled in the middle of a perfect painting. And yet the flags hung from other driveways, the fabric fluttering in the wind. And the grass plots were lush and green.

When I found the Novas' rental house, I parked across the street. My throat tensed. It was so different from their old home. Natural grass, and at one time, a rose bush—to plastic turf. But I didn't regret taking Kora. My intentions were never pure, and they continued to be ill-advised, but now I simply wanted Kora to be safe. And now, she lived in a house guarded with fake grass, as if none of the Novas could stand the idea of anything dying again.

The front door swung open. Shea's limp hair hung around her face, the strands gray, not her usual brown. She looked older. Like she wasn't her usual self.

Perhaps destruction came in many forms.

"Mr. Erickson?" Shea asked, squinting her eyes. "What are you doing here?"

What had made me hate her and her husband, years ago now? Her entire facade had disintegrated, leaving behind a fatigued woman with hardly anything left. *This* was the real Shea: the one who was left alone. A woman who used control like a vice to keep the people around her close.

But that didn't make what she did right.

Nor did it excuse *my* actions.

"What do you want?" Shea asked, clutching her coat around herself. "Stay away from Kora." She reached back toward the house. "I have a gun. My husband is the sheriff. You need to stay away."

I opened my mouth to say I was sorry, but I couldn't do it. Because I wasn't sorry. I wasn't going to apologize for yanking Kora from her mother's cage.

But I could argue for Kora's future.

"You need to let Kora go," I said. "Let her make her own choices, even if they aren't the best ones." I shook my head. Hell, I needed to do that too. As long as I could ensure her safety from Andrew, I would back off. "She deserves to grow."

"How would you know what she needs?" she snapped. "You don't know anything about her."

My throat ached, because, at one point, Shea would have been right. I didn't know Kora when I had stolen her. And perhaps I still didn't know her.

But none of that mattered now. Only Kora did.

"Andrew is taking advantage of your family," I said calmly, stepping forward. I locked eyes with her. "Don't let him hurt your daughter."

"Andrew is a good man," she said. "We've known him since he was a baby."

A heaviness fell on my shoulders. "If you let him, he will hurt her."

She took another step toward the house. "All I want is for her to be happy." She tucked hair behind her ear, the same way her daughter did. "She'll be safe with him."

A grave expression crowded my face. "Controlling who she dates won't guarantee her safety and happiness. Nor will it guarantee yours."

She scowled at me, her face turning red. "Stay away from my daughter," she whispered, tears in her eyes.

She disappeared into the house. I stood there, trying to picture the life that Kora would live. If Andrew was out of the picture, could I let her go? I ran through that possibility. As long as Kora was okay, as long as she was safe—what could I do for her?

I got back in my car and drove myself back to Quiet Meadows. I wandered to her grave, then stared at the daffodil engraving, running my hands over it, remembering the way she tore the petals apart. One day, Kora would find a good life, one without Andrew, but one that Shea approved of. And if I could find no fault, then I would have to let her go.

Because at least Kora would be happy.

Kora

I paced down the sidewalk, not looking back at Andrew, clutching my purse close to me like a shield. I wished I had that canvas bag from Vincent with me. I wanted to go to Quiet Meadows, but I knew Andrew would tell my mother that I was still out soon, and with the way the date ended, I couldn't risk her overprotectiveness. I had to make her think I was safe at home.

Back inside of the house, my heart rate never slowed. I should have felt safe there, but I didn't. Luckily, my mother was watching a movie in a distracted trance, her mind elsewhere. She didn't ask about the date. I said goodnight, and she waved.

A few hours passed. When I was sure the house was quiet, I pulled open the window, letting in the dark night. I needed to calm myself, and for some reason, I kept dreaming of lying in the graveyard with Sarah, Bernie, and Ulysses, while Vincent muddied himself in the dirt. How he'd glance over the edge of a plot, asking me strange questions back.

I laid back down on my bed, staring at the ceiling. I wouldn't be able to sleep. Not until I saw Vincent for myself.

I removed the screen, then put a hand on the windowsill. My bedroom was on the ground floor, like our old house. I slipped into an old pair of flats, leggings, and a loose sweatshirt. I lifted my leg, prying myself over the window, and landed on the fake grass.

Then I walked.

It was as if my body was ahead of my mind, like I was observing myself make a choice that I knew would haunt me. But I couldn't stop myself. I didn't want to.

It took me over an hour and a half, but when I finally saw those headstones like figures crouching in the darkness, relief washed through me. Down the path, the bright flowers shined in the night, sitting along the memorial stones. The floral perfume wafted through the breeze. I breathed it in, relishing it, hoping the scent would become engraved in my memory.

My heart pounded with each step, and when I saw his shadow, leaning against my headstone, my whole body clenched up, twisting into knots. It wasn't about him coming in a dream to rescue me anymore. I didn't need to be saved.

He was waiting for me. All I had to do was go find him.

Chapter 35

Vincent

Kora stepped through the moonlight, the leggings snug on her thighs, a hoodie wrapped around her body, partly unzipped, her hair in a short ponytail. Those bushy eyebrows were expressive and wild, and yet pure, even with everything she had been through. My breath caught in my throat, my mind urging me not to let a single thing go, as if a single wisp of air could make her vanish, floating away into the night.

But she was finally here.

"You're here," she said.

I swallowed hard, my throat dry. What were you supposed to do when you finally got to see the woman you loved? A woman that you thought you would never speak to again?

"Join me," I said. I gestured to the patch of grass next to me. "The dogs are here somewhere. I'm sure they'll say 'hi.'"

She smiled, sending heat through me, then sat down next to me, wiggling her hips into the grass. I leaned back, resting my open palms on the blades. The earth was cool on my hands, wetting my pants; I'm sure her pants were stained too. The thought of this place, *my place*, marking her in such an innocent way, made me smile to myself. Another way I'd be with her, even after she inevitably left.

"What's that look?" she asked, side-eyeing me.

I shrugged. "You couldn't stay away," I joked.

"It's easier to get here than the flower field," she said. "At least, on foot."

"You walked here from your house?" She nodded. "You could have called me."

She looked into my eyes. "I didn't want to disturb you."

How was I supposed to tell her it could be in the middle of the night, or the crack of dawn, even midday during a service, that years could have passed without exchanging a single word, and if she told me she needed me, I would be there for her? It didn't matter what I wanted, or that I knew she deserved better. I was always hers.

It had taken me way too long to see that she had been doing that for me too.

The stars twinkled in the night, the breeze tickling our skin. I imagined kissing her neck, inching my way closer to her lips, but I stayed still. Kora had come here for a reason; it wasn't up to me to take her like that again.

But damn it all, I wanted her.

The dogs came by, each nudging Kora while she greeted them with cuddles. She squeezed Sarah in a hug, right as Ulysses licked her face and Bernie sat in front of her legs. Pride filled my chest, making everything expand. I had never wanted anything for myself besides destruction, but at that moment, it was all for her.

Once the dogs realized Kora wasn't going to play right then, they ran off, back up the pathway to the house. Kora ran her fingers through the grass.

"I've been thinking about it again," she said, breaking the silence. "It's not that I want to die. The opposite, really. But I wonder about it, you know? What's it like? What does Nyla feel?"

Nyla was nothing more than ashes buried in the ground.

"I suppose it's cold down there," I said.

"Before that. When she was in the casket." Kora stared into my face, her green eyes luminous. "Do you ever think about that? What they must feel like?"

It was something I had wondered about since my parents had died, the thoughts resurfacing once my brother was dead too. But that was the peace about death; there was nothing to feel anymore. It was simply existence.

I would never be able to show Kora what that meant without taking her life, and I knew, now, that I would *never* kill her. Because living was more challenging than death. Because there was beauty in tragedy, in survival, in knowing what you had overcome. And I could make that experience happen for her, in my own way. I could show her what it was like to feel nothing but existence, to show her how to return to her true self. I could show her that even if she fell back into the shadows, I would be there, waiting for her.

"I could show you," I said. Her eyelids fluttered, and I grabbed her hand. "But I need to know something. Do you trust me, Kora?"

Her gaze fell to the ground, and a fiery heat burned inside of me. There was no reason for me to expect her trust. But my shoulders strained, anticipating her answer. Needing it.

When she didn't answer, I couldn't help myself: "I would never hurt you, Kora. You know that, right?"

Her eyes blazed into mine, those emerald reflecting the moonlight.

"I know," she said. "Not unless I wanted you to."

A sweeping sensation rolled through me, and I swallowed it all, holding it down. There was so much that she had taught me already, and I wanted to learn more.

I gestured at the plot of grass next to us, beyond the hill. "What about there?" I asked, changing the subject.

"Hmm?"

"We could plant the burial trees over there," I said. Amusement pulled at her lips. "But how do we differentiate? Different types of trees? Carving?"

"Memorial plates. Like anything else."

Kora already had the answers. "Would you plant Nyla that way?" I asked.

"I'd have to clear it with her family." She leaned back. "But I think they'd go for it." A subtle smile formed on her lips. "You're trying, aren't you?"

I exhaled slowly. *For you, Kora?* "Yes."

Her eyes flicked down. "You said some awful things."

"I know."

"*Go back to your tower, princess,*" she said, using a deep, mocking voice. "*All I wanted was to show you how easy it was for me to lick you.*" She shook her head. "Or my favorite: *Stop obsessing over me.*" I clenched my jaw, sucking in a sharp breath. "You were a jerk. And that's putting it lightly."

"You're right."

She flinched, then squinted her eyes, making sure that she heard me right. "What?"

"I'm not sorry for burning down your mother's house. For stealing you away from that life," I said, my jaw clenched. "But I am sorry that I hurt you."

Her eyes never left mine. "How do I know you're not just saying that?" she stammered. "You've been so against everything. And yet, now, you act like considering tree burials will make it okay. But it's not that simple, Vincent. You know it's not."

She was right. There was nothing in this world that would make up for what I did. But I could tell her how I felt.

"My favorite color is blue," I said.

She blinked her eyes rapidly, failing to comprehend my statement. "What?"

"That night I first saw you. Halloween. On the viewpoint." I nodded to her. "The lamppost cast these blue shadows on your face. From the moonlight. The streaks of tears, your wet lips." Even in that past moment, when I knew nothing about her, she was still captivating in her innocence. And now, with each day, she was even more beautiful than the last. There was no stopping her.

"I will never forget how you looked," I continued, "How I wanted to take you away, even then, knowing that I had the power to save you, and the power to destroy you with so much worse." Her eyes widened, and I laughed to myself. "I don't have a favorite food, but I know you love yogurt. So I learned how to make it." *For you. Only you,* I thought. Did she remember asking me these questions? *Tell me everything,* she had said. *Then tell me anything. Anything at all.*

"I used to think I hated the sunlight," I started again. "Sunlight meant people. Meant families. Meant services. Customers. Clients. And it's been years since I wanted to sit in the sunshine. But then I saw you in it." I stared deep into her green eyes, and pictured her spinning in the grass barefoot, watching how she fell in love with the sun's warmth all over again, how my heart couldn't help but stop for her, couldn't help but be in awe. "Since the first moment I saw you, everything has been for you, Kora. It may not be what you deserve, but it's all I have. And it's yours."

She opened her lips, not knowing what to say. Then she put a hand around the back of my head and opened her mouth to speak. But when the words didn't come, she came forward, bringing her lips to mine. Hesitant. Unsure. Questioning if this was right. But once she opened her lips, her tongue sneaking out for me, I pulled her into my lap, wrapping her legs around me, hoisted her up, bringing her to the plot of grass behind the grave —unmarked, untouched, like she had been before I ripped her from that life.

I laid her down, the moonlight casting her skin in shades of blue, the grass wet on her back. I unzipped her hoodie, a ripple of goosebumps coursing over her exposed skin. I pushed up her loose shirt, then kissed her soft stomach, up to her breasts, her light nipples, my whole body pulsing with heat, with the overwhelming need to fuck her, right here, right now.

You are everything to me, I wanted to say. I kissed her neck and she whimpered like the gentle touch was worse than every rough thing I could give her. So I bared my teeth, sinking into her, and she cried out, the whimper becoming a moan, then I raked my hands into her skin. I pulled off her clothes, her body naked against the grass, her green eyes seeing everything that was part of me, that was completely hers. I flipped her onto her stomach, then ripped open my jeans, taking out my cock, holding her wrists behind her back, shoving her face into the grass. My cock was heavy and hungry. With her cheek on the grass, I pushed inside of her. Each thrust pressed her deeper into the grass. She closed her eyes, desire rolling through her body, bringing her to the edge, as if we could dive into the abyss together. I plunged into her, again, and again, until her cries were murmurs in the night. And I knew those sounds would haunt me forever.

You are everything I've ever wanted, I thought. *Because you're real, Kora. And you're here with me.*

Chapter 36

Kora

Vincent collapsed next to me, his hand reaching for mine. His fingers were sticky and slick. My body was singed with sweat, and a burning sensation crawled through me at this intimate gesture. How was it that holding hands after making love in a graveyard was so romantic? Slowly, our breaths mellowed. And I silently hoped that the night would never end. I didn't want to think about what would happen in the morning. All I wanted to do was to lie there, existing in this timeless place, with Vincent's hand in mine.

Vincent propped himself up on his elbow, resting on his side.

"There's something I want to do for you," he said.

I smirked, raising a playful brow. "Oh?" I laid my hands on my stomach, the chilly breeze a welcome relief to my skin.

"But tell me," he said, his tone tender as if he was trying to read my soul, "Do you trust me?"

Those words sunk down, swirling inside of me. I knew, without a doubt, that he would never harm me. There was a time when he was going to, but *now*, after everything we had built for each other, I knew he would never let that happen. Not unless he could see in my eyes that I truly wanted it.

But I wasn't sure if I believed him. I wasn't sure what to

believe. But even if Vincent had done a lot of cruel things in his life, I knew he wanted to protect me now.

"I trust you," I said firmly.

I expected for him to smile at those words, but he only bowed his head, as if he was resigned to what he had to do now. He held out a hand, and I took it, both of us standing up. I reached for my clothes, but he shook his head.

"You won't be needing those," he said.

I covered myself with my arms, watching him dress. "Why do you get your clothes?"

"This isn't for me," he said. "It's for you."

Those words chilled me, but I had to trust that whatever we were doing, *was* for me. That I could believe in my own instincts about Vincent. That I could trust him, and myself. Vincent took my hand, leading me up the path to his house, then opened the door for me, leading me to the studio. He got a cup of water from the kitchen, then offered me a white pill.

I looked into his black eyes, unsure of what to say. What was it?

But I trusted him. I swallowed the pill, drinking the rest of the water with it.

"Stay here," he ordered.

Footsteps stomped through the house, between the backyard and the bathroom and down the hallway. I wrapped my arms around myself, gazing up at the paintings of me. A thundering racket ricocheted from the bathroom, like he was dumping something out. Then the water ran. I stepped forward, trying to figure out what he was doing, but the room swayed in slow motion. What was he doing? I couldn't tell. The hairs on my neck stood up.

Vincent appeared, framed by the doorway, like smoke drifting above a burning fire.

I lifted a hand to say something, but my lips wouldn't move. Vincent's face was blank. He ushered me toward the bathroom, guiding me. A curtain hung around the tub. He slid it to the side; the rings around the curtain rod jingled. He picked me up, laying me down inside. An ice bath. The icy temperature stabbed my skin. A cry ripped through me, but it never reached my throat. All that came out was a gurgled whine.

Vincent smacked a hand down on my face. "Not another sound."

I sucked in a breath. The ice burned me, but I couldn't do anything. He stood up, staring down at me, and the coldness crept into my chest.

He scooped me up in his arms. His body was hot, and I savored that warmth. We went through the front door, and the world passed in frames. Down the driveway. The cement path. The breeze brushed my skin, making me shiver more. The scent of flowers, stronger now, swirled in my nose. Into Quiet Meadows. The door swung shut behind us, clamoring down the empty morgue. Inside of the crematory room, he laid me down on a stainless steel gurney, which was comforting somehow, warmer than my skin.

Vincent moved my chin, propping my head so that I was facing the ceiling. I stayed there like he had positioned me. He tapped on the keyboard in front of the computer. Then the cremation machine beeped loudly. My breathing hitched, but I calmed myself. Deep breath in and out. His footsteps clunked to the side, and he opened up the chamber, the heat rushing to my body. Then he twirled the gurney around until the heat blasted the middle of my body, wrapping me in a cocoon.

A sharp blade pressed against my neck, but there was no pain, only pressure. When he pulled it back, it was clean. Then he pulled and pinched my skin, as if putting a needle into it, and he waited. Then he parted my legs, his palms grazing my thighs, kneading me. The warmth circulated between my legs, radiating there, and I fought to buck my hips, to feel more of him, even though I knew I wasn't supposed to move. I was supposed to be helpless. But no matter how hard I tried, I couldn't make myself do it. After that pill—my movements, the sounds, the sensations—everything was muffled.

He flickered in and out of my vision like flames dancing above a bonfire, and when he ran his hands back between my legs, my heat surged there. I needed his touch. He pressed between my folds, one finger, then two, every nerve ending in my body electrifying. Then he pressed down, rubbing my clit, massaging me, making me dizzy. He held up his hands, his fingers wet with my desire. He unzipped his pants, using my juices to play with the tip of his cock. My whole body buzzed, pulsing for him. I wasn't cold anymore.

This isn't for me, he had said. *It's for you.*

But he couldn't help himself; he wanted me too much. His pants clattered to the floor as he fucked himself harder. Because even my lifeless body was more than he had ever wanted. He pried open my teeth, then stuck his cock in my mouth. I gagged, but he penetrated deeper, filling me up. And when another noise escaped my mouth, he pulled out, glaring down at me, his eyes seething. He left the room and quickly returned with a roll of duct tape. A thick silver strip sealed my lips, holding me tight. I was so helpless.

He shifted me around so that I laid on my side. Nothing happened for a moment. My lungs filled and expelled; my eyes were blurry. He moved me to my stomach, his hands pulling apart my ass cheeks. Then he rubbed my juices against my hole, pressing a finger inside of me. Tension filled me as he went deeper. The pleasure was so great I could cry. But I didn't make a single sound. I couldn't. I had always thought it would hurt back there, but it didn't. Instead, it was a pressure-filled sensation. In and out, he fucked my ass with his finger, until everything trailed to that point and there was nothing else. And that's when it hit me: *This* was what it felt like. This nothingness. This little death. In his eyes, this was what helplessness was, when my mind was made of nothing besides desire and him. And yet I was alive, more *powerful*, knowing that he had done this, not for anyone else, but for me.

He pulled me from the metal table, and this time, he carried me through the empty hallways, to the viewing room, where a cushion-lined casket lay open on the bier. He placed me inside of it, his treasure on a pedestal.

Climbing up, he positioned himself above me, moving my thighs, rocking my hips forward. He held his cock at my ass, but this time, when he penetrated me, it was different. His cock sank into me like a knife of heat, breaking me apart, and those muscles between my legs clenched against him, squeezing him, trying desperately to get more of him. I tried to grit my teeth, but I stayed silent, the duct tape pulling at my skin. His eyes rolled to the back of his head. My face twitched, trying to smile, and his cock impaled me, thick and heavy, and it should have hurt, should have ruined me, but it awoke my senses and those nerve endings in my ass. And I wanted more. His concentrated rhythm built into a sensation that made me fall apart, and he held onto my neck, my shoulders, pressing deep within me like he could never be deep enough. Like there would always be more to take, more to find, more to harvest from me. And I would be here like this, ready for him to take, and take, and take.

"I love you, flower," he growled, his voice low. His words chilled my veins. And I knew that the reason he said it was because I couldn't say it back. Because he didn't want to know if I felt the same way. Because when I was like this, I was dead. And though he was the one moving, living, breathing, the one who was supposed to have strength, I knew that I had more power in that moment than I had in my life. He had done all of this for me. Accepted me for who I was. Saw me even when I couldn't see myself. "I love you so fucking much," he said.

My toes tingled and his hands pressed into my skin, and the bite of his fingernails pressing into my hips burned inside of me. He fucked my ass like he needed it, like it would make me live again, like he needed this more than either of us would ever understand. Tears traveled down the sides of my face, the pressure so intense I could hardly stand it, but he edged me closer, and though I couldn't do anything, I still came apart and I swear that relief was everywhere. The tears swum over my cheeks and the release was sweet—years of not knowing what anything felt like, of saving myself from any slight discomfort, of not knowing that with pain, came something beautiful like this. Two souls trying to figure out what it meant to truly live, to go after what you wanted, to accept yourself for who you were. Even if that meant offering a woman drugs, icing her living body, rendering her helpless, and fucking her inside of a casket. Even if that meant trusting the man you weren't supposed to trust, but knowing that despite everything he had done, that you would still give him everything you had.

His gaze burned with passion, and it was as if the fire from the crematory still reflected in his eyes. He stared into me, trying to speak the words he couldn't say, like he knew I was more than he ever deserved, but that he couldn't help but love me. And I could only let it all out. I could let it go. So I cried and cried. Because with catharsis, *with acceptance,* came power. And I had power over Vincent. I had power over myself.

And he had power over me. The power I had given him.

Chapter 37

Vincent

I cradled Kora in my arms, and as the drug wore off, she cried harder than she ever had in her life. My instincts surged with the need to protect her, to hold her close so that nothing could touch her, not unless it destroyed me first. She shuddered with each sob that raked her body. And with that level of release came pure exhaustion. She slept in my arms, her breathing rhythmic and calm.

I wrapped her in a blanket, then carried her across the path, through the cemetery, back to the house. The dogs joined us, circling at my feet, curious, but quickly picked up that Kora was not to be disturbed, and dismissed themselves. I brought her to my bedroom and laid her down beside me, tucking her inside of the blankets. She stirred, her eyelids fluttering between wakefulness and sleep. I stroked her hair until she fell back into her dreams. And eventually, I slept too.

In the morning, she stretched like a cat, then glanced around the room, taking in the sights. I motioned at the nightstand; a bottle of water was waiting for her. Above us, a traditional chandelier hung inside of a circular cage, the metal hanging from the high ceiling. Opposite of the bed was a retractable floor-to-ceiling window in three rectangular slabs, showing a view of Mount Punica and the cemetery. Red fruit flashed in between the green and brown mountainside, silver stones speckling the lush lawn below. I had never invited anyone in here before. This was my place. And if she wanted, it would be hers too.

"I've always wondered where you slept," she said.

It was such an innocent statement, and yet, we both knew how much this meant.

"Do you like it?" I asked.

"I love it."

Pride filled my chest. I got up, pressing a button to the side of the room. Each window pane folded above us like a garage door, letting the breeze fly in through the giant open window. Then I joined her back on the bed. A bird chirped in the distance and the air rustled through the trees. The sun was up, but the light was still soft, warming us. As the bird's song stopped, Kora glanced at the clock on my nightstand. It was past seven a.m. Her shoulders went rigid.

"I should go," she said.

"Why?" I knew the reason, but after what we had done, all of that seemed so unimportant now.

"If she finds out, she won't forgive me," she shrank down. "She'll kill you." My hand twitched. Naming her wasn't necessary; we both knew who controlled Kora's life. "I'm pretty sure today is her day off though, so there's a chance she slept in." Her cheeks flushed red. "She might not even notice I'm gone if I hurry back now."

But Kora wasn't a child. She was a grown woman who was more than capable of staying the night somewhere else. It was her choice.

"You can't keep bowing down to your mother like this," I said.

"Should I be bowing down to you instead?" Those words stabbed my heart, but I knew she was right. Replacing one person with another didn't make her situation any better or worse. She had to decide for herself and stop putting everyone else first.

"Is that what you really want?" I leaned in closer. "Coming to your mother like a servant?"

"She hasn't called me yet. But if she does—" She stopped, sighing to herself. "It's not like you're any better."

"You came to me, remember?" I huffed a deep breath. "Tell me. What do you want, more than anything in this world?"

Her eyes were full of longing and restraint, passing over every inch of me.

"You want me to say you," she said.

That was right. But I wanted her to come to that conclusion herself.

"If you leave," I said, pointing at the door, "Your mother will shorten her reins."

"Don't you see what's going on here?" She blinked up at me. "She's not the only one."

My jaw went stiff. I ran a hand over my neck.

She tucked her hair behind her ears. "I have to think about my mother. She needs me."

"But you came here in the middle of the night," I said. "Because you need me. That means something. Don't you want something more than to please your mother?"

"Can't I want both?" she asked, her eyes searching me. "I want to make you happy. But I want to make my mother happy too."

"But what will make *you* happy, Kora?" I squeezed her hand, trying to make her see what actually mattered. "What about you?"

"What about me?" She threw up her hands. "What about *you*, Vincent? I'm giving you my answer. Isn't this enough?" She motioned to the bed and pillows surrounding us. "I don't know what *this* is. But it's what we have right now."

I closed my eyes, willing away the frustration and anger. Because Kora was right. *This* was all we had. You could search for something else, but in the end, it always came down to the exact moment we were living in.

She cupped my head in her palm, her thumb stroking the stubble on my cheeks. It was hard for me to accept this as all we had, because every time I was with Kora, I knew it might be our last chance. And I couldn't let that go without fighting for it.

She needed this to be enough right then, but it wasn't enough for me.

I pulled her by the arm until she was straddling me, her naked body pressing into mine. My cock swelled between us. I grit my teeth, grinding her hips into my lap. She rocked back and forth, then kissed me, and my tongue swarmed inside of her, knowing that I might never get what I wanted.

She broke from me, her eyes flinching to the clock. She wanted me, but she wanted to go home too. Part of me knew she would get in trouble if I kept her here, and in some ways, I wanted her to be punished. As if that could prove to her she deserved more than she realized.

Which was why I was the one who deserved the punishment.

"Hit me," I said. She blinked her eyes, so I grabbed her by the throat. "I said, *hit me*, flower."

Her jaw dropped but she slapped my face hard, the fire from her palm ricocheting through me. I turned back to her slowly; I tasted blood.

Kora held her hand close to her chest in shock. But we both knew what this meant. And I didn't want to accept it right then.

I wouldn't.

I pushed my cock into her pussy, her body twitching on top of me. I guided her hips, making her fuck me, slamming into her. She groaned, her eyes scrunched at the pain, my cock going deeper, hitting her cervix, her velvet walls clutched me. Finally, those groans surrendered, mixing into a pleasure-filled growl. I grabbed her throat again, keeping her steady, and she hit me again, punching my face. The pain rocked through me, and I grinned, baring my teeth, beckoning her to do it again. And she did—until I squeezed her neck so hard that her face turned a purplish-red and her hands pulled at my wrists and the first pulse of an orgasm burst through me.

I let go. She gasped for breath, holding her neck; her pussy clenching with every cough. My come dripped out of her, wetting our thighs. I grabbed her ass, lifting her up, then threw her down on the mattress. I found my boxers and pants, then dressed quickly. She stood, but I ignored her.

Her shadow on the floor was as still as a statue, waiting for my response. But she was going now. Back home. To her mother. What was there to say?

She pulled her hoodie over her arms, then lifted her phone. "My mother will be here in a few minutes."

I said nothing. The urge to argue with her burned inside me. But I didn't need to argue that. She had accepted that her mother was on her way. And I wasn't going to stop her.

Because it was her decision, wasn't it?

We stood outside in silence. She leaned down, wrapping her arms around the three dogs as they licked her face. She glanced over her shoulder at me. I crossed my arms.

A car pulled into the driveway, and Shea's eyes seethed at me. *Stay away from my daughter.*

But no matter what I did, I was always drawn back to Kora, like she was to me.

"I'll see you soon?" Kora asked. Shea waved at me, wiggling her fingers like she knew she had won.

Kora wanted to live in both worlds. I had to accept that. But I wanted to do something for Kora, to prove to her that life was more than going between two sides. She had found an art contest for me; I could do something for her too. And even without that, she should have something for herself, and for herself, alone.

At work, I used the laptop to search the database of a real estate website. A lot, about two blocks away from the flower shop, was for sale, and for a considerably low price. Surprisingly low, in fact. It would be perfect. The lot was far enough away that she would have some distance from her mother's shop *and* from me. But the important part was that she could build her greenhouse there. I would fund it, but I would put everything under her name. I put in an offer, then went back to work.

A few hours later, I dialed Kora's number, my chest tight.

"Mr. Erickson." My blood ran cold. Shea. I clenched my fist.

"Where's Kora?"

"I'm afraid she lost her phone privileges," Shea said. "If she wants to stop sneaking out at night, I'll give her the phone back."

"Where is she?" I growled.

"I dropped her off at her father's fundraiser." She took a deep breath. "And this is a courtesy to let you know I filed a restraining order against you this morning. If you come near me or my daughter, my husband will make sure that you never see the light of day again."

She was full of shit. "The restraining order will only work if Kora is willing to use it," I said.

"I'm sure her new husband will use it."

My blood ran cold. "What husband?"

"Andrew signed the marriage license last night. The judge too. All we need is her signature." She chuckled. "But I could sign for her."

"You can't do this to her."

"I'm only doing what keeps her safe."

My throat was dry. Screw the deal I had made with Mike. "Andrew killed Nyla!"

"Goodbye, Mr. Erickson."

Then the line went dead.

My blood boiled. Adrenaline surged through me, making my fingertips tingle. Visions filled my head: Shea's blood smeared on a white-tiled floor. Sheriff Mike with a gunshot wound in his chest, the blood pooling out beneath him. Andrew's head on a stick, his limbs chopped from his body. All of their flesh incinerating in the retorts until they were nothing but a pile of bones.

And in that vision, Kora was beside me. Tears running down her cheeks.

Kora would never come back from something like that, but I couldn't let it go. Something had to happen.

I dropped off the dogs with Catie, then went back to the house and got the canisters. The town would burn before Andrew married my flower.

Chapter 38

Kora

That afternoon, my father's plastic grin calmed the voters as they shook his hand. Once the crowd cleared, Sheriff Mike slapped me on the back.

"Thanks for coming," he said. "I know it was short notice, but the voters love seeing you. It's comforting, you know?"

If they only knew that one of the police officers had known where I was all along. Another voter came by, donating to the cause, then shaking my father's hand and waving at me.

"What about the Echo murders?" I said. "Have you made any progress with that?"

He waved a dismissive hand in front of his face, then acknowledged a citizen across the room. "I wouldn't worry about that. You're safe now."

"The Echo Killer is still out there," I said. "Or you wouldn't be having this fundraiser. It's not like he'll magically stop."

"Or he will," my father laughed. "Once we get in the final votes, there will be no need for him anymore."

The bottom of my stomach pitted. It was like he knew he could stop the murders right now if he wanted.

"The Echo Killer would never hurt you," he said. He patted me on the back. "You're safe. You're the sheriff's daughter! Give me some credit." He let out a belly laugh. "And as soon as I can, I'll give the final command, we'll arrest the suspect."

"Who is the suspect?" I glanced around. The murderer could have been among us right now. "Why aren't you arresting him?"

"The arrest can't happen until Monday or Tuesday. I haven't decided which day would be best for the votes yet."

I swayed, lost in thought. "So you'll let the Echo Killer take more lives, because you want to win the election?" It seemed so wrong. My father was a jerk, but he cared about justice.

Didn't he?

"He won't take more lives," he said quietly. "I promise you that."

"How can you be so sure?"

He relaxed his posture, his eyes half-lidded. "Don't worry so much," he said. "It doesn't look good. You should be confident in me. In my team." He put his hands on his hips and thrust forward. "We've worked hard for this."

My muscles were weak, my knees wobbling, the world blurring in front of me. My father wasn't just a jerk. He was an asshole. And I knew Andrew was an asshole too. But this?

Was everything a lie, like Vincent had said?

"You planned this," I said, my voice flat. "All of it. The Echo deaths. The timing." I shook my head. "It really was a way to help your campaign."

The pattern filled my mind; right before the election, my father found new causes to back his election: youth violence, drunk driving, and now, the Echo deaths. But it had never seemed as timely, or as fabricated, as it did right then.

Maybe Vincent had been attacked by the Echo Killer, only it was Andrew, like Vincent had said.

"Be careful of what you're saying," Sheriff Mike said, the grin fading from his face. "Now, all of those *victims* had one thing in common: they chose to be out. Chose to drink and take drugs. Chose to drive home. I never made their choices for them. Neither did the Echo Killer."

"What about Nyla?" I asked. "She never did that kind of stuff.

She rarely even drank! She only went out to 52 Peaks because it was her birthday and she wanted to dance."

He lifted his shoulders. "You know, Andrew questioned me when it came to her too." He gazed at the ground. "But we can't make exceptions. It's how these things work. No one is safe."

My eyes bulged from my head. "She was my only friend!"

"I know. It's tragic." He gave a deep sigh, rubbing his forehead. "But sacrifices have to be made for the good of the people. Even a good girl like Nyla can't always get off the hook. Besides," he ran a hand over his chin, "I always thought she was a bad influence on you. She put ideas in your head, making you think you were unhappy. I never liked her."

My jaw dropped, my head pounding. "You killed Nyla," I whispered.

"It's a good thing your mother didn't want you to go. You can thank Andrew for reminding her of the Echo deaths." He shook his head. "I would have supported all three of you going that night."

A sour taste filled my throat. The world spun around me. "You would have wanted us to die too? To kill us?" I couldn't swallow, no matter how hard I tried. Nausea came swimming back, burning my throat. "Even Mom? *Your wife?*"

"Be careful, now." He clenched his teeth together. "I never lifted a finger. But it's easy to add your friend, Vincent, to the list next." His lips transformed into a grin. "Catie would run the business much better than he could anyway."

Every inch of my body stiffened. "Don't you dare hurt him," I said, "or my mother, you bastard."

He ignored me. "You know Andrew. He's always itching to prove his capabilities." He chuckled to himself. "And taking down Vincent would be the best way to redeem himself. And if that doesn't work? Maybe he can add you and your mother too."

My stomach turned. I held my mouth, trying not to get sick. I couldn't look at him. Couldn't face what this all meant.

He stepped closer, the hairs on the back of my neck standing on end. "Don't do anything you might regret," he said in a menacing voice. "And don't embarrass me. I would hate for you to become the last victim of the Echo Killer."

My breath caught in my throat. I couldn't move. "I've got to go check on Mom," I finally said.

"I'll call her to come pick you up."

The minutes passed by in a fog. By the time Shea picked me up, a headache pounded through my skull, my stomach nauseous. In the passenger seat, I heard my name, but I didn't move. I couldn't do anything.

"Are you awake?" Shea asked.

I startled. "What did you say?"

"I have a surprise for you at home." She beamed at me, like nothing in the world could possibly be wrong. Would she believe me about my father and the Echo deaths if I told her? Or was she part of it too?

"Why are you looking at me like that?" she asked.

A squad car was parked in front of the house. My stomach twisted into knots. Nothing was safe. What was happening?

Andrew stood from the couch when we entered the room. "Miss Kora. Miss Shea," he said, his thumbs tucked in his belt loops. "It's always a pleasure."

I turned to my mother, my mouth pinched together. "Why is he here?"

"Kora!" she scowled. "That's no way to treat your future husband."

"Future husband?" I yelped. "*What?*"

"Andrew has asked for our blessing to marry you." She clapped her hands together. "Your father and I couldn't pick a better husband for you. He'll protect you like your father protects me."

My face was numb. Everything turned dull.

"I promise to do all of that and more for you, Miss Kora," Andrew said. "You deserve the world."

I turned to my mother. "He killed Nyla."

She blinked at me. "What?"

"Tell her," I turned to Andrew. "Tell her what you did. He's been killing the Echo victims, Mom. *All* of them. Because Dad told him to. Dad wanted us to die that night with Nyla. We're only here because Andrew warned us about the Echo deaths!"

Shea winced and smiled sheepishly at Andrew. "You don't know what you're saying, sweetheart," she said. She rubbed my back. "Do you need a drink of water?"

"I'm afraid you're onto something," Andrew said, nodding at me. I didn't know whether to be relieved or terrified. Was he going to tell my mother the truth? "Kora might need a little help relaxing after this."

He was going to treat me like Vincent, then. To tell everyone that I was seeing things.

"He's the Echo Killer," I said again, my tone stern. "You've got to believe me. Why would I lie about this?"

Shea shook her head violently. "You realize what you're accusing Andrew of? A cop with that many murders—"

"He did it because Dad told him to!"

I locked eyes with my mother, both of us in a death stare, her hands shaking.

"No," she whispered. "You're lying."

"I'm telling you the truth."

"He wouldn't do that." She crossed her arms. "He would never do such a thing."

"He has." I widened my eyes, pleading for her to believe me. "*He has*, Mom."

She snapped her head back quickly, her shoulders crumpling. "You've done a lot of stupid things recently." Her mouth slackened. "But this, Kora? This is the worst. Even this is beneath you."

"What do you think I'm getting out of this?" I yelled. "I am not going to marry Andrew. I want him to go to jail!"

"Now, now, Miss Kora, there's no need to cause a ruckus about this," Andrew said, grabbing my wrists, keeping them together. I gasped and my mother sobbed aloud. "I already made a deal with your daddy, and seeing as how you figured out more than we had anticipated, I'd say that I'm in a position of power now," he grinned, his teeth gleaming. "If you so much as whisper this to another soul, I imagine I could take care of a few loose ends."

The realization that I was right crossed my mother's face. Panic filled her eyes. Her jaw trembled.

"You can't kill her!" my mother cried. "She's my baby!"

"Oh, Miss Shea. Who do you take me for?" he grinned. "I wouldn't kill her. But I would tell the town about the sheriff's corruption. And then, your family would lose everything."

The flower shop. Our rental. Even the burned-down scraps of our old home, still standing after the house fire. None of that mattered. My mother swallowed a gulp as the tears slid down her face.

"If you told everyone about my father's corruption, you would be putting yourself in jeopardy too," I said.

Andrew smiled. "Not if I made an agreement for immunity. But you can prevent that. It's in your power, Kora. No one else's." He tightened his grip on my wrists and I grit my teeth together, sneering at him. "I'm done waiting." He pulled me in closer. "So what's it going to be?"

He leaned down, bringing his face closer to mine. My heart sank.

Vincent.

Vincent

I emptied the canister over the flowers. Most of it slid to the ground, but every once in a while, the fuel would collect like drops of dew on the petals. This place, this flower field on Mount Punica, was one of the last jewels of this town. And if I couldn't have Kora, then why should the town get to keep this?

I lit the match, throwing it onto the field. Immediately, the trail of gasoline ignited, and the flowers burned, curling under the flames, the yellow daffodils transforming into crumbled black remnants, like the beams of the Novas' house. I imagined Kora kneeling down in the middle of the blooms, looking up at me, unafraid. A fire like this would consume the field quickly, and likely spread down to the rest of the mountain. And with enough wind and the right luck, it might even stretch as far as my house. At least the dogs were gone. All that was left was the funeral home.

But nothing stirred within me. I wanted to watch it all burn, even if that meant me. But instead of weightlessness, I felt nothing.

All I wanted was Kora.

One by one, I would burn parts of Punica down. Until every siren, every police car, was searching for the arsonist. And either I would wrap my burning fingers around Kora and carry her through the fire with me, or I would make sure that nothing could trap her again. Even if that meant burying her in the grave.

And if Shea tried to stop me, I would kill her too.

Only then would Kora be free.

Chapter 39

Kora

Andrew's hot breath blasted my lips. I shrank into myself, closing my eyes. A siren wailed in the distance, making Andrew pause. I wrangled myself back, but he gripped my wrists, his ears turned toward the alarms. Another stream of sirens. He let go. I stumbled back next to my mother.

"What's happening?" Shea whispered.

Andrew grabbed his radio and turned it on. Static filled the room, then: *10-80.*

Sheriff Mike's voice: *Location?*

Another voice: *Mount Punica. Near the Wild Berry Trailhead.*

My mother looked at me, horror in her eyes. The flower field.

Andrew turned off his radio, then stowed it.

"Something tells me this is because of that no good fuckup," Andrew muttered. "He's dead this time."

"This time?" I asked. I grabbed Andrew's arm as he tried to walk away. "My mother and I heard you. We'll tell—"

"Who?" Andrew snapped around. "Who? You and your mother won't say a word," he laughed, throwing a hand in her direction. "She's your father's scared little bitch. You think she'll rat on me?"

I glanced at my mother. She clutched her face, her knuckles

white, her bottom lip quivering. No. I didn't believe him. She wouldn't let him kill Vincent without a fight.

Would she?

"Doesn't matter what you think. She's my mother," I said confidently, though the words were weak on my tongue. "She would never let you or my father get away with killing innocent people."

Andrew tilted his head. "You have a peculiar definition of the word 'innocent.' You see, in *my* eyes? Vincent has been wasting his life. So did the rest of them. What does all of that partying stand for, anyway?" He narrowed his gaze. "A waste of time."

Shea gasped.

"Nyla didn't do anything wrong! She was only twenty-three years old!" I shouted.

"And you were dumb enough to think that she'd live forever." He slapped me on the back and I clenched my fists. I wanted to punch him in the face, harder than I had with Vincent, and I wanted to run away too, to never give men like Andrew the time of day ever again. To pretend like he never existed.

I had done it with Vincent; I could do it with Andrew.

My fist pummeled his jaw in a loud *crack!* He rubbed his mouth; blood smeared his fingers.

"Assaulting an officer?" he smirked. "A valiant effort, at least. But we'll discuss your options later." He moved toward the door. "Now, if you'll excuse me. I've got to go take care of that fuckup."

"I will *never* let you get away with this," I said. Andrew stopped, his hand on the doorknob, then turned in place. Nerves fluttered inside of me.

"Don't worry, darling. If I have to, I'll take care of you too." He winked. "Now, I'm positive we can figure out an arrangement that will be beneficial for all of us, even your mommy and daddy. But we can do that later. Right now, I've got a criminal to catch."

He slammed the door behind him, and my mother and I rushed to the window, watching him walk down the driveway. His squad car peeled down the street, his sirens blaring with the rest. A chorus of chaos serenading the mountain.

I went outside, turning to find the silhouette of Mount Punica in the distance, a haze of dark gray smoke rising above it.

"What do you think he's doing?" Shea asked.

I wasn't sure if she was talking about Andrew, Mike, or Vincent. And I guess it didn't matter. All I knew was that I needed to find Vincent, to warn him, to make sure he was okay. But why was he doing this? What was he trying to prove by burning everything down?

Was he trying to tell me something?

My muscles quivered, my pulse speeding in my chest, heat radiating to my heart. My mother tied her fingers together. No matter how hard I stared, I couldn't see the woman who fell asleep for months on end without eating dinner, who cried silently when I wanted to leave for college. Who held it together every last day because she knew she had to. All I saw was the woman who desperately wanted to be the wife my father wanted, who wanted me to be like her. Because that would mean I was safe.

But I could never be that woman. I wouldn't let myself. Not for her. Not for my father. Not even for Vincent. I had to be my own person, and that meant making my own decisions. That meant deciding my future *for me*.

"Did you know?" I asked. Tears filled her eyes. "About Nyla, Mom. Did you know?"

"No," she whispered. "No. Never."

Relief trickled through me, but it was short-lived. I was glad she wasn't like Andrew or Mike, but that didn't change the fact that now we both knew the truth. We *both* had to decide what that meant to us.

But I already knew what I needed to do. I needed to find Vincent. I needed to protect him, to save him, like he had saved me.

I ran inside and grabbed the keys out of my mother's purse. I had never driven a car before, but I crossed my fingers that I would learn easily. It would be quicker driving than running.

"Where are you going?" my mother shouted.

I opened the driver's side door and my stomach turned. Where would I even start?

"Don't leave me," she screamed. "I can't bear to lose you again."

My body buzzed with energy, making my fingers twitch. I hated doing this to her, but I couldn't keep catering to her anymore either. I had needs too, and I was done putting myself behind everyone else.

"What about Poppies & Wheat?" she asked. "What if he goes there next?"

I took a deep breath. I hoped not, but who could tell where he was going next?

"He won't," I said. "Not if I get to him first."

She threw her hands down at her sides. "I won't let you go, Kora," she threatened, "not by yourself."

"Get in the car," I said. I couldn't waste any more time. We had to leave now.

She scrambled to the passenger door. "Kora—"

Her phone rang. She pulled it out and the caller ID blinked on the screen: *Vincent Erickson.*

Vincent

A swarm of fire trucks and police cars zoomed down the highway. A hunger buzzed in my chest, my skin hot, my breathing quick. If all of them were here with the fire, including Sheriff Mike and Officer Andrew, then this would be a breeze. I could leave with Kora in my arms within the hour.

But I needed everyone to be distracted, including her mother. That was the only way I'd be able to take her now.

The streets were deserted. The townspeople had likely followed the commotion. A serenity swept over me as I parked downtown, following the street to Poppies & Wheat. A golden flower was painted on the sign that hung above the door. A bell jingled when I entered.

It was chilly inside. A young woman in an apron popped up from behind the counter.

"Hi! How can I help you?" she asked.

Pots hung from the ceiling, the vines dripping over the sides of the containers. Most of the walls had glass-door refrigerators. Bright sunflowers, white roses and lilies, and a table in the center full of vases of different shapes and sizes overflowing with rustic bouquets.

"I see you're browsing," the woman said. "My name is Nikki. Just holler if you need me."

She turned toward the back room. I cleared my throat.

"You should go," I said.

She raised a brow at me. "Excuse me, sir?"

"You heard those sirens?" I motioned in the direction of Mount Punica. "This place is next."

Her face turned pale.

"You should go," I repeated. I was burning this shop down whether or not she was in it.

She quickly ran to the storeroom, grabbing her bag, and when she stumbled for the key to lock up behind her, I held out my hand.

"I'll take those," I said.

She threw them across the street, then lurched forward, tripping down the sidewalk. It's not like I actually needed them, but it would be more convenient if I could get through the entrance easily.

The alarms were finally hushed, signaling that all the required forces had arrived at the Wild Berry Trailhead. I steadied my breath. The canisters were heavy in my hands, but as the fluid fell, the weight lifted from my shoulders. Drenching the pots. The vines. The ribbons in that back room. The coolers with shivering flowers.

I lit a match, dropping it down, the rush of heat blowing against my skin. I stepped back, exiting the building, entranced as the fires engulfed the structure. Soon, it would spread, taking the building to one side, and the wildflowers on the other.

Do you ever get the feeling like you're reliving the same day on repeat?

Kora's voice filled my brain as I went to the viewpoint railing and admired the burning flower shop. Three years ago, I had seen her there for the first time. And now, I was watching one of her childhood memories burn to the ground. Like I had burned her house.

You are better than this, she had said. *You've been so against everything.*

I clenched my fists. I was only against what kept Kora stuck in a cycle where she was never anything but what the other people wanted. That would never be okay with me.

But it's not that simple, Vincent. You know it's not.

My chest tightened, thinking of her words. The way the moonlight lit her face in shades of blue, a coolness that never left her.

You have to start treating me like I treat you.

The flames curled around the top of the building, flushing over the sides. And still, I felt nothing. What would I accomplish by doing this? A dryness swelled in the back of my throat, a numbness coursing through me. It didn't matter how much of the town I burned. Kora had to decide for herself.

It was never up to me.

I grabbed my phone out of my pocket and dialed Kora's number. It went straight to voicemail, so I searched for Shea's number on the internet and sent the call. The phone rang three times. But finally, she answered.

"Hello?" she asked, her voice hesitant. "Mr. Erickson?"

"Your shop is on fire," I said.

Her tone immediately shifted into anger. "What is this? What are you—"

"If you want to save any of it, you'll have to go now. Call the fire department."

"You can't—"

I hung up the phone. Then I got in my car and headed to my house. If I was lucky, the firefighters had contained the Wild Berry Trailhead by now, and it wouldn't touch my home or the cemetery. Inside, the house was silent, the dogs still with Catie. I grabbed my other gun, then buckled the holster, stowing my weapon, checking the bullets.

I went through the cemetery. Black clouds hung above Punica, the sky a deep orange. The fire must have spread from Shea's shop, taking the neighboring store with it.

I sat down next to her grave. I shook my head, irritated at myself for phrasing it like that. It was *our* grave. I ran my fingers along the daffodil, a hint of regret deep in my stomach. I had burned that flower field, a piece of her, a piece of *us*, and nothing would be the same.

But fuck it all. I didn't want things to stay the same. I wanted Kora to be free. Even if that meant free from me.

A shadow stretched across the grass like a scaffold at dawn.

"Well, here is Punica's most wanted," Andrew said, the ice pick hanging from his grip. "I was beginning to think you'd skipped town on us."

I clenched my fists. "Not without Kora," I said.

Chapter 40

Kora

CALL ENDED BLINKED ON THE PHONE SCREEN.

Your shop is on fire, Vincent had said. *If you want to save any of it, you'll have to go now.*

Was he trying to warn her?

"What do we do?" Shea asked. "He isn't serious." She blinked her eyes. "Is he?"

Did I need to remind her of what he had done to our old house? She must have been stuck in this idea that being the sheriff's wife made her invincible, which was far from the truth. The house fire should have shown her that. I put on my seatbelt, turning the key in the ignition. The engine rumbled to life, and a sick knot twisted in my stomach.

I was really doing this. *I had to.*

"I can drive," Shea said. "It's not safe for you to be behind the wheel."

If I had to, I would drive at five miles per hour. But I wasn't going to let my mother drive me anywhere.

"I've seen you drive enough," I said.

"Watching is not the same thing as—"

I put the car into reverse, going down the driveway far faster than I anticipated, a surge of adrenaline racing through me. My mother yelped, then quickly put on her seatbelt. Once it clicked into place, I jerked the car down the street, out of Rose Garden Neighborhood, back to the main roads. Luckily, the streets were empty. Eventually, I got used to the gas and brake pedals, but as my heart pounded, it became hard to concentrate on anything. So I sped up. We needed to get there *now*. Vincent was in trouble. We needed to find him before Andrew got to him.

Poppies & Wheat came into view. Black and white smoke rose above the shop, mixing together in a swirl, hovering in the sky like a storm cloud. I parked across the street, getting out of the car, standing on the viewpoint. What would Vincent do next? My mother was paralyzed in the front seat, pressing her back against the cushion.

I opened the door, leaning down to her. She closed her eyes, her body rigid.

"We need to go," she whispered. The front windows of the store cracked, the shards crashing onto the sidewalk. Shea jumped. The orange and red flames grew, blocking the view of the inside.

"Did you call Nikki?" I asked.

Keeping herself against the seat, she quickly dialed her number.

"Miss Nova?" Nikki's familiar voice said, the volume on my mother's phone so loud, I could hear her perfectly. Relief waved through me. "Your flower shop. It's—"

"I know," my mother whispered. "Did you see who did this?"

"A man. Dark hair. A scar on his neck. He had a bruise on his eye—"

"And you let him do this?"

A beat of silence passed. "He told me to get out. So I—"

"And you didn't call me? The police? The fire department?"

"Miss Shea, I—"

"It's fine," my mother grumbled. "I'll do it."

"I can—"

"Don't," my mother barked. Then she hung up.

I stepped back from the vehicle. "Call the fire department," I said.

Shea stayed frozen in her seat. Drowning in fear. I took a step back. If she wasn't going to do anything, then I needed to go *now*.

"I don't have my phone with me," I started, "but you have Vincent's number—"

She jumped out of the car, tripping over her heels as she stumbled onto the sidewalk. She grabbed my shoulders, shaking me.

"You can't go," she said. "If what you said is true, then none of them can be trusted. Not your father. Not Andrew. Not even Vincent." Her eyes bulged, her voice trembling: "All we have is each other."

That wasn't true, but she wouldn't understand. I turned toward the street, checking the direction of the funeral home. Vincent must have been insane to think that burning down the town would give me a signal. A sign that he loved me.

But it wasn't all about destruction. Not anymore. He didn't want Nikki to die, nor my mother. He even warned her of what he had done. He just wanted the world to burn.

And I didn't blame him for that.

"I have to go," I said. I stepped around Shea, going toward the driver's seat of the car, but she stepped in front of me.

"I won't let you." Her eyes narrowed on mine. Her nostrils flared, her feet planted firmly apart, ready to brace for my impact. Ready for me to fight her.

But there was no time for that. If I couldn't drive, then I would go on foot. I went around her, walking down the sidewalk.

"Please don't leave me," she begged, her voice rattling. The shop's windows shattered, every last piece of glass spilling on the sidewalk. Shea flung a hand over her mouth to keep herself from whimpering.

"Call the fire department," I repeated. "Then leave. You don't have to watch this." I motioned toward the car. "I have to go."

"You're making a mistake," she said. "He doesn't love you. He wants to kill you."

The flames reached high above the roof. The breeze fueled the fire, the flames growing to the clouds. From across the street, the heat brushed against our skin, the yellow, white, and red flames mixing with black clouds. The fire roared.

303

Each time I had been inside of the crematory room, Vincent had opened the furnace door, letting the heat brush my skin. Like when he had placed me on that conveyor belt, threatening to burn me. We didn't know each other than, and yet, when I was ready to let the fire take me, to release me from this existence, he had stopped me. He had threatened me, tried to hurt me, and taken everything from me, and yet he had given me so much. Shown me what it meant to be free.

Because Vincent wanted me to understand what it meant to live.

"He never wanted to kill me," I said. I put my hands on my hips, trying to be strong. "All he wanted was for you to wake up. For Dad to see what was there, that you and I were waiting for him. That I was there for you, Mom. Every time. Because in the end, I was nothing to you. Nothing but a prop. But to Vincent?" I gestured at the fire as if he was inside of there, as if the flames were a representation of him. As if I could feel him with us. "Vincent always saw me. When you locked me away. At the dead of night. Even when I thought no one in the world could understand. He always did."

"That's not love, sweetheart." She bowed her head. "That's obsession."

And maybe she was right. Maybe that's all it really was: Vincent's sick obsession where I was the centerpiece, the muscle that kept twitching, that kept everything connected, even when all the other signs said to give up.

But it was *ours.* Our obsession. Our screwed-up love. And for once, it didn't matter who I was, or what image I was failing to uphold. Because Vincent saw me. The real me.

"I know what our love is," I said firmly, "and I don't care."

Her skin flushed, her hands wiggling at her sides. "I'm the only one who has always been there for you, who never stopped looking for you. The only one who will keep you truly safe." She bared her teeth. "Does that mean anything to you?"

"Safety isn't always what you think it is," I said quietly. The fire crackled loudly to the side of us, and I raised my voice:

"Safety doesn't matter if you sacrifice your happiness along with it."

"Don't I make you happy?"

I stared into her green eyes, the color she had given me. She had wanted to be the perfect image of a family for so long, that now, now that she knew with certainty, that her husband wasn't the man she thought he was, she was latching onto me. But that didn't fool me. I knew it was never about my father, nor was it about me. It was about making Shea secure. She needed someone like that. Someone to protect. Someone to make her feel like she wouldn't disappear.

But even if I was going to be there for her, I needed to be there for myself first. And I couldn't give up Vincent. I refused.

"I will always come back to you," I said. "But my heart doesn't belong to you."

A sob crumbled through her. "He doesn't deserve you."

"None of us deserve this," I said, thinking of the words Vincent had spoken from the viewpoint years ago. "But he's mine. And I'm his."

Her chin quivered. She shook her head incessantly, then picked her phone out of her pocket.

"I'm calling the police department," she said.

I moved toward the car and she stood in front of me.

"Nine-one-one operator, what's your emergency?" a voice asked.

"Yes," Shea said. "I'd like to report a fire. My—"

"We already have a team responding to Mount Punica, ma'am."

"Poppies & Wheat," she stammered. "The flower shop is burning."

"My apologies. It's been a stressful day," the operator said. "Do you know what caused the fire, ma'am?"

Shea held the phone against her shoulder, covering the microphone as she spoke to me: "If you go, I will never forgive you for this."

In the distance, white smoke rose above Mount Punica, dissipating into the overcast sky. The fire trucks would be here soon, and then my chance would be gone. Shea's eyes were full of water, ready to burst.

"I know," I said. Everything inside of me needed to tell her I was sorry, that I didn't want to hurt her, but I couldn't say those words. Because I wasn't sorry for what I was about to do.

"Ma'am?" the operator said. "Are you there, ma'am?"

She turned back to the phone. "W-what was your question?"

"Do you know what started the fire?" the operator asked. "The more we know, the more adequately we can handle the situation."

Shea closed her eyes. I was ready to hear her say those words: *Vincent Erickson.*

"No," my mother said quietly. "No. I don't know what caused it."

The flames roared to the side, burning my eyes. Tears ran down my mother's cheeks, and she turned away from me. I knew it hurt her to say those words, but I was grateful she had given us a chance. My mother moved down the sidewalk, keeping her back to me as she continued to speak to the operator. I quickly got into the car, then I drove down the street, hoping that I would get to Quiet Meadows in time.

Chapter 41

Vincent

Andrew's shadow loomed over the cemetery. The ice pick hung in his palm, his gun shining on his hip.

"Kora isn't going anywhere," he said.

"Have you asked her that?"

"I don't have to."

It pissed me off that everyone thought they could make decisions for Kora. *Even me.* But I could be different now. I wanted her to have her own choice. To be seen for who she was. And I knew Andrew would never do that for her.

"You think you know her?" I said. Andrew's palm twitched around the ice pick's handle. "You're nothing but a mouthpiece for the sheriff." I laughed, tilting my head back. "Trust me, without you, she'll be fine."

"And will it kill you when she chooses me?" He cracked his neck. "Soon, we'll have you connected to all the arsons, and then the Echo Killer." He grinned wildly. "You broke the agreement, Vincent. The only reason Sheriff Mike agreed to let you out was because Kora swore to do whatever her mother said. Now that's been broken, and the sheriff never did declare that you were immune from being arrested again." He smirked. "No one can save you this time."

"I almost wish she would save me," I forced a chuckle, "to show your sorry ass how stupid you are."

He scowled at me, straightening, his image silhouetted in a film of gray. He grabbed his handcuffs from his back pocket.

"You're under arrest for the arson of the Wild Berry Trailhead and Poppies & Wheat, in connection with the Echo murders."

"You're giving me all the credit," I said. "How thoughtful of you."

"Make this easy on me." He stepped forward, the handcuffs dangling from his fingers. "You might even live."

"Not my priority."

"You'd die for something as pitiful as her honor?" He grinned. "Wow. You really are pathetic."

It was more than that. It was the ability to give her a path that was unwritten, one that she would choose for herself. One where her mother didn't decide, where Andrew wouldn't be her inevitable end.

As long as he went down with me, I didn't care what happened. I clenched my fists, my ears pounding.

"This'll be over soon anyway," Andrew said.

"Then let's do this."

He dropped the cuffs, then came forward, swinging a fist at me, the ice pick in his other hand. I ducked, then found a shovel resting on a nearby tree. I swung it toward him, the ice pick blocking my strike, and he bared his teeth. The tools banged together, one blocking the other, until finally, he swung so hard that I used the return momentum to shove his ice pick to the ground. I hurled the metal end of the shovel at his head, but he flung a foot out underneath me, knocking me to the ground, my shovel falling out of my hands.

I grinned, clutching my fists. Andrew did the same. Weightlessness filled my chest. I swung forward, landing a punch on his jaw. He used that second to sling a fist into my stomach, following with a kick in the ribs. I pulled him to the side, down the hill, back to the main part of the cemetery. The headstones stood tall, judging us, our feet running over the flattened memorial plaques.

Our breaths were frenzied with recklessness. I swung at his face, knocking into his nose.

"Good always triumphs over evil," Andrew said, pulling back and wiping his forehead. "And I *will* triumph, Erickson."

I got the impression that he really believed that everything he did was for the good of the citizens, for the sheriff, for the county. He was such a self-righteous prick, and yet he took innocent lives as if it restored order. But I didn't care what he did. Who lived. Who died. I didn't even care if I took the blame for it anymore. None of that mattered to me. The only person who mattered was Kora.

He surged forward, and I attacked him with my curled fists. His punch landed in my eye, my vision blurry, my head pounding. Another punch to my jaw. Blood filled my mouth.

"You're a selfish prick," Andrew said. "Abducting her. Keeping her to yourself. Depriving her of a life she deserves."

I knew all of that and I didn't care. I couldn't change what had happened, and I would never take it back. But I could change what I did now. And if that meant killing Andrew—if that meant going to jail—if that meant leaving me buried in the ground while Kora moved on to thrive somewhere else, then so fucking be it.

I was a selfish prick, but I was never trying to hide that.

"At least I know what I am," I said.

Latching onto my shoulders, he threw me to the side, and I stayed still, letting him think I was in pain, but once he got close enough, I opened myself to a punch, then immediately returned the strike to his jaw. He clutched his face, then spit blood onto one of the graves. We traveled forward, moving with the fight, down to the empty burial sites, waiting to be filled.

A second passed, both of us out of breath. We stared at each other. He pulled out his phone.

"I'm going to need you to come down to the cemetery," he said. "Yes, Sheriff." Then he hung up. He wasn't using the radio then, which meant the sheriff knew exactly what was going on. How far did the corruption run?

"So how many were you planning on killing today?" Andrew asked. "With those fires. The drugs. I'm dying to know."

"Can't even take responsibility for it now, can you?" I said. "Why not admit what you did? What I *know* you did. What the sheriff knows you did. I'm sure Kora knows what you did too." My eyes twinkled with rage. "Or are you afraid?"

He narrowed his eyes at me, thinking over the words, evaluating if I was a threat. He straightened, his fists at his sides.

"I killed them," he said in a low voice, "Each and every one of them. Sometimes with the sheriff's help, but most of the time, all by myself. And I'll do it again. If it means securing the sheriff's position. If it means guaranteeing my future."

I smashed my fist forward, and he blocked it, but I rammed forward again and again until I finally made a hit.

"You're a corrupt bastard," I muttered.

He punched my jaw, the pain surging to my temple. "You do understand me, don't you, Erickson?" he sneered. "Sometimes, sacrifices have to be made. And sometimes, that means taking the lives of young ones. But all of them were criminals. Underage drinking. Drugs. Fake IDs."

"Nyla wasn't like that," I said. Our fists flew at each other again. "And once Kora finds out, she will never forgive you."

"I don't need Kora's forgiveness," he snickered, kicking at my shins. "All I need is her signature on the marriage license." He held my fist, and I grunted hard, pushing out of his grasp. He tilted his head to the side. "Trust me, Erickson, if she wants to live a good, long life, she'll do whatever I say."

My vision was red, blood throbbing in my ears, and I railed into him, then spun him around, wrapping him into a chokehold from behind, pulling my elbow tight, pushing on the back of his head so that his throat was against my arm. He swung a fist back, knocking my grip loose, and coughed himself awake. He came forward, his fists at his side, and I punched hard but missed, and he shoved me backward. I stumbled into one of the empty graves. Darkness fell over me, the sides shadowing the bottom of the pit.

I looked up at that rectangle of light. Andrew peered down, then disappeared. My heart pounded, my blood pulsing everywhere. I still had my gun, but so did Andrew. I needed to time everything right.

He returned, the ice pick in his palm.

"Maybe you won't go down as the Echo Killer, but another victim," he said. "You're right; I should take credit. If it means taking your life."

He jumped into the burial plot. I left myself open. And when he swung the pick at me, I blocked it with my hand, the pick's pointed blade puncturing my palm, nailing me against the dirt. A grin stretched across his face as he pulled the pick out and I howled into the air. But when he came closer, raising the pick above his head, aimed at my heart, I grabbed my gun, shooting him twice in the chest. He was stunned for a second, his eyes dropping down. I kicked him back into the wall of dirt. He knocked my gun out of my hand, but I grabbed the ice pick from his loose hands and swung it down onto his chest with a piercing thump.

His eyes flickered with energy, then he fell back, gaping at the gray sky.

I wet my lips, staring down at him. My gun lay beneath him. With my brother, the regret was instant, the anger simultaneous. The rage was focused on myself for being impulsive, hating myself for what I had done. But this was different. My chest expanded like I was floating. Kora was free. She wouldn't have to marry a man who would likely abuse her. I let out a breath. The sirens wailed in the distance.

"Didn't think it would come to this," another male voice said. I turned around quickly; Sheriff Mike came toward the open rectangle of light. "You know, I always liked you, Erickson. Even when the rest of the department thought for sure that you had murdered your brother, I backed you up. *Now, now,* I would tell them, *Why would a good man like Erickson kill his own brother?* The only motive you had was to keep the funeral home to yourself. But Justin was ready to give it to you, wasn't he?" He removed his gun from the holster. "Now, that didn't make sense. None of it did. But I suppose I should have arrested you back then. Maybe it would have saved Andrew." He gritted his teeth. "He was like a son to me."

I scowled. My gun was in my peripherals, beneath Andrew's shoulder.

"You treated him better than your daughter," I said.

"I never wanted a daughter. Never wanted a family. But I always wanted power. And this," he grinned, pulling back the hammer, "This is worth it." He raised the gun, straightening his aim at me. My body hardened. I needed to get that gun now. "Don't worry," he said in a low voice. "This town will be safer now. Especially Kora."

I plunged forward, reaching for the gun. My whole body went numb. A shot went off and I swallowed a breath, but I didn't feel anything. There was no blood anywhere. I looked up: the sheriff held his chest, then glanced at his hand. It was covered in blood. He turned around to see who it was, but by the time he did, his body fell forward, falling into the grave on top of Andrew with a hard thud. Someone had shot him, saving my life.

Kora stepped forward, her jaw clenched, the gun still aimed down at her father. The canvas bag's strap slid down her shoulder. Once she was satisfied that he was dead, she dropped the gun to the ground, then fell to her knees.

Her green eyes looked down, waiting for me.

Chapter 42

Kora

Chills ran up and down my spine as I gazed at the blood trailing down Vincent's lips. His brow and cheek were swollen. His eyes held me.

"Are you okay?" he asked.

He was asking about me when he was the one who was hurt, the one who had been through who-knows-what with my father and Andrew? I didn't want to think about it. Didn't want to relive what I had just done.

"Are you okay?" I asked.

He nodded. And with that simple movement, a heaviness sunk through me. I wanted to lie down and stare up at the sky, but we couldn't let go. There were two dead bodies to take care of. We couldn't waste any time.

"The ladder," I said. I ran through the graves, my skin tingling, and when I found it, I lowered it into the plot. He climbed out, leaving the two bodies in the hole.

He put a hand on my cheek. His hand was grimy, caked with sweat and dirt. Chemicals and body odor wafted from his skin, his lips bloodied and cracked. His dark eyes found mine, black with the white clouds of smoke reflected in them.

"Are you okay?" he asked again. Tears filled my eyes. I shook my head, and he pulled me closer, a firm grip around me. Once I felt his touch, once I felt safe and seen, everything inside of me poured out, the tears falling through me.

But Vincent was okay. He was okay, and my mother was okay, and my mother hadn't ratted him out. But Andrew was gone, and my father—

My father was gone too. I had killed him.

"He told Andrew to kill Nyla," I whispered through the sobs.

Vincent didn't say a word, just held me close, running his fingers through my knotted hair. I couldn't stop them from killing Nyla, but I had stopped my father from killing Vincent. My mouth was dry, my stomach weak, and I hated, *hated* that I felt better now, knowing that they were both gone. Two men I had known all of my life, men who had sworn to protect me. I hated that I felt safer with Vincent than I ever had with my family.

But I had the power to accept what was real. And I let myself feel every screwed-up emotion that was left inside of me, everything pouring out in tears, in rage, stomping my feet, screaming into Vincent's chest, sobbing until the nausea and every last tear were gone. Vincent held me, never once offering unsolicited advice. He knew this was all I needed: acceptance.

Finally, I turned to him. "What do we do?"

"Not sure," he said. "What do you want to do?"

The world was quiet. Most of the town was at Mount Punica or downtown, watching the chaos unfold. But us? We were here, alone in the cemetery. It was hard for me to comprehend that he cared enough to let me make my own decisions. So I tried to think it over.

"The bodies," I said, gesturing at the burial plot. "The cars first?"

He took a deep breath, then squeezed my shoulder. "Let's do it."

After a quick shower, Vincent put on gloves, then hot-wired both cars, removed the tracking devices, and took them out to Mount Punica. He dropped them off on the other side of the volcano, spreading them apart from the Wild Berry Trailhead. Then, after he had gotten a rideshare back and called Catie to bicker, he said that she had agreed to ask the new medical examiner for a favor, to patch up the stab wound on his palm, off of the clock.

And while he was gone, I examined the hole. The bodies lay there. I imagined Nyla lying in the totaled car on the side of the road. Her twenty-third birthday. What gave them the right to decide when she died?

And maybe I didn't have that right to decide when their lives ended either, but I wasn't going to take it back. If I had to live with myself, I would rather have killed them than have done nothing at all.

I climbed down, lifting my father's shoulders, but he was so heavy I could barely move him. I tried with Andrew, and though Andrew was smaller than my father, he was solid muscle. A car door slammed shut, then the dogs trampled forward, barking down at me. My heart raced in my chest. Who was it? And how was I going to explain this to them?

My hands shook as I climbed the ladder. Catie bent down, petting the dogs. And when she saw me, her brows furrowed.

"Vincent went out," I said. I wiped my brow with the back of my hand, a slimy substance crossing my skin. I was covered in dirt and blood.

"You look," she paused, tilting her head, "busy."

"Sort of," I said sheepishly.

"I'll close the cemetery, then," she said. "You want me to handle the funeral home while you're—" she gestured around, "—working?"

I nodded. "Thanks. Vincent should be back soon."

"Okay," she said, whistling. "I'll be inside."

Annoyed at myself for not being able to push a two-hundred-pound body up to the grass, I went inside Vincent's kitchen, finding a cleaver. I climbed down, carrying the knife's handle between my teeth, focusing on the task itself. I took a deep breath, letting the air expel slowly.

"I hope Nyla stomps on you," I said. Then I brought the cleaver down as hard as I could onto Andrew's arm. It split the skin and flesh in a hard whack, deep red blood oozing out. The scent of dirty pennies filled the air, but I did it again, and again, until finally, his arm broke off.

One arm down. Three to go.

A bizarre sensation washed over me, like I was watching myself do all of these things. Dismembering a body. A corpse. Knowing that they felt nothing.

"And I hope Vincent's brother smashes your face," I said, bring down the cleaver on my father's neck. The snap of the bone made me cringe, but I was almost done.

I threw one of the calves up to the ground, then started working on tossing up the rest of the body. Sarah leaned down and whined.

"What is it, girl?" I asked.

Bernie barked, then took the calf, dragging it off.

"Hey!" I shouted. "Wait!"

Ulysses sat next to Sarah, whining in a chorus. Then they both carried off arms of their own. My head was dizzy, my body still vibrating with adrenaline that kept me going. I couldn't stop them now.

Vincent peered down the hole.

"I didn't mean for them to get the body parts," I said. He laughed, then reached down, waiting for the other body parts, and I lifted them to him.

On the ground, the dogs' canines tore into the flesh, dark blood gathering on their fur. Sarah looked at me, certainty in her eyes, almost like she wanted to protect me. She had accepted me too.

Vincent returned with black garbage bags. We gathered the body parts together, including the chewed-up pieces. Once we were done, Vincent turned to me.

"Let me take care of this," he said. "Why don't you take a shower?"

I nodded, grateful for the break. The water ran brown and pink, mixing at the bottom of the tub until finally, it was clear again. And I didn't think about what that meant. Or the fact that I didn't know what I was doing with my life. Or what my actions meant for my future. I focused on my breath.

Nyla was dead. My father and Andrew were dead.

But Vincent was alive. So was my mother. And I was okay too.

By the time I was tucked into sweatpants and an oversized shirt I found in Vincent's bedroom, the firepit was roaring in the backyard. It was finally night. The outline of a few limbs flickered in the flames, but it was hard to tell what was what. Vincent tossed in another arm, then a thigh, one by one, watching the fire flicker in shades of red and black, until finally, they were all gone. I thought for sure that we would get in trouble for lighting a fire after the amount of smoke Punica had endured that day, but no one came. Everyone, including the police, was too tired to care about a controlled fire.

I laughed to myself. I was worried about fire laws when what we were doing was so much worse. I turned to Vincent.

"What if they find out?" I asked.

"This is their evidence," he said, gesturing at the pit. "The bones, we'll pulverize in the home. Spread them somewhere." The fire crackled, the scent of roasting meat enveloping us. He gestured at the flames. "If it comes down to it, I'll take full responsibility."

"That's stupid. I was there. I killed my father. Don't do that to yourself."

"I've done enough for a lifetime in jail. You were only defending me."

I wasn't sure how to take that, or whether he was telling the truth, but I knew he was never going to let me say otherwise. And if it came down to it, I would never let him take the blame like that. It was our decision. Our mess. Not mine. Not his. But *ours*.

As we watched the bodies burn, Sarah came and sat beside us. Vincent tossed a stick into the flames.

"My brother wanted to kill himself," he said. "But I didn't let him." He threw another twig forward. "I killed him myself."

We looked at each other, the flames dancing on our skin. Without him speaking the words, I knew I was the first person he had ever admitted that to. Because he knew what I was feeling right then, the tremendous weight of the what-ifs trickling through me. The rage. The guilt. The self-loathing. The righteousness.

"Nothing can change it," he said, grabbing my hand. "You did what you thought was right. Better than me." He gave a melancholy chuckle. "I did it out of anger."

My fingers twitched. That wasn't completely true. I had been angry at my father too. For the life he robbed from Nyla. From all of those people, young adults like me.

I leaned my head on his shoulder, and Vincent's body tensed, then relaxed under my weight.

"What do we do now?" I asked.

"Wait for a few hours, then grind up the bones."

"No." I sat up, facing him. "*Us?* We? What do *we* do now?"

His eyes searched mine, and an eerie sense of coolness drifted over him.

"It isn't up to me to decide. It's your life."

"I know that," I said. "But what about you?"

"This isn't about me, Kora. It's about *you*," his voice was stern. He held my chin, cupped in his palm. "It's always been about you, Kora."

My heart tightened, pulling my nerves back to my chest.

"But what do you want for your life?" I asked.

"I want to make you happy." His eyes never left mine. "I want to do whatever that means to you."

I pressed forward, our lips meeting, and he grimaced at the touch, his lips swollen and bruised, but after a moment, his tongue dug into my mouth. Violently, he broke apart.

"I don't deserve you," he said.

"This world is never good enough for any of us," I said. A small smile flickered across his lips. "But I don't care. I love you, Vincent."

He clutched my face. "I love you, flower."

Then he kissed me hard, like he would never get enough.

We sat around the fire until the early morning. A few charred chunks were leftover, so we brought them inside the funeral home and finished them off in the crematory. Then we pulverized the fragments. Once we boxed the granules in an old vase, we took them in the car and headed out.

The police stopped us for questioning. In the chaos, it seemed like the sheriff and the captain had disappeared, and now, there were suspicions that the two of them had started the fires as a ploy to play heroes and get more votes. But when it had gotten out of hand, they left town.

I didn't think they suspected us, and once we got rid of the ashes, it wouldn't matter. We would probably have to *truly* get rid of the cars, but after that, we would be okay.

Vincent drove us to the far end of downtown, a few blocks away from the flower shop, to a plot of land. There was a styrofoam cup, a burger wrapper, and a few dandelions. It reminded me of the lot next to Poppies & Wheat before Nyla and I had spread wildflower seeds in it.

"What is this?" I asked.

He showed me an email on his phone. *Offer, Lot 20809, Downtown Punica.* I raised a brow.

"It's not official yet, but the realtor is hopeful," he said.

"You're opening up a new funeral home?" I asked.

"Your greenhouse." He rubbed the back of his neck. "Or, whatever you want."

I stared at it, seeing the possibilities. As a piece of flat land, the lot seemed so small, but with time and structure, it could be bigger than anything I had dreamed of. It was hard to imagine.

"I was thinking you could call it Spring Renewal," he said. "I guess it's the whole transformation of it." He kicked the cup further into the lot. "Trash to beauty."

He put his hands behind his head, unsure of himself, knowing that the gesture was a strange one. I reached up on my tip-toes and kissed him.

"*We* can call it Spring Renewal," I said. My heart swelled with warmth. "I love it."

That night, we drove down Willow Highway to 52 Peaks. Every so often, we parked on the side of the road and spread more ashes. Little grains of bone dusted the asphalt, then mixed with the dirt in the forest. At the club, the parking lot was empty, but the music still blasted through the building. I had no desire to go inside, but I could almost feel Nyla there. I could see why she loved it.

We let out the last handful of sand, letting it swirl with the wind.

In the car, the radio turned to the news: *Local law enforcement agencies are baffled at the disappearance of Sheriff Mike Nova and Captain Andrew Pompino. It appears that there may have been some connection between the arson attacks and the Echo deaths. Mayor Renolds has asked the county commissioner to put the election on hold—*

I turned off the radio. Vincent turned to me.

"Has your mother called?" he asked.

I shook my head. "But I'm not going to give up on my mother."

"I would never ask you to do that."

A weight lifted from my stomach. So much had changed about us. And yet, there was still a tracking chip in my arm, but I knew that if I wanted, I could get that removed too. The difference now was that Vincent trusted me. And I trusted him. I loved him, more than I had known was possible.

In Quiet Meadows, we crept through the empty hallways, back to the cemetery. We sat with our feet dangled in our grave, holding hands, talking about nothing, until finally, I slipped inside the plot.

"Come here," I said.

Vincent shook his head. "What are you doing?"

"Come join me!" I laughed.

He set the ladder to the side of the plot, then slid in too, and as soon as our feet were level on the ground, he pressed me to the side of the wall and kissed me. Clumps of dirt fell around us, ruining the perfection he had sculpted, and I loved it even more. Maybe one day I would be buried here. Maybe he would be buried here too. But right then, all I wanted were his lips on mine. His hands raked through my short hair, I dug my fingernails into his back, and the dogs barked to the sides of us, rounding the grave in a flurry of excitement.

The moon lit the cemetery in a tender light, and his lips were violent and yielding. *One day, you'll wake up and you'll realize none of this matters,* he had said, *I promise.* His black eyes had held me then, looking deep inside of my soul, as if he could see the future. As if he could see us.

And he had kept that promise. None of my worries mattered anymore.

Epilogue

Vincent

one year later

The doors to the funeral home opened. A single set of heels clicked on the tile, and I knew instantly who it was. Usually, Catie was the one who mediated between us, but without her there, Shea was stuck with me.

"Mom," I said, opening my arms wide in a mock gesture. Shea glared at me, her arms wrapped around a skinny-limbed tree, the soil wrapped in a burlap sack.

"Where do you want this one?" she asked.

"Follow me."

We went through the side exit to the cemetery, then over to the plot of grass to the side, where a grove of trees stood tall. A sign hung above the arch, vines clinging to the edges. *Spring Renewal*, it said. The same name as Kora's new greenhouse.

Though Shea refused to believe I was her daughter's boyfriend, when it came to the night where two people disappeared and her shop burned down, she stayed to her original story: Kora and I had been with her the whole time, comforting her about the shop. No one questioned it. We stuck with that story too.

I didn't understand her reasons for backing us up—or, better yet, for backing me up, but I didn't have to. She wasn't holding it over me, but we weren't exactly friends either. Any time she was around, it was cold and dry, like the dead of winter, but she was kind to Kora, and actually listened to her now. All it took was a little arson.

She set down the tree next to the new hole. She had stopped dying her hair and put the loose gray strands behind her ears. And though Kora kept her hair shoulder-length, Shea had grown hers out past that. So in a way, some things did change. I thought of the painting hanging in Shea's new shop location, one she had bid on from an art auction, because the painting reminded her of her daughter. She didn't know who had painted it, but because of her bid, the artist had won the contest. Except, no one knew who had submitted it.

Whenever I saw it in her shop, I smiled to myself. Just like I was smiling then.

"She's still at the greenhouse," Shea said, gesturing behind her. "She might be there forever if you don't go rescue her now."

"Thanks," I said. Shea left, heading back to her new flower shop, and I drove to the greenhouse. Three young women, including the one who had been Poppies & Wheat the day I burned it down, stood before Kora in green aprons, as she listed off final training instructions.

"So, Nikki is in charge," Kora said. "But you can always call me if you need to."

Kora turned toward me, her shoulders relaxing as we locked eyes. The three women dispersed, leaving us by ourselves.

"Did you pack yet?" I asked. She shook her head. "But you leave tomorrow."

"I know," she said, laughing. "I'll just throw in everything tonight." She pulled on my arm. "Let's go see her."

We grabbed a portfolio from the house, then walked to the cemetery. After a vined arch, trees lined the path like an orchard, but none of the trees were the same. We had struck a partnership; Spring Renewal Greenhouse worked with the families at Quiet Meadows to provide burial trees and other plants. Using my regular vendors, we had plaques created for them too.

Next to the long skinny branches of an Eastern Redbud tree, facing a bush of yellow daffodils, I pulled a thick piece of canvas from the portfolio: a picture of Nyla that I had painted. After Andrew stabbed my palm, my hand was screwed up, and I couldn't paint nearly as well as I once had. But the textured finish was set with lacquer so that even with the occasional weather, it would be kept in decent condition. Kora beamed, holding the painting to her chest. Then we set it into the memorial plaque's display slot.

This section of the grounds was filled with trees and bushes that surged with color, bringing life to decay. Because that's what the families wanted. And Kora brought it to this place.

"She would have loved it," Kora whispered. I put an arm around her, holding her close to me. She turned, her eyes concentrating on mine. "What if I don't want to go? California is so far away. From Punica. From my mother. From you."

My chest tightened, but I held onto that firm smile. "I'll be here when you return," I said. "The semester will be over before you know it."

She turned back to the tree, running her hands along the bark, then she faced me again.

"Come with me," she said. "I know I can go there by myself, but what if I don't want to be there by myself? What if I want to be there with you?" She stared at me, her eyes pleading. "Please, will you come with me?"

For a second, I wondered if she was afraid of being alone, but no, that wasn't the case. Most nights we spent together, but she had been living by herself, to prove to her mother *and* to herself that she could live on her own without anyone's help. She could handle the solitude, then. It was the distance that made her ache.

And was there any request that I would deny her? Never. California had too many fires already, but I supposed there were other ways to find destruction. And I had honestly already looked into funeral homes I could work for inside of that agricultural town. Death care was, thankfully, an industry everyone needed.

"Yes," I said. She wrapped her arms around me, and I hoisted her up by her waist, kissing her deeply. Relieved that we could go together.

Later that night, as she put her leggings and loose shirts into a duffel bag, I made a mental note to add plastic wrap and cable ties to my own bag. We'd have to get a rental home together. The two of us weren't going to fit in a twin-sized bed in a shared dorm room for three months.

I pulled out a small box from my pocket, with a new onyx ring inside of it. This one was smaller than Nyla's, but the onyx was still the centerpiece, with diamonds flashing around it. I kneeled down beside the bed, waiting for Kora to turn from the closet.

She threw the last shirt onto the bed and gasped. "What are you doing?"

"I want to make you my wife," I said. "Forever. In sickness and in health. In life and in death." I pulled the ring out, offering it to her. "Flower, will you marry me?"

"Of course," she said. "Of course. Of course, I will. I love you." Tears poured out of her eyes, and I held her close.

"And I love you."

We kissed each other hard, and an easiness floated through me. It was only a semester, but now we were going together. No one was getting left behind. And even if she hadn't asked me, I knew in my heart that both of us would have still waited for each other.

But if Kora wanted me by her side, I was going to be there.

As she zipped up her bag, I smirked. "You know you're marrying a no-one," I joked.

Her cheeks turned red and she pulled me closer. "You've always been more than that to me."

THE END

Also By Audrey Rush

Dark Romance

Stalker

Standalone

Crawl

Grave Love

Hitch

Assassin

The Feldman Brothers Duet

His Brutal Game

His Twisted Game

Mafia

The Adler Brothers Series

Dangerous Deviance

Dangerous Silence

Dangerous Command

Secret Society

The Marked Blooms Syndicate Series

Broken Surrender

Broken Discipline

Broken Queen

Secret Club

The Dahlia District Series

Ruined

Shattered

Crushed

Ravaged

Devoured

The Afterglow Series

His Toy

His Pet

His Pain

Billionaire

Standalone

Dreams of Glass

Erotic Horror

Body Horror

Standalone

Skin

Acknowledgments

Thank you to my alpha and beta readers for making this book possible. Camrynn, you helped Kora find her spunky self and gave me the motivation to make the story even better. Heather, you pointed out plot holes and helped create the perfect details to help the story come to life. Lesli, you helped this book level up thematically in a way that would make my grad school professors proud. Michelle, this book would be a disaster if it weren't for your honesty and support. Seriously, you are all freaking amazing, and I appreciate your feedback so much.

Thank you to my husband, Kai, for being the best personal graphic designer and supporting husband a writer girl could ask for. Thank you to my dad for your critical feedback on the blurb. Thank you to my ARC readers for your honest reviews and helping give this book a fantastic launch. And thank you to my daughter, Emma, for taking long, productive naps and tolerating my writing sprints.

But most of all, thank you to my readers. You are the reason I love to turn my daydreams into stories. I would love to hear from you. Feel free to leave a review online or to email me directly at audreyrushbooks@gmail.com with your feedback.

About the Author

Audrey Rush writes kinky dark romance and erotic horror. She currently lives in Florida with her husband and daughter. She writes during school.

TikTok: @audreyrushbooks
Instagram: audreyrushbooks
Reader Group: bit.ly/rushreaders
Threads: @audreyrushbooks
Reader Newsletter: bit.ly/audreysletters
Amazon: amazon.com/author/audreyrush
Website: audreyrush.com
Facebook: fb.me/audreyrushbooks
Goodreads: author/show/AudreyRush
Email: audreyrushbooks@gmail.com

Printed in Great Britain
by Amazon